AN EISLIAN'S TALE
PENNY THE BRAVE

By
PAUL HOLLAND

*For Miranda
Thank you for all
of your support.
Welcome
to Eisley!*

aBM

Published by:
A Book's Mind
PO Box 272847
Fort Collins, CO 80527
www.abooksmind.com

Copyright © 2016
ISBN: 978-1-939828-59-0
Printed in the United States of America

No part of this publication may be reproduced, stored in a retrieval system, or transmitted in any form or by any means – electronic, mechanical, digital photocopy, recording, or any other without the prior permission of the author.

All rights reserved solely by the author. The author guarantees all contents are original and do not infringe upon the legal rights of any other person or work. The views expressed in this book are not necessarily those of the publisher.

For my grandmother, Beth Holland
Your support unshakeable
Your kindness unwavering
Your love unfailing

From the Journals of Penny Daulton

In many ways, life itself is a storm, and we are but ships thrown about in its waves as rocks and reefs threaten to sink us.

I believe the secret to life has always been to enjoy those calm days at sea, when the ocean is like glass and the skies are blue and cloudless.

We must take time to cherish the cool sea breeze on our skin, the sunlight glinting off the horizon's waters, a gull's call or a dolphin's grace.

Truly, I advise to be careful not to spend too much time dreaming of the shores of tomorrow when the sands of today are warm beneath your feet.

Then again, I've never even seen a beach... or the ocean, at that.

The others still won't tell me what a starboard is, either. Rather odd name for a fish.

II PAUL HOLLAND

PORT MIHKOZA - SAELOW PROVINCE - SUMMER, 1217
Docks Security Office - Holding Cell

The cuffs binding my wrists seemed to tighten themselves as I watched the armor-clad man pacing about in front of me. He wore chain mail underneath a surcoat emblazoned in black and gold, the colors of the King's Personal Guard. His notably large broadsword gleamed dangerously, serving as a stark reminder that as far as we had come, my friends and I hadn't quite made it to the end of our journey.

Four stone walls glared at the two of us from all sides. The oil lamp on the splintered table in front of me and the lone torch, burning in its sconce, allowed shadows to dance lazily in the soft light around us. Smells of ocean spray and sea salt poured in from the lone window, accompanied by the full moon's light.

I didn't know whether to be flattered or terrified that the Commander of the King's Elite himself had come all the way from Eisley City to Saelow on our account.

The knight ceased his pacing. He leaned over to leer at me menacingly, his weight on the table coaxing a creak from the wood. Formidable brown eyes narrowed at mine, accompanied by deep stress lines creasing tanned skin, and a small scar that snaked upward into his bronze-colored hair.

"Enough with the facade," he rasped lowly. "You don't deny that you're Penny Daulton of Northroe?"

I shook my head.

"Yet, you deny responsibility for the crimes you've been charged with."

I cleared my throat. "Aye."

The man balked at me incredulously. "So the Lords of Northroe *and* Foye, along with the authorities in *all* of eastern Eisley are just mad, is that it? Making it all up? Are you saying that King Lidstrom III is a liar, as well?"

"No sir, never!" I answered truthfully. "Just misinformed. And, if I might add-"

He slammed a hand angrily to the table, causing the oil lamp to jump. "Don't."

Cringing at the outburst, I willed myself to relax when the man started pacing again. He wore frustration freely.

"Paxon, please listen," I tested carefully. "I know it's been a long road for you, too. I know what you've been told."

He folded his arms. "That's Sir Paxon, to you."

I inhaled deeply. "We're not your enemies! I'm just a bloody writer, a storyteller! I'm not a blasted crime lord!"

The knight chuckled, rolling his eyes. "The ungodly trail of ruination you and your friends left behind over the last year and a half would suggest otherwise. But, I'm sure we're just imagining things, aye?"

I mustered courage and patience. "Things aren't what they seem. We-"

"Let's recap, shall we?" the knight interrupted, taking a seat across from me. He unfurled a warrant scroll. "We have... arson, questionable ties with highwaymen, kidnappings, multiple murders, jailbreak-"

"Listen-"

"-destruction of private property, destruction of public property, trespassing, petty theft, grand-scale theft, unlawful evasion, smuggling." He paused and stared at me. "Even a bit of piracy in the Adgridd Sea... all attributed to one 'Penny Daulton' and his cohorts."

I mumbled something under my breath.

"What was that?" the huge man asked, tossing the scroll aside.

"*The Grey Moira* wasn't a pirate ship," I spoke up. "They were privateers. Treasure hunters."

"My apologies. In that case, you're free to go."

My eyes widened. "Really?"

"No."

Someone rapped loudly on the door of the guardhouse.

"Come," barked Paxon.

A man hurried in, in the same outfit as the commander, strapped with a sword and shield, my traveling gear in tow. "The others are in custody, sir. We've seized their possessions." He gestured toward me. "The pack and satchel belong to this one."

Sir Paxon took my belongings. "Stand watch outside, Jon."

"Aye, sir. Lieutenant Griff just arrived, and will be here shortly."

"Very well."

As the man stepped out, Paxon took my satchel and emptied the contents onto the table. A capped jar of ink bounced loudly onto the wood, joined by rolls of crudely folded parchment and two worn quills. The knight scanned some of my writings and eyed me curiously before giving up and moving on to my backpack.

I sighed and watched the torch flames dance. So close to the end of our journey... all to be intercepted by the King's Elite, and this man didn't know-

"The hell," Paxon breathed. Traveling supplies, small morsels of food, tin cookware, a coin purse with six silver shillings, and more scrolls clustered about the table in front of us. He reached in and scooped out a few large, leather-bound books. I winced when he let them fall sloppily with a thud.

"See?" I ventured. "I'm just a Storyteller, mate. I don't-"

"Where's the money?" he flashed angrily. "Don't tell me you don't know, Penny. I'm not stupid. I've hunted down colder men than you."

My jaw tightened. "What money?"

The man suddenly drew his sword with terrifying speed. Steel flashed in the moonlight, and the blade was at my neck. I recoiled in such fright that I tipped myself over in my chair, slumping to the stone floor in a heap.

"Wait!" I hollered. "Just hold on, mate!"

Two gloved hands seized me by the collar of my tunic and pulled me upright into my seat. Sir Paxon glared at me viciously.

"I'll kill ya," he said lowly. "Test me."

"Read the books. Everything's there."

The man backed away quizzically and pointed at the large volumes on the table.

"Aye," I nodded. "They're journals."

Paxon spat. "Journals? Don't have time for games."

I groaned loudly. "Everything's there. All of the past year and a half, Paxon, I swear it. All will make sense. You'll see!"

The knight flipped open my thick journal and scanned a few pages. He eyed me again with an eyebrow raised.

"It has everything," I said hastily. "It'll prove that we're not lying."

"But you've admitted to your identity, and-"

"I am Penny Daulton!" I nearly yelled. "But I'm not the bloke you think I am! I promise, sir, on my life!"

The man exhaled, watching me closely.

"Commander," I tried, "I know your time is not to be wasted. Just read the journal, 'tis all I ask! It's all there. If you find me to be a liar, then kill me."

His hard gaze softened in surprise, but he masked it swiftly. Paxon scooped up my journals into his gloved hands and sighed. "Will take a bloody week to read all of this."

"Take all the time you need, for it's all important. I'm not going anywhere, right?"

I was the only one who laughed, and it faded quickly.

Jaw clenched and brow furrowed in thought, Paxon silently turned and left me in my cell, locking the door behind him.

The ocean breeze outside misted in with the sounds of waves washing the beach, and boats creaked noisily while they bobbed with the tide in port. I watched the night sky through the small window forlornly, thinking of my friends and how they were faring.

Her face entered my mind. My breath caught in my chest.

Would I ever see her again?

Shifting in my chair uncomfortably, I hunched over and gingerly let my head sink to the tabletop. I shut my eyes, wondering if I would be able to sleep.

All I could do was wait, and hope Commander Paxon would heed my request. The journals told of our entire adventure, from the very beginning.

I closed my eyes to recall that day in Northroe, nearly two years ago.

- PART ONE -
In which plain lives become much less ordinary

CHAPTER 1
NORTHROE, EISLEY - FALL, 1215

The city of Northroe was enjoying a sunny sky that day, without the faintest wisps of clouds or hint of impending storms. Birds were chirping musically, gentle breezes accompanied the sun's brilliant rays, and the people outside were probably having the times of their lives.

I sighed and looked longingly out the window to my right.

Northroe was a rather dull place I suppose, but the weather there was always splendid. I could see the trees swaying slightly with the wind. People were bustling about along the cobbled streets, crowding vendors' stalls and browsing shop windows. The collective ambience of sandals, boots, horse and carriage all scraped along the cobblestone, but sounded quiet beyond my closed window. I felt a world away from the people outside, and I wished I could be out among them.

Instead, I was holed up inside the Windfarer's Inn, like most days, and I wasn't enjoying the soft comfy beds it had to offer. For one thing, the inn's beds were quite the opposite of comfortable. What I hated even more was that I lived in the inn, which also happened to be my workplace.

I wasn't the Innkeeper, though. Nor was I the maintenance man. We had a bloody idiot named Marv for that, who spent his days drunk on the job and making problems worse.

No. I, Penny Daulton, was the innkeeper's accountant. Not half-bad, I suppose. My monthly rent was nearly paid for and I didn't work in some forsaken field somewhere. No hard labor at the mercy of bad weather whenever one of the Fates woke up on the wrong side of a cloud. The only thing I liked about working at the inn was that it was a short walk from the November Raven, the favorite tavern of my mates and me.

All things considered, I hated the place, since I hated my job.

I suppose the fact that I was terrible at math and the keeping of books of any sort should probably factor in there somewhere. I got the job because a friend of mine, Jacques, helped me with the mathematics "test" required to prove my worth, as it were. Long story short, Jacques did my work for me, I pretended it was me doing it, and I paid him a decent sum. After some time, Jacques got fussy about how I got the better end of the deal. I then gave him the key to one of our rooms on the West end of the lodge, and from then on the man enjoyed free shelter while continuing our little arrangement.

In retrospect, the whole thing was rather unorganized and ridiculous, but it worked for a long time, all the while unbeknownst to my boss, Head Innkeeper Domheimer.

It did *not* go unnoticed by Assistant Innkeeper Trenten.

I wasn't a hostile man by nature. I hated confrontation, had never used a sword, and avoided eye contact with rough-looking blokes. While violence wasn't a big part of me, I wouldn't mind if Trenten fell off a cliff or got trampled by a steed, or something of the like.

See, one day, some months before, I had slipped up and Trenten learned of the arrangement between Jacques and I. Rather than turn me in to Head Innkeeper Domheimer, Trenten chose to hold it over my head, blackmailing me into running errands and doing petty tasks for him while he would take the day off, or sleep.

Or both.

I stood from my desk in my study, my old chair scraping along the wood floor as I stretched. I could hear hushed whispers growing louder outside my door in the hallway of the second floor of the inn.

Two shadows appeared at the floor under my locked door. I heard the high, whiny voice of a man accompanied by a low, manly laugh that actually belonged to a woman.

I grumbled inwardly. I knew who these two were. I started making my way to the door, but before I could reach it, they rapped on it loudly.

"Mr. Daulton? Are you there?"

I rolled my eyes, opened the door, and was greeted by Thomas and Sophie Flannery, an incredibly irritating couple whom, I still believe to this day, the Fates hired to make my life hell.

"What a surprise," I said hollowly.

Thomas was a wiry man with a red-haired bowl cut and a mustache as long as an eel. His wife Sophie was more than twice his size, boasted the same haircut, and usually showed off her remarkably unattractive self in skimpy clothing.

Thankfully, she had failed to do so on this day. However, I was still fairly troubled.

Thomas Flannery was dressed exactly as I was, in a brown, sleeveless tunic over a white, long-sleeved shirt, with tan trousers, a leather belt looped around his waist, and even the same shoes as mine, fashioned by a shoemaker named Laurence.

I stiffened when I saw a small pouch fastened next to a coin purse on his belt, exactly where I wore my own.

Even more unnerving was the sight of Sophie Flannery, dressed to the threads in the same attire.

"Good day, Mr. Daulton!" Thomas crowed.

"Mr. and Mrs. Flannery," I forced in greeting. "Call me Penny, please. Just Penny."

They stared at me blankly.

"You can just call me Penny. No 'Mr. Daulton' required," I rephrased.

Mrs. Flannery's eyes flashed as if she'd come to some great revelation, and her husband nodded, offering his hand for a handshake. Eyeing his hand and then his runny nose, I respectfully declined.

"So, Thomas and Sophie. What can I do for-"

"Ah," interjected Thomas. "Just Mr. and Mrs. Flannery. Please."

"Please," his wife echoed, following his example. "Just call us Mr. and Mrs. Flannery."

I gawked for a moment, suppressing a shake of my head. "Uh huh. Apologies."

A long, awkward silence ensued. They both stared at me, and I glanced back and forth between them.

I eyed the pouches at their belts. "So, what do you have there, Thomas?"

"Mr. Flannery, you mean?"

"Aye," I sighed. "What's in the pouch?"

The man stroked his long mustache excitedly. "Extra jar of ink, and some parchment, Penny. Just like what you carry."

"I don't carry jars of ink and parchment in a pouch."

Thomas cocked his head. "Really? You should."

"Ah," I grunted. "Writers now, are ya?"

"Just like you," Thomas nodded.

Sophie gleamed. "We've decided to become poets. Perhaps you could allow us to-"

"Mr. and Mrs. Flannery," I interrupted quickly, "what can I do for you today? I am rather busy, see."

Thomas chortled loudly. "Ha! About time you ask! Penny, we're not going to be able to pay rent this week, and we were wondering-"

"If I could pass that along to the Innkeeper for you?" I finished for him.

They both nodded.

"And, I'm guessing, try to persuade him to allow a late payment for you both after he gets angry and most likely yells a bit, aye?"

They nodded again.

I shifted in the doorway and rolled my eyes. "Feels like we've been down this road before, you two and I. Probably because this is the third week in a row this has happened, and-"

"So you won't do it?" Thomas Flannery asked, fidgeting nervously and looking at me with pleading, wide eyes.

"Well," I shrugged, "Innkeeper Domheimer will only tolerate this so often, know what I mean? I don't think it'll go unpunished this time."

Thomas leaned over to whisper something into his wife's ear, and she turned to me and abruptly dipped low, making sure I could see down her shirt in a manner that might have been flattering to a more attractive woman.

I balked incredulously, and absently began rolling my sleeves to my elbows.

Thomas eyed my arm and hands closely. He started to roll up his own sleeves, mimicking me.

"Oh, bloody hell," I protested. "Really?"

Thomas and Sophie exchanged glances. "Have we offended you, Penny?"

I didn't even try to answer the question. "Get some work at the lumber mill, for the Fates' sake, Thomas. This can't continue week to week, see?"

They were looking down at the floor now, like two children who had just been reprimanded. I decided to change my tone.

"I'm sorry. I can't help you two this time. I want to, but I can't."

The man stroked his enormous mustache for a moment. "We can make a partial payment."

I nodded. "That might help. Well, it's thirty-five silver a week, in case you've somehow forgotten. What can you offer?"

The man fished inside his coin purse, pinched two copper shillings together, and handed them to me triumphantly.

Unimpressed, I eyed the two coppers in my hand. "You're joking."

"It's all I have, Penny."

More silence. I wasn't sure if they were trying to appear pitiful, but I was feeling sorry for the Flanneries despite their blunt stupidity.

I took a deep breath and handed the coins back to Thomas. "Look, I'll talk to Domheimer for you, but I can't promise-"

Before I could finish, Thomas and Sophie both rushed forward with the intention to embrace me, but ended up practically tackling and pinning me to the wall.

"Thank you Penny!"

"You're so kind, Mr. Daulton!"

I gave them both a reluctant pat on the shoulder, crinkling my nose in disgust at a suspicious smell before pushing the couple away lightly. "Listen. I can't promise anything. Not this time, okay? Both of you seriously need to look into finding work."

"Will do. Promise. Thanks again!" They turned to leave, but Thomas spun back to me. "Oh, and Penny?"

"Aye?"

He was studying my hair rather obnoxiously. "Where do you get your hair cut?"

"Bye, Thomas."

They left hurriedly, leaving me behind clinging to my doorframe. Only when I realized my knuckles were turning white did I think to let go and slip back into my room.

Why on earth Thomas and Sophie Flannery chose to imitate me, of all people, was beyond me. In truth, I think the fear of the answer to that question far outweighed my will to ask it.

CHAPTER 2

Back inside my humble living space, I took a look around. A single mattress on a rusted iron frame rested idly in the corner, along with my desk littered with stacks of parchments, scrolls and various ledgers. The wood floor was smooth, at least. Many rooms in the Windfarer's Inn had floors that had never been sanded, and so some people walking barefoot would end up with splinters in their toes.

Many of the documents and ledgers on my desk were logs and records for the inn. Jacques would come over and sit at my desk to work his mathematical magic while I'd write.

You see, one day, I would be a writer. An author, to be more precise. I was confident. Fairly certain, at least. It was my passion. I loved storytelling, and I was always spinning new tales in my mind. A single person passing by, a certain smell, a sound, the rain – seemingly anything could spark inspiration inside me. I could create and envision entire adventures in my mind just by taking a walk down a market street in Northroe.

These unfinished and sometimes discarded works were the other documents littering my desk and other areas of my room. One could say I was motivationally challenged, to put it lightly. Inspiration could vanish as quickly as it had appeared.

Writing was my passion, indeed. I officially considered myself a Writer-in-Training. Words were my art. Characters and their stories were my weapons, like a soldier's sword and shield. Well, something of that sort. And that was of course when I actually stayed on one project for more than a day.

I looked outside again and noticed the sun had been setting, and the air was getting cooler outside. A flood of relief washed over me. Any time now, Head Innkeeper Domheimer would turn in for the night, meaning I was free to act as I pleased.

No sooner had I mused this than there was another sound at my door. Not the rapping of knuckles upon wood, but the sound of someone turning the handle of the locked doorknob followed by the dull thud of a body colliding with the wood door. A man cursed with a sigh outside.

I grinned, hastily changing into a dark tunic and grabbing a lightweight cloak in case of rain. "It's locked," I said loudly.

"Very good," the slightly muffled voice answered dryly from the hallway. "Open up, mate."

I walked briskly to my desk as I always did before leaving. I looked things over, mainly my writings, checking if they were in order. There was no reason to. Nobody ever had or ever would tamper with anything, but I always did this anyway.

Glancing at the cracked mirror on the desktop that leaned against the wall, I looked at myself for a moment. My brown eyes peered back at me. Wavy, brown hair cut short, dark circles under my eyes. I hadn't been getting much sleep recently. Hadn't shaved in a couple days, either.

So, this was the face of a man who wished so much, yet did so little. Then again, wasn't that the face of most men? Or was the joke on me?

"Comin' or what?" came the voice again.

"Yes!" I called. "You could do wonders with more patience."

I opened the door and grinned at the strong, large man in front of me. He was my friend Alomar Sanstrom, veteran of the Eislian Army and the best drinker in town.

"You have it wrong, mate," he said with a twinkle in his eye. "Patience is overrated, so I hear."

Alomar flashed a white smile, and I shook my head and pushed him aside, trying not to show that it took great effort. "Let's go," I said. "Thought this moment would never come."

"Penny," Alomar asked as he easily caught up with me, "what were you doing in there anyway? Took you an hour to open the bloody door. Sprucing up, were ya?"

"What?" I returned in mock horror.

The man laughed, brushing a hand through his short-cropped, black hair. His light green eyes were radiant, even indoors. Alomar stood at least a head and a half taller than I, and his strong build simply sealed the deal: wherever we went, the man seemed to trip over beautiful women. He would practically have to fight them off, and Alomar was very adamant in doing so. He'd been married to his wife Corrine for nearly five years.

"You're early," I said as we strode out of the inn and into the streets of the city. Everywhere I looked, people were moving and winding through the crowded roads. Vendors peddled their goods, merchants shouted and called to passersby, and the smells of different fruits, vegetables, meats and spices blanketed the air.

"Aye," my friend answered, sidestepping out of the way of a passing Watchman. "Royce sent me. He said he's got some news for us tonight."

I looked at Alomar questioningly. "Really? Royce has news? Interesting."

"Right?" replied Alomar. "He never has news about anything."

"Except if he just lost his new apprenticeship for punching his new boss in the face."

We both laughed heartily, mainly because I wasn't joking.

Alomar shrugged. "Well, news or no, to the Raven we go."

"Aye!" I answered, toasting an imaginary glass in the air.

Off to the November Raven we went, snaking our way through the crowds of Northroe's streets. A nightly outing at the tavern was a regular tradition of Alomar, Royce and I, and there was no way we'd miss it tonight.

CHAPTER 3

Cheers all around, indeed.

That fall night in Northroe found Alomar, my good friend Royce, and me sitting at our usual spot at the bar of the November Raven, the busiest tavern in the West Quarter of the city. My two companions and I were lost amidst the clinking mugs and glasses, hollering men and women, drunken laughter, and frequently spilled ale.

Every night, a notable crowd of hardworking folk flocked to the Raven to let loose and stir their hardships into an ale or rum before chugging it down. Of course, new problems were sometimes created at the tavern, resulting in the occasional brawl or shouting match, but rarely anything another pint couldn't wash down.

I half-stood from my stool and leaned across the bar counter to find the bartender amidst all the cheers and chaos.

"Ozlow!" I shouted. "Another amber ale, mate!"

"Oy!" came a rough voice from my left. "Make that two!"

I turned to my longtime friend, Royce Bartha. "Blazes, Royce. We've only just got here and you're on your-"

"Fourth mug, I know," he finished. Royce downed the remainder of his glass and slammed it on the oak counter with might. "Not nearly enough, mate. Know what I mean?"

I watched Royce briefly. He had dusty blonde hair, long and tied back like usual. He was scratching at his chin and jaw, which bore a light but noticeably unshaven stubble. Royce wasn't a large man like Alomar, but he was tough and had enough fighting bones in his body for the three of us. The man's blue eyes seemed distant, and I suspected that perhaps the news our friend had to share with us did carry some weight, after all.

Alomar and I exchanged knowing glances as Ozlow scurried over with three mugs of foamy ale.

"Lads, drink up!" Ozlow bellowed cheerfully. He was an older man with the energy and strength of a youth, and, to put it bluntly, Ozlow himself was one of the best features of the Raven. He'd owned it for years and had never missed a night.

Not one.

Alomar reached for a mug and gave the bartender a wink. "Ozlow, I didn't even call for one. It's like you knew."

Ozlow chuckled. "Years of practice, lad."

I took a drink. "Lucky guess, you mean?"

"Aye, that's it," Ozlow laughed before lowering his voice, "but don't tell these other hooligans. I'll be out o' business by morning's light."

Alomar and I laughed heartily as the bartender shuffled down the counter to tend to other patrons. Royce nodded with a smile.

Taking another long swig, I looked behind me and surveyed the tavern. It was a cozy setup. Sturdy oaken tables and chairs filled the large pub with plenty of space for the barmaids to walk to and fro. Most of the tables sat four to six patrons. Judging by the barmaids' hasty manner, this night's crowd was demanding. Looking at all the laughing, yelling, shouting and even crying customers as they drank to sorrows and celebration alike, I observed that there were but two empty seats in the entire establishment.

I leaned closer to Royce and spoke loudly so he could hear me. "Full house tonight. You see 'em all? Bloody hell."

"Aye," he replied rather glumly. "Bloody 'ell, indeed."

Again, Alomar and I exchanged glances, and he gave me a subtle nod. I returned it and took one more gulp of ale.

"So Royce," Alomar said, rubbing his chin. "What's this news you were speaking of today? That you wanted to share with us?"

"Aye," I chimed in. "You're awfully quiet tonight, mate. Usually we're trying to drag you away from a brawl or shut you up by this point."

Alomar shot me a look, but I just shrugged.

Royce was holding his mug just above the oak counter, tilting it this way and that, watching the dark beer slosh about inside. His eyes were intent on it, and it was then that I began to feel uneasy. All jokes aside, I couldn't remember the last time I had seen the man in such a state.

"What's going on?" I asked lowly.

Brushing a strand of hair from his eye, Royce opened his mouth to reply when a woman's voice interrupted him.

"Hey there, lads," came a woman's silky voice.

The three of us turned to see Kara, one of Ozlow's beautiful barmaids standing with an empty tray at her side. She had long, flowing blonde hair and hazel eyes that teased with the most subtle of glances.

I immediately felt my heart begin a nervous beat, and hoped I wasn't too obviously excited.

She was staring right at me, and gave a smile. "Penny? You're sweating rather badly. And you're staring."

Royce and Alomar chuckled, making no effort to hide it.

Kara shifted and folded her arms. "You have a fever, hon?"

Blast. There it was. The tightening in my throat. Nervous pumping of my heart.

"Kara, sweet Kara," Royce interjected, setting his mug down on the counter and turning to fully face her. "I believe that Penny here is just...at a loss for words, you see. After all, in the face of such beauty, how could-"

"Oh, easy now," the woman said with a frown. Completely ignoring Royce, Kara pointed at Alomar, raising her eyebrows. "Now *this* model of a man better know I'll be here if things don't work out between him and his wife."

Gawking, Royce shook his head and gave a dismissive wave. "Woman has no appreciation for a real man like myself."

Slightly jealous but mostly curious and entertained, I sipped my ale and watched Alomar.

Alomar turned slightly red in the face. "Ah, I... appreciate it, Kara. I do. But I... well, I-"

"The man loves his wife," Royce finished for him, turning quickly back to Kara. "Whereas I don't actually have a wife, see? I am free from those cursed shackles."

Kara tossed back her head and laughed. "You just do not give up, do you Roy?"

Royce shook his head. "No, Madame. I would never."

"Well," Kara said, stepping closer and lowering her voice, "I suppose I might one day consider getting to know you a little better."

"Really?" asked Royce, his eyes twinkling.

The woman nodded and leaned even closer to the man. "Yes."

Alomar and I both drank.

"Except," Kara continued smoothly in that silky voice of hers, "you just compared marriage to cursed shackles. 'Tis a problem."

Alomar gave a low whistle, and Royce opened his mouth as dismay played across his face, but no words came. So, I spoke for him.

"Thing is though Kara," I said carefully, "if marriage is so sacred to you, why are you hoping Alomar's wife chokes to death on hard bread or gets lost in the woods or something?"

The barmaid laughed again, stepping away from us to circulate around the tavern once more. "Well, you can't always follow the rules now, can you?"

"Now," Royce said with narrow eyes, "that was a low blow. Completely unfair."

I looked at my two friends and raised my mug. "To the woman's victory this night?"

"Aye," laughed Alomar. "To Kara. She won again."

"Fair and square," Royce sighed, and we all clinked our mugs together in cheers.

I set my glass down after our toast and narrowed my eyes. "Royce, what on earth does that mean?"

"What does what mean?"

"Fair and square."

Alomar looked at our friend questioningly. "Aye. What in blazes does a square have to do with anything being fair?"

"It'll catch on," Royce replied.

I shook my head. "But what does it actually mean?"

"Well, when you think of it - a square, I mean - all four sides are the same length, you see? Equal."

Alomar and I looked at the man expectantly.

"Well," Royce continued, sounding as if we should have already understood, "fair and square. Get it? If something's fair, it's equal, so to speak. Like the four sides of a... square. Fair, and square, as it were."

"No, mate," Alomar said with a shake of his head. "Not gonna catch on."

"Ever," I agreed. "Fair and square? Don't think so."

Not hiding his dejection, Royce took a long drink and studied the patterns in the wood on the countertop thoughtfully for a moment. "You sure?"

"Very."

"Oy, lads!" came Ozlow's voice again from down the counter.

"Three more!" Alomar called.

I coughed. "Only halfway finished with this one."

Alomar smiled and turned back to Royce. "Now, c'mon. What's this news you have for us?"

Royce promptly tipped his mug to his mouth and downed the remainder of his ale. He let out a subtle belch before cracking his knuckles and taking a deep breath.

"I received a letter today. From my father."

Alomar and I didn't need to exchange glances for this one.

"What!?"

"You're joking."

Royce shook his head. "Afraid not."

Alomar's face was a picture of bewilderment. "Since when were you two on speaking terms?"

"We're not, and never have been."

"How'd he even find you?" I put in. "After all these years-"

"Been just over twenty years, yeah," Royce interrupted.

Alomar and I held our tongues and waited for the man to continue.

Royce sighed. "He says he needs help. Practically begged for it. Says he's in trouble. Details are vague, but it doesn't sound good."

"Help?" Alomar protested. "But-"

"He says," Royce cut in gently, "that he's being blackmailed, or something of the sort. Says he lost his business to some blokes already, and he's gonna lose his home. They stand to take it from him within the month."

After nearly a minute of silence, I finally spoke.

"Some nerve, asking you for help."

Royce smiled wryly, but said nothing.

"I feel the same way," Alomar said, "but more importantly, and no offense mate, how does he expect you to help him against the likes of thugs and the lot? Blackmail's only as effective as the blokes behind it, and he says he's already lost his business."

Ozlow strode up to us and set more mugs of ale down. We gave a nod. Seeing the way he frowned ever so slightly, I'm sure Ozlow knew something was up, but the man strode off to his other patrons without any hearty banter. I silently thanked him for being sensitive to such matters.

Royce gripped his new mug but didn't drink for a few contemplative moments. "He probably doesn't even know that Trev is gone. For all I know, he tried contacting him first."

At the mention of Royce's dead older brother, we all cozied into a period of silence. Alomar peered into the fireplace behind the bar, eyes lost in the flames. Royce stared down at his untouched ale, swallowing a pain that tugged on his heart.

"So," I mused, "he expects you to what, band up with some pals and eliminate his problem?"

Royce shrugged. "Suppose so."

"And apparently he's not involving the City Watch, for whatever reason."

"Apparently not."

"What are you thinking, Roy?" asked Alomar. "Even if we had the means, would you still aid your father?"

"And after twenty years...." I trailed off.

More silence. I watched the faces of the crowd around us. Their features were illuminated in the glows of oil lamps and torchlight, and I momentarily lost myself in the clinking of glasses and hollers of men. The front doors to the tavern opened, and a few men strode in, the air from outside breezing in behind them and causing the candle flames throughout the pub to sway gently with the wind.

"Right, then," Royce said at last. "Here's to decisions, mates, and I've made mine."

Alomar and I solemnly lifted our mugs to meet Royce's in the air for the most important toast to that moment in our lives as friends. We took mighty drinks, letting the ale wash down our throats and into our bellies. I watched Royce. His forehead was furrowed in thought and his blue eyes were narrowed. The man finally lifted his gaze to meet ours and spoke.

"My father left Trev and I to die in this city. I wasn't even six years old yet. We lived on the streets. He'll get no help from me."

Alomar and I looked at each other again, but said nothing. What could be said, really? I knew without asking that Alomar agreed with our friend's decision, as did I.

Royce suddenly produced a rolled up parchment from his coat, and held it up so we could see. Scrappy words were scrawled onto it in black ink, with a signature on the bottom.

"My father's letter," Royce murmured, confirming my thoughts.

The man held it to a candle near us on the bar counter, and the flame seemed to grow aggravated as it spread slowly across the parchment, which charred and crumbled under the blaze.

Wordlessly, Royce slammed a closed fist down onto the burning paper, snuffing out the candlelight. Bits of it broke apart onto the oak countertop.

"Another round?" Alomar proposed softly.

"Aye," answered Royce. "One more."

CHAPTER 4

Royce, Alomar and I left the November Raven and spent the next hour weaving our way southeast through the city, following the River Keska. The moon had chased the retreating sun from sight, revealing bright stars in the night sky. The bustling streets were now sleeping, along with most of the city folk. Shadows of all shapes and sizes seemed to follow my friends and I as we walked, flickering and dancing everywhere we looked in the glows of lanterns, oil lamps, torches and candlelit windows.

The River Keska ran through the city of Northroe, flowing southward from its northern origins near the sea beyond Eisley's borders. It was a relatively calm, glassy river that curved slightly through the city before exiting out the southeastern corner of the city limits, continuing on through the green hills and dense woodlands surrounding Northroe. At night it looked particularly beautiful, aflame with the calm city lights that guided us on our trek.

We finally reached South Bridge. It was sturdily built across the River Keska's waters, linking our city streets with the worn dirt path leading out to the country and wilderness. South Bridge was another favorite location of ours. It was much quieter than most of the city, especially in the hours of late. Even during the day, however, I would gladly take the heaviest traffic of journey-folk, wagons, horses and carriages traveling in and out of the city on South Bridge over the densely populated, tightly packed market quarters in the rest of the city.

The moon bathed everything around us in its white glow, casting a surreal, beautiful filter over all that my eyes could see. The starlight above finished the moon's painting of deep blues, blacks, and plentiful shades of gray.

We stood atop the stone bridge, leaning on the low stone guardrail to peer over into the dark waters of the river. Moonlight glared brightly off ripples and gentle torrents in the water below.

The wind had picked up, and I pulled my cloak tighter around me, stifling a shiver.

Royce straightened and gripped the railing. Exhaling deeply and looking up at the sky, he reminded me of an irritated officer of sorts about to give orders to his troops.

"You ever wonder what it is exactly we're doing here?" asked Royce softly. "What the point of it all is?"

"You think too much, mate," laughed Alomar. "Some kingdoms punish those who think freely."

I chuckled. "Aye. 'Fair and square,' and all that."

"I'm serious." Royce turned back to us and leaned on his elbows against the ledge. "We're born, we work, or fight, and we die. Seems like such a waste, know what I mean?"

"Roy," I replied, "I know what you're saying, but we've had this talk, many times before."

Royce was silent, but not discouraged. I could tell from his thoughtful gaze and the way his eyes were shifting from stone to stone on the cobbled surface at our feet.

"I know what you're gettin' at, I do," Alomar offered. "But I'm sure every bloke and his mum has thought the same thing. All around the world. Since the beginning of bloody time itself."

Folding his arms, Royce countered. "Of course. But some really achieve it! That greatness. Haven't you ever wanted to be something more? Actually live your life?"

Despite my best efforts, a torrent of laughter escaped me and echoed down South Bridge. I couldn't help it.

"Think it's funny, do you, Pen?"

"Well," I said between chuckles, "yeah, mate. I do."

"You can bugger off then," Royce growled.

"What!?" I protested. "Royce, half the time you come up with the most random thoughts I've ever heard in my life. You don't take anything seriously until about an hour after you've put down ten rounds of ale. You got into a fight with your last boss down at the mill just three days ago! You-"

"Oh?" Royce interrupted, flashing with vigor. "Criticize me, will ya? You don't even do your own bloody work, mate. Have to pawn it off on another bloke while you... well what is it you do all day to pass the time, exactly?"

"Does a lotta sprucing up, I think," Alomar said with a grin.

I shoved Alomar in response, but the hulk of a man didn't budge. I set my sights back on Royce.

"Look, I'm sorry, all right? But every day you have this new idea, or some plan, or some verse of wisdom about the secrets of life, know what I mean?"

Royce spat on the cobblestones, before turning his back on me to gaze out at the river's waters once more. I took a deep breath and scratched my head before looking at Alomar and giving a slight plea with my eyes.

"Look, Roy," Alomar began as he joined Royce at the ledge, "it's just that you're the most hotheaded, impulsive, craziest bastard we've ever met. That's all Penny's trying to say."

I saw a grin play across Royce's lips, and I breathed out in relief when the man laughed and shook his head, still staring at the river below us.

"Just seems odd sometimes is all," I said. "Next you'll be telling us you saw the Fates with your own eyes, and-"

"All right! Come off it already!" retorted Royce, still smiling. "Point taken. But tonight, I mean it. I always have meant it... I suppose I've just never acted on it. Don't know if I've ever known how. Maybe I was waiting for the two of you blokes to agree with me and somehow feel that way yourselves."

The three of us let all spoken words sink in, perhaps hoping the night's breeze and the soft current of the River Keska might suddenly reward us with answers to Royce's musings.

When no answers came, I leaned back against the ledge on my elbows and looked at the dark silhouette of the city that loomed against the sky. Shadows of buildings of all sizes seemed to be trying to reach upward and pierce the few silvery wisps of clouds that were out, but only the small castle of Lord Hannady of Northroe came close to doing so.

I fidgeted, sighing inwardly and wondering what it must have been like to be born into nobility. Your life was laid out before you, riches guaranteed with prosperous promises of comfort. I'm sure Lord Hannady had his worries, but they couldn't possibly be about how he'd make rent, pay taxes or when his next meal would be.

"Wonder if Lord Hannady has to pay rent?" I said finally. "Or taxes, or... or anything."

Alomar chuckled. "To the King, sure. Otherwise, I doubt it. But he's bound to have his own share of problems."

Suddenly Royce stepped away from the ledge overlooking the river and turned to Alomar and I, his eyes lit with undoubted passion behind whatever he was about to say.

I braced myself.

"What do you live for?" Royce asked, pointing to Alomar.

"Eh?"

"What do you live for?" he repeated.

Alomar looked at me for a moment. I just shrugged.

"Well, 'tis a broad question, isn't it?"

"But it can be answered," Royce insisted. "Go on. What do you live for? What's your reason for living?"

I stifled a laugh. I knew Royce noticed, but the man paid no mind.

Rubbing his chin thoughtfully, Alomar answered. "My wife, I suppose. Aye. My wife. Corrine. And I make a decent living at the lumber yard."

"Ah," Royce nodded. "Indeed. Your wife and money. What's the money for?"

Even Alomar cocked his head now. "What do you think?"

"I know, I know," Royce said quickly. "Just indulge me. What's the money for? Why do you work for it?"

Mustering patience, Alomar sighed. "To pay for my house. For the King's taxes, for food to eat. But obviously you know this already."

"Okay," replied Royce, turning to me. "Stay with me on this one, mates. What about you, Penny? What do you live for?"

Resisting the urge to ridicule my friend, I cleared my throat. "Um. Well, I live for... shelter. I mean, I have a roof over my head. I suppose a bloke's lucky to have one at all, yeah?"

"Go on."

I was suddenly shocked. Judging by the look on Alomar's face, he understood what Royce was getting at, too.

What were we living for, exactly? I couldn't answer that question! I didn't even do the work for which I was employed, and this conversation was making me feel suddenly very guilty about it.

"I think I see what you're saying," I said with a smile. "For once, you may be right."

Royce shook his head. "I'm always right, mate."

Folding his arms, Alomar spoke. "Okay. I hear ya. We're living...well, to live, is that it?"

"We're living for shelter, for food, and to just sustyne living, you see?" replied Royce triumphantly. "And that's it."

"Sustain," I corrected.

"Eh?"

"Sustain living. Not 'sustyne'."

"Shuddup, Penny. Now, what about what we want, mates? What do we want to live for? We've got this life, yeah? The Fates put us here. Now what do we want to do with it?"

Again, we were all silent and let the conversation's weight bear down on our thoughts. I had to admit, what Royce was saying seemed true. And actually, most importantly of all, it was striking a chord within me. I almost felt angry. Like I'd been dull-witted all along for not noticing what Royce had pointed out here tonight.

But it was like that the world over, wasn't it? You were born into riches, or you weren't. End of story.

"In this world, you're born with riches, or you're not," said Alomar, echoing my thoughts. "That's just how it is. The Fates have allowed it for thousands of years, after all. If every poor farmer, street urchin or fisherman out there all had the same thoughts we're having now, all at the same time, what could they do? There's an order to things, aye?"

Whatever this new surge of excitement was, this force of inspiration inside me that Royce had sparked, it was being swiftly quelled by Alomar's seemingly impenetrable logic. I could feel the momentary, newfound secret that I had just stumbled upon start to fade away. You were rich or poor. Simple as that.

But to my surprise, Royce wasn't bothered. In fact, he had a familiar twinkle in his eye. Since it was the dead of night out there on South Bridge with only the moon's light overhead, that I could see the twinkle in his eye really spoke volumes.

"Thing is mates, I don't think that's all there is to it. I think there's more than being rich or poor."

The man watched us, studying our faces. I had this very odd sensation, a clinging hope inside me – a stubborn hope, waiting to see if Royce could draw it from the deep and make good on some unvoiced promise of a better life.

"What do you think it is?" I asked, trying to mask what felt like childish enthusiasm in my words. "I mean, what else is there besides being rich or poor?"

"Aye," Alomar said. "What else?"

Royce folded his arms. "What have you ever wanted to do with your life? What or who did you want to be, that you can't be here? Have you ever dreamt of another life, another you? One you can't find or live because you're... you?"

I looked at Alomar, then to Royce. "Sure. Doesn't every man?"

"Aye, they do, I'd wager," Royce replied. "What about you?"

"Me? I asked. "What about you?"

Royce grinned. "Not yet. You two first."

CHAPTER 5

It was then that Alomar's words punctured the cold night air.

"It's been hard for me, mates," he said solemnly, shifting his weight. "After the war, I mean. All I ever wanted to be was a soldier, you know?"

We grew quiet, and I caught Royce's eyes. Alomar rarely talked about his time in the Eislian 2nd Cavalry. He'd fought abroad, east across the Adgridd Sea, on the shores and mainland of Dekka. The Dekkans fought our Eislian warriors fiercely, but Eisley ultimately prevailed as it always had in the last six centuries. Six hundred years and not one war lost. Our country was indeed powerful, and practically unmatched by anyone in the world, except perhaps the large, sweeping nation of Athekov, across the Mihkoza Channel to the North.

"I joined to make a difference," continued Alomar. "To actually have a part in the outcome of something that mattered. And I did. When I was there, I felt purpose, you see."

I watched the man carefully. His eyes were lost, probably somewhere I'd never been and never would be. Alomar ran his hand through his short, black hair like he always did. But the movement was slower this time, and he kept rubbing his head while watching the dark waters of the Keska flow by.

"I'll tell you one thing," he said, snapping out of his trance. "I never want to see another desert again for as long as I live. And the places you got sand in...."

I laughed. Royce did as well, but I watched him carefully.

Trev's death in Dekka during battle was most definitely not a topic Royce spoke of much. We didn't know specifics. Alomar had returned at the war's end alone. He told us that Trev died a hero, having sacrificed his life to save those of many.

Every death of someone in war was a 'hero's death,' that I had heard of, anyway. Truthfully, nobody could bear being told otherwise. But I had known Trev for a long time before he and Alomar left, and I chose to believe he died while saving others. It was definitely something the man would have been capable of.

Alomar continued. "The point is, being a soldier was everything to me. That was what I lived for. But the war is over. I came home and met Corrine. You know the rest."

"Do you regret meeting Corrine?" I tested gingerly. "Marriage and whatnot?"

"No, not at all," Alomar answered quickly. He jabbed a thumb over at Royce. "But now that our own personal philosopher here has me thinking, I don't know what to do with my life now that I'm not a soldier anymore. I mean, if I had a choice."

I rubbed my chin thoughtfully and looked back out at the river, allowing myself to get lost in thought momentarily.

"What about you, mate?" Royce asked, looking at me now with immense interest.

The question, oddly, froze me. *What about me?*

"I... don't know what I want," I lied.

"Nothing at all?"

I shrugged. "I don't know. Never given it a whole lot of thought I guess."

"What a load o' crap," Alomar said with a wily grin. "Everyone's got a dream, an ambition. Right?"

"Actually," Royce said, "I don't."

Alomar and I both looked at each other, then back at Royce.

"But you're the one-" I started.

Royce held his hand up to interrupt. "I don't know specifically what it is I would like to do. But I do know it's not here, in Northroe."

"Please continue," motioned Alomar.

"I think traveling, journeying through the world, is the only true freedom," Royce stated confidently. "To see the lands the Fates have put before us. Even the richest noble has one set of shackles. He can't just get up and go when he pleases. He has responsibilities and duties that keep him chained to his manor or castle, you see?"

I laughed. "Roy, I have to say, you're actually impressing me this time around. That makes sense."

It truly did. At that moment, I suddenly felt a strong calling from the horizon. Looking out at the river and beyond, to the trees of the dense forests and the old dirt road winding through them into the distance and out of view, I suddenly thought that this abstract freedom Royce was talking about was real. It was a tangible thing, somewhere far off, somewhere I'd never been, and I had this strange sensation that I was a prisoner. That I could be out there chasing whatever this beckoning was. Freedom's call, if you will. But I was stuck there in Northroe, living my plain, boring life as thousands of others did.

"You never answered us, Penny," Royce said. "What do you live for?"

Not a simple question, by any means.

"I suppose just for food and shelter, like anyone else," I answered. "I just go through the days as they come, yeah?"

I became abruptly angry with myself for waking up in a bed I was lucky to have, passing the hours until the night muscled the sun out of the sky, and going to sleep having done nothing with the time given to me. Royce was right. I didn't even work for the coin paid to me, and it was more than many men earned doing harder labor.

"Right," Royce continued. "What about your ambitions, mate? I suppose I do have some, after all. Getting out of this blasted city, for starters. But you?"

First time for everything.

"I think... I want to be a writer."

This drew puzzled looks from both men.

"A what?"

"A writer. An author, really. Stories, tales and the like."

Alomar scratched his head. "A writer, Penny? Really?"

"Aye."

My heart was beating fast, and my pulse quickened. I had never told anyone. I suppose I had been terribly shy about sharing this dream of mine with others. I was already beginning to regret it.

"Not like, oh, I dunno. A war hero? A pirate? Become a lord of some castle?" asked Royce, as if trying to coax an alternative answer from my lips.

I shook my head. "Well, no."

"How about an explorer, or cartographer, or-"

"Oh, come on," I moaned. "You asked and I answered, yeah?"

Royce held up his hands in surrender, but then took one more jab.

"Probably could make more coin as a man-whore, mate."

I balled my hands into fists.

"Actually," Royce said with a thoughtful frown, "probably not. Scratch that."

My glare softened when Alomar's laugh rang out and echoed into the night, and I couldn't help but join him.

Royce yawned. "At least you know what you want to do, I suppose. I'll give you that."

I rolled my eyes. "You kind of have to. You don't know your calling yet, slacker."

"It's getting late, mates," Alomar said with a yawn. "If I were smarter I would have gone home when we left the Raven. Corrine's gonna have my head on a stick."

Royce strode forward and clapped his hand to my shoulder, and the other to Alomar's. "Listen. I've been thinking about something, and-"

"Never good, is it?" I whispered. Alomar chuckled, but Royce pressed on.

"Listen. You two blokes have been my best friends for practically as long as I can remember."

Alomar and I once again exchanged glances, but said nothing.

"I want to leave Northroe. I'm done with this city. We've been here our entire lives. There's a whole world out there we've never seen. Adventures to be had and whatnot."

I looked incredulously at Royce. "You want to leave town?"

"Oh, I'm going to."

"When?"

"Soon, and I want you two to join me."

Alomar shook his head. "I'm married, mate. It's a minor detail you might have overlooked."

"Corrine can come."

"You're serious," I said. It was an observation, not a question.

"Mate, we can't just up and leave... everything. Everyone," Alomar said in a scolding tone.

I looked at Alomar. "He's serious!"

"Of course I'm serious!" Royce hissed. "Did you blokes just forget what we've been talking about? Alomar, you and Corrine don't have children to worry about. See? She can come too."

Alomar chuckled, and I rolled my eyes.

"We get one chance! One life to live!" urged Royce. "I'm not going to wait around and hope something falls in my lap! And I want you two to come with me!"

"One life to live," I echoed in a murmur.

Alomar shifted his weight. "Unless you believe in reincarnation, like the Kovians."

Royce grabbed us and did his best to whirl us about so we faced the wilderness east and south of Northroe. The moonlight that night emphasized the vastness of the land. I could see the sprawling Kovald Forest in the distance, seeming to scroll all the way across the world from the northeast to the southeastern horizon. The broad and mighty Mount Kovald stretched upward from the sea of trees. It was both magnificent and powerful, looming large despite its distance from us, parting clouds and casting a dark, titanic shadow upon the boundless woods.

I bit my lip. "Royce, I don't know about this one."

"I'll talk to Corrine about it tomorrow morning," Alomar said suddenly. "First thing."

I gawked at the man, fully aware that my mouth was hanging open in shock.

"Good!" Royce gushed. "Ha! I knew you'd go for it!"

I was still staring. "But-"

"Penny, he's got a point." Alomar's voice grew low. "I once felt purpose. I knew what my time meant to me. I miss that more than I could ever explain, you see?"

I was suddenly at a loss for words. A familiar feeling of panic was building inside me. It felt like butterflies and hot air both swirling around in the pit of my stomach.

Royce was aiming his gaze at me now.

"One chance. One life, Pen. This is it! Let's not waste away like so many do! Blast the chains we were born with! Let's set out and see the world!"

What was this man's fascination with chains and shackles?

I was silent for a good long moment before finally uttering my reply. "Maybe you should become King of Eisley. You know how to speak, friend. Did you write this speech? Practice it first?"

Royce laughed. "Many times over."

"Really?"

"Fates, no. I'll leave the writing to you writers."

"Writer-in-Training," I corrected.

Royce blinked. "Sure. Anyhow, it's been on my mind for a long time, mate. I know we won't regret it. And I know I'll look back and regret never having taken a chance on life if I don't now."

The whispering current of the water passing under South Bridge continued on its way, indifferent to our presence and the potentially life-changing decision we were pondering. I repeated Royce's words in my mind before replying. "One life to live, eh?"

Royce nodded. Alomar was looking at me with a glimmer in his eye I had never seen before.

I sighed, trying to ignore the panic. In my typical fearful fashion, I mustered a rather anticlimactic answer.

"I'll think about it."

CHAPTER 6

I made my way down the street in the night. The wind had started to pick up, and I found myself wishing I had worn a winter coat. The street was lit by oil lamps and torches burning in sconces outside of buildings and homes, coupled with the occasional candle glow behind the glass of windows, all casting a dull orange accent to the city around me. I imagined that the flames had all been lit for me, showing me the way home.

I kept replaying our conversation on South Bridge in my head, over and over.

Royce was always going on about the water being bluer elsewhere. He was always talking about how one day the three of us, especially him, would become kings, or get rich, or have our names chiseled in stone for all coming generations to admire. I don't think I ever realized how much thought he had given those matters. Perhaps I should have taken the man more seriously.

Now as I walked, I realized I was beginning to look at my life through a new set of eyes, sparked by the conversation on South Bridge.

I turned the corner and headed north, passing Wes the Blacksmith's shop and the neighboring bakery. During the day, one could see Wes frequently steal away next door to buy a slice or even entire loaves of bread from Sara, the bakery's keeper.

Ah, yes. The Crusty Crust Bakery.

I chuckled to myself, moving on in the night. The quirky, ridiculous name Sara had bestowed upon her shop and livelihood was most definitely intentional. From the day she'd opened it, the Crusty Crust Bakery was a sensation with the entire South Quarter of Northroe. Within a week, the bakery's name was on everyone's tongues from corner to corner of the city.

It was difficult for me to imagine leaving Northroe, as Royce had urged.

I was a middle-aged man who had lived in Northroe since I was a boy. I had met Royce, his brother Trev, and Alomar while being chased out of a noble's manor in the North Quarter and into the nearby backstreets. They saved me from being caught during a particularly pitiful attempt at stealing food from the nobleman's house, and we became inseparable from that moment on.

In truth, an entire book could be written about our experiences as orphaned street urchins trying to survive in Northroe.

The wind still rippled steadily, and my breath clouded into mist in front of my face. The cool autumn air had made the full transition into a cold chill, a preview of the winter soon to come.

As I walked, I gazed at the tall buildings and the ominous alleys between them. The alleys were dark, but I knew that if one ventured just a minute or so into those backstreets, they'd come across scrappy, makeshift fires built by homeless folk.

More memories flickered from my childhood, a distant past in my mind's eye.

I could picture the street urchins and paupers warming their hands by the blaze of a fire they made out of a discarded wagon wheel, or the clothing from a dead man. I could recall happening across two men in a back alley in the Market Quarter, both fighting over a thick overcoat left behind by some poor soul whose lifeless, frigid body lay off to the left against a stone wall.

One man, who already had a warm outfit he'd somehow been lucky or ruthless enough to acquire, was trying to use the coat to fuel his dying fire. The other man, lacking any winter clothing, was trying to win the coat from the other so he could simply try to stay warm and alive.

I could recall lucidly the anger that had overcome Royce, Alomar, Trev and I when we had stumbled upon this scene. How could one be so greedy? Perhaps we were too young to keep in mind that living on the streets and freezing to death could do just about anything to anybody.

The four of us ended up charging the two men. We succeeded in wrestling the overcoat away from the greedy man, and handed it to the other. The pitiful soul thanked us from the bottom of his heart, and swore he'd never forget our act of kindness before hurrying off into the maze of backstreets behind us. We never saw him again.

The other man, whom we later nicknamed The Greedy Bastard, looked us all dead in the eyes and made his own promise. He, too, would never forget our faces, and swore that if we ever showed up in his part of the backstreets, he'd cut our throats before we could bark a plea in protest.

We never ventured back that way in the alleys again.

Now there I was, more than a couple decades later, thinking of so many things I hadn't mused over in a very long time. I even took a step toward the alley in the distance without really thinking about it, but I was stopped in my tracks by the gruff voice behind me.

"Oy. Got business in these parts?"

I turned to find myself face-to-face with a sturdy-looking member of the City Watch.

Watchmen wore expertly crafted, lightweight armor as white as snow that gleamed brilliantly in any source of light. Their helms did their job, protecting the guards well while looking intimidating, even at a distance. The man wore a short sword on his left side, a nasty club for beating on his right, and a small buckler shield slung across his back. A thick woolen scarf the same white shade as his armor was wrapped around his neck, which fit snug and covered his mouth as well to further insulate against the cold.

"Hoy there," I returned. "No business, not for me. Just going home."

I hoped he'd leave it at that. Some guards could be royal bastards, but most were respected and liked by the law-abiding citizens of Northroe.

The Watchman was drumming his fingers passively on the hilt of his sheathed sword, surveying me with his seemingly emotionless eyes. No doubt he was sizing up who I was, if I was a bad man, whether or not I paid my taxes, and what my favorite day of the week was, all in seconds.

"Right then," he said with a swift nod. "Carry on. Best get indoors, eh? Damned cold out here."

"Aye, it is. 'Night to you," I answered, returning his nod.

"G'night."

We parted ways, and I continued on through the night for a few more minutes before finally reaching the eastbound street that led back to the Windfarer's Inn.

He was right. Where had this sudden chill come from? I put my hands to my mouth and warmed them with my breath before rubbing them together briskly.

As I walked, I again thought of the prospect of leaving Northroe. It had been home for most of my life. Though it was a dull city compared to Foye in southeastern Eisley, or Belfour in the Northwest, or Eisley City, the capitol in the Heartland, Northroe still meant a lot to me and who I was. Who *we* were, my friends and I.

Then again, that was Royce's point, wasn't it? We'd never ventured outside of Northroe, Alomar's service abroad being the only exception. So how did we know anything about the rest of Eisley, except for hearsay?

I exhaled deeply, emitting the misty vapor of my breath into the air. That panicked feeling hadn't left me since the conversation on South Bridge. I hadn't felt that nervousness, that anxiety, in a long time.

Fear. That's what it was. Uncertainty scared me. My life as a child on those very streets probably had something to do with that.

Waking up in my father's cottage in the woods south of Northroe one morning as a lad and discovering he wasn't there probably didn't help, either. Left on my own to fend for myself with no warning, from him or the Fates.

I'd been very young at the time, not yet eight years of age. My mother died while giving birth to me, and my father was so poor he had no paintings or portraits or anything of the like of her, so I never knew what she'd looked like, except for what my father had told me. He didn't tell me much, because the pain of her death haunted him so.

Regardless, my father was a good man and raised me, and planned on moving to Northroe to get a small house for us if he could earn enough funds from selling timber to the mill nearby.

Like the great city of Port Journey was known for its fishing industry, Northroe was famous for its logging and woodworking. My father was a woodcutter trying to make his way in a very crowded sea, but he just couldn't seem to beat out the bigger fish. He had just begun teaching me the trade in the vast wooded sprawl of the Kovald Forest when I woke up one morning and he simply wasn't there.

I can remember searching our two-room cottage many times over, the surrounding paths, meadows and thickets, but to no avail. I never found out what became of him. It was a harsh thing for a child to wake up to, but such was life in the world. Things of the sort happened.

After three or four days of wandering about our cottage and the surrounding area scared and hungry, I finally made my way north to the city and fell in with Northroe's underclass, keeping to the shadows and trying to scrap out anything I could for myself without getting killed or run off.

That was one rather unique connection Royce, Alomar, Trev and I had all shared – we were all orphaned in one way or another.

The Bartha brothers lost their mother in a fire, and their father just up and left them one day in the streets of the city, reassuring his sons that they'd be "better off without him" before instructing them to forge a path of brilliance and success through life. Royce's father said this as he left them without coin and food, huddling together scared behind a small shop as he turned and vanished into the rainy night.

Awfully classy, yes?

Alomar, simply put, never told how he lost his parents, and we always knew to leave it at that.

As I shuffled through old memories, I again pulled my coat tighter around me to ward off the cold air. The street sloped upward, so as I neared the inn, more of it seemed to rise into view.

The more I thought about Royce's plan to leave Northroe, the more appealing it became. The more it grew on me, the more scared I felt. The more scared I felt, the more I just wanted to be in my bed, sleeping my way to a fresh new day the next morning – a day without such bold thoughts and ambitions.

Listen to me, so scared of change that I was hoping to erase these thoughts of a new way of looking at life, something new to hope for… all over a night's rest.

Yes, I was scared of striking out into the world… but far more terrifying was the notion of my two best friends leaving without me.

CHAPTER 7

At last, I reached the inn and quietly let myself in. The front lobby was peaceful. The few chairs were empty, and Marv the Maintenance Man was leaning on one elbow on the front desk, supporting himself as he slept.

It was good to know we had tight security.

I made my way through the lobby and up the creaking staircase to the second floor, turned into the hallway, and almost collided with Head Innkeeper Domheimer.

"Oh! Penny. Good timing. I was just knocking at your door, actually. Well, I was about to, rather."

Frederick Domheimer, Head Innkeeper of the Windfarer's Inn, was a decent man. He did have a bit of a superiority complex, but maybe I was just more tolerant than most people. Domheimer was balding, short and stout, and had this annoying habit of wringing his hands almost methodically while talking. His voice was nasally, and when he disagreed with something you said, the man would even more annoyingly try to break it to you gently, like trying not to upset you because he assumed everyone else got just as ridiculously peeved over nothing as he did.

Did I say Domheimer was a decent man? Perhaps I had my reservations.

"Oy there, Innkeeper. How goes it?"

"Listen Penny, I need you to... yes, I need a favor from you," he answered, and I was sure he hadn't even heard my words of greeting. "I need you to turn in the month's ledger and records by tomorrow night."

"Eh? But that's a week-"

"Week in advance, yes. Yes, indeed."

Cue more hand wringing, and mousey shifting of the eyes.

"Indeed," he repeated again.

I waited for him to continue, but he just stared at me, so I did the next most sensible thing.

"Um. Well of course, Innkeeper. It'll be done."

"And when will it be done, Penny?"

"By tomorrow night."

Domheimer's face lit up. "Good lad. Excellent. My thanks. Remember, by nightfall," he said, walking away.

"Aye, Innkeeper."

"Don't forget!" he called again. "By tomorrow-"

"Night, yes," I sighed. "Tomorrow night. Got it."

This wasn't one of the times I wanted to take after Royce's ways and throw the man out of a window or anything, but Domheimer was still an unreachable itch.

Now, Assistant Innkeeper Trenten? Different story. Trenten was insufferable and a complete scourge upon the land.

I finally opened the door to my room, only then realizing my vision was a bit fuzzy. We did drink plenty that night, after all.

The small piece of parchment caught my eye just then. It was on the floor, not a pace inside my room. I shut my door and knelt to grab it. It had been folded and slipped under the door, that much was certain. Striding over to my desk, I hung my coat and rubbed sleep away from my eyes long enough to spread out the page and read it.

Oy mate. It's Jacques. You weren't in your room when I came by. I don't want to be an arse about this, and was hoping to tell you in person, but I'm heading downriver to Glydell to help out my brother with a few things. Stuff on his farm and whatnot. He needs help transporting some grain and the like, and a mate of mine has agreed to let me borrow a horse and wagon. Of course I'll be stopping by the Crusty Crust Bakery on my way out. You know me.

I groaned and blinked. Then I groaned a bit louder before continuing on.

What I mean to say is, I can't do this month's ledgers. I know it's short notice, but I don't expect to be back within the week, maybe even two. Genuine apologies, Penny. I'm sorry. Hope you can look past this.

-Jacques

I stared down at the note in my hand, jaw set and eyes narrowed as I tried to make sense of what I just read. I think I reread the note four more times before cursing and flinging it into the air. I then kicked the wall with all my might, because hurling the parchment into the air and watching it gently float down to the floor didn't satisfy my anger nearly enough.

This was some crusty crust, all right. The month's deadline was tomorrow night and my only ticket to getting it done was going to be a week's ride south in the Glydell Farmlands.

CHAPTER 8

The next morning, after a rather sleepless night, I sat at my desk, watching the sun rise slowly into the sky. It declared a new day for the world with an array of dull pinks, blues and gold. Slumping back on my old rickety chair, I traced patterns passively onto the desktop with my fingers, my eyes glazing over at the sight of the stacks of paperwork waiting for me.

So much to do in so little time. I doubted even Jacques could do it.

I groaned and tried to wipe away stubborn sleep from my burning eyes. I couldn't believe that man chose now of all times to disappear! I had planned to ask Royce and Alomar for help in finding someone to temporarily fill Jacques' boots, but that was obviously out of the question now since I couldn't leave the inn.

Sighing, my gaze wandered this way and that in the dull light of my room. *Blast it, Jacques! How could you? Not now!*

I felt a creeping guilt. It wasn't Jacques' fault I was mathematically inept. I couldn't expect him to shape his life around mine, with absolute thought for my own convenience.

No. I had gotten myself into this mess.

As usually happened while making any attempt to even glance at the workload on the desk, my eyes wandered to my writings. Stories and ideas scattered this way and that, largely unorganized thoughts about fantastical journeys and brave heroes in lands afar. I had only ever finished three projects among hundreds of budding ideas.

I suppose that was an accomplishment. To finish a work of fiction, or a poem, or any artistic writing endeavor was something anyone could be proud of. However, all three of my completed works had been denied publishing by Lucille of The Weathered Page, a large bookshop in the North Quarter.

Apparently nobody had an interest in stories about men who could turn into wolves, or immortal creatures that sucked the blood of humans in the dead of night.

I had also been sure that *The Pirate Who Ate Everyone* was going to be a smashing success, but alas, it was not so.

Not getting any closer to that dream of yours, Penny.

There was one exception, a project I had never taken to Lucille. It was nearly finished, but I just could not decide on an ending for the life of me.

I found it instantly among the paper maze on my desk. My desk may have been unorganized, but when it came to my writings, I knew exactly where each project was amidst the chaos.

Reaching for it, I set the papers out in front of me and quickly scanned over the first few pages. A smile formed across my lips. It was different from anything I'd written before.

This was it. This was the one.

Looking back now, I think I was so sure of how good that book was that I never brought it to Lucille because I couldn't bear the thought of it being rejected like my other works.

The Eagle and the Raven was about a decorated, elite general of his King's army who turns traitor, switching sides after he falls in love with a woman hailing from the country his nation is at war with.

The story had everything! Heroism, action, suspense, romance... I had poured everything I could into it. There hadn't been a book like it ever written!

Mulling over it in the candlelight, I took out my ink and breathed deeply. Royce had said it himself, hadn't he?

One life to live. Live for your passion.

I wanted to write more than anything. I wanted my name to be known throughout the land, and I didn't care if it was a ridiculous dream to others. It was my dream. Stretching, I began to comb through the pages of my story one last time.

I had no way of knowing my life, and the lives of my friends, would be forever changed before the next dawn arrived over Northroe.

* * *

I spent the rest of that day locked away in my room at the inn, sitting at my desk, looking over my story. I had never written with such passion. The world around me slipped away. The faces of Domheimer, Trenten, Thomas and Sophie Flannery, even those of my friends and acquaintances at the November Raven all faded to a mist in a dark corner of my mind. All light of my thoughts shone on my story.

When the sun started to fall in the East and the shadows of the pines and buildings in the view outside my window began to grow longer, reaching across the grass and cobbled streets, I only then realized I had shunned my responsibilities to the inn. I hadn't so much as given a thought to finishing the month's ledgers for Innkeeper Domheimer, and I had ignored every knock at my door that day.

As far as I was concerned, I was not sitting in my room at the inn. The real world did not exist. I was lost in my book's world, breathing its air and giving voice to those who inhabited it.

It was profoundly liberating. I would most likely be out of a job and thus homeless as punishment by morning's light, yet I cared not.

When the sun finally set completely behind the forested mountain ranges in the mighty Kovald Forest off to the East, I stretched with a smile on my face. At last! It was time to meet with friends at the tavern we all loved. I could already hear Ozlow's cheery shouts and feel the warmth of ale and good company.

I pulled my coat over my tunic and looked down at the stack of pages on my desk. I couldn't remember the last time I'd felt so proud. A warm sensation of... satisfaction, I think, was welling up inside me. Was this good feeling so foreign to me that I could hardly recognize it?

I felt like I had to gather these positive feelings into a bottle, and hold it beneath the surface so it could not bob in the waves of foolish thinking. I felt that if I became too enthusiastic, I'd somehow sabotage everything, my luck included.

Time to get out of this blasted inn.

I decided very quickly I couldn't wait for Royce and Alomar. If they came and I wasn't there, Marv would tell them I'd left already. He was good for something, at least.

I turned and left quickly, practically running down the stairs, and promptly bumped into Head Innkeeper Domheimer.

"Ah! Penny. I trust the ledgers are-"

"Not finished," I said, almost happily.

"What?" he asked in confusion. "Penny, I specifically-"

"Aye," I interrupted, bounding down the stairs past him and perhaps enjoying myself a bit too much. "You wanted them turned in by tonight. Night's not over yet, Innkeeper!"

I didn't venture a single look back as I left the inn, but I was sure Domheimer was at a loss for words, for he uttered nothing as I closed the doors to the front lobby behind me and cheerfully strode into the street.

Minutes later I was grinning as I neared the doors to the November Raven. A small group of men was loitering around outside as usual, talking about work, the country or women, most likely. As I neared them, I gave a nod, and a couple of them raised their bottles and flasks in acknowledgement.

"Penny!"

I turned to see Royce jogging to me across the street and barely out of the way of a peddler's cart. The driver cursed at him loudly, and Royce turned and told the man to go to hell with sensational finesse.

"How goes it?" I greeted.

"Oy. You must be thirsty, eh? I went by the inn, but you'd already left."

I gave what I hoped came off as an apologetic grin. "Sorry. Couldn't stay holed up in there any longer. Where's Alomar?"

Royce shrugged. "I don't know, mate. I was hoping perhaps he beat me to it and went to meet up with you at the inn. Apparently not."

I jabbed a thumb at the tavern. "Feeling thirsty?"

"Aye."

We both strode inside. It was cozy as always, already half-full with patrons and warm with laughter and the chorus of clinking mugs. I saw that a couple barmaids were cleaning unoccupied tables, and another was fetching a tray full of drinks from the counter.

And then I saw *her*. A woman I didn't recognize.

"Hey," I nudged Royce, pointing toward Ozlow's bar. "Look at her. Ever see her here before?"

She was most alluring, in an oddly plain sort of way. The woman stood by herself off in a dark corner behind the bar counter. She had dark red hair and striking eyes that seemed red-brown, though I couldn't tell if it was a trick of the light. Her skin was tanned and seemed almost bronze in the glow of the torchlight near her. Her lips were pursed tightly and her gaze was hard. She seemed to be surveying everyone in the building.

"Oy," I repeated, "you ever seen her here before?"

Royce jarred me out of my fixation with a nudge of his shoulder, and pointed toward the tables on the other side of the pub, to our left. I followed his stare.

Alomar was sitting by himself at a table that looked much too small for his strong frame. His face was buried in his hands, and his elbows were planted firmly on the oak tabletop among three empty mugs. The man was clearly upset, to the point where I couldn't tell if his flushed cheeks were complements of distress, or the three ales he'd already downed.

"Bloody 'ell," whispered Royce. He turned to me. "You ever seen him like that?"

I shook my head. "No. And he never sits anywhere but the bar. The devil is he doing over there by himself? I don't like this, Royce."

We made our way to him quickly and stepped carefully, as if we were in danger of waking a sleeping giant. Royce and I reached the table, pulled out our chairs and took our seats. Alomar barely lifted his head to acknowledge our presence.

"Fates, mate," Royce said, "what's wrong? You look like you just found out you're scheduled for execution tomorrow."

"Oh?" asked Alomar. He kept scratching at his short hair sporadically. "Is th-that all? Be a blessing thompared to... compared to this, I meant."

I looked incredulously at the man, then down at the empty mugs on the table. "You've only had three ales, mate. You're slurring like you've been drinking for hours."

"Aye," Royce chimed in. "Everyone knows you can stand on your feet and recite the Eislian Anthem backwards after twenty ales and a knock to the head. What's the matter, Al? You look terrible."

Alomar finally straightened and looked at us, then down at the table. He started to gently slide his empty mugs into a circle, taking great care so that the handles were all touching in the center.

I looked at Royce and just shook my head. He shrugged back, wide-eyed.

"Well, you thee mates. You see, rather. I've been 'ere for a couple hours already an' I–"

Before he could finish, Alomar abruptly doubled over and dry-heaved.

Royce and I both stood in concern, but our friend held up his hand and motioned for us to sit back down.

"Oh, come off it. I'm just a lil' drunk. Sit down."

We reluctantly obliged. I turned in my seat to try to catch Ozlow's eyes up at the counter. I did, and the bartender only shrugged with a sad expression and returned to cleaning dirty glasses.

"Mates," Alomar continued slowly, "there's only three empty mugs here because I've already drank twelve or s-so...whole table was full of empty glasses earlier. The maid, th-that new one rith the whed hair over there... she already cleaned up for me here. I'm starting o-over."

Royce glanced over my shoulder at who I guessed was the stunning new woman with the red hair. I watched Alomar silently.

"So," I rephrased, "you literally covered this entire tabletop with empty mugs of ale."

"I will fill this table again!" shouted Alomar suddenly. "It will happen!"

"Alomar-"

"All glasses!" he roared in slurred, angry agony. He got to his feet shakily. "All glasses empty! Empty like my soul!"

Royce cursed incredulously and slammed his fist down hard, sending Alomar's perfect circle of mugs bumping into the air with a slight clink. "Alomar! Snap out of it!"

I just stared in awe. Concentrated, pure awe. The Fates themselves rarely bottled it the way I felt it now.

When Alomar reluctantly obeyed and slumped back into his seat, Royce did as well.

"Bloody 'ell," Royce said, grinning at me, his eyes twinkling in the candlelight. "Can you believe this?"

I shook my head. "Don't think it's very funny, mate."

"Oy there, lads," came a woman's voice.

All three of us, even Alomar, turned to see the new red-haired woman walking up to our sad state of a table.

I gave a nod, trying to play off as if I wasn't unnerved by her presence.

Royce stood quickly, sending his chair sliding across the floor behind him and bumping into what was luckily an unoccupied table nearby.

"Madame," he said, eyes overflowing with admiration. "To what do we owe the honor of your presence?"

The woman raised her eyebrows and then motioned toward Alomar. "I'd suggest no more drinks for this one," she said, ignoring Royce. "He's had a bit much, as you'd prolly noticed."

Royce remained standing. "A name, please. I must know the name of such grace. Such-"

"Please," the woman interrupted. "Save yourself some time and-"

"You're beautiful," uttered Royce. I suspect that one slipped, judging the confused expression on his face immediately after saying so.

She just stared – a most unimpressed stare, at that. "Can I get either of ya a drink?"

"Two amber ales, please," I answered coolly, seizing my chance to not be an idiot in front of her and capitalize on Royce's flustered performance. "I'm ordering for him, you see. He's so captivated and all that, my friend's forgot his favorite drink."

Royce scowled at me. The nameless lass simply smiled and turned to make her way back to the counter. I noticed as she walked away that she was actually rather strong for a woman. Not large by any means, no; but the way she leaned across the counter to inform Ozlow of our drinks showed off toned muscle in her arms.

I heard the clinking sound of the mugs being arranged yet again into another pattern, and turned my attention from the woman back to Alomar.

Royce took his seat and looked at us both before he spoke. "As much as I want to talk about that woman's perfection, you need to explain, Alomar. What in hot blazes happened? What's got you so knocked about?"

"Aye," I added. "Let's hear it. You're scaring me."

The man took a deep breath. He spoke slowly, trying not to get his words confused and slurred beyond understanding.

"It's Corrine. I... I think she's seeing someone else."

"What!?" Royce hissed in a strange whisper.

I felt a heavy pang weigh upon my heart. I opened my mouth, but couldn't say anything.

"Corrine's seeing another man, I think," repeated Alomar hollowly.

Royce and I looked at each other, eyes wide and mouths hanging open in disbelief. There were no words to say at that moment.

"Discovered a letter, I did," Al continued.

The new barmaid returned, unknowingly interrupting the man. "Here ya go, lads. Easy does it, aye?"

We just nodded weakly as she set down two new mugs of ale on the table in front of Royce and I before scooping up the empty ones in seemingly the same motion. The woman lingered momentarily, like she was puzzled by our sudden change of attitude, but said nothing and made her way back to her corner behind the counter. I thought it was interesting that she seemed to stay up front in her little shadowy perch and didn't circulate like the other barmaids, but I left any speculation at that, turning my attention back to my grieving friend.

Alomar pulled a folded piece of paper from his coat and held it dangerously close to the candle's flame. I thought about how just last night, Royce had produced his own parchment in much the same manner. This was certainly the season of dreaded parchments.

"This," Alomar uttered solemnly, "is a letter from... from some bloke to my wife. He...."

I could tell Alomar was having trouble keeping his composure, and gritted my teeth at the sight of him in such sadness.

Alomar cleared his throat. "This is a letter from some blight to Corrine. In it he describes his... feelings for her, as it were. Trying to court her. I won't get more specific about it."

More silence as Alomar gathered himself momentarily. His jaw was clenched as tightly as his fingers were gripping the letter in his hand.

Royce hadn't taken a single sip of his ale. His eyes were narrowed, and he cast me a nervous glance. I was speechless. The air weighed down on us like nothing I'd felt before. Alomar and Corrine had always been perfectly happy together. Their love had only seemed to grow stronger since the day they had married, and their marriage was known in many circles as a fruitful, genuine coupling.

The news was sudden and more than unexpected. It was terrible. If I was taking it this badly, I could only imagine how Alomar was feeling.

"Mate," Royce finally said carefully, "do you know who it is? The one who wrote the letter?"

Our large friend shook his head. "Just initials on the bottom. No name or signature. Some bloke named T.S."

"T.S.," I echoed.

I could tell by the intense glimmer in Royce's eyes that he, like myself, was rapidly picking through his mind, trying to see if he knew anyone with those initials. I myself knew a foreigner named Tuhrm, and of course there was Thomas Flannery, and Tuttles Finnigan, a trader in the Merchant Quarter. But not only did none of those men have matching initials to the ones disclosed in the letter, none hardly seemed up to Corrine's standards. She was a beauty, and most men could only wish on the stars that a woman like her would ever take a liking to them.

Royce finally shook his head at me in silence, wordlessly informing me that he hadn't thought of any potential men to fit T.S., either.

"When I find this T.S.," Alomar murmured, "I'll gut him like a pig."

At that moment, the door to the tavern opened, and a tall, muscular man with long blonde hair and bronze skin entered with much pep in his step.

"Hoy there, lads!" the newcomer boomed to the front counter as he strode toward it.

Alomar had his back to most of the pub and was still staring into space, but Royce and I watched the newcomer as a group of men up at the bar welcomed him loudly.

"Oy, Tyrius! It's about bloody time!"

"Aye, we was wondering when you were gonna show-"

"Thought you died, Tyrius!"

'Tyrius' started with the right letter, at least. I watched the man for a moment. A potential suitor for Corrine, at least. He was certainly strapping enough.

I rolled my eyes at the thought and finally took a long swig of ale. Now I was surely going to be suspicious of any man whose name began with a 'T.'

"That's right, my friends!" Tyrius crowed enthusiastically as he took his place among them. "Ozlow! Time to celebrate!"

"Celebrate, eh?" Alomar asked, cursing. "To be so lucky."

Royce took a drink and folded his arms on the table, watching this Tyrius fellow closely before speaking. "Alomar, I'm sorry, my friend. I don't know what else to say."

"Aye," I chimed in somberly. "I'm sorry, mate."

We drank and Alomar nodded in dejection.

"Attention, everyone! Please!"

I looked up to see that the man called Tyrius had stood up on Ozlow's bar, and was addressing everyone in the pub. Royce was looking on as well, and we swapped glances. Alomar paid no mind. He was huddled over the table, shoulders slouched in defeat while his eyes watched the wood of the tabletop, as if it somehow might provide answers.

"Attention!" called Tyrius once more. "On this night, I have a woman's promise of her hand in marriage!"

Most of the tavern's patrons cheered and lifted their mugs and glasses alike, and some made their way to the growing celebratory crowd at Ozlow's bar counter. I noticed that the red-haired barmaid was instantly at Ozlow's side with trays of drinks ready, handing them out across the counter with a brilliant smile.

"I, Tyrius Sewell, will be leaving the city with her on the morrow!" the man gushed. "Here's to the divine fortune provided by the Fates themselves! Here's to the beautiful woman who will surely be mine!"

"Who is it?" a voice called.

Tyrius Sewell flashed a rascal's grin. "A married woman, that's who. But she won't be married for much longer!"

The crowd cheered wildly, and ale was sloshing about this way and that way, spilling over the brims of mugs as they clinked together in celebration. Tyrius tipped his glass back and chugged the entire drink, and his companions did the same. Ozlow joined in, raising his own mug and ignoring the spilled beer and ale that splashed about on the bar.

Alomar's eyes flashed open. I met them with my own.

"Tyrius... Sewell?" he whispered drunkenly to me.

Royce looked at me, then at Alomar. "Oh, no. Come now, Al. What are the chances, honestly?"

Alomar straightened in his chair and turned to look at the blonde-haired Tyrius.

"Alomar," I hissed, "come on, mate! You don't really think-"

"Barmaid!" shouted Tyrius, his face the essence of glee. "Another round for my friends and I! Another round to my future wife, a goddess among women! Woe, that she could not be here with us tonight!"

Lightning erupted in the pub, but no one could hear it over the celebration. A storm crashed in that very moment, taking form in Alomar as the war veteran stood with a maniacal, bloodthirsty glare.

All the air went out of my lungs without my consent. Royce and I looked at each other in horror. Our eyes practically bulged out of our skulls. I saw Alomar's eyes and grew alarmed when I realized the fire in them wasn't from the candlelight.

"Oh, hell," Royce uttered lowly. He stood and rounded the table to Alomar's side so quickly that I barely saw it happen. "Al. Listen to me."

I stood uneasily. Looking to Tyrius and his many friends, I saw them gathered in a huddle, toasting once more and downing their drinks. I could feel a sort of rage begin welling up inside me.

"Royce," Alomar said in a low snarl that made my blood cold, "let go of me."

"Stop, Al," Royce breathed. He looked at me wildly. "Pen, help me! He's gonna kill him!"

I was on the other side of Alomar in one stride. I knew what Royce said was true.

"Alomar, listen!" Royce urged. "I know he deserves it, I do. But you'll be arrested. Think, mate. Wait!"

Alomar started walking toward the bar. I grabbed his right arm, and Royce was holding on to his left.

"Alomar!" I pleaded. "Wait! Stop!"

He didn't wait, nor did he stop. The man ignored us and stepped closer to Tyrius and his friends, still fifteen or so paces away, oblivious to us and the danger so imminently close.

Alomar shook me off easily and shouldered Royce away, but Royce practically dove forward again and caught Alomar's shin, then wrapped his arms around the man's ankle. Alomar merely dragged the man a few paces before shaking him loose.

I could only hold my breath.

A warrior in commoner's clothes, Alomar walked straight up to the circle of men at the bar with Ozlow.

"Oy there," Alomar said loudly with a good-natured smile. I was shocked at how genuine it looked. "How 'bout I buy the next round?"

Tyrius and his mates turned. "Eh?"

"Next round's on me!" boomed Alomar. "To celebrate, yeah?"

"Ha!" cried Tyrius in glee, clapping his hand to Alomar's shoulder. "Many thanks, friend. Another round!"

CHAPTER 9

The November Raven was a scene of merriment, as far as everyone else was concerned. All eyes were on Tyrius Sewell and his party at the bar. Onlookers seated at tables throughout were all smiles and cheers as Ozlow nodded toward the red-haired barmaid at Alomar's request.

I considered stepping forward and trying to somehow bring Alomar back to where Royce and I nervously stood, back to where cool heads and collected wits may have reigned supreme, but I decided against it. Our friend was far beyond those bounds. I could see the hate lurking there in his eyes, a fire waiting to be set to the dry wood and brush that was Tyrius' celebration.

Swallowing hard, I blinked once, then twice, with what I imagine was a hard, aloof look on my face. Alomar was a detonation on two feet, waiting to explode in the midst of all those men.

Is this really about to happen?

The attractive barmaid whose name still eluded us stepped forward during the short, rushed life of my thoughts. Tyrius cheered and some of his mates clapped as she set a tray of mugs upon the counter in front of them all, each filled to the brim.

Most disturbing was how well Alomar was playing his part. He was clapping Tyrius on the shoulder, grinning widely and nodding enthusiastically with the man's friends as they reached for the newly presented ales.

"'Ey there!" called Tyrius loudly, looking toward Ozlow. "No way we're drinking without you, friend! C'mon, have a drink!"

Ozlow smiled widely, but humbly shook his head in refusal.

"Come now!" shouted a large man with a bushy beard at Tyrius' side. "Join us! Hear, hear!"

"To Ozlow!" roared Tyrius as he thrust his mug high.

"To Ozlow!" came the answering chorus of men and women throughout the pub.

Another man stepped up onto a chair and pointed with great stress at the bartender, who still stood behind his counter. "Oy! We ain't drinkin' without ya, Ozlow, so ya best grab a drink!"

Laughter and cheers erupted, and Ozlow the Bartender finally stepped forward, putting on a show of reluctance as he took a mug. The old man turned to the barmaids nearby and invited them to partake as well. Kara and her fellow barmaids grinned and accepted without needing encouragement, much to the joy of the large party gathered at the counter.

The red-haired woman did not join them.

So much joy, merriment, celebration. They seemed to blend into one sound that droned on, trying to deafen my thoughts, though it couldn't. One glance at Royce's face told me it was the same for him. We were nervously transfixed on the scene at hand, our concern set on our friend. Royce and I were the only two in the tavern that night standing stock-still.

In one loud round of cheers, seemingly the entire crowd tipped their mugs back and downed their drinks. Nobody seemed to notice that amidst the festivities, Alomar did not drink. Not one sip. The man was a stone dividing a river. He did not budge. He stared undaunted at Tyrius with such ferocity that I thought his eyes would pierce right through the man and burn anyone else in their path.

In all the years I'd known Alomar, I'd never seen such rage in the man. Not like this.

Additionally, as Tyrius, Ozlow and their companions all drank, nobody seemed to notice the red-haired woman step back from the counter and slip off to the rear corner of the tavern near the back door.

Her eyes were narrowed, her forehead was creased with thought and her jaw was set squarely. The woman watched them all very purposefully, seeming very intent on Tyrius and his mates with Alomar at the front of the crowd.

Watching her suddenly unnerved me. Her eyes were off. Something was wrong. I felt it like an animal can predict the rain.

As if she could hear my very thoughts, the nameless barmaid's red-brown eyes suddenly diverted to my own, and I was taken aback.

Our gazes met for but a few seconds. I can't explain the coldness behind her features. She was rather attractive in the dull, cozy glow of the torchlight, but she looked very angry. Her eyes somehow narrowed even further and her nose crinkled slightly as they did. She looked dangerous, yet captivating. I could not bring myself to look away.

It was there. I saw the same ferocity in her eyes that I could see in Alomar's... but the woman's ferocity was cold and calculating, much different than Alomar's heated and passionate rage.

My heart skipped a beat.

Before I could even think about all of this in the mere seconds that had passed, she opened the back door and slipped out silently into the night, releasing me from the captivity of her gaze.

Nobody else seemed to notice.

Royce cursed quietly, and it snapped my attention back to the crowd.

Among the celebratory cheers and splashing ale, Alomar's face had turned a slight shade of red. With a look of disgust, his deathly stare remained fixed on Tyrius Sewell's oblivious eyes.

Looking back now, I realize that Alomar was patiently waiting for Tyrius to notice him and make eye contact before making his move.

Tyrius finally met Alomar's unflinching stare.

"Oy, friend," Tyrius said, genuinely puzzled, "you didn't drink! Are you-"

Before the man could finish, Alomar clutched the man by the shoulder in an iron grip, cocked back his other hand, and brought down his still-full glass of ale on Tyrius' head.

CHAPTER 10

The mug connected with Tyrius' temple with shocking force. Shards of glass and spears of ale sprayed outward in every direction. Tyrius crumpled under the blow immediately with a thud.

I imagined that everyone would halt their celebrations in surprise, and silence and confusion would blanket the crowd as everyone struggled to comprehend what had just happened in their midst.

It didn't really work out that way.

Yells of confusion and anger sounded off quickly all around the bar. A couple of the barmaids screamed as Tyrius' mates rushed Alomar in a breath's instant, knocking Ozlow over in the process. Everyone dropped their mugs and spilled rum and ale all over, making the floor and counter slick and slippery.

Judging by the lightning-fast reaction of Tyrius' mates, I concluded that they'd done this before.

With a maniacal roar, Royce shot forward without hesitation and bounded over a table, sending glasses flying and the still-shocked patrons seated there ducking as he threw himself mercilessly into the crowd. Two of Tyrius' men were sent reeling backwards out of the fray a moment later.

Alomar threw a wicked punch that sent an attacker falling into another nearby table, knocking it over. More glass broke, and the man and two women who had been seated there were on their feet quickly and running for the door.

Three of Tyrius' mates assaulted Alomar not a second later, driving him backward toward another table. The men who had been seated there were already diving out of the way as the brawlers slammed into it, knocking dishes and chairs this way and that. The table broke under the impact.

"Dammit, Pen!" shouted Royce somewhere in the chaos. "Get your arse over here!"

I was no fighter. I wasn't a trained warrior like Alomar. I didn't know a thing about scrappy street fighting like Royce did.

I should have stepped in sooner!

I found Royce amidst the fray, on his feet and grappling with a man. He took a hard punch to the nose and fell backwards. In an instant, my friend was back on his feet, not bothering to wipe the blood from his face. He grabbed the man's shoulders before jerking his head forward in a vicious head-butt. Royce's opponent dropped instantly, unconscious.

Alomar was trying to push past his attackers and get to Tyrius, who was crawling away from the brawl in a daze and trying to reach safety behind the bar counter.

Ozlow was trying to restore order, but when a chair sailed just over his head, the poor old man ducked behind the counter. Kara and another barmaid decided they'd had enough. They screamed and ran out of the tavern, bursting out into the streets, no doubt to find the City Watch or any help they could get.

"Penny!"

It was Alomar this time, and the anger in his roar was so potent that it snapped me from my stupid, awestruck state.

I, Penny Daulton, Writer-in-Training, was going to fight. I also was clueless on how to do so, but given the circumstances, to hell with it.

I hollered fiercely in what I thought was a war cry to be reckoned with and rushed to the action, leaving my furiously beating heart struggling to catch up.

Alomar was standing over a man, gripping him by the collar and pummeling away when one of Tyrius' mates tackled him. The two men rolled violently, crashing through more chairs and tables.

As they did so, the man Alomar had pinned a moment before got to his feet, teeth clenched and eyes narrowed as he wiped blood from his mouth.

He didn't see me coming.

I threw myself recklessly into him. We collided, but I fell to the floor instead of my intended victim. He stumbled backward a bit, but stayed on his feet.

The man looked rather angry. I hastily stood and braced myself.

From somewhere to my right, there was a roar, and Royce rushed my victim just as he was about to come at me. The two grappled savagely. I started toward them to help Royce when the most spectacular impact of callused knuckles crashed into my cheekbone from my right.

Thunder crashed in my ears, and bright spots lit up my vision.

I fell and hit the ground hard, my head knocking into the floor as I rolled onto my stomach. Someone had completely blind-sided me.

I couldn't blink away the haze I was seeing.

Two hostile hands grabbed my coat and started to lift me upward. In my daze, I could make out one of Tyrius' friends leering over me with his hand cocked back.

I lashed out with terrible form and hit the man upside his face with an openhanded slap.

He yelped in surprise and dropped me back to the floor. I could see my handprint already forming on his face. Before he could come at me again, I thrust forward with a mighty kick straight into his shin.

His bone broke with a nasty crack, and my attacker dropped to the floor, howling in agony.

I stood slowly, gripping the table next to me for support, feeling quite pleased with myself. Before I could get my bearings, another one of Tyrius' friends tackled me from behind, and we both pitched forward headfirst and slid across the floor.

Growling and trying to seem menacing, I thrashed about wildly, kicking and flailing my arms.

My boot connected solidly with someone.

"Fates!" barked Alomar, clutching his shin. "Fight the proper blokes, Penny!"

Another man had Royce pinned up against the bar counter and was desperately trying to land a hit. Royce was dodging his every attack, bobbing and weaving swiftly.

Royce finally sidled to the left. His hands shot forward and he grabbed the man's head in an iron grip and slammed it down into the counter with a yell. His nostrils flared and his eyes widened as he pointed frantically over my shoulder.

"Pen!"

I instinctively heeded his warning and dove to the floor as a chair crashed into the counter next to me, missing my head.

Alomar streaked by me with frightening speed toward my chair-throwing assailant. The other man swung, but Alomar ducked under the blow and thrust his shoulder upward, catching the man's chin with so much power that it lifted our opponent off of his feet completely.

With a muffled grunt, our foe crashed to the floor. Alomar was over him instantly and dropped his knee solidly down onto the man's stomach, followed by a brutal right hook to the jaw.

Royce was at Alomar's side a second later with a wild look on his face. I joined them immediately, struggling to catch my breath and wiping the sweat from my brow.

There were only two men left standing between us and Tyrius Sewell, who was in a daze on the floor behind them. There were unconscious bodies everywhere, many groaning in pain as they moped about on the floor without the strength to get to their feet.

Ozlow slowly, carefully ventured a look from the safety of the bar counter, and said nothing as he sadly surveyed the wreckage around his tavern. The two men stared at us, seemingly judging what their chances would be if they continued the fight.

The high of battle was coursing through my veins, exhilarating and new. I thumped my chest and spat at our enemies with a menacing glare.

To my dismay, a wad of spit harmlessly dribbled to the floor.

Royce shot me a most disapproving glare. I hastily wiped my mouth and chin.

We all stood in silence for what seemed like hours. Everyone that still stood was huffing and puffing, trying to catch their breaths among the low grumbles and moans of the incapacitated.

Among the unconscious bodies and the wounded, the November Raven sat in a dismal state. Tables, chairs and dishes were strewn about, littering the tavern. Some were splintered and broken, others were propped in wild positions this way and that way. Ale, rum and other spirits practically soaked the furniture, the floor and the people lying about. I saw a lit oil lamp swinging dangerously from the ceiling.

A stubbornly brave barmaid gingerly rose to her feet from behind the bar, and now moved to help Ozlow stand.

I was the only one of us brawlers who turned to venture a look at the bartender's face. Ozlow was shocked, his eyes sweeping around his establishment sadly. His mouth opened, but he said nothing. The barmaid was whispering tersely to him, probably trying to get the man to leave the building with her. Ozlow seemed to be paralyzed by grief, for he wouldn't budge.

It was Alomar who spoke finally.

"You two," he growled, pointing at the two remaining enemies who stood over Tyrius protectively, "leave now. My quarrel is with that man at your feet."

They looked at each other. A moment passed, and one of them sprinted suddenly for the door without a word, bolting out into the night. As he fled, I could hear the muffled murmurs of what sounded like a small crowd gathering outside rush in with the cold autumn air. No doubt everyone else heard it, too.

"Oy," Royce uttered hoarsely, pointing at Tyrius' last companion. "Get outta here."

The man was breathing hard and biting his lip in aggravation, clearly not wanting to abandon his friend. At last, he shook his head, faced us defiantly and spat at our feet.

I noted the man's skill in spitting in defiance in the face of an enemy was far greater than my own, no doubt practiced on occasion.

As if on cue, Tyrius sat up groggily, rubbing his head and wincing when his finger felt the warmth of blood.

"Out of my way," snarled Alomar. "This man doesn't even deserve your loyalty."

"Lads," Ozlow said lowly in a shaky voice, "the Watch will be here any moment. You've destroyed everything."

Tyrius' lone defender suddenly clutched at his stomach for a moment. His eyes narrowed in surprise and he bent over slightly as if his belly was in great pain, but he recovered as quickly as he could manage. Ozlow spoke again.

"Boys," the bartender pleaded, "you ruined everything. How could-"

Royce just held up his hand and looked over at the bartender, shaking his head slowly.

"This man," Alomar whispered gravely, "is an adulterer. Trying to marry my wife."

Tyrius squared himself. "I'm sorry, what did you say?"

"My Corrine," Alomar continued, his cool demeanor gradually becoming shaky and slightly rattled. "Corrine Sanstrom is my wife, and-"

"Wait, wait," Tyrius interrupted, getting to his feet with great effort. "You? You're Corrine's husband?"

Alomar was quaking with anger. "Don't interrupt me, you dismal sod."

Tyrius cursed and spat blood and a tooth at the floor.

Alomar sprinted forward in a fury, Royce right behind him.

Ozlow yelled.

Alomar slammed into Tyrius while Royce tackled the other man. The barmaids were yelling again, one of them shouting at the doors for help from the crowd assembling outside. Alomar picked up the cowering Tyrius Sewell from the floor in a show of strength and rage, and held him upright so that they stared each other in the eye.

"She's my wife, you son of a-"

"Not anymore!" screamed Tyrius.

Alomar grabbed a broken glass, it's jagged edges glinting off the torchlight, and cocked back his arm. Tyrius' eyes went wide.

"Alomar!" I shouted. *"No!"*

My friend never delivered the killing blow.

Tyrius suddenly coughed and made a gagging noise. I could see his face contort into pain and his stomach heave as he squirmed in Alomar's grip.

Alomar only had time to pause in question before Tyrius suddenly coughed a torrent of blood out of his mouth that sprayed onto Alomar's chest and shoulders, misting into the air.

Shocked, Alomar winced and stumbled backward, dropping the man to the floor. He tried wiping the blood from his face.

All eyes were on the pair when Ozlow suddenly dropped to his knees and vomited a crimson splash of blood onto the floor.

"By the Fates!" shouted Royce, echoing our shock.

"Ozlow!" cried the barmaid at his side. She barely got to her knees to help the poor man up when she too, doubled over and coughed her own blood out into the air, a red and black cloud that spattered about.

Royce, Alomar, Tyrius' last remaining friend and I all stood utterly amazed and taken aback. No one could speak.

Suddenly Tyrius' ally gave a scared shout and dashed for the door to the tavern. We all watched in horror as he pitched forward violently before getting halfway across the pub. The man fell on his face, vomiting and coughing as he did so. His body convulsed on the floor, and he was covered in his own blood as it mixed in with the puddles of ale around him.

All three of us recoiled in shock, stunned.

The door to the tavern swung open and banged loudly against the wall with force that seemed to shake the terrifying scene around us.

At a loss for words and completely numbed by shock, my friends and I turned to see a burly man clad in the white armor of the City Watch.

CHAPTER 11

I can only imagine what the City Watchman was thinking as he surveyed the tavern and us. We three men stood in the midst of broken glass, shattered interior décor, bodies of men and women that were bruised, unconscious, and some seemingly drowning in pools of their own blood.

It couldn't have looked good.

After taking in the scene slowly, clearly struggling to comprehend what he was seeing, the armored Watchman finally looked at us in astonishment.

"Sir?" I started. "I know this… can't look good, but-"

"Ozlow," the Watchman cut me off. "Where is the owner? Where's Ozlow?"

None of us could answer. I don't know if it was guilt or simply a loss for words, or that we were scared to answer the man's question, but we said nothing.

"Where is the owner of this tavern?" the Watchman asked coolly. "I won't ask again."

Alomar, his eyes on the floor, motioned toward the bar. "The counter, sir. Behind the bar."

The Watchman drew his blade, the short sword scraping against the sheath with a deathly sound, and he leveled it with purpose to his side at the ready. "The three of you, up against the counter. Turn around. Hands behind your back."

Royce balked. "But-"

"Now!" the guard commanded.

We sullenly made our way to the bar counter. The sounds of glass crunching beneath our boots and slushy footsteps across the ale-laden floor were all that could be heard. The Watchman did not budge until we had assumed the position at the counter.

The guard slowly made his way toward us, understandably apprehensive. I was between my two friends – Alomar on my right, Royce to the left. We didn't dare speak. My eyes wandered about the patterns in the wood counter.

I once ventured a look over the side of it to see if I could spot Ozlow's body, but he must have been just out of view... all I could see were splotches of blood near the fireplace, which still burned brightly.

The Watchman rounded the counter and stopped in his tracks, his horrified and angry gaze obviously having found Ozlow's body. I imagined the bartender lying there, lifeless, all bloody and twisted into a strange position on the floor of his own pub.

His jaw set and eyes glaring, the Watchman didn't move a muscle in his body for a few long moments as he stared at the corpses of the bartender and the barmaid next to him. The guard's hand was frozen in the air, still holding his short sword outward absently.

"Sir," I tried again, "this isn't what it looks like."

"That so?" the man replied quietly. His tone was unnerving.

"I can explain," Alomar broke in. "Sir, if you'd allow me to-"

The Watchman snapped his gaze suddenly to Alomar, and his eyes darted to the man's forearm. "2nd Cavalry?"

Alomar raised his eyebrows, confused for a moment, but then followed the guard's stare to the *2nd CAV* tattoo on his right arm, flanked by a long scar that had once been a deep wound on some long lost field of battle.

"Yes, I was in the cavalry."

The guard looked from Alomar's tattoo back to the man's eyes. "Dekka?"

"Aye."

Without hesitation, the guard pointed at Royce and I. "You two, take a few steps that way. Stay on the counter. Face the wall."

I realized he was trying to separate us. The man considered Alomar a danger because his military training and service deemed him a potentially deadly threat. An Eislian soldier's battle prowess was unmatched nearly the world over.

"Look, sir," Alomar started carefully, "just allow us to explain-"

The Watchman held up a gloved hand, and Alomar grew silent. Royce and I shuffled slowly and carefully against the counter and rounded to the other side. I didn't take my eyes off the Watchman's blade once as I did.

"You three are under arrest," the Watchman stated without emotion, like we should have known already.

"But-"

"I place you under arrest with the authority entrusted to me by the honorable Lord Hannady, for murder on... um, on..."

The Watchman paused in mid-sentence and surveyed the area. His mouth was moving silently and I realized he was counting bodies.

"... multiple counts."

"Aw, bollocks!" Royce groaned. "Please, it was self-defense!"

"You first," the Watchman commanded Alomar, ignoring Royce. "Hands behind your back, fingers spread apart. Palms up."

"Sir," Alomar pleaded, "may I speak?"

"You may," the Watchman said, "only because I recognize your service to our nation. Keep it brief."

"It was self defense, as my friend says," Alomar lied. "These men attacked us. We merely tried-"

"What, tried defending yourselves?" finished the guard. "This pub is painted in these men's blood. This looks like a slaughterhouse, for the Fates' sakes."

"I assure you," repeated Alomar. "We only defended ourselves. They struck first."

The Watchman slipped the cuffs around Alomar's wrists, and I heard a metallic click.

"As a veteran of this nation's great army," the Watchman said solemnly, "you are perfectly capable of handling yourself in a manner that would *not* result in the deaths of this many men who were clearly unable to match you in battle of any kind."

Well, the Watchman had one thing right. Tyrius Sewell and his friends hadn't stood a chance against Alomar and Royce. And myself, if I really counted.

"Don't move," the guard commanded. He strode toward Royce and I, stepping nimbly over a body and a broken chair as he did.

Royce cursed in a whisper.

I was suddenly overcome with a wave of dread, a trapped sensation, as if I were a caged animal. My life and the lives of my friends were over as we knew them. This was it.

Alomar shifted ever so slightly, accidentally thumping his knee against the counter behind us.

"Oy," growled the Watchman, turning quickly in a graceful motion with his sword readied, "not one movement from you. Got it?"

It was so sudden. I didn't even think about it. It just happened. The Watchman never saw it coming.

Gritting my teeth and squaring myself, I snatched a lit torch from its sconce on the wall just above me. The guard heard the torch scrape from the sconce and whirled toward me, but was a moment too late. I brought the torch, still aflame, down with all my might on his head.

The Watchman jerked his head left in a reflexive dodge, but my torch still caught the temple of his helm. There was a crack and shower of bits of wood and sparks, and the force of my blow knocked him towards the countertop. The hit I'd dealt with my swing didn't knock the man out, but the impact of his face against the side of the counter did.

The force of my attack so jarred my hand that it knocked the torch from my grip, sending it twirling wildly and crashing to the counter. The bar ignited as the torch flame mixed with the spills of alcohol everywhere.

The wave of heat that burst from the bar was enough to make me shield my face with my arms.

Royce hollered in alarm and pulled me away from the bar, both of us stumbling in our haste.

Alomar was staring at me, aghast that I, of all people, just assaulted a member of the City Watch, seemingly unconcerned about the flames as they spread.

And oh, did those flames spread. Frighteningly fast, at that. The fire raced along the surface and sides of the bar counter, thriving on the rum and ale that seemed to cover the entire premises. The blaze reached across the floor, swirling around the clusters of shambled furniture and feeding on the unconscious bodies lying about like dry brush and tinder. I saw a spear of flame furling its way up the walls, and an oil lamp swinging by a thread crashed to the ground in a burst of fire.

"Get back!" yelled Alomar.

Most likely in shock and not realizing it yet, we turned on our heels and rushed to the pub's entrance when I slid to a stop.

"Oy!" I shouted. "We can't just leave him here!"

"What?" asked Alomar.

I pointed urgently toward the bar. "The Watchman! We can't just bloody leave him to die!"

"Oh, hell," Royce protested. "Really?"

"We didn't kill these men," I yelled over the flames, "and we're not going to start now!"

Alomar butted in. "Now is not the time, Penny. We have to get out of here!"

"No!" I countered. "Besides, we need the key!"

"Eh?"

"The key to your cuffs!" I roared, pointing at Alomar's bound hands.

Both men cursed.

As if we were rehearsing a dance, we again spun on our heels, this time dashing for the counter from which we had fled. Alomar slipped on the blood of one of Tyrius' friends. Royce got him to his feet. I was the first to reach the bar.

"Careful Pen!" called Royce. He ignored his own advice, sprinting after me as fast as he could while hopping over burning wreckage.

I slid across the floor on my knees to the unconscious Watchman. The flames hadn't got to him yet, though how I'd never know. My eyes flickered momentarily to Ozlow, and I couldn't help but stare in terror when I saw fire devouring the old man's body.

"Help me!" Royce yelled while slipping his arms under the Watchman's shoulders in an attempt to scoop him up.

I was about to reach for the man's boots when Royce hissed in pain, dropping the Watchman back to the floor. It startled me, and I looked at him in a panic.

"Watch out!" growled Royce. "His armor's a bit hot, yeah?"

Alomar could only watch without the use of his hands. He was constantly craning his neck to and fro, watching around us for any sign of a sudden collapse or burst of flames.

Royce stripped off his coat, and I did the same. Wrapping our garments around our hands and forearms, we scooped the guard up off the floor and struggled to carry him away from the bar and back through the tangled mess of destroyed chairs and tables. Flames licked at my shins and arced dangerously near. I winced from the waves of heat and tried my best to hurry along. Looking at Royce, I saw that he too was winded from carrying a man clad in armor; his face was red and his features tried. We let the Watchman clatter to the floor, trying to catch our breaths.

"Oy!" shouted Alomar. "Hurry up! The fire is-"

"We know!" Royce snapped. "I don't see you dragging this bloke around, eh?"

"What about the key?" Alomar urged.

The man barely finished his question when we heard a loud, splintering crack from above. The three of us looked up in horror and saw a large beam in the rafters break in the flames and drop toward us. It suddenly jerked to a stop, hanging by what must have been stubborn threads of wood, crackling under the fire's onslaught.

"Out!" hollered Alomar.

Don't have to tell me twice.

Royce and I cursed, gathered the unconscious Watchman up the best we could, and moved for the tavern doors. Alomar cursed even louder, running back and forth in utmost frustration, kind of kicking at us because it was all that he could do.

"That's not helping!" I declared.

We neared the entrance. More cracks and loud, splintering explosions sounded off behind us. I envisioned a giant fireball rolling after us, right on our heels, about to swallow us up.

"Hurry!" gasped Royce, as if we could somehow go faster.

Just a few more paces to the doors. Ahead of us, Alomar threw his weight into them and a gust of the night air rushed in, shockingly cold on our heat-caressed skin. A volley of yells, shouts, and alarmed cries from the crowd gathered outside flooded in with the cold air. It was a wonder no other members of the City Watch had come to our unconscious friend's aid.

Or, the Watch had guards all over outside, just waiting to nab us and explain the ins and outs of prison life. Or maybe they would just kill us on the spot.

Suddenly this thought was more pressing than the fire clawing at our backs. It occurred to me that we might just be looked at as fortunate survivors as we rushed out that door to meet the crowd waiting for us.

Survivors with an unconscious guard in tow? No. We'd be branded lawbreakers immediately. Assaulting a guard and-

Wait. The crowd wouldn't know this... they might even think we were saving the Watchman. We could be heroes of the night, rushing a noble member of Northroe's City Watch to safety, putting our own lives at risk to do so...

unless Kara, who had fled earlier, had indeed found the Watch and told them everything.

Or had she met her strange, sudden end like everyone else inside, coughing up her own blood somewhere out there on the street?

All these thoughts flashed through my mind in mere seconds.

Time to go.

Tightening our grips on the man we carried, Royce and I thundered roughly through the doors and into the brisk, cool night to face the crowd gathered in the street... whether we were ready for it or not.

CHAPTER 12

What just seconds ago sounded like a vague rumble of excitement outside the tavern suddenly became a roaring crowd from all directions as Royce, Alomar and I stumbled out into the street with the unconscious City Watchman in tow.

"Fates!" came an anonymous voice. "They survived!"

"It's on fire!"

"-where Ozlow is, haven't seen him yet-"

"Are they hurt? Can you see if-"

"-saved a Watchman! You believe that!?"

The crowd gathered around us swiftly, swallowing us up like the sea claiming a sinking ship. I felt hands touching my shoulders and saw men and women alike darting back and forth between me, my two friends and the Watchman at our feet. Their frantic questions, shouts and observations churned into a loud drone in my head, like an earthquake composed of voices.

"Back off!" screamed Royce. "Give us space!"

"Give this man some air!" Alomar shouted.

Apparently, the two men had thought along the same lines as I. We would play the heroes.

Not waiting for a cue, I hastily fumbled through the guard's pockets, trying to find the key to Alomar's handcuffs. I desperately scrounged about and hoped for the touch of metal, knowing time was against us.

"Check his pockets!" urged Alomar tersely, dropping to one knee.

"We know," I grunted.

Royce scrambled to my side and went through the other pockets in the man's trousers. We were both cursing, for it was hard to gain access past the armored greaves protecting his thighs.

"Nothing," I said. "Empty."

"Oy!" I heard a woman call from the crowd. "Look at that one! He's wearin' cuffs, he is!"

"-been arrested?"

"What? Did they save him or hurt-"

"They knocked him out!"

"Don't go near that one, he was in the cavalry, see?"

I felt like dying inside. So much for any hope of faking our Watchman's rescue. How could I have forgotten Alomar's handcuffs?

Royce and I did what any other sadly desperate men would have done in our situation: we searched the same pockets again. My heart was beating so fast! I was scared and overcome with a frantic, frenzied surge of haste and fear.

"Mates," Alomar said as low as he could over the crowd's cries around us, "I don't think we have much longer here. They're growing savvy to what's going on, aye?"

I gave a frustrated growl as I came up empty-handed again.

"Where on earth is this key?" Royce hissed.

"Check the shoes, mates!"

I whirled about in surprise, as did Royce and Alomar. We tried finding where the voice came from in the rowdy crowd.

"Eh?" I asked dumbly.

"Check his boots!" said a dirty, homeless-looking man who stepped forward from the crowd's ranks. "It's probably in his boots."

Rather than do so, I just stared. I wasn't expecting help. Neither were Royce or Alomar.

"Check the blasted boots!" the disheveled man urged once more. "That's where my brother used to keep the key to his chastity belt."

Royce cocked his head. "Wait, mate. Your brother wore a chastity belt?"

"Might as well look," I muttered. "Only place we haven't."

I pulled off the boot on the right foot after undoing the straps, and was met with the sight of a terribly soiled and sweaty sock... with no key. I recoiled accordingly.

Royce saw my little venture and crinkled his nose in anticipation as he reached for the other boot and removed it. Another blackened sock was unveiled. The smell of sweat and musty horror that could only come from a foot confined within boots for an ungodly amount of time overtook us both.

I shivered and almost doubled over. Royce clasped his hand to his mouth.

"It's not there!" observed our scrappy homeless ally.

"You think?" retorted Royce, his voice muffled by his hand.

The street dweller was suddenly at our side and joining the search. The crowd must have been entertained or curious as to what the outcome of our little endeavor would be, because they still looked on, though far from orderly and organized.

"We have to go," said Alomar. "We're lucky no other Watchmen-"

"Now," the homeless man said loudly, ignoring Alomar and scratching his long, dirty beard, "now this is common. Common indeed."

He looked so thoughtful. So serious.

"Eh?" I asked.

The scruffy man looked at us, his eyes lit by excitement. "You see," he said, motioning enthusiastically with his hands, "if the key's not in the boot, then heavens be buggered, it must be in his sock!"

"Oh, bugger off," spat Royce dismissively. "Al's right. Time to go, Penny."

"No!" protested the man with passion. "Look!"

With that, he clutched the unconscious Watchman's sock in his grimy fingers and tore it free. He flung the garment over his shoulder into the crowd, causing a few bystanders to reel back in disgust.

The constant chants and rumbling of the crowd paused momentarily. Then a chorus of low gasps erupted from everyone, including me.

The man's foot was filthy, and a big, rather developed sore was wedged between two toes. The odor was excruciatingly offensive.

I blanched. Royce gagged like he'd try to down two ales in one gulp. Even Alomar was speechless.

"The other sock, then!" declared the dirty man. "It is there! You must check!"

At that moment, a gruff, dazed voice sounded off from below us on the ground.

"Check. Check? Check what?"

The unconscious Watchman was suddenly very conscious again. Another gasp from the crowd confirmed this. Obviously they were enjoying themselves.

I didn't wait. Feeling bold from the earlier bout in the tavern, I stepped over the man and cocked back my fist, ready to unleash a mighty blow. The guard's eyes first narrowed with recognition.

"Sorry mate," I muttered.

I rocked downward with a fierce punch, my fist hurtling toward the man's face.

As fate would have it, the Watchman simply jerked his head left and fully dodged my attack. My fist slammed to the cobbled street with full force.

Crying out in intense pain, I doubled over onto my side and clutched at my hand and wrist in agony.

Royce just stared in surprise.

The guard took advantage of this. He abruptly sat up and sent a brutal kick to Royce's face with his bare, smelly, grimy foot. It found its mark. There was a loud snap of skin-to-skin contact, and Royce slumped backward in pain and astonishment. The Watchman yelped in pain, having struck my friend the wrong way, and he reached for his foot tenderly with pursed lips and red cheeks.

Alomar stepped forward with a vicious kick to the guard's head.

For the second time, someone from our party was responsible for knocking out the Watchman. This time, we didn't wait around.

"Up!" bellowed Alomar. "Get your arses up!"

We didn't need to be told twice. Royce and I scrambled to our feet and fought through the crowd, sprinting, stumbling and shoving our way through them all.

The three of us broke through and fled into the street wildly. The roar of the crowd grew distant as we raced into the alleys. Alomar was running like a maniac with his hands cuffed behind his back, Royce half-ran and stumbled along groggily from the kick he'd just taken to the face, and I dashed on in a lopsided jog, clutching at my bruised and cut hand in agony.

As we scrambled into the dark refuge of the backstreets and out of view of the main road, the November Raven burned to the ground behind us. It would become a part of Northroe's past, with the souls of those who died inside.

CHAPTER 13

It had been many years since my friends and I had been orphans, scrapping about in the city streets. That night, we again found ourselves skulking through the dank backstreets of Northroe, where the poor and homeless lived, and at times where the curious and stalwart ventured.

We were huddled together behind a shed next to a small clothing shop in a dark corner of the maze of alleys, well out of view of the main streets. Royce, Alomar and I had wound our way through the alleys for nearly a half hour or so to lose any possible tails.

The sight of someone running for their life or trying to avoid arrest was an everyday occurrence in these parts of Northroe. The poor, the homeless, and the criminally inclined folk all claimed refuge in these alleys that we, ourselves, had grown up in. If any of these people saw Alomar cuffed and the three of us fast on the move, they wouldn't just turn and look the other way... they would do so with a smile.

Nighttime provided us decent cover of darkness, but we could only hide out for so long. Once the witnesses and onlookers of the crowd told the City Watch who we were, it'd be time to move. The alleys would be the first place they'd look.

"Fates," murmured Alomar as we sat to gather ourselves. "What have we done?"

"What?" I asked. "We didn't do anything. We didn't make those people all start vomiting blood and dying on the floor in the Raven. We-"

"You both should have let me be," Alomar cut in. His eyes were distant. "I didn't mean for you two to get caught up in this."

Royce snorted. "No proper friend would've turned away, mate. Besides, that Tyrius Sewell and his mates, celebrating like that? We couldn't just do nothing, could we?"

A crazed-looking man with no teeth wrapped in a tattered cloak trudged by slowly. He was old and slow, and he paid us no mind as he passed. We waited as the sound of his tiresome footsteps scraping against the ground grew distant, then disappeared, before we continued.

"What was that?" I mused. "All that blood... everywhere! Everyone! What in blazes happened?"

"Aye," Royce nodded grimly. "Never seen the likes of that before."

I rubbed my chin. "But why everyone else and not the three of us? I mean *everyone*. Tyrius, his friends, even after they were unconscious-"

"The barmaids," Royce added solemnly. "Kara too, probably."

"Ozlow," whispered Alomar.

We all fell silent.

I clenched my jaw when I pictured him on fire. It was at that moment that I knew it was an image I would never be able to get out of my mind for as long as I lived, and I sighed at the realization.

"Fates rest their souls," mumbled Royce.

The three of us paid our silent respects in memoriam of those who had met their end that night. A few minutes passed. Distant voices of some passersby echoed through the alleys to us, but they moved on somewhere into the night.

"Oy, mates," I said in realization. "We've started a public brawl, vandalized property, knocked out a Watchman, committed arson... all in the same day."

"Twice."

I looked at Royce. "Eh?"

"Twice," Royce repeated. "We knocked out the same Watchman twice."

Alomar rolled his eyes. "Indeed."

"Fled arrest," I continued. "They'll blame us for all the deaths in the fire, I'm sure."

"They won't know the poor bastards all died by throwing their insides up before the flames ever started," Alomar said, cringing.

"You know," Royce said thoughtfully, "I was thinking... is the property vandalism erased, or struck from record, or something, since all Ozlow's tables and chairs and belongings went up in smoke, anyway?"

"What?" I asked, eyebrows raised in question.

Royce folded his arms. "What I mean is, wouldn't the arson cancel out the stuff we broke in the brawl and all that? Sure, we broke furniture, but since now it's gone anyway, and-"

"Come off it, Roy," I muttered.

Another surge of pain rippled across my right hand. I rubbed it gingerly, cautiously eyeing a few raggedy men who stalked by and leered at us, their faces and hands caked with dirt.

Alomar gave a defeated grunt and slumped back against the stone wall, sliding down to a seated position on the street. The only light was from a fire nearby that two men and a woman had fashioned, comprised of assorted bits and pieces of what once must have been furniture of some kind.

"Did you lot see the red-haired woman during all that chaos?" I asked. "The new barmaid?"

Both men were quiet for a few moments before Royce spoke.

"I... actually, no," he replied. "She served those ales to all the blokes at the counter. You know, when Alomar called for another round... that's all I remember."

Alomar had a quizzical look on his face. "She brought us the drinks... everyone cheered and all that, and... she didn't, well... you know."

"Throw up her insides all over the floor?" I finished harshly. "No, she didn't."

His jaw clenched, Alomar's eyes seemed to be searching for the answer, darting this way and that. "I don't remember," he said finally. "I don't remember seeing her, or-"

"She ducked out," I said.

Both men just looked at me, waiting for more.

"After she served the drinks, I saw her step back into the shadows, near Ozlow's back door," I continued. "It was strange, mates. She was just... watching them all. You, Alomar," I gestured, "and Tyrius and all the others. That woman was just staring. Like... like-"

"Like she was waiting for something," Royce finished.

It dawned on all three of us at once, because our eyes shot wide open and we gazed at each other in a mixture of shock and amazement.

"Bloody 'ell," Royce started, "you don't think-"

"Poison," growled Alomar.

I opened my mouth to say something, but just let their words sink in.

"She served up the ales. Didn't want to give any of us her name. Stood back there behind the blasted bar the whole time. She was waiting," Alomar surmised. "It was poison."

Royce uttered a vulgarity of sorts and spat at the ground in disgust. "If we ever see her again...."

In the dark of midnight, we sat in silence, dwelling on the conclusion we had just reached for a few more minutes. I was trying to shake off the pain in my hand, letting it dangle and waving it about. Then I cursed inwardly, furious at myself. It was my writing hand. So much for writing anytime soon.

Was I really thinking about writing right then?

Royce saw me whipping the air with my hand in a futile attempt to somehow ease the pain, and grinned. "Hell of a punch that was, Pen."

I just shot him a look.

"No, really," he continued with sincerity. "I mean, sure, hitting the street was a real doozy. But you nailed that Watchman back there. He went down like a rock."

Alomar chimed in. "Aye. Not bad for a man who throws candlesticks in a fight."

I stared at Alomar, but sidestepped his comment and turned back to Royce. "Royce, what's a doozy?"

"Thing is mate," Royce plodded on without answering, "that was a good shot. Really, and good judgment at that. We'd be cuffed and rotting away in Lord Hannady's dungeons by now. We'd be cellmates with blokes like that chastity belt fellow."

We all shared a much-needed laugh, and then we spent more time deep in thought. My friends were desperately reaching for ideas on how to get out of our predicament, as was I. The three of us knew there wasn't a clear way out, but we searched nevertheless. Hands still cuffed behind him, Alomar pushed himself up to a stand, his back scraping against the wall. He inhaled deeply before he spoke.

"Any ideas?"

I shook my head.

"No," answered Royce. "Except make a run for it."

"Eh?" I asked. "Leave Northroe?"

Royce tossed his head back and laughed heartily, his laughs booming off the walls of the alley and echoing down the backstreets with fervor.

"What's so funny?" I asked.

The man looked at me with a glimmer in his eye. "You really think there's another way, Penny? Ha! Looks like we have to leave this city now, don't we?"

I did grin, but the thought wasn't appealing. Perhaps the Fates had heard our conversation on South Bridge the other night.

"Okay," said Alomar. "We'll leave. All we can do. But I have to do two things first."

"What's that?" asked Royce.

Alomar spat at his feet, looked up at the night sky and sighed heavily before turning his gaze back to us. "I have to get these blasted cuffs off, but I don't know how that'll happen yet."

"What about Mateo?" I asked. "He could have those cuffs off you in a minute, yeah? Used to prowl about this part of the backstreets, didn't he?"

Royce shook his head. "Not gonna happen. Mateo's been dead for nearly two years, mate."

"What? Really?"

"Bloody 'ell, Penny. I told you the day it happened. Those blokes went after Rory Gray for stealing from their boss in the North Quarter. Killed Mateo by accident."

"What?" I repeated, dumbfounded.

"Aye. Thought he was Rory. They got the wrong man. Rory got away that night. Fled the city."

I mulled over this for a moment. "Lucky bastard, Rory Gray."

"Well," Royce shrugged, "not really. Bandits in the Kovald got him the next day in the woods."

"Regardless of how I get these cuffs off," Alomar broke in, "there is something else I must do. You don't have to come with me."

Royce shook his head. "You already know we have to stick together, so out with it. Where we going, mate?"

"Just follow me."

CHAPTER 14

I suppose that I assumed by that time hordes of City Watchmen would be scouring Northroe, street by street, alley by alley, hunting for us. I thought that surely by now, an entire division of Eislian soldiers would be tearing up the floors, walls and ceilings of every dwelling in the city in their search.

As Royce, Alomar and I stalked cautiously through the backstreets of Northroe, I shuddered from the cold. The night was a dark one, and thankfully so. The only hint of moonlight was a gray glow that illuminated a barely visible sea of clouds in the sky above. The alley-dwellers and street urchins in this part of the city near the Market District seemed to be particularly down on their luck, for in nearly an hour of alley jumping, we had only come across two fires warming small parties of the homeless.

This was fortunate. The less light, the better. We weren't stupid. The odds were against us and our lives really, truly hung in the balance.

I brushed past an old woman in a hooded cloak with her hands outstretched and cupped in a plea for generosity. Guiltily, I avoided her gaze.

"Left," whispered Alomar.

We turned left. The houses and shops and buildings of all kinds loomed high on our left and right, seeming to stare down at us as we scurried through the cramped back alley.

I imagined Lord Hannady himself suiting up for the manhunt, flanked by the Watch Captain and his best troops. To be honest, I couldn't help but wonder if he would actually do so or not over the likes of us. Crime in Eisley was not taken lightly, and the Lord of Northroe's direct involvement was very possible. After all, a tavern had been burned to the ground, nearly ten dead inside, and the public surely thought it was an act of arson committed by the three of us. Things weren't looking up.

"Bounties on our heads, for sure," I mumbled.

"Eh?" asked Royce, not turning to look back at me. He was too busy scanning our flanks and the alley shadows for threats.

I shrug dismissively. "Nothing." Did I really say that aloud?

It then occurred to me that a crime as serious as the one we would be found guilty of – multiple murders and the like – was one that would be a bit more than the subject of excited and anxious banter among drunken men in pubs. Our little debacle was worthy of town criers' proclamations in every city in Eisley from coast to coast. Everyone in our huge nation would know our faces. Our names. No doubt friends of ours and eyewitnesses from the crowds outside the November Raven had already given us up.

They'd call the army in, I was sure of it! Eislian regulars, the militant masters of death in their ebon armor, dark as night, would descend upon Northroe within a day! Fort Carrington was just a day's ride west!

"Penny. Stop it, mate."

I looked at Royce, my rampant thoughts shattering around me. "What?"

"I don't know what you're thinking about, Pen," he said as we rounded another corner, nearing South Quarter, "but it ain't good. I know that face."

"It's over," I replied shakily. I couldn't help it. "We have no chance!"

Alomar slowed his pace. "Penny, shut up."

"Soon Hannady's Guard will be combing the streets," I continued hastily. "You know they will. Bashing in doors and burning out cellars and basements! They-"

"Pen, shut it."

"-probably even the sewers, then. And Fates forbid the army gets called in. You know they'll be here shortly, and-"

A forceful impact jarred me suddenly, and my words lost their weight in the wind. Royce had his palm to my chest and pushed my back to the brick wall of an old warehouse. Alomar was standing in a scolding stance, shaking his head.

"Stop, Penny," Alomar repeated lowly. "You're not helping the situation. Understand?"

"Was just saying."

Royce stepped closer. "Yeah, we know. You 'just said' a lot. Just keep quiet, mate. Bloody 'ell. We'll figure this thing out, aye? Got enough to worry about."

I sighed. "Alomar, where are we headed?"

The man hesitated. "I have to pay Corrine a visit. I need to hear what my wife has to say about all of this."

I blinked. "Say again?"

"Not a chance!" exclaimed Royce. "That's a bad idea, Al."

"The two of you don't have to come," Alomar said, scowling. "I'll go alone. It's my problem."

He turned to stalk off, but I grabbed his enormous shoulder in an effort to stop him. "Alomar, wait."

"Don't."

"Think about this, mate."

"I have."

Royce caught up to us and stood in front of the man, halting his advance. "It's not safe!" he urged. "The Watch will be at your house, Al. We can't just go-"

"What am I to do?" Alomar growled. "Just leave my wife in the city? Take off without her, is that it? Leave her thinking she married a criminal? A murdering arsonist?"

Neither Royce nor I could find words for a reply.

Alomar shrugged out of my grasp and continued onward, bumping Royce out of the way.

Royce shuffled backward, holding his ground. "No. Al, listen to me."

Uncaring of Royce or the cuffs shackling his wrists, Alomar wrestled forward. I rushed to Royce's aid.

"Let go!" Alomar hissed, trying to shoulder us out of the way. "Get off of me!"

Royce and I dug in, wrapping our arms around the man's bearlike, muscled frame as he tried to propel through us and across the street.

"No!" Royce nearly yelled. "Dammit, Al! They'll kill you!"

I was grasping at Alomar's shirt now. "Stop!"

In a shocking display, Royce pressed his hand up to the man's face, shoving him backward. The rather vicious action finally snapped Alomar's eyes from his home to us. He was seething with anger.

"Back," Royce said, hand pressed to the man's chest. "You know we're right. Calm yourself! Breathe!"

Alomar slowly recovered. "Corrine." His gaze fell to his boots for a long moment, and when he looked back up, I saw that his eyes were wet, threatened with tears.

I clapped him on the back. "She'll know, mate. Even if the City Watch is questioning her, she-"

"I need to see her," Alomar breathed.

"Al!" I said, narrowing my eyes. "Focus. Listen to me."

He grudgingly obeyed.

"She'll nod her head," I continued. "She'll just tell them what they want to hear, but she knows! Corrine bloody loves you, mate. She knows your heart. She knows us! Don't think she'll accept what they say for a moment, hear me?"

Alomar lowered his head. "Loves me, does she? Not according to that blight, Tyrius."

My heart cracked at my mistake. I opened my mouth to speak, but dared not.

"Listen," Royce said hastily. "We'll figure this out. You'll get to talk to her, Al. Get answers, tell her what happened, everything. Just not tonight."

"How?"

Royce inhaled deeply. "We'll find a way."

"He's right," I nodded. "For now, we continue to stay off the main roads. We'll come to a plan of action. One step at a time."

Alomar cursed, turned on his heel and stalked back the way we had come, into the comforting darkness of the backstreets. We followed quickly.

CHAPTER 15

As the night carried on, the silvery clouds above seemed to grow thicker and larger, barely giving the half moon time to bathe the city in its dull but brilliant white glow. The wind picked up, graduating from brief and random bursts that blew leaves about and parted blades of grass to full, steady gusts that swayed the trees and made me adjust my coat accordingly.

Reeling from all that had happened, the three of us spent the next hour or so wandering the backstreets in silence. I didn't dare speak, and even Royce held his tongue, for Alomar had been through much that night. The veteran was normally the one with the level head, the man in our midst who could stay steady and collected even if the air itself seemed to swelter.

I had watched the man's entire life fall apart in a matter of hours. My own was probably over as I knew it. Probably? No. It was. Problems with the City Watch aside, I had failed my assignment back at the inn. I'd be evicted within the day, especially if Assistant Innkeeper Trenten had anything to say about it, and he most certainly would.

I'm not sure if either Royce or Alomar were thinking about it as we walked, but I noticed we were slowly making our way to the southern edge of the city, where South Bridge reached over the River Keska. After our conversation there the other night, perhaps South Bridge had become our symbol of escape, representing any dreams we hadn't pursued and adventures we had only dreamed of.

We finally rested at another secure outlet in the tangled mess of alleys in the South Quarter and sat wordlessly, stretching out on the hard ground. It may have been a hard surface, but resting still eased our muscles and tired bodies.

I saw Royce repeatedly glancing at Alomar, and then turn to me raising his eyebrows as if to ask me if I thought it was okay to speak to him. With a subtle shake of my head, I mouthed, "No."

My friends and I sat and listened to the wind sweep across the high walls of buildings through the backstreet, whispering along in the night as if the Fates were trying to remind us that perhaps right then might not have been the best moment to rest. I can't be certain of how much time passed before Alomar finally spoke.

"Where do we go?"

Royce and I glanced at each other. It was a bit alarming to hear the man ask with such uncertainty, even anxiety. Maybe even fear.

Perhaps it was just me.

"We have to leave Northroe," Royce offered. "Of course we all know that, and I wanted to leave most of all... but it is a bit sudden. Not quite on our terms, either."

I bit my lip. I felt a panic build inside, churning my stomach like butter and lancing my heart with nervous beating.

"What about Foye?" proposed Alomar.

Royce shook his head. "That's just as bad an idea as Eisley City itself. An army division is always stationed there. Their City Watch is something like three times the size of the watch here in Northroe, yeah?"

I frowned inwardly. Alomar was an Eislian veteran, a battle-tested warrior from the famed 2nd Cavalry. Royce shouldn't have had to tell the man any of what he'd just said, which led me to suspect that Alomar wasn't thinking clearly. I suppose I couldn't blame him.

Royce yawned and hung his head, closing his eyes for a moment. "I still say we go to Saelow Province."

Alomar and I glanced at each other.

My eyes widened. "Wait. The King is finally settling Saelow?"

"Aye," Royce beamed. "At long last! Now think about it, mates. Saelow Province, ripe for settling. They promise land there! Good work! Opportunity to carve out a good life, aye?"

"It's not even part of the Eislian mainland!" I protested. "It's way up north, an island in the middle of nowhere!"

"It's just a three day voyage north off Eislian shores, Pen," Royce countered, rolling his eyes. "We can live new lives! No more of this blasted city. A fresh start! We can live like we've always wanted to!"

"It's in the Mihkoza Channel, mate," I argued. "Too close to Athekov! Those blights are just a two weeks voyage north of Saelow."

"Oh come now," Royce argued, his features animated. "They're already that close to us to begin with, Saelow being so near to us! Besides, Eisley and

Athekov haven't made contact for decades. We've never even seen a Kovian in our lives, have we?"

He made a point.

Eisley and Athekov had abruptly severed all diplomatic relations, trade, and communication roughly 60 years ago. The Eislian public was informed by King Lidstrom II that the Kovians of the North were "no longer fit to continue relations with, nor fit even to be recognized as a nation."

That was the way our part of the world had been for decades, and the way it would continue to be, as far as everyone was concerned.

Alomar frowned. "If we're settling it soon, Saelow Province might as well be part of Eisley, anyhow."

"Still, our chances would be much better, wouldn't they?"

I hesitated. "We'd have to worry about getting there first."

"We just need to head far away, is all," Royce countered. "To Sia, or Port Journey. We shouldn't take the road west to Stratton... aye, we should avoid Fort Carrington. How about Belfour? Head south a few days, then turn west and-"

"What?" I interrupted. "Belfour? That's just as dangerous as Foye! And it's at least a couple weeks' journey by horse, and let me remind you mate, we don't have a horse, much less three. We'd be better off trying a smaller town, like Balta, in the Heartland. Or-"

Royce threw up his hands. "By the Fates, Penny. Stop being such a stick in the mud."

I stared. "A what?"

Exasperated, Royce squared himself at me. "You're so bogged down in your little fears you won't bloody move. 'Stick in the mud.' You see?"

"Oh, come on-"

"Listen," Alomar broke in with a wave of his hand. "We can talk about this later. Right now, though, is what matters. Right now we need to get out of Northroe."

Then it dawned on me. The alarm rang out in my mind, beat my heart heavily and dashed any thoughts I had on the subject at hand.

"My works!" I cried out.

Alomar motioned to be quiet. "Calm down! Your what?"

"My works!" I repeated in dismay. "My writings! My projects! My book!"

Royce's eyes widened. "Oh, no! *The Eagle and the Pigeon!*"

I was so distraught I didn't even correct the man. I pictured all my notes, pages upon pages of drafts and ideas outlining past and future works of hopeful stories, all littering my desk back at the Windfarer's Inn. Free for the taking. Assistant Innkeeper Trenten would surely do something horrible, like burn them, or-

"Okay, look," Royce said hastily, "I don't know if we can risk it, Pen."

I shot to my feet. "We have to! I won't leave those behind!"

"First thing's first," interjected Alomar, his expression on his face begging me to lower my voice. "We have to pack. Gather some things for the journey, aye? Otherwise we're doomed before we even begin."

"I have some things for you, mate," Royce offered. "Since you can't go back to your house for...."

The man trailed off, embarrassed. Alomar answered quickly to spare him. "Aye. We can go to your place, Royce. We can-"

"Wait!" I lashed. "So it's okay to risk going to Royce's place for things, but I can't gather my works from my own?"

"Oy, come on!" Royce urged. "You're the bookkeeper at that inn, Pen. How are you gonna get in without being seen? Besides, gear is more important. I'm sorry about your story, mate. I am. But it won't help us survive out there."

I folded my arms while smoke surely billowed out of my nose in rage. "Let me put it this way. Those works are my life, mate. I would gladly go to prison or face death to retrieve them."

My two friends stared at me, no doubt trying to figure out if I was sane or not.

"I can never get those thoughts, those ideas, back again," I continued, lowering my voice to a pleading whisper. "At least, not exactly as they are now. And they're perfect now. You don't understand how difficult it is! They're a part of me. I'm not leaving without them."

Royce was grinding his teeth, nodding against his will. He didn't like it, but he knew I was sincere. The man understood I couldn't leave them behind willingly.

"Okay, Pen," Alomar said finally. "Understood. But get it done quickly and meet us before the dawn rises. You and Royce live on different sides of the city. We have to split up to save time, meaning we have to meet up later.

South Bridge is a good point, since it's just outside the main body of the city and relatively quiet before dawn."

"No guards posted there," Royce mused. "Any lookouts and sentries are closer to the city, well out of view of the bridge."

"Right, then," I replied, standing tall. I hoped I fooled them with my fake confidence.

Royce breathed in deeply. "I don't like it. We shouldn't split up at a time like this, and we all bloody know it."

"Look," I answered calmly, "I'll be okay. If I'm not there by dawn's light, then... leave, the two of you. Just go without me, yeah?"

My friends said nothing.

"It's settled then." I extended my hand to Royce. "South Bridge before dawn, mates."

Royce shook my hand sullenly. Dread and concern etched his face.

Alomar stepped forward and did the same. "South Bridge it is, Penny."

"Luck to you both," I breathed, feeling my brave charade start to melt away.

"The Fates be with you."

I turned on my heel and hurried as quickly as I dared through the backstreets of Northroe, toward the Windfarer's Inn. I kept replaying the night's events in my mind's eye, and I only hoped I'd see my two friends again, my writings in hand.

I'd never been so scared in my life, but I felt something inside me, something new and foreign to my spirit. Was this what they called courage?

Was this what being brave felt like?

CHAPTER 16

I wasn't sure what surprised me more as I reached gingerly to the handle of the front door to the Windfarer's Inn: the fact that I hadn't been caught yet, or that I had only seen two Watchmen patrolling the streets in my entire hour-long journey to the inn.

Grasping the rusty iron doorknob in my hand, I paused for a moment and frowned. Was there a reason for that? Where were they all, anyway? I had pictured vast armies complete with cavalry charges and war banners storming the roads of Northroe looking for my friends and I... and yet, there had been nothing of the sort. Quite the opposite, actually.

Then again, how long had it been since I'd wandered the city at this late hour? Years, at least. Perhaps this was normal. It then occurred to me that most of the City Watch stationed itself at the city limits and walls for sake of protection.

A droplet of water plinked against my ear. I nearly cried out in surprise and whirled around, but saw nothing and nobody. Then another drop fell from somewhere above, a flurry of more droplets matted my hair, and I realized it was raining.

Gazing upward, my eyes were met with large, gray clouds, so heavy and thick that they could be seen in the night. Thunder rumbled from somewhere in the heavens, and I imagined the Fates laughing at the mess my friends and I had got ourselves into.

"Ah, yes," I said upward in sarcasm directed to the Fates themselves. "Thanks for that."

Lightning erupted, illuminating the clouds and the sky in an immensely brilliant white flash.

You're welcome, Penny Daulton.

The loud drunken hoots and hollers of a group of men stumbling down the road snapped me back to reality. They were far enough away to where I wasn't terribly concerned, but I suddenly felt like an idiot. I hadn't even looked for Watchmen or guards posted at the inn, and here I was at the front door.

And why in blazes was I about to go in through the front door, rather than the back?

Cursing silently, I hurried off the front porch and across the slick, wet grass around the side of the inn, keeping close to the walls and in the shadows. Thankfully part of the Windfarer's charm was the lush and elegant layout of trees and vegetation that enveloped the inn and the grounds around it. They provided more than adequate cover.

Cautiously peering around the rear corner of the building, I surveyed the green hedgerows and apple orchard out back. There was no one to be seen, and the large double doors I knew to be locked were at the rear of the building.

Though I was surely no longer welcome, I thankfully still had the key to the inn, and I clutched it triumphantly between my thumb and index finger and scurried along the wall to the back porch. Glancing behind me more than once, I finally stepped up to the large wooden doors.

I tenderly slipped the key into the lock, praying that Head Innkeeper Domheimer hadn't changed the locks after hearing about what had transpired at the November Raven. Again, I hesitated. In my mind I pictured a whole Watch company inside the inn right at that moment, blades drawn and leveled at the back door. I imagined that they somehow could see me through the walls and had been waiting for this moment for hours.

They'll slay me without hesitation! I won't get three steps inside!

Before I could start trying to imagine what it felt like to be stabbed or beheaded, I shoved the thoughts away.

I was already here. I couldn't leave my writings behind, and Royce and Alomar were depending on me. There was no way I could fail, no way I'd leave them under South Bridge, making them wonder what had become of me before they left Northroe forever.

No way, unless I was gutted like a fish by a Watchman.

"Blast," I muttered. "Penny, focus, you oaf."

Holding my breath, I turned the key and opened the door. Thankfully, I entered the inn with hardly a sound.

* * *

Minutes later I stood outside the door to my quarters, my home on the second floor. I kept eyeing the door to the right of mine not ten paces away. Assistant Innkeeper Trenten was sleeping soundly, completely unaware of my presence, as was the rest of the Windfarer's inhabitants.

At least, I assumed this because I had reached my quarters unseen. Marv had once again been asleep at the front desk downstairs. Since I had entered through the back, I probably could have snuck right past the man and up the stairs even if he had been awake.

I fumbled in my pocket for the key to my room, but stopped when I saw my door was slightly open. Peering closer, I frowned and pushed lightly against the door with just a finger. It opened further without resistance.

Of course, I thought. They must have already evicted me. Probably moved my things. I felt my face fall in grave realization. What had become of my writings?

More thunder rolled across distant mountains and sounded muffled beyond the windows. I gritted my teeth and opened my door after taking one more look down both ways of the hall.

A loud crash rang out.

Startled, I jumped in such shock that it's a wonder I wasn't literally scared out of my trousers. Loud metallic clanging and ringing came from just inside my room! Stepping in quickly, I cursed with a scowl.

Someone had set dining wares of all sorts just inside, directly in the door's path in the obvious effort to have an alarm sound if anyone tried to enter. Goblets, plates, and bowls tumbled and clattered about, rolling noisily on my wood floor.

Trenten.

The Assistant Innkeeper must have set a trap, intending to catch me upon my return. Growling, I looked quickly around my room, trying to prepare myself for the man's approach, for I knew it was coming.

Everything was just as I had left it. Nothing was missing. I snapped into action.

Ignoring the sound of a door opening from out in the hallway, I pounced on my small pack that I kept under my bed and hurriedly scooped a shirt and trousers into it. I then practically dove toward my desk where all my works sat, untouched.

"Ha!" I heard Trenten's voice from the hallway. "I knew you'd be back, you buffoon!"

Blocking the man's taunting words from thought, I feverishly scooped and stashed and brushed my writings from the desk into my pack. It filled quickly. I couldn't fit them all.

Frustrated, I reached into my pack amidst my scrolls and parchments and lifted my spare shirt and trousers out. I flung them behind me.

"Planning a trip?" came a muffled voice.

Trenten sounded nearer than I had imagined, and I turned quickly to see his face completely covered by the trousers I had tossed. They draped about his shoulders, and the man plucked them off, letting them fall to the floor.

"I haven't washed those trousers in months," I said. "How did they smell?"

"Like a horse's arse. Something you probably don't even notice anymore."

I didn't reply. I hastily stashed the rest of my works into my pack and stood to face Assistant Innkeeper Trenten. All thoughts of packing efficiently for the new life of a nomad faded. I had a bigger problem, and he stood right there in front of me.

Trenten watched me warily and smoothed his black hair, the silver wisps on the sides strikingly noticeable in the light. I waited for the wide-eyed accusations, the cries for help, but they didn't come. He just stared at me.

"What do you want, Trenten?"

"Penny," the man replied sinisterly. "What could possibly have you up at this hour?"

I gestured to the junk on the floor. "Probably you. Setting traps, and for what, exactly? Are you in charge of my curfew, now?"

He grinned. "Just keeping tabs on you. Someone's got to."

"You join up with the City Watch, or what?"

"Why?" Trenten pressed. "Should I be aware of something?"

I rolled my eyes. "You're not even aware of your own stench and shameless pompousness. You being the Fates' gift to our fair city and all that."

The man was silent, watching me intently. He wasn't a bad looking man, which unfortunately contributed to his cocky demeanor. Trenten was about my height, ten pounds stronger and ten times luckier in life's fortune than I'd ever been.

"You see," I continued, folding my arms, "I had a theory about that. I think the Fates didn't know what to do with you, so they tried hurling you straight down to hell. You know, fires and torment and all... but I think they somehow missed, and you hit some poor bloke's loins. Ended up as a woman's child, instead."

I could tell my words struck a chord, but Trenten kept calm. Except for the very brief redness that had surged to his cheeks in anger, the man didn't budge.

"Well said, Penny," Trenten offered finally. "But, you're still playing the role of my personal bitch in this world. So the Fates must hate you even more than they hate me."

I wanted to swing at him, to throw him out a window like Royce probably would have done without much thought on the matter. I had been through too much that night to deal with a bully of Trenten's magnitude.

"I have to leave," I said, trying to mask how much his words had stung. "Business."

I tried to hurry past him, but to my surprise, Assistant Innkeeper Trenten moved to block me.

"Your only business is here, friend. This is your place of work, in case you forgot, since you don't actually do any."

I could feel the hotness inside my chest, the heat of anger, and it was threatening to overflow and spill out onto the floor at our feet.

"Out of my way," I snarled.

"You didn't do the ledgers, did you?" he finally said.

I just stared, and blinked once. Maybe twice.

"Ho," the man chuckled, "you can kiss employment goodbye, Penny Daulton. Wait until Domheimer hears about this."

He didn't know...

"Imagine," Trenten continued, folding his arms, "what will come when I tell the Head Innkeeper that you couldn't complete your task. That you've been apparently sneaking about at night. That you-"

He didn't know!

"-a man to do your work for you, at that. Perhaps... yes, perhaps you've been *stealing* as well." He stressed 'stealing' like a bard or an actor putting on a play for Lord Hannady himself. A devious twinkle flashed in his eyes. "I caught you stealing from the inn's coffers, didn't I? A thief in our midst."

I shook my head. A lie, of course. Imagine the man's surprise when I smiled very deliberately in his face.

Trenten was puzzled. "What's so funny?"

I laughed heartily, stood straight and looked around my room like I'd forgot something. "Oh, Trenten. If only you knew how big of a sod you are at this very moment."

The man scowled, but maintained his confident stance. "Trying to leave, are you? Skip out of the city in the night before you have to face consequences of being a good-for-nothing slacker, is that it?"

With a smug grin, I started toward him. "I'm leaving now, Trenten. Out of my way."

Before he could retort, a loud knock rapped on the front door of the inn. The thuds on the wood echoed all the way up through the second floor hallway.

I darted to the window, ignoring Trenten, and peered through the glass and the droplets of rain that streamed down the smooth surface. The glass felt cold as I pressed my forehead to it and tried desperately to see who was at the front entrance.

Two Watchmen in their telltale white armor stood outside impatiently. One looked about, surveying their surroundings with his hand at his blade's hilt. The other knocked again.

"City Watch!" came their call, bellowing like a death toll in the night's rain.

I whirled toward Trenten, who was smiling widely.

"Well what do you know," he said, rubbing his hands together. "This is just too good."

After the crazy, hectic night my friends and I had suffered, I suddenly knew what I would do. It was crazy, but I was facing death or the dungeon, after all. I didn't know if it would work, but I suddenly came up with a plan that was very unlike me.

The rapping came again, and I heard footsteps. Marv had no doubt awoken from his drool-filled slumber. I pictured him hurrying for the front door.

"You can't run now, Penny," Trenten said. "So just give up."

"Trenten," I said loudly, boasting a confidence I was strangely not faking for once, "it's been a pleasure knowing you, mate. A real pleasure."

The man looked at me, puzzled. I walked toward him with purpose, and he backed up and out of my room into the hallway as I came nearer. His bewilderment was priceless.

"I go to whatever fate awaits," I said, and extended my hand to the man I hated. "Perhaps they'll lighten my sentence if I turn myself in, eh?"

Still confused, Trenten kind of raised his hand to meet mine, and I wondered if he was aware that he was even doing so. I grasped his hand in mine and shook it, leering closer to his face. I narrowed my eyes and gave my most fearsome gaze.

"Turn yourself in?" he asked slowly. "What do you mean?"

"Sorry, Trenten," I whispered truthfully. "I hope you don't plan on using this hand often."

Before the man could react to my words, I wrenched my grip around his hand as tightly as I could and slammed it to the wall next to us. Trenten cried out in pain. He made a fist with his hand and pulled it free for a second, but I seized it and slammed it to the wood again, even harder.

Specks of blood were on the wall. Trenten cursed and dropped to his knees, clutching at his injured hand. Anger welled up inside me, and I roughly kicked the man aside as I hustled past him.

I heard voices of men downstairs echo up toward me, clearly alarmed. No doubt the Watchmen were on their way up. I ran to meet them. My heart beat loudly in my ears, and I shot downstairs into the lobby where Marv the Maintenance Man stood with the two Watchmen. They were standing with their blades drawn and buckler shields at the ready.

We all stared at each other for a moment. Rather than halt, I mustered courage and tightened my stomach in an effort to quell the butterflies fluttering about.

"Oy there, Marv," I said with a nod. I strode toward them all unflinchingly. "I'm going out on business."

"H-hello, Penny. These men are-"

"Please let Innkeeper Domheimer know I'm leaving," I interrupted. I turned my gaze to the two City Watchmen. "Ah, and sirs? A man up there assaulted me. Assistant Innkeeper Trenten, in fact."

Marv's eyes widened. The two Watchmen did not budge, so I looked them squarely in the eyes and tightened my grip on the pack slung over my shoulder.

"He said he'd burn this place down if I ever told anyone," I continued, trying desperately to project confidence and not let my tone waiver. "Said he'd already punched a City Watchman out earlier today."

The two Watchmen looked at each other, then back at me. I was just a couple paces away from them. I tried not to let my gaze linger on the front doors to the inn that were so close, yet so far away.

"Say again?" one of the guards finally asked. I tried not to swallow nervously when I saw his grip tighten on his sword.

"Trenten said that he knocked out a guard today with his bare fist, and he was going to burn this inn down if I told anyone. I caught him snooping about in my quarters upstairs. He threatened me."

The Watchmen exchanged glances and proceeded to walk toward the stairs, one passing on either side of me. I held my breath, waiting for one to lop my head off with his blade, or do something else unpleasant. One continued upstairs. The other that had spoken earlier turned to me again.

"You say he talked of arson? An actual threat?"

"Aye," I nodded. "Said he'd done it before and he'd do it again. Oh, and his hand is bruised and cut up. Looked like he'd punched a wall, or someone really hard in the face. Know what I mean? He's dangerous."

The Watchman nodded. "Stay here. Don't go anywhere."

With that, he made his way quickly upstairs to assist his comrade-in-arms. A moment later, I could hear the confused shouts and pleas from Assistant Innkeeper Trenten as the men took him into custody.

It was time to leave.

I turned to Marv. "Well, then. 'Night, Marv."

Bewildered, Marv just half-raised a hand in a wave. "But the Watchman said to stay put."

With a smile, I ignored him and started for the front door. My heart was thundering in my chest, and I was struggling to keep myself grounded and not sprint for freedom like the fugitive I was.

"Oy, Penny?"

I turned to face Marv the Maintenance Man one last time. "Eh?"

"Where ya goin'? Looks like you're goin' on a trip or something, yeah?"

Nodding, I flashed another grin. "Aye. I'm heading to the Heartland," I lied. "To live the good life and all that. Wish me luck, mate."

Marv didn't answer as I stole through the double doors and out into the street, leaving the Windfarer's Inn behind me forever. As I hurried on and hoped my friends were as lucky as I was, I couldn't stop chuckling and laughing to myself, still shaken with the giddy rush of excitement.

The rain began to descend harder, pelting the cobbled road and buildings around me as I again trotted into the backstreets out of view from the main road, quite pleased with myself.

Penny, you rascal, you.

CHAPTER 17

I never thought I would be grateful for my days living in the streets, prowling the alleys and back-roads as a homeless boy. Those years I'd spent as an orphan with Royce and Alomar proved invaluable to me as I crept my way across the city for much of the remaining night. The rainfall kept up, and the air was filling with gray mist, a fog that gently wrapped Northroe in its embrace.

Thank the Fates for that. Foggy mist would only help us in our getaway. I thought often of how Royce and Alomar were faring as I made my way through South Quarter, and finally I could see the edge of the city draw near.

My ruse back at the inn had only bought me more time. I wasn't stupid. I didn't know why neither Trenten nor Marv had any idea about what I had been involved with back at the November Raven, but regardless, the City Watch would find very quickly that my story was rubbish, that Trenten was not the man they were looking for.

Leaving the sprawling, jagged edge of the city's clustered buildings and streets, I carefully made my way down a grassy slope to the edge of the River Keska.

On the south and southeast edges of Northroe, the River Keska itself was the city limits, curving around like a large moat before spearing southward into the country. It was only a twenty-minute walk to South Bridge, so the distance between the city and the bridge itself was relatively short. The highway wound like a snake through small clumps of forest along the way, bending three times before leading straight across the bridge and out into the Eislian wilderness.

What made South Bridge an ideal meeting point was that the City Watch did not normally station guards there, but rather kept its sentries reined in closer to the city itself, watching the road and other small backstreets that were points of access.

Of course, I did not travel on the road itself. I ventured out into the countryside and down to the river. For what seemed like an eternity, I trudged along the Keska's bank, at times heel deep in mud, water sloshing about my ankles.

By the time I saw the bridge, my eyes had grown unbelievably heavy. I didn't need a mirror to know they were rimmed with gray circles and my face was weighted by fatigue. My feet hurt, my muscles ached and I kept having to stifle yawns. My body yearned for sleep.

Despite this, my heart beat nervously as South Bridge loomed closer and higher with each step I took. Its strong stone archway reached over the river, grounded by tall stone pillars that showed no quarter to the water surging around their base.

I grew nervous, and then as I hurried along in the sand and mud to the base of the bridge, I bit my lip.

Alomar and Royce were nowhere to be seen.

Lightly chewing on the inside of my cheek in worry, I cast a glance behind me and up the slope toward the hills between myself and the city off in the distance. I checked my surroundings for seemingly the hundredth time. I hurried under the bridge and slumped down against the stone wall beneath, safely out of view from the road above me.

Where are you?

I hoped to the Fates nothing had befallen my two friends.

I watched the current. The flow of water sounded loud and amplified here under the bridge. It rushed by, sloshing hard against the stone and lapping at the banks on both sides as if trying to escape its set path and be free on land.

Tiny ripples and splashes could be seen on the river's surface before it ran under the bridge. The rain was coming down harder now. Dawn's light could just barely be seen far out to the East. The night sky was becoming a lighter palette of grays and charcoals. The sun would arrive within the hour.

The sound of wind and more rolling thunder in the distance caressed and lulled my senses. I blinked furiously in an effort to stay awake.

"No, Penny," I mumbled quietly. "Stay. Awake."

The River Keska flowed by, oblivious to the perils my friends and I faced. It would run its course like it always had.

I couldn't hear my breathing very well against the current, but it was steady in my mind. Slow, relaxed. Calm. Sleep tugged at my eyelids, and they gave in. I closed my eyes to the world and nodded forward slowly.

"No," I uttered, coaxing myself back awake. Falling asleep now? Under South Bridge, at a time like this?

My eyes found the water yet again. I watched it for a few moments. Any fatigue or burden my body was suffering from seemed to melt away with the river's current. Hunger called to me from somewhere deep in my gut, but faded away as I tried stubbornly to ward it off. Rather than come at me again, the hunger pang eased off and left me to my thoughts.

A cold wave of fear chilled my bones. What if Royce and Alomar hadn't made it? What if something happened to them?

I clenched my jaw and sat up a bit taller for a moment, looking across the river to the other side of the base of the bridge. My two friends were most definitely not there.

Sleep beckoned again. The water's humming and rhythm teased my senses with the lightness of a feather.

No! Stay awake, you oaf!

I couldn't sleep. Not now. I could be captured by the City Watch, though the chances of being found and killed by bandits were better, and this didn't put me at ease. What if Alomar and Royce came scrambling down the slope from the countryside, being chased by guards? What if they needed my help?

Heavy, gray clouds. Fading traces of the moon. The light, beautiful chorus of the River Keska. Soft sand in my fingers as I scooped it up in a desperate attempt to stay awake.

My right hand hurt. My head and legs ached. The serene place around me faded to mist.

I waded into the waters of sleep.

- PART TWO -
In which we make new friends in dangerous places

CHAPTER 18

I was lucky. Royce and Alomar had found me under South Bridge, sleeping away like my life wasn't in danger. Their journey to Royce's home hadn't yielded much. His tiny house had been boarded up with an eviction notice stuck to the door. My friends were able to pry the boards off and gain entrance, but most of Royce's things had been disposed of in one way or another.

The two ran into no trouble with the City Watch or angry Assistant Innkeepers. They listened incredulously as I told my story. Royce didn't even believe me at first when I told them about how I dealt with Trenten and temporarily pinned our crime on him.

The idea of setting out into the world on your first adventure sounds exciting and romantic enough, but it's accompanied by bleary eyes, a headache from no sleep, and sore feet from all the walking. Not quite what one would expect, I suppose.

We set off south, to the woods. It was no wonder that bandits and highwaymen were always abound in forests throughout Eisley… the woods were the only safe places for such types. We were keenly aware of this and treaded lightly, having no choice but to press on and accept that the dangers in the countryside would have to be challenged.

After all, we couldn't bloody well go back to the city, could we?

So we hiked along the hills, moving as quickly as we could manage, not taking time to admire the crystalline blue skies overhead. I carried my pack slung over my shoulder, my writings nestled messily within. Royce carried his own pack, which had a large tin cup and two blankets stuffed inside. A spare cloak was draped over his other shoulder.

Alomar was still in handcuffs. We had little time to think about trying to break them, and swiftly surmised that we didn't have the means to do so. The man looked claustrophobic as he trudged along through the shin-high grass.

Since he was still in shackles, he couldn't carry anything except for the bunch of coins Royce had stashed away beneath a floorboard under his bed. It was hardly enough, and it wouldn't last the three of us two days back in the city, but it was sure better than nothing. I could hear the coins jingle around in Alomar's pockets as we continued.

Two hours later we were moving on through the thickets and small clearings of the woods, finally coming up on the dense, immense forest that surrounded Mount Kovald.

Mount Kovald was a tall peak that looked as if it were trying to snatch clouds from the sky. It was the grandest of a large range of mountains that ran alongside the northeastern border of Eisley, shielding Northroe and the Kovald from the Adgridd Sea.

Kovald Forest was one of the largest forests in our entire nation, and that was saying something, since wooded areas in Eisley were plentiful and some of the most sprawling and dense in the world. Tall, thickly populated clumps of Eislian oak, ash, pine and poplar trees provided protection from prying eyes and a haven from open country for hours by foot in any direction from the base of Mount Kovald.

Royce, Alomar and I had decided to follow the river to the woods so that we would have a source of water nearby. The dawn gradually progressed to late morning, and the sun rose high in the sky. We welcomed its warmth after the night of hard rain. On the outskirts of Kovald Forest and on the River Keska's edge was where we first braved a break from travel, coming to a stop to rest.

*   *   *

"Blast. Sun or no sun, I'm still bloody cold," Royce complained.

Alomar snorted. "Yeah? Try being in handcuffs, mate."

Royce knelt by the river and swirled his hand around in the current before washing his face. Alomar was pacing this way and that, taking stock of the area. I had noticed that since we left the city, Alomar had been extremely observant, often making a complete sweep of our surroundings at periodic intervals. I found myself glad that he had been a soldier once. It wasn't the first time since he had returned from Dekka that I appreciated the skills and experience he brought back with him, but in the present circumstances I found it incredibly valuable to have an ex-member of the 2nd Cavalry in our midst, handcuffs or no.

I strode over to a tall ash tree and knelt low under the reach of its leaves, making my way to the base of it. Yawning loudly I sat down on the dirt beneath it and pressed my back to the trunk. It felt good to sit, especially after all the traveling we'd been doing. Between running about in the Northroe backstreets and escaping into the wilderness to continue south, we had traveled for nearly half a day.

Resting my head against the ash tree's bark, I inhaled deeply. The forest morning enveloped us, and I realized the air was notably fresher than that of the city's, perhaps since we had it all to ourselves. I stretched out my legs the best I could, and they felt annoyingly stiff. As I did so, the burlap material of my pack rubbed against the fabric of my trousers audibly, and my eyes wandered to it.

Well, then. Here I was, day one of our journey, in the beautiful Kovald Forest. Wasn't this was writers did? Real writers, I mean? They traveled the world, saw the sights and met new people, learned what new lands had to offer. They wrote incredible stories inspired by what they had seen, or would bring back writings and journals telling of exotic cultures and majestic, far-away countries.

Kovald Forest was right next to Northroe, but it was a start. I opened my pack, scooped out my quill, blank parchment and uncapped my jar of ink. A smile played across my face, and I felt a surge of excitement. This was what I would do. This would put me on the map the world over. I would document our travels, our adventures!

That is, if we didn't get captured by bandits. Being sold off as slaves, or killed and left for dead in the wilderness where no one would ever find our bodies didn't strike me as appealing, but more importantly, that would prevent any good stories from being written.

Perhaps I had my priorities a bit mixed up.

My writing hand was sore from unintentionally punching the street when I had aimed for the Watchman outside of the burning tavern. I sighed and took the quill in my hand, testing it out as I scribbled words into the air.

"Right, then," Royce was saying. "So what are you suggesting? We live off berries and leaves for a while, mate? Shall we hunt for deer as well? We could sharpen Penny's quill over there. That could land us dinner, for sure."

Alomar was shaking his head. "I'm just saying we need to stay off the roads, is all. Even traveling here by the river is risky."

Royce took off his tunic and the shirt beneath it before wading knee-deep into the water, then up to his waist. He dipped his head into the cold river and brought it back out, his breathing rapid as he tried to shrug off the chill of the water.

"Fates help us," Royce muttered. "Pretty soon we'll be bandits, yeah? We'll start starving, since I haven't seen any berries or fruit since we entered the woods. Who would've thought?"

Alomar laughed, making his way to the river's edge. He sat and was able to awkwardly kick off his boots before letting his feet dangle into the current. "Aye," he chimed sarcastically, "we could do that. Start robbing commoners on the road."

"Rob them unarmed, at that."

"Hm. Suppose weapons would help."

"Don't bloody have any, do we?"

While the two men talked, I was relaxing in the shade and taking in my surroundings. The scent of earlier rain mixed with pine and dirt was intoxicating. A slight wind passed through our tiny thicket, rustling leaves overhead.

What would I write, anyway?

Here I was, a Writer-in-Training, off in the woods in a beautiful clearing surrounded by nature in all its glory. Wasn't I supposed to be able to write something? Anything?

"-thinking of becoming an inventor."

I looked up to see Royce coming ashore and kicking back in the grass near Alomar.

"Eh?" asked Alomar. "An inventor?"

"That's right," replied Royce. The man snatched a blade of grass from the earth and chewed on it as he spoke. "For example, I was thinking of, well, inventing this thing. A wide brim you hold over your head while it's raining, and it protects you from getting wet."

Alomar mulled over this. "Is it like a hat?"

"Aye. You could hold it by a stick or something while you walk."

"A brim on a stick."

"That's right," Royce said. "It'd be made of...cloth, or some fabric. Leather hide or...or something."

"So a wide circular leather-or-cloth-or-something brim, that you hold on a stick over your head while you walk in the rain, to prevent you from getting wet. Why circular?"

Royce thought for a moment. "Well, I dunno. Suppose it doesn't have to be circular. Maybe it could be like a rectangle, or pointed like a triangle and all that. We could sell them in different shapes. Actually, I didn't say anything about it being circular, anyway."

I tried picturing this, and watching Alomar's face I could see he, too, was giving it serious thought.

"No, mate," Alomar finally concluded. "It'd never catch on. Why carry a big... brim to protect from the rain when you could just wear a hat? Or a hooded cloak and the like?"

His face seemed to fall for a moment in defeat, but Royce shrugged after a minute. "Eh. Guess you're right."

I left my writing tools next to my pack at my perch under the tree and got up to join the two men next to the water. "Royce, I, for once, think it'd be a great invention."

Royce craned his neck to face me. "Yeah?"

"Aye," I said, reaching the river's edge and stepping out of my boots. The grass and dirt felt soft beneath my bare feet. "I think people would go for it."

My friend grinned. "Thanks, Pen."

I made my way into the river, gritting my teeth in response to the shock of the cold water. Grimacing against the chill washing across my body, I looked down at my reflection in the river's surface. It was more of a shadow in the current than an actual image of me, but I could still imagine details of my face and put it to the watery Penny that stared up at me. It danced in the ripples, and I found myself wondering if I was dreaming.

We had actually done it. Left Northroe behind to embark on a journey.

Scooping two hands into the water and dashing my shadowy silhouette from the river, I splashed it about my face. Was this a journey, yet? Or just an escape? Either way, we'd left the city, but not exactly on our terms.

I washed the cold water about my skin, closing my eyes as I did so and trying not to shudder with the cold. It was at this time that I felt a weight of some kind bump into my leg.

Opening my eyes, I looked down to the water... to see another face staring up at me beneath the surface.

What?

I wiped the water from my eyes and blinked twice before looking again.

A man was gazing up at me, wearing an expression of absolute terror. His blue eyes peered at mine absently and his mouth was open. I quickly realized there was no life left in his face.

His throat had been cut.

CHAPTER 19

I hollered in surprise and fell backward, splashing about in the water wildly.

"Penny?" called Alomar in alarm. "What is it?"

"Fates!" gasped Royce. He shot to his feet. "Look at that!"

Cursing in grunts and guttural noises I didn't know I could make, I scrambled back to the riverbank hastily, my arms a flurry of desperation.

Royce extended his hand and pulled me ashore. Breathing heavily, I looked back to the water to see the body continue to float down the river, bobbing lifelessly with the current.

"Bloody hell," I uttered. "His throat was cut."

"Eh?"

"Someone cut that man's throat," I repeated, cringing as I pictured the grim sight.

Alomar became exceedingly intent on our surroundings, specifically upriver from where the body had come from.

"Mates," he said lowly, "get up. Get to cover."

Royce and I both just stared up at the man.

"Hurry up," he hissed. "Highwaymen must be in these parts. It's pretty clear, yeah? And I can't exactly fight if they come up on us."

"But-"

"Royce," Alomar interrupted, "the body was still bleeding. Bloke hasn't been dead for long, know what I mean? They're nearby."

I was already on my feet and jogging to the tree where I'd left my pack and writing supplies before Alomar finished, but now Royce was close behind, needing no further convincing.

Hurriedly kneeling under the tall ash, I quickly capped the ink and returned my quill and parchment to my pack. As I did so I was looking about wildly in every direction. It was a terrible feeling, the sensation that we were being watched from afar.

Royce pulled his shirt back on and stuffed his tunic into his pack before bounding over to me. Alomar was close behind.

"Got everything?" Royce asked. His eyes were wide with genuine fright. It scared me.

"Aye," I whispered.

Alomar jogged over to us as well. I wasn't used to the sight of someone moving quickly with their hands shackled behind them. Seeing this somehow made Alomar's earlier point even more clear: he couldn't fight. If barbarians or brutes came upon us, we'd be dead men. I couldn't fight worth a damn and Royce would most likely be outnumbered and outmatched, if the stories of bandits in these parts were true.

We had held our own at the November Raven the night before, but it was different out here in the woods. Killing was what bandit clans did. It was their way of life. Fighting one of them would be much different from an angry brawler in a tavern.

I sat abruptly and pulled on my boots, forgetting I hadn't done so, when Royce's voice jarred my attention back to the river.

"Bloody 'ell," he said, nudging me and pointing past Alomar. "Look at that, Penny. Alomar! Look!"

Another body was floating on downriver. Its clothing was soaked with water and blood alike. I gawked shamelessly as it continued on, thumping against a large boulder that sent it twirling about slowly.

Alomar cursed lowly when yet another body entered view from around the bend. It was a woman. Her corpse continued along the same forlorn path as the two before her.

Royce looked upriver anxiously. "Al, what do we do?"

The man knelt behind the tree. "I'm thinking."

"Thinking?" I squeaked. "Maybe we should be running instead, yeah?"

Alomar shook his head. "Could be a trap."

"What?"

"A trap. I heard about highwaymen out west in Belfour doing this," he replied. "They'd send a couple bodies downriver. If any travelers venturing by came across them, they'd naturally flee in the other direction. The bandits would set up ambush points along the roads and intercept the poor bastards running from the bodies coming downriver."

Royce and I looked at each other. He just raised his eyebrows and shook his head.

"There's no roads here though," I urged. "We could go in any other direction."

"We need to find better cover," Alomar broke in. His voice had grown soft, and his tone was very calculating. "All we have is a tree at the edge of this thicket. We need to at least draw back a bit."

Royce nudged us both. "Come on, there's thicker foliage over behind us. We can-"

He didn't finish. Two more corpses floated into view, polluting the River Keska with blood. One was facedown with its arms tied behind it, much like Alomar's shackled hands. The other was another woman whose face was twisted in horror. I didn't want to know what end she had met.

What made all this worse was when we heard yells from upriver and out of view. A man's voice carried through the air to us, and the reply of another. They were far enough away to where we couldn't discern what was said, but we all understood one thing: more than one man was coming toward us.

There was no further discussion. The three of us turned and dashed for the cluster of trees and foliage further into the tree line that rounded about the thicket. Leaves and pine needles crashed loudly under our feet.

Royce, Alomar and I practically slid to a stop in the dense foliage and knelt low in the brush. Alomar was crouched on one knee, trying his best to peer through the leaves at the direction of the voices. Royce did the same. I got prone on the ground, pressing myself as low as I could into the dirt as if a volley of arrows would shoot toward us at any moment.

The voices grew louder in the distance. They echoed through the woods, rebounding off trees and rock formations before passing around us. Eyes wide, I crawled very slowly forward so I could peer with one eye around the foliage to the river's edge, where we had been just a minute before.

"Royce," Alomar whispered, "I want you to watch our backs. Lay with your back to the river. Keep your eyes peeled. You see any movement, give me a nudge, got it?"

Royce nodded and shifted to a sitting position before leaning back on one elbow. He swept his gaze carefully around the forest behind us.

"Penny," Alomar continued, "I want you to watch the river ahead at our last position. Keep an eye on the right as well, to the South. I'll watch upriver to the North. No words, you two. Got it? We-"

Alomar fell silent as the voices of men grew even louder. One voice was hoarse, as though whoever its owner was yelled all day and night. The other was rough and strong, bellowing through the trees.

"-gotta be kidding me. There's one! Quaid! Over here!" came the hoarse voice.

"Found one! About time, yeah?" a man presumably named Quaid replied.

Cracks of twigs and pine needles beneath running footsteps sounded off from upriver. A wave of fear swept over me, and my heart nearly stopped. I could feel my temple pounding with my pulse. This was a new flavor of fear. The danger the night before had been very real while we avoided the Northroe City Watch, but Watchmen were officers of the law.

Bandits abided by no laws, except their own.

Alomar exhaled lowly. "Another body. I... think they're chasing after it."

Royce said nothing and kept watch faithfully behind us. I could hear him breathing unsteadily, clearly understanding the situation at hand.

Water splashed noisily, and I heard another set of heavy footsteps plod through dirt and mud before they, too, crashed into the river water.

"Strange," mused Alomar. "They're dragging the body ashore."

The grunts of two men could be heard easily. Going with what Alomar had said, I pictured two mean-looking blokes dragging a dead body from the river, blood swirling about them like a misty cloud.

Curiosity got the best of me. Perhaps they weren't so mean-looking?

"What do they look like?" I asked. "They look dangerous?"

"Aye," Alomar said. "They're not messing about. Armed. Light armor. Nobody utter a word from here on out unless you see-"

"That blasted fool Castor," one of the men said loudly, panting after coming ashore, cutting off any further words from Alomar.

"The Cap'n will have our heads," the hoarse voice replied.

"No, Arthur," answered the man who must have been Quaid, "he won't. He ain't finding out."

"Bollocks. Cap'n always finds out."

I peered out even further, craning my neck so that I could try to see around the cover of undergrowth masking us from sight.

The men named Arthur and Quaid were standing over the fifth body that had washed downriver, breathing heavily after having dragged it to the riverbank.

"Fates," Arthur muttered in his hoarse voice. "Five more to go. We need to hurry."

I swallowed hard when I saw that Alomar had been rather accurate in his description of the two men.

Arthur was wearing what appeared to be a dark brown long-sleeved overcoat of padded leather, and tough, worn leather gloves. He donned a padded coif on his head, which was like a hood one wore but fit tight about the head and offered more protection. His hide boots were caked with mud from the river. A sword hung at the man's hip in an old-looking sheath, and two daggers were snugly tucked into his belt on his other side as well.

Quaid wore a sturdy, earthen green gambeson – a padded, lightly armored jacket. A tattered brown cloak hung about him over his jacket. It had a hood, but the man did not don it. This revealed a haircut I'd only seen on men in the military: the sides of his head were extremely short-cropped, nearly shaved, and a single strip of dark brown hair ran down the middle, also cut short. He wore fingerless woolen gloves that exposed calloused, dirty fingers. I gulped when I saw a large bow slung around his back and a quiver of arrows that rested snug against his side, angled backward. The man also carried a short sword that looked considerably smaller than the one his companion wore.

Short blade or not, I knew better than to judge a sword by its length. Eislian companies preferred short swords anyway for their speed and lower encumbrance.

Sighing, I abruptly dropped my head face-first to the dirt and shook it in dismay.

The two men now trudged on downriver, right past where I had dashed ashore in fright upon seeing the dead man in the water.

We held our breaths.

"Castor wasn't supposed to kill this lot, yet. Cap'n wanted to keep 'em, right? For ransom?

"Aye."

"Skies be cursed."

Arthur gripped his sheathed sword absently as they hustled on. "We'll figure it out. He was gonna kill 'em all anyway. We can still lie about it."

"Let's go. Still five more, aye?"

"Hold on, Quaid. Rock in my boot."

The two men stopped momentarily. I wiped the dirt from my nose after I finished my self-pity session before looking up at Alomar. He just returned my glance and shook his head slowly.

Royce was still laying back on one elbow, trying not to move as the bandits spoke, and having not seen the men for himself. While I lay prone, Royce shifted cautiously to his other elbow and tried looking over me and out toward the river.

As my friend shifted his weight, a twig snapped under his boot loudly.

The highwaymen up ahead both snapped their gazes toward our hiding place, crouching low and freezing like animals discovering they were being hunted.

Alomar clenched his jaw and flashed Royce a gritty scowl.

I froze, holding my breath. My eyes were open as wide as I could make them, and I edged nervously back behind the brush of leaves and foliage at the base of the trees.

"Who's there?" shouted Arthur gruffly. He wasted no time and unsheathed his blade with a metallic rasp, beginning to edge toward us very slowly. "Come out, now!"

Quaid stepped swiftly a few paces to the right of his companion, drawing his bow off of his back and reaching for an arrow at his side in one fluid motion. Now that Arthur was out of his line of sight, Quaid readied an arrow to the string and angled it downward at his feet, not yet drawing back.

"Out with you, now!" Arthur called again hoarsely, taking another step.

"Oy!" shouted Quaid. "You heard the man. You step out and we talk, or we find ya, and you die."

I cursed silently, my eyes wandering over to Alomar, who was still crouched, hanging his head low in hiding. His eyes were darting this way and that at his feet, and he looked deep in thought.

Royce looked like he was in pain. He was shaking his head as he mouthed his silent apology to me.

"Dammit, we don't have time for this!" Quaid yelled. "Last chance. You want to live? Show yourselves. Right-bloody-now!"

Alomar looked back at us. "We have no choice. Follow my lead."

"What?" I whispered back. "Are you out of your mind?"

"Oy!" Arthur called again. "We can hear you, yeah? Come out to where we can see ya!"

Alomar didn't wait. I watched my friend rustle the leaves and bushes around him as he got to his feet and strode slowly out into the open.

CHAPTER 20

I'm not sure if the bandits were expecting us to actually show ourselves or not, but that's what happened. Royce and I would be damned if we let Alomar walk out there into the face of death without us.

I wonder what they must have thought when a large man with a military tattoo and hands bound behind his back came out of the woodwork, flanked by the rough-and-tough long-haired Royce and myself, timid and knuckles white from clutching my pack so tightly.

The two men looked at each other for a moment, then back at us.

Quaid lowered his nocked arrow and eased the tension on his bowstring.

Arthur leveled his blade outward, pointed menacingly at Alomar. "State your business."

"Well," I started, "you see. Uh, well. It's quite a story, if you-"

"Look, mates," Alomar interrupted, glaring at me as he did so. "We don't want any trouble."

"That a fact?"

"Aye. We're on the run, ourselves."

The archer stepped forward. "Why the handcuffs?"

"Like I said," replied Alomar calmly, "we're on the run."

Royce and I exchanged glances. I held my breath as I turned back to the bandits, watching their faces carefully.

They looked as uncertain as we were. It wasn't every day one came across the likes of us in the middle of the woods. I suppose Royce, Alomar and I were an odd sight, soaked in water, dirty, and one in shackles. Come to think of it, we must have looked dangerous ourselves.

Regardless of the impression we gave Arthur and Quaid, they had weapons. We did not.

Arthur lowered his sword very slightly. "On the run, eh? What for?"

"This is stupid," Quaid cut in from behind his companion. "Let's kill 'em and be done with it."

"Wait!" I cried out. "We just-"

Royce nudged me roughly. "Let Alomar talk," he whispered.

"Eh?" Arthur asked, looking at Royce now. "What was that?"

My friend held up his hands harmlessly. "Nothing."

"Look," Alomar cut in again, "we're fugitives. Wanted in Northroe for arson and murder. Had to leave the city yesterday. As you can see," my friend continued, turning for the men to see his cuffs more clearly, "I was in custody briefly, but-"

Quaid leered skeptically. "How the 'ell did you escape the Watch?"

"Long story," I replied before Alomar could.

Arthur was looking me in the eyes now. "You. Put that pack down."

My fingers tightened around it defensively.

"Now. I won't ask again."

When Quaid re-nocked his arrow to his string and pulled back, Alomar looked back at me with an urgent gaze.

"No!" I whispered.

"Yes, dammit!" Royce interjected in a low voice. "Fates, Pen, he's going to kill you!"

The final remnants of stubbornness washed away when Quaid's bow creaked as he drew back further. I obeyed, letting the pack slide off my shoulder and gently set it to the ground at my feet.

"Throw it over here," Arthur ordered. "You, too. Throw your pack."

Royce sullenly gripped his pack at his side and slung it through the air as lightly as he could. It landed halfway in the open between us and the bandits, sliding in the dirt. I followed suit and tried to aim my pack for a large clump of soft, green grass.

I missed.

Wasting no time, Arthur set down his blade, got to his knees and picked through Royce's belongings while Quaid stood behind him and kept his eyes on the three of us. No one dared move for fear of having an arrow provide a rather painful death.

I was surprised when Arthur closed Royce's pack back up without taking anything. He tossed it back to Royce's feet before going through mine.

"Oy," Quaid said coolly, "those bodies are goin' downriver. We have to hurry."

"Aye, I know, mate," replied Arthur as he opened my pack.

I was overcome with the grave realization that my entire life's works as a Writer-in-Training was now in the hands of a bandit who would kill me for looking at him the wrong way. My mouth grew very dry, and I could feel butterflies swirling about my stomach in a fury.

The look that crossed the highwayman's face was priceless as he opened my pack and saw the pages, scrolls and rolls of parchment inside. He produced my quill and the capped inkwell after a moment, holding it up for Quaid to see. Neither man said anything. Arthur looked at me with a puzzled look and simply put them back inside my pack before tossing it to me.

Arthur stood, grabbing his sword off the dirt as he did. The noise of the soil scraping against the blade made my hair stand on-end.

"There's coins in my pockets," Alomar volunteered. "It's not much of anything, really. It's all we could swipe before we had to leave the city."

Arthur moved slowly forward and scooped into Alomar's pockets, finding the coins my friend spoke of. He did this carefully, and I noticed that he never once moved into Quaid's line of fire.

"All right, then," Arthur said. "So, you're arsonists? Really?"

All three of us nodded. I tried to be convincing.

"What'd you burn down?" the man pressed.

"A tavern," Alomar answered.

"Which one?"

"The November Raven."

Arthur folded his arms. "November Raven is in the North Quarter, right? Near Lord Hannady's manor?"

"No. The Raven is... was, in the Market Quarter. Near the Windfarer's Inn. And Hannady's manor is in the Central District, near Keska Square." Alomar glared. "Now, are you done testing us?"

Nodding slowly, Arthur looked back at Quaid. "We'll verify your story later. Right now, if you want to live, you get to help us."

All three of us looked at each other.

"We have four bodies floating down the Keska right now that we need to retrieve before they get too close to the main road in the countryside."

Quaid seemed to catch on quickly, and he slung his bow around his back. "You need to help us drag 'em ashore. They're too far downriver now for Arthur and I to do so ourselves before they reach open view near the road."

"I can't help," Alomar said, shifting slightly. "Can't use my hands because of these blasted cuffs. If you could break these off for me, I-"

Arthur shook his head. "Not a chance."

"Then how am I supposed to-"

"You're not," interrupted Quaid. He turned to Royce and I. "You two do it. Help us drag the bodies from the river."

Royce folded his arms. "How do we know you won't just kill us after we do?"

Arthur sheathed his sword, and then held his hands outward as if declaring peace. "Good faith, mate."

I winced suddenly, feeling a pain in my mouth. I had been nervously grinding my teeth the entire time without knowing it.

Alomar looked downriver before turning back to the bandits. "I have a proposition."

"We don't have time."

"If my mates here help you two with the bodies," Alomar continued anyway, "you take these cuffs off my wrists."

Quaid spat at the ground passively and laughed. "Look here. You're not in the position to make any deals, eh?"

Royce shook his head, letting his anger show. "You could just kill us afterward. This isn't-"

"Hoy!" thundered Arthur. His fierce voice echoed throughout the woods around us. "What's it gonna be? Help us on good faith, or don't, and we kill you right where ya stand. I don't see how you think you have any more options than that."

I looked at Royce, who was clearly resisting the urge to charge the man. Alomar glanced at us and shrugged.

"Right then," I said, surprising myself. "We'll do it."

Quaid nodded. "Good. Now you," he said, pointing to Alomar, "against that tree."

The man motioned to my friend to stand up against a medium-height pine tree about twenty paces off to the left. I wanted to object, but Alomar moved before I could utter any words and obediently stood with his back to the trunk.

Arthur looked at Quaid. "Rope?"

"In my pack."

Arthur strode to his comrade and rummaged through the man's pack while Quaid watched us closely, not taking his gaze off of us. Shortly after, Arthur produced a coil of strong rope and started toward Alomar.

"Now, wait a moment!" Royce said. "What are you-"

"It's insurance," Arthur replied. "Your military friend – aye, we noticed – stays here. After we retrieve the corpses, we'll come back."

"But-"

"We're splitting up," the man pressed, drowning out Royce's protest. He pointed at me. "You. Leave your pack and come with me. And you," he continued, looking at Royce, "you'll go with Quaid. Mark my words: try anything and we'll gut you like fish, then come back here to finish your friend off."

"Now, now," I said with a forced grin, "that's no way to start a new partnership, eh? Is it?"

No one answered.

"Is it?" I asked again weakly.

Arthur finished his knot, tying Alomar to the tree securely. He turned to us and started jogging downriver.

"We've wasted enough time! Let's go!"

Royce and I trailed behind the man, and Quaid brought up the rear. I ventured a last look back at Alomar, who stood helplessly bound to the tree, watching as we hurried out of view.

CHAPTER 21

Very quickly, our jogging pace broke into an all-out run. I was huffing heavily, red in the face as I tried to keep up. The forest seemed to whisk by me in a blur, a colorful painting of greens and browns with hints of the newly developed yellows and reds of autumn. The outlaws were fast and nimble, clearly heavily versed in the swift navigation of the forest by foot. I was out of breath in no time.

A hand pushed me from behind. "Gah, get movin'!" came Quaid's voice. "Bloody slow, you are!"

"Sorry," I gasped, pushing myself on.

After another few minutes of running and being scraped across the face with pine needles and leaves of all sizes, Arthur's voice rang out from up ahead through the trees.

"There!" he called, his words punctuated by the rushing current of the river and strong wind. "Got one in sight. Quaid, you two keep going, yeah?"

"Aye!" called the archer outlaw. He turned to me mid-run. "You better hurry."

I quickened my pace, watching as Quaid streaked onward, followed by Royce. My legs burned, but I did my best to ignore it. I dashed through the woods and scrambled down a steep slope to the river's edge, toward where I had heard Arthur's voice.

"Hurry!" Arthur called again, beckoning for me. He was already waist-deep in the water.

I was afraid, yes. I was scared of being killed, and of Alomar being eaten alive by a bear while in his helpless state tied to the tree, somewhere behind us. But something in me had something to prove. I wanted to prove to myself that I could do something in a pinch... that if I had to, I could do what I had to do to survive, no matter what it would be. I had a strange desire to prove myself to the bandit in the water ahead, to show that I was a man who could handle business.

My heart beat with these different emotions as I threw myself into the river and waded to the man quickly.

"Grab his feet. Aye, grab the – right, there ya go. Pull!"

I was holding on to the corpse's boots, trying not to look at it. It was a red-haired man. His eyes were closed and his neck had a deep, nasty gash across the throat, like the first body I'd seen.

My nose crinkled in disgust and I forced down an urge to vomit. I cast my gaze away from the poor man and behind me to the riverbank, and pulled.

"Easy does it!" rasped Arthur as we got to the bank. I tugged hard, but as I set my foot to the muddy soil, I slipped and fell to my knees, water swirling around my waist. My injured right hand shot out to stop my fall in reflex, and I yelled as I landed on it with most of my weight.

Arthur didn't pay much attention. He had the body by the shoulders and swung it around up onto the soil before rolling it ashore by himself. The man was red in the face, and I was tenderly moving the fingers on my right hand.

"What happened to your hand?" he asked between breaths.

"Punched a Watchman," I answered, still wincing. It was a half-truth.

The bandit raised his eyebrows. "You? *You* punched a Watchman?"

"Aye. He was still wearing his helm."

Upon hearing this, Arthur grinned and erupted into a loud, hearty laugh that I swear swayed the tree branches. "You don't look like the fighting type... but I can tell you're not lying."

"Can you, now?"

"Let's go," the man said. "We have to hurry."

* * *

The better part of the next half-hour saw the four of us scurrying along the River Keska, following as it wound southwest, dangerously closer to the main road in the countryside. The highway led south toward the Glydell Farmlands and Mable, a small village. To the north, it was just a half-day's trek by foot to Northroe. Being a large city, Northroe was often the destination for traders and merchants and business of all types. Since we had recently acquired the shiny new titles of "arsonists and murderers," we preferred to stay away from the road.

As Arthur and Quaid had pointed out, the bodies were not going to wait around.

After we dragged the first corpse from the water, Arthur and I continued south. Minutes later we passed Royce and Quaid, who were tugging their first body from the current. Royce gave me a grin as Arthur and I rushed by, and I returned it with a confused look.

I suppose Royce *would* grin while helping an outlaw pull dead bodies from a river.

Arthur and I reached the next body. It was one of the women. I grabbed her shoulders while the outlaw clutched at her ankles tightly, not seeming to mind feeling her cold dead skin on his fingers.

He must have seen my disgusted look.

"If you grab by the shoes, they could slip off."

Ah. Somebody had done this before.

The dead woman was on her back, water sloshing about her as we brought her closer to the bank. I tried my best not to look at her horrified face. Her brown eyes looked as if they'd already started to glaze over, but that might have just been my imagination.

As we dragged her to the bank, Royce and Quaid shot by uphill.

"Two more!" Quaid called.

"Aye!"

The next body was snagged on a low-hanging tree that dipped its branches into the water rushing beneath it. Somehow the corpse had been caught and forced under it. It took all four of us standing chest-deep in water to deal with the problem. Royce pulled the body out from under the tree's grasp, huffing and puffing against the current while Arthur, Quaid and I shoved the tree upward and off the legs of the body with all our might.

"One left!" Royce said loudly over the river's current.

He was handling himself rather seriously. I thought I even detected enthusiasm in my friend's voice.

All four of us jogged alongside the river, following the slight bends and turns along its banks as it flowed on, flanked by thick brush and forest on both sides. After a few more minutes of travel, even Arthur and Quaid were starting to get winded.

"Fates," uttered Quaid, bending over to rest his hands on his knees. "Where's that bloke at, anyhow?"

"Last one, too," Arthur said. "Figures, eh?"

Wanting to match Royce's initiative, I trudged on while the others caught their breath. It was then that I realized perhaps Royce was trying to show the men that we had worth, or that we were, in fact, who we claimed to be. If we 'proved' that we were fellow highwaymen by helping the outlaws, maybe they'd let us go our own way.

This new possibility added more pep in my step, and I resumed running. I glanced backward and saw that the others were following my lead.

Five minutes later, we found the body... but its placement couldn't have been worse.

The woods around the river had thinned out considerably, and up ahead the Keska raced straight for the highway leading back to Northroe. There was always the chance of Eislian soldiers marching along it, or of seeing a caravan flanked by some noble's security team, or of a chance encounter with a City Watch unit that had perhaps struck out to the countryside in search of Royce, Alomar and I.

All four of us were huddled behind a small formation of trees and foliage much like the one Royce, Alomar and I had used to hide from the two outlaws earlier.

A very small bridge arched over a thin point in the river, linking a small country road to the main highway from further east. As fate would have it, the body had been pushed right up against the stone base of one of the columns supporting the bridge above the water.

"We're lucky," Quaid said, his eyes darting both ways. "This road isn't deserted often."

"We're short on time," said Arthur in his raspy voice. He turned to Royce and I. "You two. Go get it."

I snorted. "What? Why don't you come?"

"They don't want to be seen out in the open," muttered Royce. "They're sending us in case the Watch comes. Or the army. Or anyone else that would cut us to bits."

I sighed.

"We'll watch over ya," said Quaid.

Frowning, I shot him a look. "Sure you will."

"Really," the man said. He brandished his bow and nocked a barbed arrow. "I'm a good shot. I ain't lying. Am I lying, Arthur?"

"He's not lying."

I looked over at Royce. We didn't have a choice, did we?

CHAPTER 22

Royce and I both sprinted toward the bridge ahead. I could see the corpse shifting slightly with the current and could only pray it didn't get swept past the bridge and onward.

"Think they'll kill us?" I breathed in question.

"I don't know."

I tried not to think about it. It occurred to me that we could try to break for an all-out run into the wilderness... but even if we got away, Alomar would still be tied to that pine tree back north along the river, completely defenseless. They would just return and kill him.

I shuddered at the thought as we neared the bridge. I kept imagining I was Alomar, and what that would be like to have Arthur or Quaid nonchalantly stroll up to me and slice me open, or-

"All right Penny, here goes," Royce said, dashing my thoughts. The slope was steep here, so we carefully made our way down, sliding this way and that until we got to a sturdy enough bank near the water's edge. The bridge now loomed over us, and the body was just out of our reach. A few trees looked on from the bank, and I imagined them laughing down at us in our predicament.

"The current is bloody fast here," I observed. "I don't know if we can swim against it, Royce. Maybe we should tell them."

The man was assessing the situation. "I think we can do it, Pen."

"I don't."

"No, look," Royce said, pointing to the steep grassy slope that met with the stones of the bridge overhead. "The roots of those trees there are coming through the side of the slope. They look strong enough to where we can grab them, and if we-"

Thinking of Alomar being killed in cold blood, I didn't wait for Royce to finish. I strode up to the river's edge, swung one foot out over the water and reached for one of the tangled roots of the sturdy oaks above us. Testing it gingerly for signs of weakness, it seemed to hold. I made a gamble and slipped into the rushing water, holding the large root with two hands to keep myself from being swept away in the current.

"Well, look at you go," Royce said with light in his eyes. "Penny, I'm impressed."

"You coming?" I asked, having to do so loudly over the rushing water.

He clambered after me. A web of strong roots from the trees above curved and twisted along the slope and jutted out into the air and downward into the water as well. I moved hand over hand from one hold to another, and Royce followed after me upon seeing which roots were safe to grab, though they all seemed sturdy enough.

"Almost there!" I shouted over my shoulder.

The corpse bobbed this way and that in the flow of the river. I shuddered at the sight of the deep slit in its throat. It seemed to have stopped losing blood.

Making my way closer, I grabbed hold of the next root and gave it a tug when the one I was already holding on to gave way suddenly. I slid downward and had luckily already gripped the next one. Taking advantage of my weightlessness in the water, I lifted myself back up and got a better grip on a different root.

"Close one!" called Royce. "Can you reach it?"

"I don't think so!" I answered. "There's no way, Royce – unless you can hold onto me while I stretch across to grab its arm."

Royce must have pictured this for a moment, judging the concerned look on his face. He clung silently to the side of the steep slope as the water rushed by.

"There's no other way," he surmised with a nod. "Let's do it."

He sidled along the riverbank, closer to me and the bridge. I edged onward until I was wedged into the corner where the stone and earth of the slope met. Royce was right behind me.

"Here goes," I said.

"Good luck, mate."

Royce was a stronger man than I, so it made sense that he be the one providing support. He grasped my hand and lowered me into the river. The strong current swept by me, seeming more powerful than I'd thought it would be.

I would never have imagined a scene like this one evening ago, much less an hour ago.

Royce then carefully climbed lower to get waist-deep in the water so that we could gain more reach. His grasp was firm.

"I've got ya! You can do it!"

My nerves were dancing to the beat of an anxiety attack. The water iced through my clothes and skin, causing my teeth to chatter uncontrollably. I took a deep breath, then another. Before my friend had to utter any more words of encouragement, I waded forward like a dog paddling and stretched for the body's arm that flailed about in the torrent.

I missed, and gasped as I felt the water start to carry me under the bridge, but Royce's grip tightened and he guided me back to the safety of the gnarled roots.

"One more time!"

I nodded and released my hold on the roots once more, entirely trusting my companion to not let go of me as I reached desperately for the corpse's deathly hand. It was so close!

Gritting my teeth, I thought I was going to miss again, but I somehow stretched even further at the last moment and my fingers interlaced with that of the dead man. A tingling sensation went up my body when I felt his hand. The fingers were cold and felt rigid and stiff. I panicked and almost let go, but thankfully maintained my hold.

The chill of the water jolted my body. Adrenaline had allowed me to act in the cold river water, but it was slowly abandoning me now. I growled in determination and reached further.

Behind me, Royce was gripping the roots desperately now, having to act as an anchor for both me and the lifeless body in my grasp. I grunted in frustration, nearly losing my hold on the dead hand.

It was then that we heard what was the very last sound I expected to hear, up out of view and overhead. The sound was coming from atop the bridge.

The voice of a man and the thrilled shouts and squeals of what must have been four or five children reached us from above. I could hear tiny footsteps scraping across the bridge muffled by the current, and I shot a startled look at Royce.

"Now remember sons," came a man's voice, "the key to fishing is *patience*. Patience! Understand?"

"Aye, father!" came a chorus of replies from the children.

"Good. Fishing is an art, m' boys. A learned skill, a trade to be proud of. Just think: today, you will have all caught your first fish!"

Cue another ecstatic cheer from the children overhead.

"Today," the boys' father continued, "you will become men. Well, little men, so to speak. But in a few short moments, you all will have cast a line for the first time!"

"Yay!"

"Let me go first!"

"Can we eat the fish?"

"Where are the hooks?"

Oh, blast. Hooks.

Still holding onto the corpse in the water with one hand while clinging to Royce with the other, I craned awkwardly backward to look at him.

He was shaking his head, eyes wide in urgency.

Of course a man would take his four or five sons to go fishing off the side of that particular, right at that very moment. This meant the possibility of being seen, but even worse, there were hooks involved.

Any sensible bloke knows that fishing hooks are rather sharp.

CHAPTER 23

"The Fates hate us," Royce murmured as quietly as he could and loud enough so that I could hear him over the rushing water.

"Pull me back!" I urged. "Hurry!"

Royce's jaw was clenched and his face red as he strained to bring me back toward him and the safety of the roots entangled in the side of the slope.

"Now," I heard the man above us say, "take your bait and – Jemmy, no, lad. Don't put the hook in your mouth. Let the fish worry about biting it."

I could hear the boys above us snickering when they all suddenly gasped.

"Jemmy, spit out the hook for heaven's sake... ah, blast. Here, let me have a look, son. The rest of you, slip the bait to your hooks carefully. You're going to then cast out on my mark, understand?"

The lads' voices answered enthusiastically. "Aye, papa!"

Suddenly my grip on the corpse's fingers slipped, and it was swept away from me momentarily. I yelped in surprise and without thinking gave a kick to propel myself forward into the water to retrieve it with a splash. My hands closed around the dead body's right forearm just in time, but I felt myself being carried away downriver for an instant.

Royce lunged out as far as he dared with one hand, stretching to the limit to maintain a hold on the roots while he did. He cursed as the water splashed around him. My friend barely gripped my ankle, and I was stretched outward as if lying prone on the water's surface, treading the current facedown.

My face was entirely submerged in underwater, and I tilted my head upward so I could breathe for but a moment. It was long enough to hear the father and his sons atop the bridge grow alarmed.

"Eh, papa, did you hear something down there?"

"I heard a splash, father!"

"Now, boys," came their father's reply, "that's the fish. They're splashing about. So it's time, isn't it? Bend your arm at the elbow, lads, like this... oy, Samuel! Wait for me to show you how. I'll go first."

I was sputtering and bobbing up and down in the water as I tried to keep my hold on the corpse's arm and stay afloat, and somehow get back to Royce at the same time. The sound of Royce hissing and cursing and groaning as he tried desperately to reel me back toward him against the current reached my ears each time I came up momentarily.

My friend was making progress. The cold water surged around me with force, but I could feel myself being pulled backward. I tried to help by fanning one arm back and forth in an awkward sort of back-paddle, but in doing so I almost lost the corpse again. I closed both hands around its forearm once more.

I was almost there. Royce was pulling with all his might so that I could rotate to a position where I could grab a hold of one of the roots, as I would have hit the slope feet-first.

"C'mon Pen!" he gasped.

Pulling the dead man closer to me and trying not to look at his face as I did so, I reached for one of the gnarled tree roots, and barely missed.

"-and then cast off, lads. Like so."

I expected a fishhook to smack me in the head, but none did. Instead, a line with a worm impaled on the hook as bait plopped into the water on the other side of the bridge, treading with the current.

I breathed a sigh of relief. They wouldn't cast on our side of the bridge. The fishing lines would be pulled with the river under the bridge if they did, chafing against the stone. Trying to ignore the shivering spasms rocking my body from the cold, I redoubled my efforts.

"See, boys? Nothin' to it, aye?"

"Aye, papa!" the man's sons gushed in excitement.

"Now, you try it. No, no bait yet, Otis. Only your hooks. We're going to do a practice cast, all at once, yeah? Stand five paces apart... yes, like that. Now, on three! Ready?"

"Ready!"

"One..."

Royce pulled harder. I lunged through the freezing water in an effort to grab the roots, and missed again.

"Two... ah, wait! Otis, adjust your grip, laddie. And your line isn't – here. Let me help. The rest of you cast off when you're ready. Don't hit your brothers!"

"Dammit, Penny," spat Royce, "I can't pull you any closer! You and that dead man are too heavy. Treading too much water, mate."

"I'm trying!" I replied.

I finally grasped one of the roots in my hand, so tightly I was worried I would crush it. I heard a plop in the water behind me, but then the sound of metal on fabric.

Royce's eyes went wide.

Clinging to the slope, I tried pulling the dead body closer to us, but for some reason I couldn't. It was as if it was being held back from me.

Why was Royce looking at me like that?

"No!" the man above wailed. "Don't cast on that side o' the bridge, boys!"

"You didn't say anything, Da!"

I turned slowly, still gripping the sturdy tree root tightly, and my jaw dropped in dismay.

Three of the four lines that had cast had all snagged their hooks into the corpse. One was caught in the dead man's open mouth. Two others were lodged in his shirtsleeve and collar. The fourth was bobbing lightly in the water.

I could see the lines get taut with tension and realized the boys above were trying to yank their lines back to the bridge.

"Oh, bloody hell," I muttered, turning back to Royce.

"No, Robin!" the boys' father yelled suddenly. "Not on that side of the-"

Royce's eyes got even wider. I looked on dumbly when I saw him turn his face away and shield his head the best he could with his arm.

The fishing hook belonging to a boy named Robin dug into my shoulder.

"*GAH!*" I hollered upward. "You cursed little brat!"

"What?" I heard one boy say.

"Papa!" another cried, "the fish are yelling!"

"Make them stop!"

"Eh?" I heard the man overhead bellow.

I felt the hook try to pry out of my shoulder. Robin must have been trying to tug it back up. I screamed in agony. I wanted to pull it out, but I couldn't do so without losing my grip on either the tree root, which was my only support now, or the corpse I had in my other hand that I had somehow kept ahold of.

"Hold still, Pen."

I cursed in response as Royce clumsily grabbed at the hook in desperation, trying to pull it out of my skin.

I cried out in pain again before kicking Royce away from me with a strong push of my foot underwater. My kick found its mark, but not before Royce was able to yank the hook from my shoulder.

A vibrant torrent of curses erupted from me, directed at the Fates and anyone who cared to listen.

"You little blight!" I hollered upward through clenched teeth.

Looking up with an angry snarl, I saw the man and his five sons lining the edge of the bridge, eyes wide and mouths open in shock as they leered down at us.

It was then I realized that they weren't gawking down at me, or at Royce. They were staring at the corpse I was dragging through the current behind me. Its face was upward, its throat gash wide open, and the dead man's eyes were staring up at them like they had stared into mine earlier back upriver.

The boys all screamed in horror, frightened by the corpse.

Royce and I screamed in unison, startled by the boys.

CHAPTER 24

"Enough of this!" yelled Royce.

He seized the cuff of the dead man's arm and pulled it toward him. As he did so, he wrapped his arm around a long, gnarled root.

"Penny, grab him!"

I did. Royce then clambered to the right as quickly as he could without losing his footing, heading back the way we had come from upriver. Ignoring the yells of the shocked boys and their father from above us, I shoved the body toward my friend, struggling against the current. He took hold of it, and I closed the gap between us. Repeating this over and over, the two of us inched along the side of the slope back up the River Keska.

The slope finally became less and less steep, gradually leveling out and then melting into flat ground. At last we were able to set foot onto the muddied soil of part of the riverbank, and Royce and I dragged the cursed corpse of the dead man onto land.

We both collapsed to the sand and mud. Our bodies shook with a violent chill, and our chests heaved as we caught our breaths and tried to dash our fatigue. We were soaked, tired, cold, and covered in dirt.

I sat up and looked downriver toward the small bridge crossing where the fisherman and his sons had been perched. They weren't there, but I could hear them yelling in the distance, out of sight.

"Good riddance," Royce grumbled.

I lay back onto the mud bank, cringing in pain. My injured hand was screaming. My shoulder was crying out and itching where I had been hooked, and I could feel warm blood beneath my shirt, though it probably could have been worse.

Royce was sitting beside me staring into the dead man's eyes, saying nothing.

Tenderly rubbing my shoulder, I pushed myself back up slowly and looked back over my shoulder to the northeast. There was no sign of Arthur or Quaid. I wondered if the two highwaymen had seen all that had transpired.

"Of all the things that could happen," I sighed, "a fisherman decides to teach his sons his trade. On that bridge. Today."

Royce just shook his head, not taking his eyes off the corpse.

I spat into the dirt messily, wiping my mouth. "I mean, really?"

At that moment Royce nudged my arm and pointed to the bridge. "Don't look now mate, but they're back."

"Eh?"

Following his gaze, I saw the fisherman and his sons had scurried back to the crossing above the river and were running about to and fro, looking in our directions and pointing excitedly.

"The devil they on about?" Royce asked aloud.

"Well, what do you think?" I replied. "I mean look at us. Look at him," I said, pointing at the dead man beside us.

Royce got to his feet and shot me a look. "You're awfully moody today."

"I'm what? Are you kidding me? I just got hooked by a brat who-"

"There they are! They're the murderin' scum, those two there!"

Royce and I immediately jerked our heads up and toward the bridge, where the voice was coming from. The fisherman was pointing at us urgently and calling over his shoulder.

"They're here!" he repeated to a party unknown. "Hurry!"

"Who is he calling over here?" I asked nervously, the fear evident in my words.

"Can't stick around to find out, mate," Royce replied. He reached down to me to offer his hand. I took it and was on my feet in an instant.

"What about the dead man?"

"We don't have time!" answered Royce. "We can't bloody well carry him with us faster than whoever that bloke's summoning over here."

"But those bandits-"

Royce shrugged. "We got four out of five bodies. I think we did well enough."

The two of us started scrambling up the hill, turning to run when a thunderous voice boomed to us from the direction of the lads' father.

"Stop! By the Fates and Lord Hannady, stop or we will kill you where you stand!"

Royce skidded to a stop and I bumped into him roughly. We both turned about slowly, like two children caught stealing cookies from a kitchen.

Three members of the Northroe City Watch were striding toward us menacingly a hundred paces downriver, egged on by the fisherman.

"You two men are under arrest for murder! Stay where you are and we will take you in for trial in the city. Disobey and your blood will be spilt at your-"

The man's voice trailed off, and he seemed to peer intently at us. A look of alarm crossed his face, and he motioned to his companions excitedly.

"Blast, I don't believe it! It's them, men! The arsonists that burned down the Raven!"

The Watchmen's white armor gleamed brightly in the sunlight. They quickened their pace from a trot to a full run, their loose gear clanking against their armor loudly with every step.

"Great," I breathed, eyes wide. "Where is that Quaid bloke with that bow of his?"

"Don't know. You think that's the bloke we knocked out at the tavern? Twice?"

"Not sure, Roy. What do we do?"

"Run."

Before we could do so, the City Watchmen ahead of us suddenly slowed, digging their heavy boots into the soil roughly and nearly sliding to a halt. Their gazes burned over our shoulders and behind us. Royce and I turned to see what had them in such a state.

I blinked in surprise.

Ten men were jogging toward us from upriver. Among them were Arthur and Quaid, and to my surprise, Alomar, though still in handcuffs. I did not recognize the other three, but they were clearly friends of the brigands we had chanced upon in the woods. They all wore lightweight armor of different sorts, and had green bandanas tied around their left shoulders. The newcomers were also armed, one of them even wielding a large spear and shield.

"Oy!" bellowed Quaid in his powerful tone. "Watchmen! Stand down!"

"Who are you lot?" called one of the guards.

"Stand back!" Arthur yelled hoarsely. "Those lads are with us!"

"Aye!" hollered one of the bandit newcomers. "Harm any part of those blokes and be repaid tenfold, got it?"

One of the Watchmen stepped forward stubbornly. "Our quarrel is not with you! Let these men be with the law, and go on your way!"

The two parties exchanged words with the two of us caught in the middle, and Royce and I glanced back and forth between them as they did so.

"I'll say it one more time," Arthur called fiercely. "Let the two men go! They're with us!"

With that, Quaid and two of the other men stepped forward, and all three men drew their bows and readied barbed arrows, aiming downrange past us at the Watchmen.

"Final warning!" roared Arthur.

My heart was beating itself out of my chest for the tenth time that day. Royce and I both cowered down at the sight of arrows aimed downrange toward the Watchmen behind us. I turned and looked past the Watchmen and saw that the man on the bridge had gathered his sons and was now retreating down the road at the sight of our reinforcements.

The lead Watchman finally squared up and spat at the ground in insult. "This isn't over, brigands! Don't let us find you. If we do, none of you will be spared, hear me?"

One of the new bandits gestured obscenely from afar, and Quaid laughed as the three Watchmen turned and trudged away reluctantly downriver and back towards the bridge, casting defeated glances behind them as they did so.

*   *   *

Our reunion with Alomar and the others was short-lived. We were out of the safety of Kovald Forest and exposed in the countryside. The thwarted City Watchmen would definitely be back in a matter of time, and we'd already drawn enough attention to ourselves.

Arthur had retreated back to the woods to call on the three bandits who had been nearby the entire time, unbeknownst to Royce, Alomar and I. While he went to get reinforcements, Quaid had kept an eye on us.

The newcomers hastily constructed makeshift gurneys out of wood from surrounding trees, using rope and other materials they had with them in their packs to do so. They used these stretchers to carry the bodies we had retrieved from the river. I was quite surprised at how efficient they were in doing so, and at how prepared they were with the supplies and kits they carried. Then again, these were men of the wilderness who lived outside the law's bounds. Maybe I shouldn't have been surprised at all. They even retrieved the last body that Royce and I had recovered from beneath the bridge.

Now our party of twelve traveled in the safety of the woods, following the river back to where we'd all met by coincidence.

"Where are you taking us?" I asked after almost an hour of moving through the woods with nothing but the sounds of leaves and pine needles crushing beneath our steps.

"Camp," Quaid answered.

I raised my eyebrows. "Your camp?"

"Aye. What other camp would there be?"

Alomar stepped carefully over a fallen log. "What about these cuffs? Not to be a pain in the arse, but you promised to-"

"Stop for a moment," Arthur said, stopping in his tracks and facing us head-on. We obeyed. His companions continued on ahead with Quaid, leaving just the four of us trailing behind.

Royce, Alomar and I exchanged glances, wondering what this was going to be all about. I scratched at the wound at my shoulder, cursing silently.

"This is how this works," the outlaw said roughly. "You three are obviously wanted by the law. I'd say those Watchmen back there verified that part of your story. Now in order to join up with us, we have to take you back to the Cap'n. He'll hear your story. Maybe ask some questions. Then it's up to him."

The wind rustling the leaves and swaying the branches overhead seemed to pick up. A silence followed, and I think Arthur was waiting for a reply, but his words were still sinking in.

"Pardon me," I said, holding up a hand. "Did you say, 'join up' with you?"

Arthur raised his eyebrows in question.

"As in 'join up' with you and your mates?" I asked. "Your... clan and whatnot?"

The man raised his arms outward from his sides. "What did you think was bloody goin' on here?"

"Very well," Alomar said, his tone commanding me to shut up. "And as for my cuffs-"

"We'll remove your cuffs when we get to the camp, only after the Captain's heard your story," Arthur replied. "Only if the Captain allows it. Got it?"

My mind reeled. I couldn't be certain that everything happening was actually real.

Surely you'll wake up soon.

Alomar thought for a moment before answering. "Okay, then. Agreed."

"Then welcome to our lot, lads. On to camp we go. Oh, and one more thing," Arthur said. "Mention nothing about this. The bodies, the whole fiasco. Understand? Some fool back at camp made the wrong call and these prisoners we were holding got their throats cut. It wasn't supposed to happen yet. The Captain and his two lieutenants are out on business, so if all goes well, my mates and I will figure out a way to account for this."

The three of us just nodded.

"Not a word."

We nodded again. With that, Arthur turned and led on into the Kovald woods, which seemed to be growing increasingly dense with every minute that passed.

My friends and I had just unwittingly joined a bandit clan. Accidents happen, as they say.

CHAPTER 25

The orange afternoon sky eventually laid to rest, and a full moon resumed where the sun left off, saturating the world around us the charcoals, grays and deep blues of night. The woods loomed ominously any way we looked, deathly and forbidding in the moon's glow. I found myself rubbing my hands as we hiked, for it grew to be much colder than the previous night.

We snaked on through the Kovald Forest, so much so that after a few hours of travel I was completely lost, only knowing which direction we were going due to the moon's heading. The outlaws led us away from the river after some time, and soon the sound of its rushing water was no longer audible. I wondered if the bandits were leading us in a deliberately wild pattern to their camp, in case we tried to make a run for it.

However as the night wore on, it was clear that Arthur, Quaid and their companions were already warming up to us. It dawned on me that after the confrontation with the City Watchmen back at the river, the men now saw Royce, Alomar and I as fellow renegades.

It was unsettling and, oddly, slightly thrilling knowing that we actually were not. I had never had the opportunity to look at myself in such light. It was strangely fascinating to think of myself in league with highwaymen and apparently being able to pass as one.

The forest was now so dense in areas that we couldn't see the mountain toward which we were traveling. I knew Mount Kovald lay ahead to the North in the sprawling mountain range, but I couldn't see it anymore like we could earlier from the river. It also meant we were getting much closer to the peaks, and the notion made me nervous.

"Hoy, lads!" called Quaid from up ahead. "We'll be at camp soon."

"'Bout bloody time," Royce mumbled. He, Alomar and I were now so tired it was difficult to walk in a straight line. We'd had no sleep for nearly a day and a half, save for my small nap under South Bridge. We were fatigued, hungry, and could have probably fallen asleep on hot coals.

As if he read my mind, Arthur slowed his pace ahead and waited for the three of us to catch up.

"You blokes look like you've had it," he said with a grin.

"Well if by 'it' you mean hot food and a place to sleep, we most definitely have not," I quipped. It came out a bit whinier than I intended.

"Rest easy," the outlaw replied, adjusting his sword on his belt. "We'll have plenty of both. We live comfortably for a lot exiled to the woods."

"Who's this captain of yours?" asked Alomar.

"Better to just meet him yourself," Arthur replied. "You gotta understand, we're doing you a favor by taking you to camp. Been a long time since we've accepted new members, so to speak."

Royce rolled his eyes, mirroring my own thoughts before looking back to Arthur. "Why are you helping us, anyhow? Why take us in?"

"Why not?" Arthur came back. "Clearly you lot are wanted, and weren't lying. Those Watchmen looked like they'd sell their mothers for the chance to hack at you with a blade. You need a place to go, yeah? Well, we won't refuse help."

We'd never offered, but I suppose it was better than being killed.

Royce, Alomar and I walked on in silence with Arthur for a long minute before he slowed to a stop and turned to face us. We all halted and looked at him expectantly. He looked like a shadow in the night with sword and knives at hand, and somehow seemed more dangerous as a silhouette against the backdrop of the woods than when we'd first seen the man in daylight.

"You three do want a place to stay, right?"

I took my opportunity to reply. "Well, I mean we weren't really counting on-"

Royce's hand clasped over my mouth, shutting my words off. "Absolutely, mate. We're grateful for the help."

"Aye," Alomar answered, firing an annoyed glance at me. "The whole arson and murder gig was going to make things really difficult, really fast. We appreciate you lads taking us in."

The way Alomar stressed 'arson and murder' was like he was reminding me of what waited for us back in Northroe if we were caught by authorities anywhere in Eisley.

Arthur studied the three of us, his gaze lingering on me the longest before nodding slowly. "Right, then. Now mate," he said to Alomar directly, "I'd cut those binds around your wrists for you right now, but it's best to just to hear what the Captain has to say when we get settled in, eh?"

Alomar nodded.

"Come," the bandit said, motioning to follow. "We're almost there."

* * *

Not an hour later found us all entering a remote clearing well off any beaten path and tucked away in the dense forest and brush at the foot of Mount Kovald. As we came up on the bandit camp, the outlaws that had escorted us all split to go their own ways, except for Arthur and Quaid who stayed with us.

I surveyed the scene, most impressed. It was much more organized and established than I had predicted.

Sturdily built cabins and small one-room cottages were all around the perimeter of the large clearing, which was lined with thick trees and foliage. Though they appeared to be made from few available resources, it was clear that the shelters were constructed well. They were built from wood beams and logs, nailed together in some places and tied together in others. Any gaps in the walls were packed tightly with mud and dirt that looked to have hardened over time.

What stuck out about the cottages and cabins the most was that they had been thoroughly and expertly camouflaged with branches, pine needles, leaves of all sorts, soil and mud from top to bottom of each structure – even the roofs. It was so well done that as I let my eyes adjust to the sights before me, more shacks and cottages seemed to spring out from hiding. They melded with the forest perfectly. It was very easy to overlook one just by sweeping my gaze from one side of the camp to the other.

Sharp, pointed logs lined the perimeter of the camp, facing out toward the surrounding woods in all directions as a defensive barrier to any would-be opposing forces. A fire pit had been dug in the center of the grounds and circled by stones that nestled a blazing fire. The flames cast an orange glow on the faces of four men warming themselves by it.

I could see the men at the fireplace look over at us and start to stand as we entered their camp. Quaid raised his hand in greeting, and that seemed to settle them down.

Woodpiles were stacked against most of the structures that I could see. I suppose that firewood would definitely be in great demand out here in the

Kovald, but I wondered if that also provided more stability somehow to their cottages, perhaps during a storm or something of the like.

There was even a small stable of sorts near the middle of the camp. Three horses were tied to posts outside a wooden building that housed stalls for the animals as well. Pails of water were lined for each beast outside. The horses turned to look at us newcomers, seemingly unimpressed.

The entire clearing and camp as a whole was relatively circular and evenly distanced. The northernmost building was also the largest, a solidly built log cabin placed almost directly against the base of Mount Kovald itself. There were certainly many cabins and cottages, and it suddenly occurred to me that this wasn't just a small motley crew of fugitives. They were a large, well-equipped and established organization of marauders.

Even at that late hour I suddenly noticed more men seeming to materialize out of the shadows. They all wore the familiar earthly green insignia bands. Some wore them around their left shoulders, like Arthur and Quaid, while others had fastened them around their heads, like bandanas. Some were talking in low voices and stopping to stare at us in mid-sentence. Another man was leaning passively against the wall of a low-rising hut and looked as if he had an eternal glare about his face. Two others came into view from off to the left, both cradling loads of firewood in their arms.

I gulped and tried not to look nervous, and at the same time tried not to look brash or cocky. Each one of these men was armed. I saw weapons of all kinds, from boot daggers to chipped hatchets, woodcutting axes to short swords. Two steel spears leaned against a big cabin nearby. I recognized the seal of the Northroe City Watch on a buckler shield a man had strapped to his back, meaning a Watchman somewhere, somehow, had lost his life to these men.

Royce gave a low whistle. "Impressive."

Quaid turned. "We do well for ourselves. Don't mind the men. You're safe with us. See that big building over there?" the man asked, pointing at the huge log cabin against the mountain. "That's the Lodge, and the Captain's quarters. Go there and wait directly outside. Do not enter unless told to do so. We'll be with ya shortly."

I gave a nervous look to Alomar, then Royce, before replying. "Are you sure? Maybe we should just stay with you? Or Arthur, or-"

"Lads," Arthur broke in, "you'll be fine. Wait outside the Lodge. All will be sorted out, aye? Quaid and I will be right back."

Not really having a choice, the three of us started for the Lodge. I tried not to make eye contact with any of the killers and plunderers in our midst. Royce, on the other hand, was grinning and giving a nod in greeting to every man he passed, even shaking the hands of two of the bandits enthusiastically. Like myself, I don't think they were expecting such warmth from a newcomer out of his element.

"Can you believe this, mates?" Royce asked lowly, still smiling widely. "Talk about adventure. And what a lively bunch, yeah?"

I finally made eye contact with a tall man covered in tattoos as we passed him. Following Royce's example, I did my best to grin and nod my greeting. The man just cleared his throat loudly and spit at his feet before turning his back on me.

"Aye, mate," I replied sarcastically to Royce. "Wonderful lot, these men are."

Alomar was fidgeting with his cuffs, as always observing every bit of his surroundings.

"What's the plan?" I asked as quietly as I could. "How do we escape?"

"We don't," Alomar answered.

"We don't?" I echoed in disbelief. "But this is ludicrous! We can't be brigands!"

Royce nudged me. "Little louder, Pen. Don't think the entire camp can hear you, yet."

"But I don't want to be a bandit!" I said feebly, eyes wide. I shifted my pack full of my writings from one shoulder to the other. "I'm not cut out for this!"

"Penny, I think you're more cut out for it than you know," Alomar said, chuckling. "You were the one that knocked out the blasted Watchman at the tavern."

"So you want to go on with this? Is that it?"

"Fates, Pen," Royce interrupted. "Shut up! We don't necessarily want to, no. But for now, we have to, see? Besides, you want to be a writer and all that, right?"

"Y-yes."

"This will be perfect. We'll have great adventures."

Alomar rolled his eyes. "Royce does have a rather ardent take on our current situation. But he's right, Penny. At least you'll have some new things to write about, see?"

We crossed the clearing to the Lodge and waited outside as Arthur had instructed. I could see Arthur and Quaid talking with the men at the campfire. They were rather animated as they did so, and occasionally they'd point our way and the other bandits would all turn to look at us. Royce, Alomar and I would look away immediately whenever this happened, probably looking like guilty children.

They must have been explaining to their companions about how they came across us, how we 'arsonists and murderers' helped them retrieve the bodies from the river, and of our encounter with the Watchmen near the bridge. I wondered if they were all discussing the bodies and how they weren't supposed to be discarded that day, as the men had mentioned earlier. I still didn't quite understand exactly what was going on there, but it really didn't bother me much.

A few minutes later, both Arthur and Quaid left their fireplace gathering and made their way to us at the Lodge.

"Just explained everything to the lads," Quaid said. "Wait here, aye? We're gonna speak with our boss."

"Do we get to sleep soon?" Royce asked. "Starting to see ghosts of loaves of bread and sheep and the like."

Arthur grinned. "Just wait here."

With that, the two men entered the Lodge, easing the door shut behind them.

"So," Alomar murmured, "their leader's just inside here, eh?"

I was staring at Royce. "Royce, only you would suggest that there could be ghosts of loaves of bread."

"I'm hungry. What can I say?"

"Bread is not a living thing."

"It is when you're hungry, Penny."

Alomar chuckled and slid to a sitting position, his back against the log wall. He stared ahead into the night and yawned deeply, watching the shadowy tree line that shrouded all in sight.

Trying not to appear obvious to any onlookers, I put my ear to the wall of the log cabin and strained to hear anything I could inside. Alas, I heard nothing.

"Are they talking about food?" Royce asked.

I shook my head. "I can't hear anything."

The steady plodding of hooves on the forest soil split our words, coming from the southern edge of the clearing where we had entered initially. The sound of two horses trotting into camp became steadily louder. I could see the large group of outlaws gathered around the fire turning toward the noise as well.

I poked Royce. "Look. Two more just rode in on horseback."

I could see the two riders exchanging greetings with their fellow highwaymen around the fire. They were too far away and it was too dark to see details in their faces, but the newcomers were atop two saddle horses: one a gray shade with brown spots on its coat, the other chestnut brown in color. The rider on the brown horse stayed mounted and exchanged words with his friends around the fire, while the other on the gray horse rode to the stable and dismounted before tying the animal to its post.

"Look," I repeated. I nudged Royce, who was now putting his own ear to the Lodge wall.

"Who's that?" he asked.

I just shrugged and turned to Alomar. The man was being overcome by sleep, his head sagging down toward the ground. I tapped the man on the shoulder lightly, and his eyes fluttered open.

"Sorry, mate," I whispered. "More horses are here."

Alomar yawned. "That's five horses now. These bastards sure are well off, aren't they?"

The rider of the gray horse was feeding it what must have been oats or carrots. The animal ate from the bandit's hand gratefully. After a minute the figure turned and strode toward us, clearly heading for the Lodge.

I watched intently. Something seemed...familiar about this man. It was as if I recognized the way he walked, a careless yet confident swagger. As he strode toward us, he reached up and unfastened the bandana he wore around his head, letting long hair fall about his shoulders.

Long, dark, red hair.

My eyes widened. I could hear Royce curse just under his breath.

"Is that...." started Alomar, but he didn't finish.

It was *her*.

The red-haired barmaid from Ozlow's tavern. The woman that had poisoned all those people. Everyone who had died all around us that night had met death at her hands, never even aware of what she had done.

"It can't be," I uttered.

She was wearing rough trousers and an unbuttoned leather jacket, with both sleeves cut off at the shoulder. Underneath this she wore a black, long-sleeved shirt. As she strode toward us, she removed the leather gloves she had been wearing and looped them around her belt, letting them dangle idly at her side next to a sheathed sword.

All three of us stared in surprise. Alomar stood, his back rubbing noisily against the wall of the Lodge.

This noise seemed to bring us to her attention. The red-haired woman snapped her gaze to us and faltered in her tracks before stopping completely.

We couldn't look away, and neither could she. Her eyes narrowed in disbelief and she was blinking rapidly, as if thinking we were tricks of her imagination.

My jaw was set, and I was speechless as her eyes seared into mine.

"Y-you...." Royce stammered.

The woman averted her eyes from ours quickly and immediately stalked right past us and through the front door of the Lodge, as if we mattered less than the dirt at our feet.

CHAPTER 26

All three of us pressed our ears to the wall of the Lodge now. Most of the men in the camp were staring at us as we did so, but we ignored them.

"This is bloody insane," Alomar whispered. "That can't be her."

I shook my head. "Aye. It's her."

"It's not the same woman," he said tersely. "It can't be! There is no way that-"

"Think she recognized us?" Royce asked.

"Sure looked like it," I replied. "Al, you know it was her. That hair? Those eyes? Who the hell else would it be?"

Royce snorted. "Listen to Penny. 'That hair, those eyes!' and all. Ask her to marry you and be done with it."

I elbowed the man and he retorted with a shove, but the voices inside grew louder. We couldn't hear what was being said, but it sounded like there were a few men trying to calm the woman down. Her voice was rising against the force of all of theirs in what I was sure was an argument, and suddenly the telltale sounds of someone stomping back toward the entrance next to us were sounding off against the floorboards.

Alomar cursed, and we reacted instantly as if it were an order. We resumed our previous positions, trying to look like we hadn't been eavesdropping. I cast my eyes at anything and everything around me except for the door to the Lodge.

The door flung open and both Arthur and Quaid strode out, looking as if they'd been on a long run, tired out and wary.

"Miles!" shouted Arthur loudly, his voice booming across the camp. "Over here, mate!"

I followed his eyes so I could see to whom he called. The other rider who had accompanied the woman into camp on horseback was now looking our way.

"Cap'n needs you in there!" called Arthur. He turned to us both. "That man there is Miles. He's the second-in-command, one of the boss's lieutenants. The Cap'n only has two officers at any given time."

The one called Miles was off his horse immediately, gracefully strolling to us. The man was big and strong, nearly the size of Alomar. He had a shaved head and a full, blonde beard. As he came closer, his eyes met ours. He had a steely gaze and piercing brown eyes that somehow looked wild, yet composed. A large tattoo of flames swirling tightly around the blade of a dagger was tattooed on his right forearm. There was small writing etched into the skin as well around the design, but he walked too quickly for me to read it.

"Problem?" Miles asked. His voice was deep and strong, and it matched his hardened features.

"Lynn's losin' it," Quaid answered, holding up his arms in resignation. "She's all yours."

Arthur shook his head. "Aye. Ain't listening to the Cap'n."

The mystery woman from the Raven had a name at last.

Without a further word, Miles took another look at the three of us before stepping into the Lodge. As he opened the door, the flurry of voices inside rushed out and amplified into the night air. The woman inside was arguing heatedly with another tough voice of a male, whom I assumed must have been the Bandit Captain.

The door closed behind Miles with a wooden thud, and Arthur motioned to us. "Best leave them be. They have business to take care of. Follow us."

"Are they arguing about us?" I asked.

"Small part of it. It's not so much you, it's more of... well. Look, all in time, eh? Let's get you to your sleeping quarters. Long day for us all."

We followed Arthur and Quaid through the camp once more. The party of brigands at the fire was now breaking up, and a couple men were putting the flames out and fanning the smoke away from them the best they could. I could see others stretching and yawning as they all spread out to turn in to their respective quarters. Still others were venturing past the cottages and out toward the camp's perimeter, fully armed and with packs over their shoulders.

"Most of us sleep during the night, of course," Arthur informed us. "But we always have sentries posted at night in different areas of the woods and at our perimeters. Guard duty rotates often enough. Most of the cottages and huts you're seein' are one-room buildings, but they house two to three of us."

I yawned loudly and felt lightheaded. The travels and events of the last two days were catching up with me, fast. I couldn't wait to lie down and lose myself to the night. As we neared one of the cabins on the outskirts of the campgrounds, Quaid broke off for a moment, stating he'd return shortly.

Arthur turned back to us with a grin. "You lot are lucky, ya know. Not many newcomers get one of the cabins. They're small, but obviously we don't need anything fancy, aye?"

We just nodded. At least, I think the others did with me. I was too tired to notice.

Our cabin was simple. It was high enough to where Alomar wouldn't have to stoop when inside, only when entering, for the top of the doorway was low. Old wood, splintering in some areas, made up the walls, ceiling and floor. Leaves and moss coated the outside of the cabin almost entirely, and seemed fastened securely, even when Arthur pulled the door open to let us inside.

Inside was starkly plain, but I found myself really not concerned. It wasn't that different from my room back at the Windfarer's Inn. There were two makeshift cots tucked against the far wall in both corners and a small wood table that sat very low to the ground in the center of the room. One would have to sit on the floor to use it properly. A strange contraption hung idly from the roof itself near the entrance to my right. It looked like thin rope or twine woven together in a tightly checkered pattern, suspended between two wooden posts that had been installed against the wood ceiling. The net sagged lower in the center. I'd never seen anything like it.

"What is that?" Royce asked, seeming to mirror my own thoughts.

To my surprise, Alomar answered before Arthur could.

"Ha! It's a hammock," my friend replied.

"A what?"

"A hammock. The Dekkans are fond of them," Alomar continued with a gleeful smile. "Trev and I tried these once during the war. Never went back, when we could help it at least."

Mention of the Dekkan War seemed to pique Arthur's interest.

"You fought in Dekka, did you?"

Alomar nodded. "Aye. I served with this man's brother," he said, pointing to Royce. "Best man I ever knew. Finest soldier I ever served with."

Arthur rubbed his chin thoughtfully. He reached up to the padded coif that was snug around his head and unfastened it, letting scrappy-looking light brown hair fall about his shoulders. There was a scar across his forehead that ran upward and disappeared under his hairline. The man pointed at it with a gloved finger.

"Dekkan blade got me here. Bastards caught us in an ambush. Almost got the better of us, but we pushed 'em back. North of the Vensai."

"The River Vensai?" Alomar asked, his attention focused on Arthur. "My company was the first to cross it!"

Arthur gave an astonished grin. "You were 2nd Cavalry?"

"Aye," answered Alomar, pointing to the tattoo on his arm.

The highwayman gave a hearty laugh. Royce and I felt odd and out of place as the two veterans basked in their newly discovered kinship. Alomar and Arthur forgot about the two of us as they briefly reminisced about old stories and places I'd never heard of.

While they did so, I strode over to one of the rickety beds and plopped down on it with force, sighing heavily as I did. It felt absolutely *wonderful* to lie down. It wasn't quite as comfortable as my bed back at the inn in Northroe, but I didn't care.

"The hammock's mine!" Alomar called, as Royce poked at the swinging bed in curiosity.

The door opened suddenly, letting a rush of cold air in. I shivered slightly as I sat up to see Quaid step in with a burlap sack in tow. The man strode to the table and set it down, and I saw a bit of crusty bread roll onto the wood.

My eyes widened. I think I salivated on the spot.

"Food for ya," Quaid said. "It's not much. Bit of bread, a few carrots. Tomorrow we'll get you more properly sorted out."

I hastily got to my feet and practically collided with Royce, who I think was in the process of diving headfirst for the sack of food.

I stuffed my mouth with half a roll, sending crumbs spraying about. Royce was trying to eat a small slice of bread and half a carrot at the same time and failing miserably when the door opened yet again.

My stomach growled loudly as the red-haired woman named Lynn stepped in from outside. In her arms she cradled a small stack of blankets, frayed at the edges but warm and inviting nevertheless.

Royce and I both stopped chewing, fixating our eyes on her as she surveyed the room. The woman's dark red hair was tied back, and a few long strands fell about the left side of her face, curling toward her chin. Her red-brown eyes found Arthur and Quaid.

"Lynn," Quaid greeted. "How'd it go?"

I held my breath, watching her every move intently.

Lynn clenched her jaw and shook her head. "Tell ya 'bout it later, yeah? Why aren't the cuffs off that one?"

Alomar's face brightened visibly. His eyes seemed to glow, and that's no exaggeration.

"Weren't sure if we were supposed to yet," replied Arthur.

Royce bit into a carrot loudly.

The woman strode over to one of the beds and dropped the blankets to it, sending a small bit of dust clouding about. "I'd say now's a good a time as any, Art. The man prolly can't feel his hands anymore."

I resumed chewing now, shocked at the apparent kindness she was showing us... if it could be counted as kindness. It might have just been a fake show of good will, or forced politeness.

Quaid chuckled sheepishly and fumbled about in one of his pockets, motioning for Alomar to turn around. Alomar obeyed, though hesitantly. Quaid produced a couple small objects and gripped them both in his hand, and I realized they were lock picks of sorts.

While Quaid fumbled about with Alomar's handcuffs, Lynn turned to us.

"Right then," she said. She pointed at me suddenly. "You. What's your name?"

I stared for a moment. "Me?"

"No, the bloke sittin' behind ya."

Puzzled, I ventured a look behind me and saw nobody before cringing in embarrassment.

Lynn shot me an unimpressed look. "There's no one sittin' behind ya."

"Right," I answered, red in the face. "My name's Penny. Penny Daulton, Writer-in-Training."

Royce gave me a disapproving glance, but said nothing.

"Penny?" echoed Lynn. "Isn't that a woman's name?"

I gawked in dismay. "No! No?"

Alomar chuckled.

"Okay then, Penny. I'm Lynn. And you?" she asked, gesturing to the man cramming the rest of his bread into his mouth next to me.

"I'm Roysh," he said with his mouth full. He ceased chewing to correct himself. "Royce Bartha."

"You?" Lynn asked our tall friend as he awaited his cuffs to be removed.

"Alomar Sanstrom."

The woman nodded. "Well, lads, I'd forget your last names, if I were you. Won't need 'em anymore. Prolly better that way."

I stared at Lynn. She stood in rugged highwayman's clothes, but her face was strikingly pretty in the candlelight. Her lips were thinly pursed as she nodded in response to Alomar. I caught myself admiring her and forced a stop to it. The faces of Ozlow, Kara and the others at the November Raven showed themselves to me in my mind. I couldn't forget that this was most likely the woman responsible for-

"Why'd you kill all those people?" Royce blurted.

Silence fell across the cabin. Arthur and Quaid looked uneasily at each other, then at Lynn, before turning back to Royce. Alomar and I exchanged glances nervously.

Lynn stood unflinchingly, staring down at Royce, who was still sitting across from me at the low table.

"Was it poison?" he pressed. "It was, wasn't it? Why didn't you-"

"I will speak with you tomorrow," the woman replied. Her tone was flat. I couldn't tell if she was truly emotionless or expertly masking anger. "Eat. Get some rest. And don't forget, ya can be dead if we so choose."

With that, she turned on her heel and stepped out into the night, letting the door slam behind her.

"Royce!" I scolded.

"What?" Royce asked, his eyes narrowed. "Don't act like you weren't thinking the same thing, mate."

"Both of you, be quiet!" hissed Alomar.

Arthur folded his arms and leaned against the wall next to the doorway while Quaid worked on Alomar's cuffs. At long last, there was a metallic clink of metal, and the shackles opened and dropped with a heavy thud to the floor.

Alomar smiled broadly and rubbed his wrists ruefully, giving a slight wince. "Thanks, mate."

"Sorry we left 'em on for so long," Quaid answered. "Just had to be sure."

Arthur brushed long strands of brown hair from his eyes. "Okay lads. Get some sleep. You'll need it. Tomorrow we'll hold a meeting at the Lodge, and

you'll meet the Captain. Everyone's tired tonight. Just be mindful around the other blokes millin' about here and you'll be fine, aye?"

Quaid nodded. "You have food, blankets. We'll get you changes of clothes and the like tomorrow. Just don't piss anyone off."

The two bandits laughed as Royce asked another question while chewing his food furiously.

"Who's the other lieutenant?"

"Eh?"

"Earlier," Royce continued, "you said that Miles bloke was the Captain's second man, and one of his officers, and you said there are only ever two officers. So who's the other?"

Arthur and Quaid both looked at each other and laughed even harder now. Quaid looked amused, shaking his head as he pushed open the door to the cabin and disappeared into the night. Arthur was right behind him, propping the door open with one hand as he turned to us.

"Who's the other lieutenant, you ask?" Arthur said with a twinkle in his eye. "Well, you just met her, mate. Watch yourselves with Lynn. She's a woman, aye... but she's the only one here, and third in command. Remember that."

Royce and I looked at each other as Alomar strode over to join us at the small table, swiping two rolls from the sack.

"She's not so bad," said Arthur. "Just don't get on her bad side, or anyone else's for that matter. I'll see you blokes tomorrow."

With that, the man left, and the door closed behind him.

I had thought that when the three of us were alone at last, we'd seize the opportunity to discuss our situation. Devise courses of action, decide on a plan for the long haul, figure out exactly what we were going to do now that we'd got ourselves inducted into a bandit clan.

But we didn't. We ate our bread and carrots hungrily with few words. Royce, Alomar and I didn't marvel at our misfortune, or discuss how amazingly unstable our short journey had been so far, or blather to each other about how incredible and frightening it was to have left Northroe and see our lives changed forever.

We wolfed down our food and turned in to our beds and hammock. I set my pack against the wall at the foot of my cot and looked at it hesitantly before I lay down and closed my eyes. I was nervous about my life's works being so exposed in an unfamiliar place, especially one like this.

In just a couple minutes' time, all thoughts drifted from my mind, and I fell asleep.

*   *   *

I awoke gradually sometime during the course of the night to a noise I did not, at first, recognize.

Peering around the cabin through bleary eyes, it was a shock to wake up in a place foreign to me and so different from my room at the inn. It took me a moment to remember exactly where I was – sleeping away in the camp of a large bandit clan at the foot of Mount Kovald to the east of Northroe, hidden away deep in the woods.

Moonlight streamed in through the lone square window, illuminating the table and the empty sack and breadcrumbs atop it in a white, hazy glow.

I realized what I was hearing was the sniffling of a nose, though the sniffles were few and far between.

Sitting up quietly, I looked over to my left and saw Royce fast asleep in his cot, one arm dangling off the side of it. He was lost somewhere in between a dreamland and a steady snore. I looked over near the door to see Alomar shift slightly in his hammock, making the wood ceiling creak.

What I heard next made my heart heavy. Alomar sniffled again, cupping a hand over his nose in an effort to muffle it so he wouldn't wake us. He cried softly, so much so that neither Royce nor I should have been able to hear him.

But I wasn't supposed to be awake.

I heard Alomar breathing in and out rapidly as he tried unsuccessfully to hold back his sorrow, making one of his cries almost sound like a whimper. In the moonlight and dying glow of the candle, I could see a lone tear streaking down his cheek. His eyes were shut tight.

Biting my lip and wincing at the sight, I lay back down without a sound and curled over on my side to face away from Alomar in an attempt to give him privacy. I felt guilty for waking up and seeing the man in that state. I wasn't supposed to see him shedding tears over his broken marriage, and I knew it.

I swallowed hard, shut my eyes tight, and tried to drown out the sounds of my friend's sadness with the promise of sleep.

CHAPTER 27

The following morning, I was awakened by a flurry of fur, the scratching of paws and excited panting as a wet tongue painted a mural upon my face.

I shot up in bed in surprise to see a rather happy and curious dog stretched over me, its front paws patting and prodding me awake while it supported itself on the floor with its hind legs.

"What on earth?" I sputtered, wiping my face with my sleeve. My hair felt matted to my forehead, and I brought my blanket up to mop the slobber from it.

The dog was an Eislian Husky who sported a thick, hearty coat of fur that was white on the bottom of its belly and paws, and faded into a darker charcoal shade on its back and head. It was obviously well fed and healthy. Its bright brown, almond-shaped eyes were very intent on my own, sizing me up.

Rubbing the sleep from my eyes, I swung my legs slowly over my cot and touched my feet to the floor. The dog sat patiently and its eyes watched mine.

"Oy there, mate," I said sleepily. I reached slowly to the animal and scratched at its ears and combed through its fur with my fingers.

"Who are you, huh?" I asked in a playful voice. "What are you on about?'

The dog answered with a yawn, caring not for my words and content with enjoying the ear scratching I was giving him.

It suddenly occurred to me to look around the cabin, and I was still for a moment. I was alone. Royce's cot was unoccupied with a remarkably large spot of dried drool on his pillow, and Alomar's hammock hung empty.

Morning sunlight streamed through the window and I could hear the sounds of activity outside. The bandit camp was alive all around me. I could hear men laughing, the sound of axes biting into wood, the crackling of flames at the fire circle, and calls from men to others that echoed across the grounds.

Blinking, I got to my feet and the dog backed up. It looked up at me eagerly and its tail swung excitedly back and forth, smacking my leg with each pass. I saw a change of clothes laying on the table and thanked the Fates, for my shirt and coat were dirty and smelled of few-days-old Penny.

I undressed quickly and slipped into the new garments. Someone had left a brown leather jerkin with short sleeves to be worn over the white, long-sleeved padded shirt that accompanied it. A thick, sturdy-looking belt was coiled on the tabletop as well, and I closed it around my waist snugly.

It felt great, actually. I was surprised at the quality of the leather, and I'd never worn a padded shirt, either. It was quite lightweight, yet felt thick and sturdy against my skin. The jerkin fit over it perfectly. I waved my arms about in the air and was happy to find that my range of motion wasn't restricted hardly at all.

I glanced over to the dog that was still sitting patiently at my feet. It was staring up at me, wagging its tail. Clearly it approved.

"Ho there, boy," I said, kneeling down to greet him once more. "Where are my friends, eh? Did you see them?"

The dog shifted and pressed his head to my chest. I embraced him and stroked the top of his head. I had always been fond of dogs. I loved the creatures. When my friends and I wandered the streets of Northroe as lads, we'd always dreamed up ways of somehow getting one of our own. Alas, we'd never had the coin, and we'd always seemed to have larger concerns.

"Who's a good boy?" I cooed, grinning as he licked my face.

"She's a girl, actually," came a woman's voice.

I spun in surprise in a quick movement that sent the dog leaping backward gracefully before bounding over to the door of the cabin with a playful bark.

Lynn stood in the doorway and knelt down to scoop up the dog in a big hug. I stared on as the woman stood and held up her hand. The dog sat obediently. Next, Lynn put her thumb and index finger together in a circle and splayed her fingers upward, and the husky promptly lay down at the wordless command.

I looked on in silence, feeling slightly awkward, as though I should say something. But I just watched, allowing myself to succumb to curious amusement.

"Her name's Ember," Lynn said, her lips parting into a smile as the husky looked up excitedly at the sound of her name. "I've had her for a long time... 'round four years now, I'd say."

"She's very well-behaved," I offered.

"Aye, that she is," Lynn replied. The woman now hung her arm idly at her side and twirled her index finger in fast circles.

Ember the Husky rolled over in a swift motion with much grace and remained laying down upon completing her little demonstration. Lynn knelt and grasped Ember's face tenderly in her fingers, giving the dog a kiss on the forehead before standing to face me.

"You slept quite late."

"Did I?" I asked. I didn't really know how to respond.

"Your friends are already out an' about, helpin' around the grounds and whatnot."

"Oh."

Lynn folded her arms and leaned casually against the wall. "They look like they fit. Your clothes, I mean." She gestured to my newly acquired jerkin and shirt.

"Ah, yes," I replied, shifting and looking down at myself. I pinched the sleeve of my new shirt as if inspecting it even more closely. "Thanks for that."

"Sure," the woman answered. "We would've got ya new trousers, but we don't have any to offer. Not yet, at least."

I waved a hand dismissively. "Not a problem. I'm grateful."

Nodding in approval, Lynn looked me over. It felt strange and added to the awkward air already weighing down on me. I decided to become suddenly very fascinated with my fingernails, and fanned them out in front of me as if to study each one.

To my surprise, Lynn gave a laugh and shook her head. Petrified with stupid shyness, I just watched her as she strode past and took a seat on Royce's cot. Her eyes found the dried puddle of the man's drool on his pillow, and the woman frowned and scooted away from it. She crossed her leg and grasped her knee with both hands in a sitting position. I watched as she drummed her fingers on her knee while staring at me.

"Take a seat, Penny," she said. She was still smiling faintly. Was it my imagination, or did those red-brown eyes of hers seem to be glowing?

I obeyed and sat back down on my small bed.

"What's your story?" she asked, with a genuinely curious look on her face. "I mean, the three of ya. I saw ya the other night at the tavern."

When she mentioned this, it was suddenly easy for me to distance myself from any illusion of her charm and recall that night laced with murder. I realized she obviously wasn't shy about bringing it up, either.

"How did ya end up here?" she asked. "One day you're all sayin' cheers at the Raven, and the next you're helpin' Art and Quaid grab dead bodies from the Keska? Strikes one as odd."

Remembering Art's strict instructions not to mention the bodies-in-the-river incident, I watched her, on my guard. Not only was I not sure if it was okay for the woman to know of it, I was thinking about what she had done at the November Raven. When I didn't answer, Lynn brushed some red hair from her eye and sighed lightly. She looked to Ember and clicked her tongue while giving a brisk nod toward the open cabin door. The dog immediately trotted outside as if to give the two of us privacy.

This put me even further on edge.

"Look," Lynn said. "I don't know what ya think o' me, and all of us, or what exactly ya think o' this place, and all that. But what happened back at the tavern wasn't an accident, yeah? They-"

"What did happen back there?" I asked suddenly. In alarm at my own outburst, I told myself silently to rein in the heat suddenly building up within me.

The woman just watched me with a blank expression.

"I mean," I continued carefully, "why did you do it? And what was it all about?"

Lynn uncrossed her legs and sat like I did now, both feet on the floor and hunched over with her elbows resting on her knees. Her eyes were on her hands, which were clasped together. She gave that light sigh again before speaking.

"'Twas poison, as your friend made mention of last night."

I stared. "But why? And who were you going after? And why not just-"

"Listen," Lynn cut me off, "I already spoke to your two mates 'bout this, just so ya know. Only one man in there was my target. That loud bloke, Tyrius. He-"

"Target? Tyrius Sewell?" I asked incredulously. "Why?"

The woman folded her arms. "You gonna let me speak my piece or not?"

"Sorry."

"Tyrius is – was, an enemy of our little band here," Lynn said. "He crossed us twice. Didn't pay a debt owed to the Cap'n. Cap'n Hael gave the man a two-month extension on this debt, and he still didn't pay. Claimed to not have the funds, ya see."

I realized I hadn't known the Bandit Captain's name until now.

"What was the debt for?"

"Doesn't matter," she replied. "We found out he was lyin'. He had the coin, alright, but he was spendin' it elsewhere. Invested in some little operation in Courtnall, bought a second home for he and his mistress. Things o' that nature."

I cocked my head. "You say, 'little operation' in Courtnall?"

Lynn answered patiently. "Tyrius Sewell wasn't an honest man, Penny. As I said, he owed a debt to the Cap'n. He was associated with us, but most of the time he had his own schemes runnin' about all over eastern Eisley."

"If he was so established, why was he never caught?" I asked, folding my arms now. "The City Watch is usually fairly good at nabbing blokes like him."

The woman chuckled. "The name 'Tyrius' was just one of many names he used. Look, it's all pretty normal and by the books, so to speak. Tyrius just did what most o' us would do to stay hidden, yeah?"

I bit my lip thoughtfully, looking at the floor for a moment. "Okay then. So you poisoned a tavern full of people over one man who owed you a debt?"

Lynn's tone grew much more serious. "First off, a debt is not somethin' taken lightly."

I waited for her to continue. Her eyes were narrowed and burning into mine.

"Right," I said finally. "Sorry."

Satisfied, she continued. "Second, I said he crossed us twice. The debt was one mark against him. Later on, that rat sold out one o' our contacts in Northroe."

"Sold him out? Like what, got him imprisoned?"

The woman was grinning and shaking her head, and looking back now I realize it was directed at me and my ignorance in the ways of the lives of outlaws.

"Sometimes there's no prison for the likes o' us. Tyrius ratted out our contact in the city, and he was executed that same night. The bastards didn't even wait 'til morning."

I let her words sink in and tried to piece everything together.

"So you found him...."

"Aye," she nodded. "We knew he was gonna be in Northroe for the month. Favorite hangout o' his was the November Raven in the hours of late, ya see?

The man had never laid eyes upon me b'fore, so I got myself hired on as one o' the barmaids there."

The rest of her tale played out before me. I thought of Tyrius and all his mates at the front of the bar, cheering and lifting cups with Ozlow and the other barmaids. Ozlow's cheery smile and hearty demeanor speared right through my recollections and into my heart. The sight of Kara and the others throwing up their insides jolted me.

"But why?" I murmured. "Why the others? You... killed so many that night."

Lynn's face was hard. Her forehead was creased in thought, and I could tell she was assessing me. Calculating where I stood on the matter. Probably wondering whether I'd last among her party of renegades out here in the woods. Clearly the deaths of innocents as collateral damage were acceptable to this woman. I stared into her eyes, trying to search her soul. Who was she? How had she grown to be the way she was now?

"It was the only way," she answered finally.

I blinked. "That's it?"

"Tyrius wasn't our only enemy in that tavern that night," she explained. "Who do you think all those men were up front with him? They had to go too, and it's not like it'd be bloody smart to draw a blade on 'em all by m'self, know what I mean? I had to-"

"Fates!" I spat. "You could have waited. Until he was alone, or... or something!"

Lynn stood steadily. I thought I detected a glimmer of anger in her gaze.

"I don't even *have* to discuss this with ya!" she reminded me, the volume of her voice rising slightly. "It's not even any of your damned business. I thought it'd be the right thing, to tell ya what happened. It had to be done!"

I shot to my feet in response. "You could have killed *me!*" I hissed. "My friends! Alomar's lucky he didn't drink from the blasted ale that you served him! Ozlow the Bartender was our friend, and so was Kara and the others, and now they're all dead!"

Lynn didn't flinch at all during my outburst, didn't waver in stance, nor cringe, or narrow her eyes. The woman just stared into me, seemingly devoid of emotion, sidestepping all the words I'd intended to hit her with. It wasn't like she was putting on a show of force, or acting like she was stone cold. My words simply couldn't cut her skin. I could feel it.

Trying to gather myself and feeling like the loser in this little match of wits and composition, I slowed my heated breathing and looked away from her. Defeated, I sat back down on my cot and cradled my head in my hands, realizing how sleepy I still was.

"Thanks for the food," I muttered, my words muffled by my palms.

"You're welcome."

"And the new clothes. And the place to sleep."

"Aye."

I gave a short exasperated laugh and sprawled back onto my bed.

"No," Lynn said. "Up with ya. Everyone's out and about. Help your friends with the firewood. We're gonna call the meetin' at the Lodge within the hour. You'll meet Cap'n Hael, and things will get sorted out officially an' all that."

The woman strode over to the door and held it open, waiting expectantly for me to follow. I sullenly got to my feet, tried to ignore the aches and pains in my body, and strode out into the morning in Kovald Forest. Lynn walked with me, and I heard the door creak shut behind us.

I had a burning urge to ask what she had been arguing about inside the Lodge with the Bandit Captain. I remembered how Miles had to be called in for whatever reason, and how heated whatever argument had been taking place had become.

I decided against mentioning it.

"Ya didn't get a chance to tell your story," she said. "Tale 'bout you and your friends, how ya got here. I suppose there's always later."

She really was rather pretty. Hopefully that wouldn't become a problem.

CHAPTER 28

"Way to go, Penny. Remind me to ask you for pointers if I want to anger highwaymen who can kill me whenever they'd like."

I rolled my eyes at Royce. "It just came out. I mean Ozlow, Kara and all of them... Lynn was the one that bloody did it, aye?"

Royce, Alomar and I were near the center of camp, splitting firewood and stacking it high, adding on to a pile already quite impressive in size. I had just finished telling both men about my earlier conversation with Lynn at the cabin. Perhaps I should have left out the part where I confronted her head-on about her poisonous onslaught back at the November Raven.

Royce shook his head. "Right. Here we are in Bandit Land and you go mouthing off to one of their officers. Alomar, am I wrong?"

Alomar wiped sweat from his brow and motioned for me to set down another log. A wide, flat stump of a large tree whose days were perhaps once graceful was what the man used as a chopping block. I placed a log there and watched as Alomar hefted the large axe over his head and brought it down on the wood with ease. The axe head split the wood in two with a loud crack, and Royce gathered the two pieces and set them carefully into the pile behind us next to the fire circle.

"Am I wrong, Alomar?" Royce repeated.

"Well, let's face it, Royce. You did it first."

"Eh?"

I set down more wood, and Alomar held the axe at the ready, turning to Royce.

"Last night in the cabin, you oaf. Here they were, giving us shelter and food and the like, and you go spouting off with a mouthful of breadcrumbs, asking why she killed those people and all that."

Royce folded his arms. "I was curious."

I rolled my eyes, getting a log ready while Alomar struck another, sending two pieces rolling off the chopping block and onto the dirt at our feet.

"Royce, sometimes you can be an arse," I said. "Just saying."

The man rubbed his chin. "At least we know now what the 'ell went on. Tyrius being a bloody conman and all. Go figure, eh?"

Alomar said nothing, seeming to purposely put all his focus on the log waiting for his axe.

"Well, at least I apologized," I said, trying to end the discussion with some dignity. "Thanked her for their, um, kindness, and whatnot."

"Aye," Royce laughed. "After she got done yellin' at you. That's very cute, by the way. Your first fight together."

I hurled a piece of wood at him, and of course missed terribly. "What are you saying?"

"Oh c'mon, Pen," Alomar cut in. "You should see yourself, mate. We saw the way you were looking at her. Thought you'd run over right there and start trying to tear her clothes off."

Royce snickered. "Thank the Fates you didn't, because you'd be dead, and to put it bluntly mate, we need a bloke to keep track of our journey. Write down our adventures and all that."

I stared at the two with my mouth hung open. Was it that obvious?

"Aye," Alomar laughed. "It's that obvious."

"If you weren't three times my size, I'd rub your face in the dirt," I growled. "I do not *like* her or... or whatever. I mean, really? She's a bandit for heaven's sake."

Royce grinned. "So? She's a good-looking one, at that."

"Oy! You three!"

The three of us turned suddenly to see Arthur about sixty paces away. He'd just emerged from his cottage, and a couple men nearby strode to him as he called to us.

Royce gave a wave. "Hoy there, Arthur! Or is it Art?"

The man grinned and shut his door behind him. "Arthur for you lot," he replied, adjusting the way his blade hung at his belt. "You wanna call me Art, you have to earn that, know what I mean?"

He had stopped in his tracks and was staring at us.

"What?" I asked.

"It takes three of you blokes to chop wood?"

"We only had one axe."

Arthur started to trudge off to the North end of the camp. "There is such thing as more than one axe, believe it or not," he called over his shoulder.

"Look mates, be up at the Lodge in five minutes! The meeting's gonna get underway."

My friends and I all exchanged glances. I bit my lip while Alomar nodded in response to our bandit friend and turned to split more wood.

"So," I said, lowering my voice. "About that. We don't want to... you know. Stay here or anything, right?"

"Don't reckon we have a choice, Pen," Alomar replied. He handed off the axe to Royce, who grabbed it reluctantly. "Not like we can leave."

I sighed. "Why not?"

"What are we supposed to tell 'em, mate?" Royce asked, minding the volume he spoke. "We march in there and say, 'Oh sorry, thanks for saving our hides and all that, and showing us your camp and feeding us and clothing us, but we'd better be on our way?'"

I saw what my friends were getting at. I should have known, but I wasn't thinking clearly. Besides it being questionable manners as guests, if you could call us that, they probably wouldn't be willing to let us leave. They'd shown us their hideout's location, after all. Would they risk us leaving and perhaps one day giving up their camp to the government or City Watch stations nearby?

Definitely not.

"So what do we do?" I asked.

Neither man had an answer right away. Royce chopped some more wood as Alomar and I mulled it over, and I counted the seconds as they passed.

I sighed. "We should probably get going."

"Aye," Alomar agreed.

"Look mates," Royce said, "I know this isn't exactly what we had in mind when we set out, but these blokes ain't all that bad, are they? They could have killed us already, right?"

"True enough," I answered. "Better than prison. Maybe."

A shrill whistle sounded out and carried across the campgrounds. We all turned to see the Bandit Lieutenant Miles at the door of the lodge beckoning for us to join them. Arthur was behind the man, shaking his head at us. He slapped the top of his head with an open palm to scold us for not coming sooner.

"Sorry!" I shouted. "Coming!"

Alomar grinned. "Guess five minutes around here means now."

The three of us made our way through the camp, which was noticeably empty. I figured the large log cabin we strode toward was probably full of killers and thieves who were all meeting for our sakes. The thought made me slightly nervous.

"No plans?" I voiced. "No strategies of greatness? Because we could bloody well use one. Or two."

"Not this time, mate," Alomar replied.

We were nearing the large door to the Lodge, and Miles was standing stalwartly at the entrance, scratching passively at his blonde beard. The man unnerved me. He was clearly not someone I'd ever want to be on the bad side of, but it was his presence that spoke volumes. Miles gave me the impression that he was a man who could hack a whole army to pieces if he so chose, but was far too smart to ever get himself into that position. He didn't take his eyes off of us for one instant while we walked to the meeting.

The three of us strode toward the door. I forced a grin to Miles and felt dumb for doing so, but to my surprise he returned my gesture with a quick smile.

"Okay then," he said in his steely voice. "Time for the Captain to meet you."

*   *   *

My eyes took in the Lodge interior for the first time.

Through the doorway, the building opened up into a wide room, almost like a lord's hall in a castle or manor. It had to be around ten times the size of our cabin. Sturdy, smooth wood beams lined the floor from wall to wall. On all four walls, there were two square windows large enough for a man to climb through that let the morning sun pass inside, and three sconces held lit torches which provided a cozy warm glow to the interior.

One of the things that jumped out at me immediately was another door at the back of the room. It wasn't an exit to the woods and camp outside, but another small room, perhaps sleeping quarters or an office of some sort for the captain. It was closed, so my eyes could not pry past to what was housed inside.

At the head of the room, just a few paces in front of the door, was a large desk with no one yet seated in the old wooden chair behind it. Various things were cluttered about it – small scrolls and parchment, an inkwell and a couple books, one opened with various things scribbled about in its pages. I saw a creased and tattered-looking map of a place I could not make out sprawled out on the desktop, held down by a compass.

The eyes of at least twenty or so men, perhaps more, were all fixed on my friends and I as we entered with their man Miles.

There were chairs here and there, no more than ten. Some were old and rickety, while others were much more solid. These were occupied by an array of highwaymen of all sorts. Those that remained were casually posted about the hall, some leaning against the walls, some making seats out of an odd piece of furniture or a large log from the supply of firewood stacked in a corner. Others were even simply sitting on the floor and casually leaning back on their elbows, or propping their backs up against the wall.

Everyone watched us as we took a few steps inside rather awkwardly. I noticed that Miles did not leave his position at the door to our backs, but rather stepped in front of it. Perhaps to block our only escape route?

I spotted Lynn. She was among the band of brigands, near one of the windows on the east wall of the large room, to my right. The woman stood, leaning sideways toward the window and propping herself up with an elbow on the windowsill. She seemed to be the only person in the hall not staring at us, choosing instead to cast her gaze out at the forest through the glass. Her eyes looked brilliant in the sunlight.

It dawned on me that the clan's "officers" as they called them, Lynn and Miles, were among the men rather than in some seat or post up near what I assumed was the captain's desk.

Quaid stood to my left at the west wall, and Arthur was seated against it near the man's feet. When my eyes found theirs, they both flashed reassuring glances.

Discussion began around the room in low voices. Some men seemed to just be enjoying a joke or two, while others were clearly talking about us newcomers that stood before them.

I turned to Miles. "Do we just wait here?"

The man nodded.

"Right, mates," Royce whispered. "We've got this, yeah? We'll be okay."

Alomar said nothing. I noticed he was staring absently at the floor about ten paces ahead of him, and I realized he was being respectful, purposely not looking anyone in the eye. Perhaps it would be seen as a challenge, and it reminded me of exactly how dangerous a situation we were in. My friends and I stood in the midst of over a score of murderers and looters.

I felt my stomach wrench momentarily. Squaring myself and trying to ignore it, I ventured another look to Lynn across the room. This time my eyes found hers. I smiled very slightly, but she did not return it. The woman just looked back to the woods outside again.

The slight creaking of a door reached my ears, and I saw Royce stiffen out of the corner of my eye. As what I figured to be the door to the private quarters in the Lodge slammed shut, I looked to the front of the hall toward the captain's desk.

A man strode out of the private quarters, his presence silencing everyone. He wore a wide-brimmed hat that reminded me of an admiral or captain's hat at sea, dark blue in color, which seemed oddly out of place. Long, brown hair fell about his shoulders. He was clean-shaven except for a dark goatee that had once been brown like the hair atop his head, but now was streaked with gray. The scars of worry and stress creased the man's forehead, their hard lines apparent even now as he looked directly at me. Sky blue eyes found mine. I wanted to look away, but I couldn't.

The most striking feature about the Bandit Captain was the lamellar vest he was wearing. Lamellar armor was made of small plates weaved and laced together tightly, overlapping each other in succession to form a sturdy barrier against possible attacks. One didn't see this very often outside Eislian military companies and the private security of nobles.

Under the lamellar vest, I could see that he was wearing a jerkin and padded shirt probably not unlike the very outfit I was wearing at that moment. His green insignia was tied around his arm above the elbow. Tan trousers met tall boots on his feet, and I saw the toes of his boots were helmed with steel. Like most of the men (and one woman) in the hall, he wore a sword at his side. It was a scimitar, a sword with a wickedly curved blade... only the second if its kind I had ever seen.

The man let the door shut behind him and strolled to his desk, carrying a book and a few odd scrolls in his hands. He set them down briskly, leaned on the desktop with both hands to look out over us all before speaking.

"Well, lads. These three men, by fate, find themselves in our camp on this day."

His voice was hoarse. I didn't dare cast a look at either of my friends, and kept my eyes fixated on the man. His blue eyes found mine, and to my surprise, he broke into a wide, yellow-toothed grin.

"Welcome, you three. I'm Captain Hael."

CHAPTER 29

"Come closer," Captain Hael said rather warmly.

We took a few steps forward. All that could be heard were the loud sniffs of runny noses amidst coughs and inaudible murmurs from the onlookers.

"Oy there, mate," Royce answered.

Alomar nudged Royce roughly.

"Mate, indeed," the man said. "From this point on, don't speak unless requested to do so. I want to get this little meeting of ours done with. Not much for formalities, myself. You understand."

Royce shrugged, and Alomar and I both nodded.

"Now," stated Captain Hael loudly as he rounded the desk to sit on the front of it, "let's get to the point of it. We appreciate the help with the Watchmen yesterday, but we don't know you. If we don't know you, we can't trust you. Not fully."

"However," Lynn suddenly broke in from her perch near the window, "that doesn't mean we don't want to."

Surprised at her speaking amidst the Captain's address, I watched as she strode slowly forward. Her arms were folded and she was looking at the floorboards thoughtfully. "I think partnership is possible with the lot o' ya."

"Says the poisonous one," Royce shot.

"Royce!" Alomar scolded. "Quiet!"

"What was that?" Captain Hael asked us. "Yes, you. The tall one. You can speak."

Hesitating, Alomar replied. "I just... told him to be quiet."

"Brilliant," came Lynn. "And in doing so went against your own advice."

"Sorry," Royce said before Alomar could reply. "I didn't mean-"

With frightening speed, Captain Hael unsheathed the dagger from his belt and jammed it into the top of his desk. A loud *thunk* reverberated off the walls as the blade cut into the wood, silencing my friend.

"Honestly," Captain Hael said, "do you really have any idea of the company you're in right now? This meeting is about whether we let you live or bury you out in the woods, understand? So shut your mouths and say no more unless asked."

The three of us said nothing. I cast my eyes down at the floor.

"Now," the Captain said, leaving his perch on his desk and beginning to pace back and forth, "you there, the large one. Your name is Alomar, yes?"

"Aye."

"Arthur has informed me that you're ex-military. Judging by the ink on your forearm and the scar accompanying it, I'm going to assume this is a truth."

"Aye, sir. 2nd Cavalry."

Grunts of approval rumbled about from around us, and some bandits nodded in acknowledgement to Alomar. A couple men even raised their hands in a toasting gesture.

"Were you at the River Vensaï?" called a man I'd never heard speak.

Alomar grinned. "Aye. All three days. Slept nicely when it was all over, though."

This earned some hearty laughter from all around. Even Hael smiled. I could swear half of the tension in the room melted away on the spot.

"Quiet, everyone!" requested the Captain. "As you lot can see, many of us blokes were in the service ourselves. I was 1st Vanguard. Miles there, too. Arthur was army, as I'm sure he told you. Sid over there in the corner was 9th Cavalry, with Ernest there. I could go on and on."

Alomar smiled and nodded. "Well-met. The lot of ya."

Lynn stepped forward, and I thought I saw her sigh. "All that aside, let me be perfectly clear for ya. You three are lucky to be standin' here at all. Know what I mean?"

We all nodded. I saw Alomar's grin slowly fade.

"This lot here," the woman continued, gesturing around her, "many of 'em think we should kill ya. I don't."

"How kind of you," Royce muttered.

Alomar and I glared at the man, wide-eyed.

"That's what I'm talkin' about!" Lynn said. "Will you just shut up for one minute? Keep your mouth closed."

I exchanged nervous glances with Alomar. My eyes widened when Lynn suddenly drew the dagger from her belt, and in a swift motion brought it to Royce's neck.

"You feel that?" she whispered.

"Hey!" I protested.

Alomar shifted towards her. "Don't!"

The sound of chairs scraping the wood floor echoed about, and everyone seated was suddenly on their feet at the slightest movement from Alomar. More men left their places around the hall, and in an instant we found ourselves greatly outnumbered by a spectacular variety of swords and axes.

Alomar stopped in his tracks and shot Captain Hael a pleading look, but the bandit leader ignored it and watched Lynn intently.

Instead of heeding my protest, Lynn pressed the flat of her dagger's blade against Royce's neck. "Feel that?" she repeated. "That's what many o' these men want. Don't ya understand?"

I was holding my breath, and I could see Alomar grinding his teeth and trying to fight the urge to rush the woman in a head-on assault. Royce was silent, and his eyes were fixed on hers.

Lynn leered upward at him. "I'm tryin' to bloody help ya! Just stay quiet. I need your word. Tell me you'll behave."

I pleaded silently with my friend, hoping he somehow heard it. Finally, I caught Royce's gaze for just an instant. I tried to wordlessly urge him to comply, but his eyes were back on Lynn's before he could see it.

Alomar spoke slowly, in fear of being reprimanded for it by the men around him. "Roy, say yes, mate. Just say it."

Royce's dark blue eyes seemed to be searching for something in the air around him suddenly, and I could see his forehead start to furrow and his nose crinkle in what looked like disgust as he faced Lynn's stare squarely.

"No."

"Blast it, Royce!" I yelled. "Stop being a bloody idiot!"

"No!" the man roared stubbornly. "Easy for you to tell me what to do when you have a blade to my neck, yeah? Real brave of you," he spat.

Lynn's face was hard, like it had been when she'd been assessing me in the cabin that morning. She said nothing.

"Easy with all your friends around here with you," Royce continued. "How 'bout you hand me the dagger and we play this game the other way around?"

I gawked in dismay, slapping my hand to my forehead loudly. Alomar was breathing rapidly and noisily through his nose, and I could see his legs start to twitch. I couldn't tell if Alomar was thinking of attacking Lynn or going after Royce for being a bloody idiot.

A few of the bandits started to move toward Lynn and Royce slowly. I held up my palms in a plea but dared not move in front of them.

To my surprise, Lynn held up her free hand in a halting gesture, and the brigands stopped in their tracks, watching her closely. She did not take her eyes off Royce's.

"You'd kill me over this?" Royce asked.

"Regardless of whether I would or not, the lot behind me might."

My friend shook his head. "Do it, then." He pressed his own neck against the woman's knife. "Go on."

"Royce...." Alomar began.

"Do it!" Royce hollered.

I could hold still no longer. I wasn't thinking clearly. I just knew my best mate was about to get his throat cut like that poor bloke in the river I'd dragged ashore, and I couldn't just watch it happen. Whirling quickly, I dashed past Alomar toward Royce and Lynn.

Alomar reached behind his back to try to stop me. His strength was formidable, but he only had time to get one hand out in front of me. I shoved it aside, but only got two more paces before Miles was suddenly in my path. I nearly sprinted right into the point of his blade.

The outlaws all around darted forward in swift response, weapons ready. Before they could strike, Captain Hael's raspy voice echoed throughout the hall of the Lodge.

"Stand down! Weapons away!" he barked.

With notable disappointment, his men obeyed. They backed away from us slowly. Lynn still held Royce at knifepoint.

Captain Hael folded his arms and grinned. "Clearly, you three are not without heart. You possess some vigor, I'll give you that."

I looked on in surprise when I saw a smile play across Lynn's face slowly as she gave Royce a wink. She stood on her tiptoes and I saw the woman whisper something into my friend's ear. His expression was still hard when she pulled away and sheathed her dagger.

"You all see, aye?" Lynn called to the hall's occupants as they relaxed. "We can use 'em, for sure. That kind o' heart? That rebellious spirit?"

The bandits began talking amongst themselves, shooting glances and words this way and that. I saw shrugs, grins, nods of approval and a few skeptical frowns.

"What say ya, Cap'n?" asked Lynn.

Not budging an inch in his stance, Captain Hael's eyes narrowed in thought for but a moment before he turned his gaze to the brigand next to me. "Miles? Thoughts?"

Miles left my side and walked to the center of the room. I could see that the same attention he had seemed to draw from me at will, he also commanded with the men around him.

"They're a motley bunch, Fates can see," Miles replied. "They've seen our faces and our camp, aye. They know how to reach it."

There was a chorus of discussion from the highwaymen around us.

"All they gotta do is go back to the Watch!" called a man. "We can't let 'em!"

"But," cut in Miles gracefully, "they helped us out yesterday. Why would they go back to the Watch? Besides, we could use the extra manpower. After all, how many blokes willingly help out men like us, eh?"

I could see the slightest hint of a grin on Lynn's face, and I was surprised when she discreetly tapped Royce's rigid arm encouragingly. I realized she was trying to calm him down.

"And like the Captain and Lynn say," Miles finished, "they certainly have heart."

The man's words floated into the hall and then sank slowly into all present. After a few moments, Captain Hael left his seated perch on his desk and strode forward.

"You all have a few minutes to discuss the matter at hand," he called. "We will then subject it to a vote. Majority rules."

There was much conversation as the bandit company around us discussed our fates. My heart thundered anxiously, and I looked at Alomar.

"Well, then. Here's to adventure, eh?" I offered dryly.

Alomar looked on worriedly. "Aye. Not bad for starters, I suppose... except we might be dead already."

Royce was still silent. I tried to catch his gaze, but he was staring absently into space. Anger was etched into his face, and a slight hint of... embarrassment, was it? I couldn't blame him. Lynn had held a dagger to this throat in hopes of playing the man, and it had worked. It didn't matter that the woman had done so for our benefit. The way Lynn did things made it challenging to imagine trusting her one day.

I hoped we wouldn't be around the bandit clan long enough to have to be trusting the likes of her. Then again, I could only pray that we survived the impending vote that loomed in the minutes to come, threatening to bring our lives and short-lived adventure outside of Northroe to an end.

"Hey. Roy. You okay, mate?" I chanced.

"Of course I am."

I hesitated. "What did she whisper to you?"

The man rolled his eyes. "Why? Jealous?"

"No!" I snapped. "Just wondering."

Royce snorted. "Nothing, Pen."

At long last, Captain Hael called the meeting of sorts to order. The outlaws all diverted their attention to him. Lynn and Miles stood near the man up front, surveying the crowd.

My stomach was in knots, and my insides felt very much like the gnarled roots Royce and I had grabbed for dear life under the bridge the day before.

"Right, then," called Captain Hael. "Let's keep this brief. All in favor of giving the newcomers a chance to prove themselves in our ranks? Show of hands!"

I was absolutely shocked to see every hand in the room go up, Lynn and Miles included.

"Those who oppose?"

Nobody raised their hands. I could hear Alomar breathe out in relief. My breath caught in my throat for a moment, and I blinked furiously, wondering if I had seen and heard wrong... but the Bandit Captain was quick to dash my doubt to pieces.

Captain Hael unsheathed his blade and lifted it into the air. There was a loud chorus of steel being drawn as everyone else did the same.

"I hereby welcome you lads to our company. Meeting adjourned!"

There was a loud shout of acknowledgement all around. I was still gaping in shock, incredulous and confused.

Miles strode through the crowd as it dispersed and stood before the three of us with a grin. "Congratulations."

"We're not dying?" I replied in question.

Alomar nodded to Miles, both men ignoring me. "We appreciate it. Thank you."

I felt myself grin slowly as I answered myself. "We're not dying."

"Art and Quaid will guide you around the camp for the day," Miles said above the chatter around us. "Show you how we do things, duties and the like. Lynn, the Captain and I have to discuss some matters. Drawin' some plans up for a certain something, we are."

"Plans, eh?" I asked.

Miles nodded. "Indeed. Perfect opportunity for you three to prove yourselves, in the near future. Art and Quaid will sort you out and put you to work. Get some rest come nightfall. You'll need it."

CHAPTER 30

The night eventually fell across the woods at the foot of Mount Kovald, and the fireplace crackled noisily at the center of the bandit camp. I watched the flames try to lick at the stars above while sparks sang upward.

Arthur, Quaid and I sat around the fire and warmed ourselves. My right hand was dressed in a new bandage, wrapped tight against the cuts and bruises from when I'd punched the cobbled street outside the tavern. I moved my fingers tenderly. It all felt stiff and terrible, but our new friends insisted I'd be good as new within a week, two at most.

Royce and Alomar were out with Miles, Lynn and a few men most of the day on a foraging run. The bandits had told us about how they scoured the edges of the river for various fruits and berries, and of a small pond to the Northeast where they did the same. They had learned to live off plants and assorted vegetation as well if hunted animals became scarce. I learned that roughly once a month a small raid was carried out down south in the Glydell Farmlands to secure as many crops as the outlaws could safely transport back.

I'd spent most of the day with Arthur and Quaid and a small party of other highwaymen, tagging along as they felled trees and began building a second storage shed to accompany the one already established on the grounds. Since I didn't have full capacity for the use of my right hand, I had carried out lighter duties, like carrying water fetched from the river and helping with weapon maintenance. A man named Ruben had once worked as a weaponsmith for a traveling company of mercenaries, and now served the same position in Captain Hael's company. I mainly watched the man work the forge, catching every other word of an old song he'd sing, or listening to random tidbits of advice he would offer. When Ruben finished with a weapon or tool, he sent me out to return it to the man it belonged to. I ignored the smithing instruction he gave, for I convinced myself that I wouldn't be in Hael's camp long enough to put it to use, anyway. It at least kept me busy, and gave me plenty of time to think.

I spent just about every waking minute of the day imagining ways to escape, telling myself that this was not a life for my friends and I. When we had spoke of travels and adventure and 'living our lives' as Royce had called it, I'm certain that none of us had imagined it being quite like this.

I had only done light lifting compared to that of other men, yet there I sat at the fire that night, aching and tired.

"You did well today, for a bloke with one hand," quipped Arthur.

I grinned. "I aim to please."

Thinking about the conversation Lynn and I had the day before, I swallowed any timidity and cleared my throat.

"The first day we were here... when my friends and I were waiting outside the Lodge. Lynn was inside talking with Hael-"

"Cap'n," Arthur interrupted.

"Aye," I returned hastily. "The Captain, I meant. What was she so angry about? We could hear them arguing inside and it seemed, well... nasty."

The two men looked at each other for a moment. During the silence, I was wondering why I wanted to ask so bad as to why Miles was needed during that instance. Was it because he was the other officer? Did he and Lynn have a close relationship? Were they good friends for years? Was he the only one that could get through to the woman when she was in one of her rages? I felt silly for thinking such thoughts, but for some reason, they tugged at me.

Arthur cracked his knuckles loudly. "Actually couldn't tell ya, Penny."

"But you were both in there. You both called for Miles, and-"

Quaid laughed. "The Captain and Lynn had a disagreement, is all."

"Well, I gathered that, but-"

"Look, Penny," Arthur said lowly. "Their business, not ours. It's that simple. They kicked our arses out because their words weren't for our ears to hear, see?"

Defeated, I nodded slowly.

"Penny, what is it that you did in Northroe?" asked Quaid suddenly. "Before you came here to the Kovald, that is."

Oh, Fates. Now it was becoming real. I had thought about this. The moment any of us shared personal information with any of these blokes at the camp changed things. If that moment had come, it meant we would be crossing the threshold of awkward introductions to 'Hello, Penny Daulton. I'm an outlaw, and I've probably killed more people than you've talked to. Let's talk about life around the campfire.'

That's how I looked at it, at least.

"Nothing... interesting," I replied.

Arthur stretched out to lie on his side, propping himself up on an elbow. "Nothin' interesting, eh? That's it?"

I shrugged.

Quaid chuckled. "Right. I'll go first. I was a mercenary. Sword-for-hire, if you will. Or should I say bow-for-hire?"

"Aye," Arthur nodded. "Bow."

"Right then. Anyway, my last employer found himself in trouble with the law down south. In Elaine, near Foye. But anyway, bastard didn't tell me he was in the child labor business, you see. I didn't know."

I motioned for him to continue. "And? What happened?"

Quaid's eyes were intent on the flames. "Got caught. They assumed m'self and the other blokes in the man's company were in on it, of course. Perhaps some of 'em were, but I wasn't. I ran. Was able to get away."

I tried to picture the man speaking before me running away from a score of City Watchmen in some town called Elaine, frantically darting through the meadows and hills and taking brilliant shots with the bow that lay on the ground next to him at this moment. I found myself wondering how good he really was with it.

"Child labor, huh?" I echoed. "Thought that was done for."

"Well, legally yes," answered Quaid. "Not too much of it anymore since the King's father started crackin' down on it. Now the King is mopping up the remnants of the trade in Eisley, so it seems. But every so often, there's still a stubborn bloke that tries his hand at it. They even get away with it for a while."

Mulling over this for a moment, I turned to Arthur, who was sharpening his sword noisily on a flat rock. "What about you, Arthur?"

"What about me what?"

"What'd you do before you came here? I mean, how did you two come to join up with Captain Hael's lot?" I asked.

Arthur inhaled deeply. "Well, as you know I served in Dekka. Almost four years in the army. Yves Company. Joined up, fought the war, came back home to Northroe."

I waited for the man to continue, but he said nothing. Finding myself terribly curious, I prodded him onward.

"And? How'd you join this lot in the woods?"

Arthur gave a sort of longing grin, almost a smile that hid a pained past and memories of regret. "It's personal."

"What? That's it?"

"Sorry."

Disappointment settled over me like a blanket. Slightly discouraged, I turned to Quaid. "And you, Quaid? I mean, I know you ran from the Watch and all that. But if you were all the way near Foye, how in blazes did you end up here outside of Northroe?"

Quaid was still watching the fire sway slowly with the night wind. "I met a woman. Most brilliant lass I've ever met in this life. We were gonna get married once we got some more coin together. I kind of just drifted north, you see. Met her in Winter's Wake, quiet town south of here. We continued up to these parts, eventually to Northroe."

He paused, and I said nothing. I don't know if it was the writer in me, but I was exceedingly curious about the rest of it. Thankfully, the man continued, exhaling heavily. "She had a brother. The man was a Master Carpenter. Said I could join up with him at his shop, as an apprentice and the like. While we worked our days away, she... well."

My eyes narrowed when I realized Quaid was having difficulty continuing. An expression vaguely reminiscent of Arthur's from earlier was crossing his face.

"Julia spent her days working the fields with a good enough crew on the Trosdee Farm. You know it? The one in the western hills outside Northroe?"

I looked at the dirt in front of me and felt a sinking feeling in my heart. The Trosdee Farm. Everyone knew of it.

"Aye. I do."

Quaid nodded slowly. "Then you know of the murders."

I paused. "Aye."

"Well, there you have it," Quaid replied lowly. "She was one of them, the fallen. Ever wonder why they never found out who killed all those innocent people there?"

I said nothing, gazing at the man intently.

"I found 'em first," the man continued. "Killed 'em both. Now, the Watch found out what I did, but I was already a wanted man from what went on down near Foye with my former employer, you see?"

My mouth dropped open. "You knew who was responsible for the Trosdee murders?"

Quaid nodded again.

I looked at Arthur wide-eyed, but he was just watching the fire. Apparently he'd heard this story before.

"But... how!?"

Quaid's eyes were far away. I'd seen that same look on Alomar's face before. The man in front of me was reliving some memory I had no place in. His eyes had seen the likes of things that mine had not.

"Not important," he said at last.

"But who were they?" I asked incredulously. "And it was two blokes, you say? Who?"

"My business, mate," Quaid replied.

Unable to mask my disappointment, I lay back in the dirt and thin grass to watch the stars for a moment. The Trosdee Murders had been unsolved for over seven years. Nobody knew who had slain all the poor farmhands on the estate. The story had become so legendary and infamous that ghost stories and the like were told to children looking for a scare. And now the one man who knew who had been responsible, and had killed them, was sitting right here with me.

One may wonder how I knew Quaid was telling the truth. Sometimes, you just know, don't you? When the man told me that story, the very air around me seemed to ice over. A stark, cold realization descended upon me, and my heart wavered in its beat.

He spoke the truth.

A few minutes passed. The three of us sat around the fire, letting the words sink in. Men were off to our right chopping and stacking more firewood, lacing the air with laughter and curses as they did so.

I wondered what this Julia had been like. I imagined a woman who could have been any woman, really. Pictured one smiling and laughing in my arms, talking with me excitedly about saving coin so that we could get married together and get a small home somewhere. I imagined finding out about the grisly murders outside of Northroe, tried to imagine what it would have felt like when I had learned it was at the Trosdee Farm, where my Julia had been a field hand.

There was this feeling in the pit of my stomach that was oddly familiar to me. It was a weight and a pain, and I realized I had felt it once, back when I was a boy and I realized my father was gone forever and would not be coming back.

"I'm sorry," I murmured finally. "That's... I can't imagine."

Quaid nodded my way. "Anyhow. See, one of those blokes I killed was the brother of a top man in the City Watch. Again, it's a long story, but the killer's brother found out who I was. Some arse sold me out. I had to flee. Happened across Captain Hael and some o' his men while on the run, and he offered me quarter with his crew, after hearing my story, o' course. Now, seven years later, here I still am."

I reached toward the flames to warm my hands, shaking my head in awe.

"Penny, can I give a word of advice?" Arthur asked suddenly.

Puzzled, I nodded.

The man sat up. "Not all the blokes in this camp have... similar circumstances of why they're on the run. I understand you're curious, mate. But a word of caution: you may not want to know everyone's story. Some don't want to be asked. Know what I'm saying? We're called brigands and outlaws for a reason."

I dwelled on this for a moment, and nodded yet again.

"And now, what about you?" Arthur asked, with the knowing grin of somebody contradicting his own words.

What a loaded question. I hesitated, gathering my thoughts. All my thinking on my own during the day and I hadn't really prepared for being asked that question. Now I was cursing inwardly for not doing so. Should I tell them the truth, without having discussed it with Royce and Alomar? Should I lie? Maybe make up a story to where the bandits would see me as a tougher man than I really was? If I did, wouldn't they see right through it, being hardened criminals in their own ways themselves?

"At least you don't have to explain how you fell in with our lot," Quaid laughed. "We know that part, don't we?"

Arthur chuckled. "Aye. That we do. But go on, Penny. You three knew each other well before you left the city? And why was your friend in shackles?"

At that moment, there was a commotion around us. The three of us perked up and saw Miles, Lynn, Royce, Alomar and a small party of men plod into camp. They were carrying sacks and packs of what must have been food gathered from the foraging run.

Some small cheers sounded out from here and there as other men saw that food had found its way to their camp. Arthur and Quaid both stood and so I did as well, and we made our way over with other men to welcome the foraging party.

"How much did ya get?"

"Any trouble?"

"Run into anyone?

"Oy! Please tell me you got some o' those blueberries again!"

I grinned wryly at both Royce and Alomar as they set down their packs. Alomar stretched while Royce simply sank to the ground and lay on his back, breathing out a sigh of relief.

"Oh, Fates!" Royce called to the stars above. "On this day, I thank you for the best blueberries I ever did taste!"

"How'd it go?" I asked.

"Went well," Alomar replied. "Bloody sore, though. Of course, who isn't, yeah?"

The three of us swapped stories of how our days had played out. Theirs had been relatively uneventful other than gathering berries and other small plants and fruits, although Royce did tell of an amazing meadow out to the Northeast around the corner of Mount Kovald. Apparently a stream ran right through the center of it, and Royce said the grass was waist-high and a green so deep the forest on the outskirts of the meadow looked on in jealousy.

My friends were much more interested in what I had done, and I told them about the weapons running to and from Ruben the Weaponsmith, fetching water and the like. I decided to leave out what Arthur and Quaid had told me about their pasts, especially Quaid's connection with the Trosdee Farm, but I did make sure to mention that the bandits were asking questions about us.

"Ah, yes. They were asking us as well, about... well, us," Royce replied.

Alomar nodded. "Aye. Wondering about how we came to be here and all that. Strange, how friendly this lot is. They're not covering up that they're outlaws and ain't shy about telling of some of their more... brutal exploits. But they're nice enough."

"What'd you tell them?" I asked.

"That it'd be better to reveal to them when the three of us are together to tell the tale," Alomar said. "Mainly we just wanted to buy time so we could discuss it, since the three of us haven't yet. But, well. We told them some things."

The two men glanced at each other. I didn't like the looks in their eyes.

"What? Hold on now. What is that look?" I asked sternly.

Royce turned to me and was rubbing his chin. "Well, we might have told them, you see, that there's a storyteller in our midst. An author at that."

I turned red. "What. What?"

"Aye. We thought that-"

I almost exploded. "You what!? But I'm not a storyteller! I'm a Writer-in-Training!"

"Yes, as you so often point out," Alomar replied. "You already told Lynn our first night here, remember? Not like it's a secret."

Royce laughed and mimicked my voice. "I'm Penny, Penny Daulton. Writer-in-Training. You can just call me Lover-boy."

He was alarmingly good at imitating me.

"Is there a difference, anyway? Storyteller and a Writer?"

I crossed my arms. "I'm not a full-fledged writer. Yet. I'm a Writer-"

"In-Training," both men echoed. "We know."

Shaking his head, Royce pointed forcefully. "You really need to stop saying that, mate."

Before I could scold them even louder, I saw Lynn break off from the crowd and come toward us. The sleeves on her shirt had been rolled up past her shoulders, exposing smooth and tan skin that had splotches of dirt here and there from the day's journey. The woman was not wearing her bandana, and had her red hair tied back.

"Penny, how'd your day with Art and Quaid go?" she asked.

"Fine enough," I replied. I was still flushed with embarrassment. "So, um, your trip went well?"

Lynn nodded and pointed behind her to the large pile of packs filled with various foods. Men were picking them up and lugging them off to the storage shed. "Aye, we did. Got us plenty o' food, enough to last for another week, at least."

Royce's eyes gleamed dangerously as he turned to the woman.

"So, Lynn. I was just telling Penny here about us telling you lot about him being a writer and all that."

"In-Training," I corrected.

The man shot me a look. "Come off it, already. We get it."

"Ah, good," Lynn replied. Her red-brown eyes were aglow with the fire's light as they found mine. "Did they tell ya the plan tonight?"

"Plan?" I asked.

"Aye."

I narrowed my eyes fiercely, trying to burn the two of my friends with them. "They said nothing of the sort."

With that, Lynn abruptly cupped her hands around her mouth and called out to the entire camp around us. "Oy, lads! Gather 'round the fire! Put some pep in your step, aye?"

My heart skipped a beat, and I paled in fright. "W-what? What's going on?"

The woman grinned and to my surprise, winked at me. "All right, Mr. Storyteller. Tonight we're gonna gather at the fireplace. All o' us, as we always do. I'm sure all the men wanna hear a good tale."

I gulped in horror, watching as brigands from all sides of the camp strolled toward the fire. A few men renewed the flames with a log and kindling, and others started taking their seats around the blaze.

"Right. H-here's the thing," I stuttered. "Is there any way to maybe not do this now? Or ever?"

Lynn folded her arms. "Time to see what ya got, Writer-in-Training."

CHAPTER 31

Why did the Fates seem to treasure making my life difficult as of late? What in blazes was I supposed to do? Writing stories was one thing, but making one up on the spot? Playing the part of a Storyteller was a different matter altogether!

And why in blazes did Royce and Alomar mention I was a Writer-in-Training to Lynn and the lot of them, anyway?

All around me, the hardened and sunburned faces of men and one woman were fixed on me intently, awaiting my poetic words that they seemed sure would tell a grand story for the ages.

"I... you see, this isn't what I do, actually," I stammered.

Lynn shook her head slowly, and I heard a couple men snort dismissively in the crowd. The fire crackled on, ignoring the situation it was illuminating.

"What?" I pleaded, looking around. "I write, you see? I write stories down. It's an art. And I'm not even a real writer yet. I'm training to be one!"

An awkward silence ensued. I saw Royce scratch his head as he cast his eyes at the dirt beneath his feet. It was Alomar who cleared his throat and spoke.

"What Penny here is trying to say," he started, clearly trying to come up with something fast, "is that writing a story is an art. Telling a tale on the spot, like around this campfire for instance, is another art entirely."

I nodded quickly. "Aye. A storyteller, I most definitely am not. I'm a Writer. In Training."

Some of the men chuckled. Lynn sat and shook her head again, rolling her eyes.

"A writer who can't tell a story," she snorted. "Bollocks."

I could feel my face turn red, but embarrassment quickly gave way to defensive anger. "Bollocks? I can tell a story!"

Lynn didn't answer. Instead, she turned to look over her shoulder and out into the dark. The woman clapped her hands twice and gave a shrill whistle. In a few moments, the patter of paws romping across dirt and pine needles reached our ears, and Lynn's dog Ember careened into view and practically tackled the woman.

Laughing, Lynn sat down and scooped Ember's face in her hands, massaging the husky's head firmly. Ember enjoyed herself for a few moments before turning her curious eyes to me. It looked like even the dog expected a tale this night.

The Bandit Lieutenant Miles strode to Lynn's side from out of the darkness and handed her a mug of what I assumed was ale. Before sitting, he turned to me and motioned with his cup in hand.

"If you can tell a story, then go on, Storyteller. Bloody 'ell, we all could use a good tale, after all. Couldn't we, mates?"

"Aye!"

"Hear, hear!"

A warm, encouraging cheer sounded off in the forest night as men here and there raised their hands or cups. I heard a man click his tongue loudly, and Ember immediately perked up, finding Arthur in the circle of outlaws. Arthur tossed a piece of food to her, and the dog gratefully pounced upon it.

Royce clapped his hand to my shoulder enthusiastically. "There you go, mate. Thank me later."

I shoved his hand away and could feel my nostrils flaring in anger. "You buffoon!" I hissed. "What in the Fates' names are you trying to do to me!? Get me killed?"

My friend just laughed as he sat to my left. "I'm doing you a favor, mate. It's time at last."

I gawked helplessly. "But... what? Time for what?"

Alomar sidled up to my side, casting his towering shadow over the fire and me. "Pen, maybe it's time to really tell one of your stories," he whispered. "Come on, mate!"

"That's not how it bloody works!" I answered heatedly. "I can't just come up with one on the spot like this! And... and I don't even know these blokes, and-"

"Exactly!" Alomar interrupted with that brilliant grin of his. "What better time to test yourself?"

Royce nudged my shin from his sitting position. "What better time to come out of your shell?"

This time, Alomar and I looked at each other, confused. Apparently Lynn had heard Royce as well.

"Eh? What does that mean? 'Come outta his shell' an' all that?" she asked.

Clearing his throat, Royce answered. "Well, see, my friend Penny here is like a turtle of sorts, yeah? Always hiding his talents from the world, if you will. Like a turtle hiding in his shell. I'm saying he should stop hiding."

Lynn, Alomar and I exchanged glances.

"That was actually quite good," I remarked finally.

"Aye," nodded Alomar. "Well-put."

Lynn sighed loudly. "Are you tellin' a story or not, Penny?"

"Tell the story already!" came a shout from the small crowd.

Miles was chuckling with another man, who was pointing at me and saying something I couldn't understand between breaths of laughter.

"Come on, Penny!" came the voice of Ruben the weaponsmith. He stood quickly and lifted his cup encouragingly. "Go on, mate. Can't be any worse than Gordon's stories."

The bandits around the fire laughed heartily.

"Who's Gordon?" I asked.

"He used to be our Storyteller, I suppose," Lynn answered.

I scratched my chin. "Used to be? Where's Gordon now?"

"Well, now he's dead."

I nodded, swallowing hard. "Oh. Right."

"Bloody hell," one man complained. "Get on with it!"

"I don't know which story to tell!" I protested.

Royce thumped my shin again. "Tell them the one about the pirate!"

I paled in fear as Lynn suddenly flashed her gaze from the fire to me.

"Pirate?" she asked. "You have a story about a pirate?"

"Aye!" Royce answered for me. "It's about a pirate, who's very hungry, you see. So, he eats everyone, and then-"

"Roy! I will kill you where you sit! Shut it, for the Fates' sakes!" I thundered.

Just like that, the constant rumble of chatter and guffaws seemed to smooth out into silence. I found myself to be the only one standing, and the crackling of the fire in the forest night seemed to be louder than it was moments before. All eyes were fixed on me, waiting.

Oddly, Royce was beaming proudly. "Aye. Go on, then. What story will we hear this night, Penny?"

Wind breezed through the campground steadily, softly swaying the flames with it. As it did, a new realization seemed to spread across me. I looked at the faces circled around the campfire now and saw their gazes fixed on me intently. Whether they doubted me, were eager, or hopeful for a good tale, it didn't matter. They were all looking to me now. Faces of the roughest kind of men were staring at me, and the simple matter was, they just wanted to be taken away from their lives, even if just for a short time.

I had always been a dreamer, a spinner of tales. Royce and Alomar were right. Was I going to tell the world my stories or not?

A new confidence swelled within me. I felt an odd sensation, almost like an obligation or duty to the weathered brigands around me. It was time.

I raised my hand. "You would like a story then, would you?"

The outlaws nodded, some voicing their ayes of approval. Even Ember sat at attention, tail wagging enthusiastically.

"O-okay then," I stammered shortly before wrestling my confidence back into my grasp. "I will tell you the tale of... of The Trickster Mirror."

CHAPTER 32

I watched their faces closely. Some men exchanged glances of approval. Others frowned in question.

"There was once a bandit captain named... Kade."

At mention of a bandit captain, everyone perked up. Even Lynn's eyes averted from the flames momentarily. Butterflies fluttered about inside my stomach, and I was trying to keep my heartbeat in check.

Blazes, was I nervous.

"Y-you see, the mighty Captain Kade and his... mighty band of outlaws, were known across the land. Known to be very–"

"Very what?" called Ruben.

I panicked. "Mighty."

"Oy," came a man's voice. "Is this story called The Trickster Mirror, or is it the Mighty Captain Kade and His Mighty Outlaws?"

"Who Were Very Mighty?" added another man.

My face flushed with embarrassment. Alomar coughed loudly and elbowed my leg from where he sat. Awkwardly trying to regain my composure, I chanced a look over to my left at Lynn. She wasn't joining in the laughter – in fact, she was sitting straight up now and watching me closely. I couldn't honestly tell, but I swear I thought I saw a reassuring smile begin to pull at her lips.

I stood taller.

"They were known as Kade's Marauders!" I said with renewed vigor. "He and his men were so feared that the King himself ordered a bounty of a thousand silver as a reward for just one of the Marauders' heads!"

"One thousand for each head?" asked a baldheaded outlaw.

I pointed dramatically into the air and nodded. "Each head, aye."

The outlaws murmured in awe around the fire.

"For you see, such was their strength, and so great was their resolve, that to capture or kill just one Marauder earned a man such amounts of silver," I continued. "But to capture or kill Captain Kade himself earned a man lordship in the King's hall, and an estate bestowed upon him and his kin."

A sunburned, tired-looking bandit raised his hand. "Wot does 'bestow' mean, mate?"

"To give," I answered. "So an estate would be given to a man and his family, in reward for the head of Captain Kade."

The man nodded and gave a low whistle.

"Now," I pressed, "Captain Kade had one weakness. Just one! And that was the woman he loved. She-"

"What was her name?" called another man.

"Oy!" hissed Lynn suddenly. "Stop interruptin' the man, yeah? Let him tell the tale!"

Taken aback momentarily at the woman's rush to my aid, I grinned and turned to the general direction of where I had heard the question. "Her name was... Lynn... er, Lindsay. Yes. The woman's name was Lindsay, you see."

At that moment I saw a form meld into view from the shadows, and I recognized it to be Captain Hael himself as he joined the fire circle without a word. The others were so intent on my story that they didn't notice. I felt that nervousness enter my heart again, but I firmly quelled it and continued.

"Captain Kade and Lindsay were lovers, aye. But they could never be properly married, for everyone in the land knew who the man was on sight. Therefore, they could never dream of having an actual ceremony. And because the woman was so dear to him, the Captain knew that he could never reveal his love for her to any living soul, for it made him vulnerable and endangered her life, as well. Not even his own men knew of her."

I surveyed the eyes of the bandit clan around me and was excited to see that everyone's attention was still on me.

"They would meet in secret, in the forest... this same forest, in fact!" I said, punctuating my words with excitement. "Lindsay stayed hidden away in a cottage in the Kovald, where the Captain knew he could always find her when he desired. She waited for him to return from his ventures with open arms, but Lindsay would never allow Captain Kade inside her cottage, for she harbored a secret within its walls that she'd never shared. Not with anyone."

The small crowd around me shifted about amidst a flurry of whispers.

"As the years passed, Kade and his men went through many trials. Some of his men were indeed captured by the King. The Captain and his bandits were forced to relocate from time to time in an attempt to evade the bounty hunters that plagued them like the shadows of night. It made it much more difficult to meet with Lindsay in the woods, and the times became more dangerous.

"The King of Eisley realized as the months and years came that the best way to combat the Mighty Captain Kade was to secure his villages and towns even more, making it harder for Kade's men to raid and loot and the like. As more and more soldiers were stationed at even the smallest farms and outposts, Kade and his crew found themselves hungry and desperate, trapped in the wilderness in a seemingly endless search for comfort and stability."

I let the words sink in and found that my mouth was becoming dry. Everyone, including Lynn, was looking to me now, completely engrossed in my tale. Even Ember watched me curiously, intent on my words.

"You see," I started again hoarsely, but I coughed. My mouth was dry as cotton!

A man hastily passed a cup to Alomar, who nudged my leg again, offering the cup up to me. I accepted it from his reach and drank, expecting ale but tasting water. I wiped my mouth and handed the cup back down to Alomar and gave a grateful nod.

Crisis averted.

I felt bolder now, and even better, I was having a bit of fun.

I stepped from the crowd and walked close to the flames so that I now stood in the middle of the fire circle. As I did, the men sitting in front of the others started to edge backwards as if to give me more room for a stage. I pressed on.

"You see, sadly, sometimes many months would pass before Kade was able to meet Lindsay safely again in the woods. But he always knew right where to meet her, and somehow, she was always there, waiting for him in the heart of the Kovald at the base of the mountain..." I trailed off, lowering my voice and widening my eyes. Dramatically, I pointed at my feet. "Right here, in fact," I whispered. "Lindsay's small cottage stood right here, on this very ground."

The silence was deafening. The men were shifting this way and that. Some were even looking over their shoulders. Some wore excited expressions. Lynn's eyes were wide and fixed on me.

"But something occurred to Captain Kade," I continued in a low, mysterious tone. "See, something wasn't right. Lindsay never seemed to age. She never seemed to get any older."

"What?" uttered Ruben the Weaponsmith. "Why?" He clapped a hand over his mouth immediately in apology.

"Kade didn't know," I answered, flashing my eyes excitedly. "As his hair began to gray with the aging wisps of silver, Lindsay's stayed brilliantly blonde. As the Captain's face creased with age, Lindsay's stayed smooth, silky and gentle. And while the color in Kade's eyes seemed to fade softly with time, the eyes of his woman stayed youthful, full of shine.

"Lindsay knew that the man she loved had taken notice of her strange immunity to aging. It made the woman sad to see the Captain growing old without her, and to see the man wonder in confusion why she did not follow his same path of mortality. At last, Lindsay decided that perhaps it was time to reveal her secret. At last, she would allow Captain Kade into her cottage!"

I smiled inwardly when I saw Royce and Alomar exchange glances, both grinning in what was clearly excitement. As I spoke, I turned this way and that dramatically, as to address the different parts of the gathered audience.

"A horrible thing befell Captain Kade. The King's men finally caught up with him and his band one night, not unlike this very night that we sit here beneath the stars. After much fighting, the Mighty Captain was forced to retreat into the darkness of the woods. Every single one of his men died in the fighting."

Low growls and angry faces met my words.

"But," I added hastily, "for every Marauder fallen, three of the King's men followed in death's wake."

A bandit raised his hand. "Followed in death's what?"

"For every Marauder that died, they took down three of the King's men with them," I rephrased.

I tried not to chuckle as I saw Ruben leaning over to the man to explain how the math worked out.

"Wounded and desperate, Captain Kade made his way shakily to Lindsay's cottage – right here, in this clearing."

Everyone was sitting straight, and many were leaning forward toward me. I wondered if they were aware of it. I lowered my voice to invite mystery into our midst.

"The Captain told his beloved Lindsay what had happened. She sheltered him in her arms and shed tears for the man's misfortune. In the quiet of the night, she held his hands tightly and offered a prayer to the Fates above in memory of Kade's men. And before Kade could ask, Lindsay looked up at the man and told him that she would finally show him her secret... that he could step inside the cottage. She would show him why she did not grow old like others.

"After more than two decades of secret meetings in the woods, Captain Kade nodded and started toward the door of Lindsay's cottage with an anxious heart. He was nervous, and she led him in by the hand. She closed the door behind them. And do you know what Kade saw inside?"

No one answered my question. Everyone in the clearing was completely fixed on me, watching me and waiting for me to continue.

"He saw nothing," I said lowly, "nothing but a mirror. The floorboards were bare, and the walls as well. I tell you, there was *nothing* in Lindsay's cottage but a tall mirror in the center of the floor! Not a bed, nor a pair of shoes or so much as one linen or cloth. One dusty mirror awaited, and a few cobwebs stretched across its base from the floor beneath.

"Lindsay told Kade that to no longer bear age's burden, and to truly walk in life beside her, he would have to look into the mirror. The Captain asked what would happen, but Lindsay said she could not tell, for it would be for his eyes alone. So, Kade did just that and stood before the mirror, awaiting whatever it had to show him."

Royce was rubbing his chin intently, staring wide-eyed at me. "What happened, Pen?"

"Nothing, at first," I answered, edging my words with mystery. "Lindsay told Kade to wipe the dust from the glass, and then to grab ahold of the frame and stare deep into it. The man listened and did so, and he gasped when he saw his reflection.

"It was him, but he had grown old and frail! White hair sat atop his head, and wrinkles creased his aged face!

"But even more remarkable was what happened *next*, you see. His reflection started to grow younger. The wrinkles faded. His eyes regained their shine. His hair grew darker. His muscles began to reform. Slowly, like a strange moving illusion of a picture, the reflection of Kade in the mirror gained its youth back from the clutches of time!

"Kade watched, his eyes wide in wonder... but what happened then frightened the Mighty Captain. His reflection started to disappear, like a mist above a waterfall fading from view, or grains of sand spread thin through the air! Soon, he was no more! The mirror showed nothing!

"Frightened, Kade tried to turn to Lindsay, but he could not move! His hands felt as if they were fused with the mirror's frame. The man called Lindsay's name over his shoulder, louder and louder, but she didn't answer! Suddenly he felt fingers grip his shoulder... and Lindsay whispered just two words into his ear: 'I'm sorry.'

"The mirror's glass cracked, then split, and then shattered. Captain Kade reeled back in surprise and whirled around to face Lindsay behind him. He did not see the beautiful lass he'd loved for years and years. Instead, the body of a woman lay on the floor just five paces away, but she was very old. This poor soul... had been Lindsay.

"You see, Lindsay's soul had been trapped by this mirror. It had tricked her into giving up her soul for immortality, a life without aging. The Trickster Mirror had taken her reflection long, long before she ever met the Mighty Captain Kade. In exchange for this immortality, one was bound to the forest for all eternity, a prisoner to the Kovald for all time! Nobody ever knew how old Lindsay really was, but the beautiful lass couldn't bear to go on any longer... so, she tricked Captain Kade into taking her place.

"For you see, the only way for the curse to be broken was to bestow it upon another. Lindsay had meant all along to fool the Captain into doing so, but... love is a powerful thing. Lindsay grew to love Kade so deeply that she couldn't bring herself to allow Kade into her cottage to gaze into the mirror.

"But," I continued in a low voice, "perhaps she was finally driven mad by the countless years of being a prisoner in these woods. Perhaps, in a twisted way, Lindsay thought that she was doing Kade a favor by preserving his youth and strength. Maybe she couldn't stand to see him grow old, and the thought of the man dying was just too much!

"Either way, they say that the spirit of Captain Kade wanders these woods to this day, trying to find someone to take his place so that he may join Lindsay in the heavens. Some tales say that here, somewhere in the Kovald, the mirror awaits its next victim. And that, friends, is the story of Captain Kade, Lindsay, and The Trickster Mirror."

I realized I was sweating despite the cold night air, and my heart was pounding in my chest as I finished and the last of my words settled upon my listeners. The campground was completely silent, save for the fire as when I had begun. Only now, anyone's doubt in my storytelling capabilities, including my own, was gone. I could feel it.

Breathing fast, I swallowed hard and regained my composure. I hadn't realized I had been so involved in telling the story.

The faces around me, those of hardened killers and highwaymen, of thieves and my friends, were all in complete shock, it seemed. Some mouths were hanging open. Eyes were wide and flickering this way and that as it dawned on them that the story was actually over.

It was Alomar who finally broke the silence.

"Bloody *hell* mate. Well done!"

Royce shot to his feet, rushed to my side, grabbed my hand and thrust it upward. "Oy! All of you lot! Two cheers for Penny!"

A chorus of cheers thundered into the air from around the campfire, followed by another soon after. I grinned sheepishly, thoroughly embarrassed and exhilarated at the same time.

"Blazes, mate!" Royce bellowed. "You really are good with this story business. How in Fates' names were your stories ever turned down back in Northroe?"

Men were all around, talking excitedly as others put more wood on the fire. I was beaming with pride when I realized they were talking about the story I just told them.

"-in this very forest, yeah? Who knows? It could've happened!"

"-wonder if our Captain Hael would listen to that Lindsay lass-"

"-dunno, mate. In these woods, for eternity? Blast, that's a hard one...."

Alomar folded his arms. "Pen, looks like you've got more in you than you thought, eh?"

I gave a weird sort of chuckle, trying not to seem like I really believed what was going on around me.

Honestly, I had never really thought I was any good. My heart was absolutely swelling with joy. This was my dream! To tell stories, the kind that people remembered, the sort that people talked about long after hearing them!

It'd only been a few moments since I'd finished, but it was still grand. I was happier at that moment than I'd ever been in my life.

Lynn got to her feet and joined the three of us.

"Well, well," Lynn said with a smile. "That was really quite good."

I beamed uncontrollably.

"Fates," Royce said, "I can't believe Lindsay tricked the Captain like that!"

Lynn folded her arms. "She was just tired o' livin' forever! Nobody could wander these blasted woods for eternity. It'd drive ya mad! She had to!"

Royce shook his head. "No way. She was supposed to love him and all that. I can't believe she'd do that to him. To the man she loved!"

Alomar snorted. "I can."

A momentary pang of sadness seared my heart, and I remembered Corrine and the Northroe debacle with guilt.

Lynn raised her eyebrows. "Can ya, now? You really believe she'd-"

"Okay," Royce interjected quickly, "see, actually, we should talk about... oh, I dunno. Something else."

The sound of hands clapping suddenly reached my ears. The four of us along with the rest of the men around the fire turned to see Captain Hael.

"Penny, well done. A fine tale, indeed," the man proclaimed in his hoarse voice, and more applause echoed after his words.

I nodded. "Thanks, mate. Captain, rather. Sorry."

Captain Hael smiled, but let it fade quickly. "Now everyone, get some rest. Miles, Lynn, we need to speak. We have some plans in the works. The rest of you, dismissed!"

We all dispersed in different directions, the sounds of discussion and occasional laughter spouting off into the night. As Royce, Alomar and I strode toward our cabin, I ventured a look back at the bandit officers.

Captain Hael was shaking his head and speaking sternly to Lynn, who seemed to be arguing with him. They kept their voices low enough so that nobody could hear. The woman wore an almost pained expression and now opened her arms as if pleading for something. The Captain shook his head, saying something in a rough manner.

Lynn spat at the ground. Miles now stepped forward and seemed to be trying to calm her down, perhaps a repeat of what we had overheard in the Lodge our first day in the camp. Lynn shoved Miles away and threw a crude gesture at Captain Hael before storming off toward her quarters.

I stopped in my tracks and couldn't help but watch and study what was going on from a distance. Royce and Alomar didn't seem to notice and kept plodding on toward our cabin.

Narrowing my eyes in an attempt to see better in the dark of night, I saw Lynn disappear in the distance and then fixed my eyes on Captain Hael and

Miles. Both men were standing close, talking more in hushed voices. Miles shrugged and seemed to gesture in Lynn's direction, and the Captain shook his head, barking what sounded like a harsh order before turning on his heel to go back to the Lodge.

Miles was left standing alone in the moonlight. He stood still as a statue, arms folded and gazing at the dirt and pine needles at his feet. I watched the man give an exasperated sigh before he turned my way.

His eyes locked with mine.

Taken aback, I instantly flashed my gaze at my feet, like a guilty fool. I slowly looked back up and found the tough officer's eyes again.

He just stared at me for a few seconds before turning and strolling to his quarters, saying nothing. I followed suit and hurried after my friends.

What exactly was it that the Captain and his two lieutenants seemed to be in such disagreement over?

*   *   *

That night, as Royce and Alomar slept in their cot and hammock, I lay on my back with a smile on my face and replayed the campfire scene over and over in my head. I had never known such joy! I had never known an ounce of success as a writer! I kept picturing the entranced gazes as everyone took in my words.

Most unlikely of all, I had come up with the entire story on the spot. I made a note to write the story down as soon as I could.

Listening to the woodland sounds that entered our cabin from our lone window, I turned briefly to look at my friends in the limited moonlight. I had Royce and Alomar to thank for it all. I had been angry, but the two men pushed me to break out of my shell, as Royce had put it. Because of their ridiculous faith in me, I was able to hurdle over personal fears and anxieties that night and overcome a serious doubt in myself.

That experience changed my life and how I viewed myself forever, and I never forgot it. Nervous as I was about Hael's hinting at some sort of task for my friends and I the next day, I was still struck by joy's high. As sleep beckoned to me like so many times before, I gave in and slept better than I ever had in my life.

The next morning, my brief serenity was dashed to pieces.

CHAPTER 33

The morning sun rose in the west, and my friends and I awoke with the rest of the camp and groggily made our way to the fire circle, where we helped a few of the men heat up some porridge made from squash. I helped churn the last bit of butter that remained in the camp's supply, which added a savory touch to the hard bread that was served.

A couple hours after dawn, my friends and I sat with the twenty-or-so bandits in camp around the fire, eating heartily and listening to the men gripe about chores or speculate on future raids, among other things. Royce and Alomar sat to my right, and a strong, tattooed man with messy brown hair and a face of stubble named Sorley was to my left. Lynn sat with Miles and the Captain across from us, so that the smoke and heat from the fire made their forms shimmer and distort slightly in the air if I tried to look at them. I noticed that neither Arthur or Quaid were present, which seemed odd, but nobody paid it any mind. It was probably their turn for guard duty out in the woods.

Everyone's cups were full of water, and Lynn passively remarked to Ruben the Weaponsmith that it was his turn to take a couple men to the river today to fetch more for the camp.

"Ah, c'mon," Ruben replied with a mouthful of food. "Why not get one of these new lads to do it?"

Royce slurped soup from his spoon noisily.

Lynn glared. "Because the new lads have business o' their own to attend to."

"We do?" I asked.

Lynn nodded. "Aye. And Ruben, if you have any other suggestions for me, I'll be glad to hear 'em before I rearrange your face. Startin' to think your nose would look better broken, know what I mean?"

There were hoots of laughter all around the campfire, and I found myself suppressing a snicker. Ruben turned red in the face and was grinning, suddenly very intent on how he sloshed his soup about in the bowl with his spoon.

"Sorry, Lynn. Was just... never mind."

Lynn made a furious face and shook her fist at the man menacingly, which coaxed further bouts of laughter from the men all around us. Someone nudged my shoulder, and I turned to see Sorley leaning in to whisper to me.

"Know why it's funny, mate?" he asked me with a grin.

"Why?"

"Because she'd do it in a bloody heartbeat, she would. Easily."

I ventured a look in Lynn's direction. Miles had rolled up his sleeve and was curling his arm, flexing his large bicep and jabbing it obnoxiously in the woman's face. She was laughing loudly, trying to shove the man's muscular arm away.

"She'd do what?" I asked, momentarily forgetting the context of Sorley's words.

The man snorted and chewed loudly on his bread. "That woman could hold her own against any bloke here. She said she'd arrange his face, yeah? Well, she could."

A man with long black hair that matched his beard leaned forward so that I could see him past Sorley. "Aye. She's strong, and an amazing fighter. Probably actually a man, know what I mean?"

I froze in horror, accidentally allowing soup to seep out of my gawking mouth. "She's a what?"

The two men laughed loudly, and Sorley smacked me upside the head lightly.

"Hey!" I protested.

"Pen, c'mon," Royce said from my right. "Clearly, she's a woman. And not a man."

"That's right," echoed Sorley. "Not a man. Definitely a woman."

I resumed chewing, still wearing an apprehensive expression. "Is she or isn't she?"

A mischievous grin spread across Royce's face. "Why don't I ask her for you, mate?"

I stared at the man. "Like hell you will."

Alomar laughed loudly. "Know what Penny? If you'd like, I can talk to her for you. Then maybe-"

My friend's words were cut off when I heard the echo of a man's voice calling to us from somewhere out in the woods.

In an instant, the unsheathing of blades and other weapons sounded off all around me, and the entire fire circle was like a ring of brandished steel glinting off the morning sun. Everyone was suddenly battle-ready.

I hastily stood with them, still holding a slice of bread in my hand. Sheepishly, I took a bite and followed everyone's gazes, which were aimed behind me over my shoulder.

Quaid came running into view, looking tired and exhausted. He raised a hand in greeting, tried calling to us, but only a wheezy voice came out.

"Not good," Alomar muttered, looking at Royce and I.

Without a word, Miles was the first to break the hasty battle formation and dash to the man. Lynn was on his heels, and then others as well. My friends and I hurried behind them.

"Quaid!" bellowed Miles. "You okay, mate?"

Quaid practically collapsed on the ground and rolled onto his back. It was then that I saw the sinister dark stains of blood spattering the front of his earth-green gambeson. His bow was in hand, and I noticed a few arrows missing from his quiver. The man's face was flushed red and wet with sweat, and his chest was rising and falling in exhausted attempts to breathe.

"Oy!" Lynn hollered, "Gavin! Get the 'ell over here!"

"I'm here, Lynn," uttered a man swiftly as he came to us. I saw that Gavin was the black-haired, bearded man who had talked to me earlier with Sorley. The crowd of bandits formed a circle around Quaid. Gavin dropped to his knees next to the man, let a small pack fall to the ground and reached in, unfurling a wrap of various medicinal herbs, needles and sutures, and precise, scary-looking instruments that I realized were healing tools.

"No," Quaid gasped. He sat up.

"Lay down," Lynn ordered, lightly pushing him back to the ground. "Stay still, Quaid. Gavin will take care of ya."

Miles turned to us and pointed. "You. Go get the Captain. He's at the Lodge."

Without hesitation, Royce turned and sprinted for the northern side of camp.

"Sorley, Ernest. Scout south," ordered Miles. As the men obeyed hastily and hurried toward the direction Quaid had come from, Miles turned to Quaid. "Were you followed, mate?"

Quaid was breathing hard, still trying to catch his breath. "Aye. Think I lost 'em."

"Who did this?" Lynn asked.

"Where's your horse?" came Ruben's voice.

"Dead."

Four or five men took it upon themselves to start fanning out around us, taking up positions behind trees and watching in every direction for any hostile approach.

Gavin reached for some herbal substance I couldn't name when Quaid's hand shot out and stopped him. Before anyone could protest, Quaid sat up.

Lynn reached for the man again. "Dammit, I said don't move!"

Quaid batted her hand away. "Oy! I'm not hurt!" he hissed. "Been trying to tell you, it's not my blood!"

Uneasy glances were exchanged all around. Before any further suspense was built up, Miles knelt down.

"Whose is it?" he murmured quietly.

Oddly, Lynn answered. "Arthur?"

Quaid breathed heavily still. I saw the man clench his jaw before spitting at the ground. He nodded. "Aye. He's dead. The Watch got him."

CHAPTER 34

Surprised, I watched as Quaid's eyes darted to Lynn's for a moment after mentioning the Watch, looking apologetic. Lynn cringed momentarily and bit her lip. Before I could wonder what that was all about, Miles butted in.

"The Watch? What? Why would they venture so far from Northroe? Are they coming here, Quaid?"

The rapid chorus of boots on the forest floor reached us, and we turned to see Captain Hael trailing just behind Royce. Royce slid to a stop next to me. Captain Hael slowed his pace at the sight of what must have looked like a wounded Quaid.

"What the devil happened?" asked the Captain.

Quaid didn't answer.

I saw Lynn stand slowly. Her features were... strange. I hadn't seen the woman look like she was looking now, and then it hit me: Lynn was worried. Almost scared. She backed away slowly into our ranks and stood between Alomar and I. She was still biting her lip.

Now I was even more on edge.

The Captain knelt next to the man. "Quaid, where were you? Who did this?"

I watched as a nervous air fell around all of us. Quaid shot Lynn a regretful look before answering. "I was... we were on patrol. At the, uh... the forest's edge."

Hael didn't take his steely gaze off the man. "We?"

"Arthur and I."

"Where is he?"

"He's dead, Cap'n. This is his. His blood, I mean. I'm not hurt."

A visible current of anger circulated around the crowd of outlaws as they looked on.

"You're okay then. Good," Hael nodded. He patted the man's shoulder. "Who did this?"

Quaid looked again to Lynn, almost as if seeking permission to answer. Lynn only folded her arms and cast her eyes to the ground.

"City Watch. Northroe."

"They were all the way out here, at the edge of the Kovald?" pressed Captain Hael, without pause.

Quaid didn't answer.

"Why were you patrolling so far from camp?"

Again, silence. Quaid cast one more sorrowful glance at Lynn before turning to Captain Hael. "I... we, uh-"

"I sent 'em," Lynn interrupted. Her features were composed again. She changed her demeanor so quickly that it put me off for a moment. "They weren't patrollin' at the edge of the woods, Cap'n. I told them to go all the way to Northroe. Sent 'em to scout the city."

Captain Hael's steely appearance was suddenly flushed with anger. "You what?"

Lynn was visibly nervous. "I sent 'em to scout the Northroe prison," she answered before faltering. She looked at Quaid, then back at the Captain. "Because you weren't willing to."

The crowd shifted skittishly around me. I saw some men back up. Lynn stood her ground.

"You fool," rumbled the Captain.

Lynn's voice shook with a barely discernible fear as she replied. "You were unwilling to do what shoulda been done! You-"

"Shut it!" the Captain roared. He was suddenly toe-to-toe with the woman, looking down at her. She didn't meet his stare. "You bloody fool. I wouldn't send any of our men to that cursed city because of this. *This*. Look at the man before you. Think of the man that didn't make it back!"

"Tambor's locked in there and you're gonna just let him rot!" thundered Lynn angrily. "I can't leave him behind and-"

"Silence!" thundered Captain Hael. "Tambor wouldn't want anyone killed on his account! You sent two men into the cave of the bear, and one of them died for your stupidity!"

Royce nudged Alomar. "Who's Tambor?" he whispered. Alomar shrugged, gesturing for Royce to hush.

Both Captain Hael and Lieutenant Lynn were seething with rage, standing toe-to-toe. Their chests were rising and falling quickly. I saw Lynn's hand shaking. Suddenly I felt a hand lightly grab my shoulder, and I turned – it was Alomar. He wordlessly beckoned to me to step backward into the ranks with everyone else, and I realized myself and Miles were the only ones that hadn't done so. I hastily complied.

"By the Fates, Lynn," the Captain said, shaking his head. "You're smarter than this. I should kill you right here for being such a bloody imbecile."

Before anyone could take in the words fully, the Captain brandished his scimitar with a wicked metallic ringing and flash of sunlight. I jumped with fright, as did some others around me. His blade's edge was at Lynn's neck. She flinched, but did her best to stand tall. I saw Miles step forward, eyes wide, and then force himself to stop.

"This is mutiny, woman," he said softly. "And after everything we've been through? After what I've given you?"

"I'm sorry," Lynn uttered hoarsely. Her face was truly sorrowful. "I can't leave a man behind. It's not in me. Tambor's alive, right now, rotting in that cell. I... can't live with that, Cap'n. Do what ya must."

My breath caught in my throat. No one moved a muscle for a long, silent moment. It was Miles that first spoke.

It was Miles who finally spoke. "Captain, perhaps we should wait, yeah? Just step back, and think about all this."

"Not now, Miles," answered Hael coldly.

"It's Tambor we're talkin' about here," Miles pressed gingerly. "Let's just take some time to-"

Lynn suddenly turned her gaze down to her feet at Quaid, who was still sitting upright, afraid to move. "I'm sorry, Quaid."

Quaid gave a slight nod.

Captain Hael still had his blade leveled at the woman's neck. He suddenly breathed in deeply, as if he was greedy for air, and let it out slowly before lowering his sword.

"You put me in a bad spot here, woman. We all know the punishment for mutinous behavior is death. That's never been negotiable."

We all looked on nervously with bated breath.

"If I don't spill your blood now, all that will tell these men is that I've gone soft. That I'm not willing to punish those who need to be. That orders can be disobeyed, that rules can be broken," he snarled. "How dare you do this to me, Lynn! After all the years in this company, you would make such a brash decision that ends with a man dead and me at odds with myself over whether to take your life."

I was scratching my chin in anxiety, watching the scene unfold. It struck me that Captain Hael seemed very proper, even articulate in the way he spoke compared to the company he commanded. Lynn said nothing, looking like any fight had left her.

"You may wonder why I say this all aloud," Captain Hael said loudly, gesturing to all of us. "Can you think of a leader that would let these thoughts be heard by his men? It is because I have nothing to hide. I play no foolish games, like the one Lynn has played today."

I could see that his words cut her, and Lynn stared at her boots still, looking sadly powerless and pitiful.

Captain Hael looked around at us all, then to Lynn. "Weapons on the ground, now."

Slowly, painfully, Lynn drew her short sword and let it clatter to the dirt, and her dagger followed.

"All of it. Belt."

The woman sullenly unraveled the gear belt she wore and placed it on the ground.

Captain Hael breathed in deeply before issuing one last order. "Your colors. Off."

Lynn's eyes widened. "But-"

"*Off.* You're lucky you're not dead at my feet."

Before I had much time to wonder what he was referring to, Lynn sorrowfully unfastened the green insignia band around her shoulder and let it fall to the earth.

"Miles, take her to the Pit while I figure out how to handle this," Hael ordered.

I nudged Royce. "The Pit?"

"Sounds bad, mate."

The Captain turned to Quaid. "You're all right then, Quaid?"

The brigand only nodded, and couldn't seem to look his Captain in the eyes.

"Then up with you. Losing Art is punishment enough. Perhaps you'll think before obeying such an order ever again. And on that note," Captain Hael said loudly, "there will be no such orders ever again. All plans are agreed upon before they're bloody carried out. No secrets from your Captain, dammit. Do you lot understand?"

"Aye, Captain," echoed a chorus of replies.

Hael looked around. "Who are we missing? Not everyone's here."

Miles answered. "I sent Sorley and Ernest to scout back in the direction Quaid came from, Captain. Make sure he wasn't followed."

Captain Hael nodded. "Good. If all's well after the scouts report back, everyone go about your duties. Double the perimeter guard, just in case. We must stay especially alert, understand? We'll deal with all of this in time, men. Now go."

CHAPTER 35

The scout party returned after two hours, having found nothing. The entire bandit company was drowned in a numbed, depressed state throughout the day, seemingly paralyzed by Arthur's death at the hands of the Northroe City Watch and the Captain's anger toward Lynn. People talked and speculated all day.

Was Lynn really so big-hearted as to not leave any man behind, or was this Tambor special to her in some way? Would the Captain be forced to kill her to make an example to the rest of his company? Just who was Tambor, anyhow? Why was he in jail?

"Fates," Alomar mumbled, picking a splinter out of his finger gently. "Talk about tension, aye? Reminds me of the war."

He had just finished chopping wood with some other men. Royce and I had helped Ruben and Gavin to feed the horses at the stable and gather water from the nearby stream. The noon sun shone down on the Kovald Forest, and birds chirped noisily with the breeze coasting through the leaves.

We sat around the campfire circle, which had become a favorite hangout of ours. No fire burned, as it seemed warmer today than usual. I watched one of the stone seats to my left in silence. It was where Arthur had always sat.

Just like that. Joking with him one night, telling the man and his companions a story around the fire, and I woke up the next morning and he was gone. No more Arthur.

"Blast," Royce said, shaking his head. "He was just here with us. Just yesterday."

Alomar's eyes were distant. I let my friend's words sink in.

"I mean, he was a nice man for being a bloody outlaw, yeah?" Royce continued. "And now he's-"

"Gone," Alomar finished. His gaze seemed far away. "That's how it is, mates. That's how it was in Dekka. You live, laugh with the men. Then, one day... they're gone. You're left with that empty spot at the fire, empty chair at the table. An empty bunk in the barracks."

I swallowed hard, watching Alomar as he spoke.

"Then you start forgetting things," he continued in a whisper. "Their voice, their jokes. The little things that made them who they were."

Royce was wringing his hands. I sensed that he was now thinking of his dead brother. I bit my lip ruefully, wondering if Alomar realized his encroachment on the sensitive subject.

"You forget their faces," Alomar murmured. "They become lost, distant, and you're left with only memories. And you-"

"Enough," Royce growled. "We get it."

Alomar seemed jarred from his trance. He opened his mouth apologetically to speak, but said nothing.

"I wonder who Tambor is?" I mused aloud, trying to change the subject. "Wonder if he was worth... well. Arthur's life."

"Oy, Pen," Alomar said lowly, "don't start thinking like that. Will only drive you mad, yeah?"

I shrugged. "Can't help it, mate. Lynn clearly took an enormous risk to look into rescuing him.

"What kind of name is that, anyway?" Royce said with a snort. "Tamm-berr."

Alomar rubbed his chin in thought. "You think she was gonna plan an all-out rescue attempt?"

"Why else would she have it scouted, eh?" I asked.

"I understand," Alomar replied, "but I'm having trouble seeing why she would risk so much over the man. Clearly she has a deep connection with the company here, and she took a chance with all of it."

Royce stretched noisily. "Maybe.. .just maybe, Tambor's her man."

I shot him a look in protest, failing to hide it.

"With a name like that?" I huffed, mimicking Royce. "Tamm-*berr?*"

With a snort, Royce shot me a look. "Isn't Penny a woman's name?"

"Shut up."

"Maybe she and that bloke are lovers, yeah? Why else would she-"

"Impossible," I cut in.

"Eh? How's that?"

I cringed, embarrassed. "I... don't know."

Royce snickered, but rather than push it, he returned to silent thought.

Alomar had fallen back into his trance. I watched him as his eyes stared through the fire circle and pierced into his past, and not unlike other times gone by, I wondered what he was seeing. Wondered what memories of a land and war far away were playing themselves before him.

Royce saw it too, and glanced at me, but kept quiet.

Looking past Royce, I saw Gavin and a few other men whose names I did not know all huddled in a crooked circle of sorts, throwing pebbles at the dirt in front of them and cheering or moaning in dismay after each man's throw. I didn't know what game they were playing, but I shook my head in disbelief.

I frowned. "They act as if nothing happened."

Alomar shook his head. "They know perfectly well what bloody happened. But you can't let it get to you."

Puzzled, I looked at Alomar with my eyebrows raised. "Are you joking? How can you just pretend-"

"They're not pretending anything," Alomar snarled suddenly. "You just deal with it. Our lives can't stop because another man's did."

I was shocked at the man's outburst and didn't know what to do except look at Royce, who was watching me intently with a slight shake of his head.

A few moments went by and Alomar suddenly sighed heavily and shook his head. "I'm sorry, mates. This is just so damned familiar. Just knowing that any day could be your last, yeah? Wake up in the morning, a friend's dead. Pass the time, carry out your duties and try to put it out of your mind. I thought I had left this behind me, see? I didn't mean to be an arse, Penny."

I just nodded. "It's fine, Al. I didn't understand."

Royce's arms were folded, and he looked at us both. "Wonder what the Pit is. Or where it is, at that."

"Sounds like a prison cell of some sort, where they'd hold a bloke captive," I answered.

"Obviously, Pen."

I huffed defensively, ignoring Alomar's laughter. "You asked what it was, I told you."

"Well I was wondering more, what's the Pit like," replied Royce. "Why not call it a cell, or dungeon, or something? Wonder if it's an actual pit? Below ground and all that."

I shrugged. Lynn had been on my mind all day. I had tried to be careful to not let it show to anyone or mention her at all, but I wondered what had become of her. Wondered if the Captain had decided to just end it and run her through with a blade. Wondered how it worked, and if there was a set time that she'd stay confined. If they fed her at all. I had a hard time picturing her in such a pitiful state, as she had been so strong and confident.

Royce sighed. "What do we do now?"

"Eh?" I asked.

"I think he's asking if this is what we had in mind when we set out," Alomar replied.

Chuckling, I replied. "Of course we weren't planning to join up with bandits. We already talked about that."

"Well," Royce said, "we didn't really have a choice when we left Northroe. We kind of had to, given the circumstances. I have to admit, I was a bit excited at all this bandit business, and we haven't even got to rob a caravan yet, but I'm thinking this is a little dangerous."

I rolled my eyes. "You're still wanting to rob a caravan? After what we've seen?"

"Well, aye, I mean... not as much as before, but sure."

I laughed. "You oaf."

"One thing's clear, mates," Alomar said with resolve. "We have to get out of here. Leave the Kovald and Captain Hael's bandits behind us, and strike out further into the country. This isn't the adventure we had in mind."

Footsteps getting closer to the fire circle suddenly grabbed our attention, and our words and thoughts on the topic were dissolved instantly by Miles as he strode up to us.

"How are you three faring?" Miles asked us, stroking his blonde beard.

"We're good," I answered quickly. "Royce and I fetched the water with Ruben and Gavin earlier. Horses are fed."

"Got extra bundles of logs chopped and sorted," Alomar chimed in.

Miles folded his arms. "Good. Now, ready for your first real job?"

We all looked at each other before Royce spoke.

"Ya know, Miles mate, I was actually hoping to get a much-needed nap in. You know, rest and whatnot. Good for the body and all that."

The bandit officer shook his head. "There will be time for rest later. Get up, and get your gear. Ruben has it waitin' for you outside the arms shed. You'll be joining me, Quaid, Sorley, Ernest and Gavin on the run. We'll be heading to the village of Mable nearby, south of us."

"Quaid?" asked Alomar. "Is he doing okay?"

Miles just nodded. "To put it bluntly, he's the best shot with a bow we have, and we'll need him just in case."

"Mable?" I asked nervously. "What are we doing there?"

Miles grinned. "You'll see."

CHAPTER 36

It all happened very quickly. We reached the armory shed and found that our gear consisted of water flasks and canteens, a quiver of arrows, a small medical kit and other odds and ends. Royce, Alomar and I weren't given weapons, which I was fine with because I wouldn't know how to use one, anyway. This didn't sit well with Royce and Alomar, but we weren't given a choice.

Captain Hael met up with us and briefed us on our assignment. We were 'making a play' as he called it, on the village of Mable in an effort to blackmail a steady stream of coin and anything else the company could get its hands on from the villagers. Apparently the poor inhabitants there had been victims to Tyrius Sewell's small little reign, providing weekly income to him and his men, along with other things that Captain Hael didn't get specific about.

The Captain told us that normally a larger party would be sent on a mission like this one, but in case the Watch was out and about, he chose a smaller party to minimize risks of being sighted. We 'newcomers' were to watch and learn as the seasoned outlaws carried out their orders, as well as provide a supporting role, as Captain Hael called it, for the others. I carried a quiver of extra arrows for Quaid, for example.

I wasn't sure exactly how things were supposed to play out once we got there, but we didn't get any time to muse about it. We left camp abruptly and set out south through the woods, gradually drifting east as we did to avoid open plains and the main road through the countryside. The gigantic mass of the Kovald Forest speared southward along the eastern coast, reaching the rocky beaches of the Adgridd Sea.

We stayed in the haven the woods provided and made our way to the village of Mable.

* * *

A few hours passed as we trudged on through the woods, carefully watching the tree line west of us for any signs of Watchmen, or worse, Eislian soldiers on patrol in the country.

There were eight of us altogether – Miles, Quaid, Sorley, Gavin, Ernest, Royce, Alomar and myself. That day, I learned what a 'column' was: a formation of traveling in which everyone walked in a line, with about fifteen or so paces between each of us. It was new to Royce and I, but basic to the others. We hiked in this manner for hours, with Miles in the lead, or 'on point' as he called it.

Royce, Alomar and I were in the middle of the column, followed by Quaid and Ernest. Gavin and Sorley were ahead of us, behind Miles.

In front of me, Royce slowed his pace suddenly and fell back to me walk beside me.

"If there weren't so bloody many of them, we could make a break for it now, yeah?" he said lowly.

"Aye," I answered, uneasy that he was breaking formation to talk to me.

He slid the pack he was carrying off his right shoulder and lugged it over his left. "These packs are bloody heavy."

"What do you think we should do when we get there?" I asked, stepping over a fallen log. "What do you think is going to happen? What if they hurt these people? Women or children, even? What do we do?"

"I was thinking about that, Pen," Royce replied. "And honestly, I dunno. Last thing I'd do is join them in doing so."

"But what if they make us?"

My friend clapped my shoulder. "Do better not to worry about it now, mate."

"*Pssst,*" came a hiss from behind us. We whirled to see the man named Ernest. He wasn't angry, but motioned to stay alert. Behind him, Quaid turned carefully around in mid-stride, walking slowly backward as he cast a long stare out at the woods behind us.

"Aye," answered Royce. He turned to me. "Just stay with me and Alomar, Penny. We have to stick together. All we can do, yeah?" With that, he jogged ahead to resume his place in the column behind Alomar.

Another half-hour or so passed, and the sound of running water from somewhere in the distance reached my ears. Miles knelt down and raised a closed fist. As he did so, everyone stopped in their tracks and crouched to one knee. I saw Alomar up ahead, craning his neck this way and that, watching the trees and foliage around us. I wondered what this was like for him, and how much of the war it brought back. He turned back toward Royce and I, and when he found my gaze, he just grinned and winked before turning back to survey our surroundings.

Perhaps this was just another patrol for Alomar, like so many he'd taken part in overseas.

Miles disappeared into the trees up ahead while the rest of us waited. I failed to stifle a yawn and did so loudly, feeling like I was being a fool in front of the others. Shifting my weight to my other knee, I purposefully glanced around this way and that to show that I was doing my part. I felt awkward, like I didn't belong in the midst of armed men.

A few long minutes passed, and with Miles gone during that duration, I felt uneasy. I kept trying to picture what would happen. I had never even been to another settlement or city outside of Northroe in my life. Now, I was imposing on a small village somewhere up ahead and about to take part in threatening their peace and wellbeing for our company's gain.

I was suddenly very nervous. Those butterflies that batted away all mirages of courage within me were fluttering about inside again like so many times before. My stomach was tight with fear. I tried picturing standing on some dusty road, or in tall grass, with little houses to my left and right and their people out on the road as we confronted them.

Would there be armed men? Women? Children? What would I do if one of Hael's men struck one of them, or cut down a child in the middle of the road to prove a point? What would I do if a farmer charged me with a pitchfork, or his bare hands? I couldn't fight.

I started to panic. I couldn't stop it, and I got nauseous. I kept picturing some faceless man in poor, tattered clothing thrusting a pitchfork violently at me. Would I dodge it? Try to leap backward? Jump left? Leap to the right? No matter what action I picked in my mind, the point always seared into me, catching my body violently. I pictured the warmth of my blood flowing over my skin as I hit the dirt and choked on dust.

It was then that I wretched noisily. It was embarrassing, but I couldn't help it.

Sorley turned to look at me in surprise. Royce and Alomar stared with their mouths wide open. Behind me, Quaid and Ernest jogged to my side.

"Ho, now! You all right, Penny?" asked Quaid.

Ernest clapped a hand to my back awkwardly. "Nervous?"

I wiped my mouth. "Aye. A bit."

"Relax," Quaid said with a grin. "We'll be fine. These villagers don't even have proper weapons. Probably won't even be a fight."

"I... can't... fight," I said through gasps of air.

"You won't have to," Ernest answered me. "You're just here to look on. We could gut every one of them and they couldn't do anything about it."

I wretched again. That was another thing I was afraid of. I couldn't have that on my conscience. I couldn't witness something like that... but I couldn't look weak in front of these men. I managed to get to my feet, shaking off the nausea.

Sorley watched me carefully. "How you managed to escape the Northroe City Watch is beyond me."

Quaid and Ernest both laughed, but their laughter was cut short as Miles came walking briskly back into view from the dense trees and foliage ahead.

"Everyone form up here," he called, motioning for us to join him.

The only sounds that could be heard were gear of various sorts clattering about and thumping against us as we hastily made our way to Miles, forming a tight huddle.

"All right. The small bridge is just ahead, just a few hundred paces beyond those trees," Miles said, motioning south. "The tree line thins just before it, so we'll be in plain view crossing it. Unfortunately there's not another river crossing for an hour in each direction, and we're losing sunlight."

"Miles," came Sorley's voice, "why don't we wait 'til nightfall, yeah? Catch 'em by surprise?"

Miles shook his head. "We need to make a lasting first impression, men. Showing up in broad daylight shows that we're not afraid of 'em. That if they don't comply with our demands, we'll do what we must. Without hesitation."

"So if they don't comply...." Gavin trailed off.

Miles shrugged, casting a glance at Royce, Alomar and I. "We'll do what we must."

The brigands in the party nodded, but my friends and I looked at each other. This was definitely not something we were wanting to be a part of.

"Newcomers, you three stay back about ten paces from our front line," Miles ordered. "Quaid, stay at our backs, twenty paces behind them. Provide overwatch. If things get ugly, do not hesitate to show we mean business. Try not to harm their women or children, but if worse comes to worst, do it."

I spoke before thinking. "Miles, I don't understand. What exactly are we here for?"

The Lieutenant and the other men looked at me, confused.

"I mean, uh... what are we um, threatening innocents for?" I winced. Probably not the best choice of words I could have used.

Miles squared himself directly at me. "Understand one thing, Penny. Survival is all our company has going for it. We're outlaws. We have no rights. So we make our own. Where do you think the clothing, the supplies, the shelters you've slept in back at camp come from?"

I gulped. "Money."

"Aye. And where do you think money comes from?"

I paused before answering. "Other people."

"Opportunity," Miles corrected. "Other people are opportunities. Otherwise we would not be alive. We'd be dead or locked up in some forsaken place, like Tambor."

"Aye," chimed in Sorley. "It's us for ourselves, mates. Don't you newcomers forget it, yeah?"

Miles gripped the blade at his waist passively. "And don't make the mistake that we're the only band of outlaws around, either. We do what we must, and so do they, and they'd be glad to chop us to pieces in an instant. We are opportunities to others as well, friends. Don't forget that."

I'd never considered there might be other companies of brigands wandering about. I wondered if that was stupid of me.

"Now, let's go. Everyone ready yourselves. Do not back down from them. Fear is our weapon, aye?"

"Aye!" came a hushed chorus.

"Let's get it done. Follow me."

I didn't even have a chance to discuss what was about to happen with my friends. I had little time to speculate anymore about what lay ahead, and as we crept through the trees, my thoughts were overcome with just trying to stay with the party. My stomach churned with dread, but I snuck on, grasping the strap slung over my chest that held the quiver of arrows on my back.

The tree line, the southernmost outskirts of the mighty Kovald Forest, loomed ahead, and I could see an old dirt road across the river coming from somewhere out west before curving south to the bridge. The roar of the current from the river ahead grew louder. I could see the simple, poor homes and cottages of Mable in the distance.

Miles unsheathed his blade. The other brigands around me did the same.

That's when Alomar suddenly threw himself in Miles's way.

CHAPTER 37

I stopped in my tracks.. Alomar's move was so sudden and he covered so much ground so quickly that I was taken aback. He must have had the same effect on the others, because everyone else halted immediately as well. Miles was more confused than angry or hostile. He looked bewildered as Alomar slid to a stop in front of him and pressed a palm gently to the man's chest.

"Wait," Alomar said hurriedly. "Let's... talk. Let's think this over."

"Al!" Royce hissed, motioning for him to step back. But Alomar didn't budge.

Miles's eyes were frosty. He stood toe-to-toe with the large man before him. I wasn't used to seeing anyone fail to be intimidated by Alomar, but then I remembered that Miles, among other men in my presence, had served in Dekka as Alomar once had. They were equally trained and just as battle-hardened as my friend.

This made me even more nervous.

"The hell you doing?" Miles growled lowly.

Alomar held his arms out to his sides in a peaceful offering and took a step backward. "Just hold on. There has to be another way of doing this, aye?"

No one moved. I felt the confusion begin to wear off on the men around me, and I glanced at Royce when I sensed anger replacing it.

Gavin steadied his large axe outward menacingly and took a step forward.

"No, mate!" Alomar said swiftly, flashing that brilliant grin of his. "No need for that. I'm just suggesting a different, um, a different... way, of...."

It was when Alomar looked over at me with a pleading expression that I smiled broadly. I understood immediately. Alomar was not okay with possibly slaughtering innocent people. It contradicted everything he'd stood for as a soldier, after all.

"H-he's right, mates. Aye," Royce forced, stepping forward and nudging me slightly as he did. "Much better ways, of uh, accomplishing the...."

"Task," I finished for Royce. "The task at hand. We can do better, actually."

Royce leaned quickly toward me and whispered. "I've got nothing, Pen."

"What was that?" Miles barked.

I nudged Royce and walked at a deliberately slow pace to the front of the party to join Alomar's side, talking as I did.

"He was saying we should tell you our version of... of a plan. For today's mission."

"Aye," Royce stammered. "For the people in Mable."

It sure was difficult to make up a story on the spot. Then again, I had just done so the other night, hadn't I?

Ernest and Sorley moved closer, joining Miles' side along with Gavin. I noticed Quaid was just staring at us from behind them, his forehead furrowed in question.

"This is rubbish," Ernest declared. "What are you gettin' at?"

Sorley chimed in. "If this is a joke, it ain't funny. You're pushin' it."

Miles had always looked mean, but now he looked fierce. I suddenly saw him as the battle-hardened soldier he had once been rather than a bandit officer. He ran a palm across his shaved head as he spoke.

"Spit it out already. You have a plan? Tell us. Otherwise, we need to move, and there will be no more stops. This isn't the blasted time or place, so bloody get on with it. What is it?"

Royce opened his mouth but said nothing. Alomar leered close to me, keeping his eyes fixed on Miles, and spoke softly.

"That Storyteller in you would be absolutely splendid right now, Pen."

Royce snickered. "Not the one 'in-Training' either, mate. We need a good one."

I elbowed Royce in the stomach, causing him to double over. Miles stepped forward menacingly.

"Wait!" I nearly shouted. "Wait. Here it is, mates, and I'm sure Hael would-"

"Captain," snarled Miles, lowering his blade slowly.

"Captain, aye. 'Twas what I meant. I'm sure Captain Hael would approve of this. Better in the long run, really," I stammered.

Fates, was I frightened. I was very aware that we could be killed over this, and that protecting innocents didn't quite mesh with the tavern-burning, Watchman-evading identities that we'd made for ourselves at the camp. Innocent people just minutes away from us could die very easily if I failed to be convincing. I had to come up with something, fast. Being a former Eislian soldier, Alomar was the only chance we had in any fight with these men, and I knew he couldn't protect Royce and I.

And then it hit me. Soldiers. These men had been soldiers, too. I could use that.

"Okay, mates. Think about this for a second, yeah?" I said, taking a step forward. "You all, at least many of you, were once soldiers in this great nation's army. Eislian braves. The world knows that Eislian warriors are unmatched the world over, and you were all once a part of that!"

Nobody spoke. I saw Sorley flexing his grasp around his spear. Gavin shifted uncomfortably.

I spoke in a very calculated manner. Looking back, I'm not sure how I was able to muster it out of nowhere, but it must have been the Storyteller in me. I talked to them as a general would while congratulating his troops. My words were rhythmic and flattering, but most of all honest. I wasn't lying to these men.

"You see," I continued, "the people of this very village once depended on you." I pointed at Miles, lowered my voice. "And you," I said to Quaid.

"This a plan or a speech?" asked Ernest.

"Listen to me!" I ordered, shocking myself.

Everyone's eyes widened in surprise at my sudden assertiveness. But Ernest did stop. He did listen.

I pointed behind me, toward the bridge and to the village of Mable. "Those people once trusted you to defend them and our great land! And this is how their trust is repaid? You would take from them? Slay them in the road if necessary? Do you forget the ebon armor you once wore, black as night? The crowds waiting for you when you returned from Dekka?"

Silence settled in over them. I saw Miles' gaze suddenly flicker downward and off to the side.

"And you would return and slaughter innocents?" I pressed.

"We don't have a choice," Quaid said, stepping forward. "Dammit Penny, this is how it is. We will if we have to. We'll bloody starve otherwise."

Gavin lifted his axe and rested it over his shoulder menacingly. "You don't sound like one of us right now, mate. You're not thinking straight."

I backtracked, took in Gavin's words, and used them all in the blink of an eye.

"Thinking differently," I answered quickly. "Think about this: we do what we have to do, aye? What we'd usually do. Cut a man's throat. Drag some poor women off to a slave wagon. Then what do you have?"

Glances were exchanged, and no one answered.

"You have a village that bloody hates you," I declared. "And then-"

Sorley strode toward me suddenly, gripping his spear. "Enough of this."

Miles shot a hand out to stop Sorley's advance just as Alomar stepped in front of me with a throaty growl coming from behind clenched teeth. Royce was at my other side.

"You have a village that hates you," I repeated louder, genuinely angry at Sorley's advance. "You may have weapons and fear over their hearts, but they will be desperate to find a way to thwart you. The first thing they'll do is call the Watch, or worse, you'll provoke a sweep of these woods by an entire bloody division of Eislian troops."

"We'll take hostages," Gavin said, his tone now reasoning rather than hostile. "We hold some of their loved ones and tell them we'll kill 'em if they go to the authorities. They wouldn't dare."

I shook my head, patting the shoulders of my two friends slightly. They stepped back to their original positions, and rather reluctantly at that.

"You might win on that count, aye... but what's better than a village that hates you?"

Miles folded his arms. "Tell us."

I crossed my own arms and mustered a confident grin. "A village that bloody loves you, and the Captain, for something you could provide, rather than hate you for the things you would destroy and take."

"What... would that be?" asked Sorley, truly curious. Everyone was a bit more eased, more relaxed. The plain-cut standoff of two lines of men now gradually melted into a small circle as I outlined my plan.

"How much coin were you hoping to squeeze out of that lot up ahead?" I asked with a grin.

*   *   *

It was unorthodox. Definitely unexpected. Dare I say, impressive. By the time I was done explaining my idea, everyone including Royce and Alomar were nodding enthusiastically, even Miles.

"This could actually work," Miles said, rubbing his palm over his bald head again. "What do you blokes think, then? Should we try it?"

"Aye," said Gavin.

"Agreed," replied Ernest.

Quaid nodded with a smile.

Sorley extended his hand to me, surprising me for a moment. I hoped I didn't let it show.

"Let's do it," Sorley said, grinning. "Sorry for earlier, mate. Just was an awfully strange time to put a stopper in our plan, eh? You understand."

I met his eyes with my own and gripped his hand heartily, grinning in response. "Aye, just business. No worries."

We all stood and turned to face the village of Mable, just a few minutes' stroll from where we stood. The afternoon sun was barely starting to fall, and the slight pink glow of sunset in the East was barely visible a world away.

"Okay then," I said. "Remember, keep all your weapons sheathed and shouldered, eh? Brandish one or start twirling a sword around like a damned daisy and they'll run for the hills."

Gavin raised his hand. "Wait. Even if this works, won't the Cap'n be upset with ya, Miles? With us?"

Miles shook his head. "If this works, Captain Hael can't be upset with us. There's no bloody way that could happen. We're changing his orders around a bit, but it's still the same outcome, just even better. Besides, if it doesn't work, we'll just do what we were gonna do in the first place."

I swallowed hard and then turned to Royce and Alomar. "You two ready for this?" I asked in a ridiculously low voice, mimicking a man with no fear.

They both laughed.

"Pen," Alomar said with a grin, "how the 'ell did you end up taking an inn accountant's job when you could have been running with bandits the entire time?"

Royce nodded. "Aye. Indeed. You could be a bloody strategist for the High General."

I snorted. "Strategist my arse. I don't even know if this will work."

The two men paused at my sudden confession, looked at each other, and chuckled loudly.

"On that note," Royce said cheerily, "off we go."

CHAPTER 38

Just minutes later found the eight of us strolling into the village of Mable on the simple dirt path leading to it. The thick spruce and pine trees of the Kovald thinned noticeably as we neared. Royce, Alomar and I tried our best to look non-threatening, since Miles and the others behind us didn't exactly project warmth and peace in their years-practiced outlaw swagger.

Mable was a simple settlement. The dirty path after the bridge ran through the heart of the village from the north, exiting south and curving west and off into the Eislian countryside. I confess that I had not the slightest idea of where it led, thanks to my extremely sheltered existence in Northroe for the majority of my life.

Small cottages and humble houses lined both sides of the path. Some had straw roofs and rickety wooden walls. Others had strong masonry at their foundations and simple, yet cozy porches. A few homes had wooden double doors just paces away outside of them, leading to underground cellars or storage rooms.

The trees in Mable were pines, sparse and scattered. The shelters it was comprised of provided the only shade in the village. Despite its obvious poverty, Mable had a warm, inviting charm to it. It was peaceful, and the singing birds on the rooftops seemed to agree.

The people, however, saw us and immediately took action.

I was surprised at how my thoughts were able to drift away from any uncertainty or fear. The first to see us were two boys walking toward the bridge with fishing rods resting against their shoulders. I had a fleeting recollection of the boys who had terrorized me with fishing hooks just days ago over a similar bridge to the northwest near the outskirts of the Kovald, making me cringe. This made me think of Arthur, since it had been he and Quaid who had ordered us to retrieve the body from under that bridge.

I thought of how Arthur's face had lit up later on when we had been shown to our quarters back at camp, and it was found that he and Alomar had fought the same battle in Dekka on two different fronts. I thought about the brief conversation Arthur, Quaid and I had around the fire, about our pasts. I recalled how Arthur had chosen very swiftly to not reveal anything about his. I had figured the man would eventually tell me as time passed.

But now Arthur was dead, and I didn't even know how he had met his end. I'd never know his story, his past, what he had been so reluctant to share with me.

I wondered if Quaid knew. Perhaps he would tell me someday.

Then I wondered if that chance would ever come, since Royce, Alomar and I clearly wanted to leave Captain Hael's rugged band behind us somehow.

When the boys up ahead dropped their fishing rods behind them and sped down the path toward their village and began yelling warning of our presence, I was jerked from the waters of thought and back onto the land of the present.

What a strange, even inopportune, time to have such thoughts. I wondered if it was normal for a man to have thoughts like those during times like these. A battle? A struggle of some kind? The moments leading to one's execution?

When villagers immediately dropped everything they were doing and started massing in the center of their settlement, I shook my head to jar myself out of my thoughtful stupor.

"You all right, mates?" Alomar asked Royce and I, having seen my sudden movement.

"Aye," I said, squaring myself.

Here come the butterflies in my stomach.

Royce snorted nonchalantly. "Am I all right, you ask? Ha! I'm right as rain, mate."

The villagers up ahead were forming up around a well in what looked like the Village Square. A tall stone statue of someone I did not recognize, holding a long sword idly at his side, rose up protectively behind the well.

"Roy," I whispered. "What does 'right as rain' mean?"

Royce looked at me questioningly. "What are you whisperin' for?"

"Shut up," ordered Alomar quietly. "Save that for later. We have to get this right."

There were easily fifty men and women massed around the statue. More men, looking like farmers, came dashing from this way and that to join them. They waved wheat scythes, pitchforks, butcher knives, even shovels and various tools menacingly in the air and started shouting. Their cries sounded like a continuous roar, and the crowd seemed to rumble visibly.

Imagine walking toward an armed crowd of the like and what it looked like from our eyes. I was more scared than I had ever been in my life. More than when we were scared orphans, or escaping from Northroe just days before, or even confronted by Arthur and Quaid and I thought we'd die.

What was particularly unsettling was how swiftly the crowd had banded together. It gave me an eerie, uneasy feeling. They'd done this before. It was practiced, even.

Child labor. Blackmail. Threat of death. All of this under Tyrius Sewell and his men. These villagers had been through a lot. Hopefully, if everything worked out as I had planned, it would all come to a stop very shortly.

You see, Tyrius Sewell was now dead. For the sake of our plan, I hoped to the Fates that the villagers didn't know that.

*   *   *

Royce, Alomar and I pressed on, trying our best to somehow look casual and peaceful in some bizarre manner, given the circumstances. Miles and the others were following about twenty paces behind us.

The crowd's shouts and yells now turned more hateful and even violent in tone. I saw that they were herding their children behind them to protect the poor souls. Their faces frightened me. They were hard, scared, but even more prominently furious and challenging. I suspected that the village of Mable had just about had enough of outside threats and abuse.

That quickly proved true when the villagers began to advance, their weapons ready.

I glanced behind us and saw Miles and the others instinctively reaching for their weapons.

"Don't!" I shouted to them. "There! Stay right there, yeah?"

Visibly frustrated, Miles and his men forced their hands away from their weapons and looked on as Royce, Alomar and I continued forward. I imagine it must have been enormously difficult to do so, but they obeyed.

"Well, then," Royce murmured. "Know what? Not so sure about this now, mate. They're gonna kill us."

"Shut up, Roy," I countered.

"Lop off our heads and stick 'em on posts or somethin' of the like, know what I mean?"

"Shut up, Roy."

Alomar nudged me. "Here, Pen. This is as close as I care to get, mate."

"Aye," I answered.

The crowd was advancing steadily, not a hundred paces from us. I could see their faces even clearer now.

"Oy there!" I called, raising my hand in greeting and stopping.

Still angry, the villagers kept coming at a steady, cautious pace.

"Please!" I yelled, trying to overcome their roar. "Please, listen!"

They were fifty paces away now. I was able to hear individual shouts and threats now.

"-the devil are you lot doin' here!?"

"Get the 'ell off our land!"

"We'll run you through!"

"Please!" I yelled again, holding up my hands as if surrendering. "People of Mable! We just want to speak, yeah?"

"Off with ya!" a man shouted back. "We'll lop off your heads and stick 'em on posts!"

Royce nudged me. "Told you."

I tried to ignore the man as I watched the villagers march. They didn't slow down until about twenty paces away. When they finally stopped, five burly men came forward with an older man, who they encircled protectively.

"What in blazes are you doin' here?" shouted one of them, a blonde-haired man with a large beard. Even he was having to shout over the roar of his fellow villagers.

"The 'ell do you want, eh?" asked another. "We'll kill ya before we let any harm come to our people again. You get me?"

I whirled to check on Miles and the other brigands behind me. They had indeed advanced a few paces, but were still far behind Royce, Alomar and I.

"Stay there!" I shouted angrily. "Don't bloody move!"

Miles shook his head and spat at the ground, but grudgingly obeyed. I turned back to the villagers in front of me.

"Please," I said loudly, still trying to overcome the rumble of the crowd, "we're here to speak, that's all! No harmful intentions, I swear it!"

"All lies!" shouted a woman from the crowd. "Be gone, scum!"

The old man that had stepped forward was staring, seeming to look right through me to the green woods behind us. I had a jarring sensation that perhaps he could see right into my heart and my thoughts. His eyes looked dead, accompanying a worn and weathered face.

"You devils!" came a woman's voice. "Leave us alone! Leave!"

I found her in the crowd and saw tears streaming down her cheeks. She was disheveled, but pretty, with red hair and dark blue eyes. Fear and hatred were etched across her face. I had never seen such intensity.

Maybe I just had a liking for women with red hair, but she reminded me of Lynn, and this stopped me cold. I was suddenly worried about Lynn, wondering why she wasn't here to accompany this little expedition. Wondering if maybe Captain Hael was going to-

"Please!" bellowed Alomar. "Please calm down, good people! We've come to help you!"

Their cries and yells faltered, but only for a moment.

"It's true!" I echoed, cursing inwardly at letting myself become distracted again.

One of the men said nothing. He just spat at our feet and stepped forward with a saw.

I backed up immediately and right into Royce, when to my pleasant surprise the old man touched the shoulder of the Saw Man.

My would-be attacker looked at the elder incredulously. "But sir, he-"

"Hear them out," the old man bellowed. For such a frail looking fellow, his voice sure carried boom with it. He turned to the crowd and held up his hand.

Gradually the villagers' collective rumble of shouts and roars sputtered down to an uneasy silence. Only the wind could be heard. Behind the crowd, back at the statue and well, I could see at least twenty children of all ages, huddled together and clearly scared to their core. Men had stayed behind with weapons and formed a circle around them, and I realized they were looking out in all directions, as if we were merely a distraction so that others could sneak in behind the crowd and grab the children.

"Fates," I uttered, eyes wide. "I'm sorry."

"What was that?" asked Saw Man angrily.

I cleared my throat, unaccustomed to the sudden silence in the village. The crowd of men and women, most of them armed, all of them ready to kill, were seething with ferocity just paces away from me.

"I'm sorry," I repeated louder. "I'm sorry we didn't get here sooner. My name is Penny. These are my friends, Royce and Alomar. The others behind us wish you no harm."

The elder cocked his head for a moment and let his eyes wander around the faces of our party before he spoke. "I am Eustace II, Village Elder here. What is it that you want?"

I mustered up the charismatic, inspiring and theatrical speaker in me that had so far served me well in the last couple days, and prayed silently that things would go in our favor.

"You people of Mable have been through much," I proclaimed, raising my voice. "We know of Tyrius Sewell, and the... evils he has taken to you and your good kinsfolk."

A bald man to the left of Saw Man stiffened, and I saw his fist clench the knife he carried tightly. "Mention the name of that man again," he said in an astonishingly scary, raspy voice. "Say it again. See what happens."

I gave a potent nod, almost a small bow, and held up my hand. "Apologies. We are here to help, is all. This is why we've come on this day. We are sorry we could not come sooner."

"Who the hell are ya?" asked a black-haired man to his left. "How do you know about that bastardly tyrant?"

"Aye," chimed in the man with the saw. "Who are you? Answer now."

I clasped my hands together in a respectful gesture and motioned to Miles and the others behind me. "We are men interested in helping you, see? We've heard about Tyr-"

Every muscle in the bald man's body clenched when I almost mentioned the man's name.

"Rather, that dirt-low blight of a man, and what he's put your village through. We-"

Eustace the Elder interrupted me. "How do you know? They threatened to slaughter us all and loot the village if we ever spoke of him and what they used us for. We've said nothing. How did you learn of this?"

I saw faces in the crowd behind them grow visibly worried, looking every which way in the distance as if they expected Tyrius and an army of hellfire to come and destroy everything in sight.

It was unnerving.

"We have our ways," I answered, summoning confidence. "Again, I am telling you, we are here to help. See the men behind me? Warriors. Fighters. Some used to serve in the mighty Eislian army. Their weapons are not meant for you. Their weapons are going to protect you from Tyrius Sew-"

The bald man came at me suddenly, knife raised in the air, glinting in the sun. His threat hadn't been an empty one.

I don't know where my courage came from.

Before anyone else reacted, I squared myself and thrust my chest forward, leering dangerously close to the man in the face of his advance, nearly butting his head.

"Tyrius *Sewell,*" I thundered, my words slicing the air, "will never harm this village again! Ever!"

I wasn't afraid. I was furious. A ferocious heat was building up in me, a hatred for Tyrius and what he had done to these people. It wasn't an act. My eyes felt like they were on fire. I was a pillar of flame that couldn't be touched. I stared into my attacker's eyes, making sure he could feel me searing into him.

He stopped abruptly, arm raised and blade dangerously close to my face, but his expression was shocked. He even stumbled slightly, as if my words had paralyzed his forward foot mid-stride.

I reached slowly forward and put a hand on the bald man's shoulder. "Ever. Understand? You need not suffer anymore at his hands."

Everyone present was staring at me. I turned my back and ignored the absolutely shocked expressions on the faces of Royce and Alomar, and pointed toward Miles and the others. I whistled shrilly and beckoned them forward with my hand. Miles, Sorley, Gavin, Quaid and Ernest all exchanged glances briefly before walking forward to join us.

I turned back to face the villagers.

"Who... are you?" asked the old man.

"We're a company of sellswords. Mercenaries. There are only a few of us here, but we represent many more," I answered.

Alomar finally stepped forward, albeit slowly. He cleared his throat. "We're here to help your people."

The footsteps of Miles and the others grew a bit louder on the dirt and they finally reached us.

Eustace II looked us over for a long time before speaking. "A moment, please."

I nodded. "Of course."

The village Elder turned and took a few steps back toward the crowd. His frontmen stayed where they were, watching us carefully. Eustace called with a whistle of his own, and I saw three other older men and one woman their age suddenly emerge from the crowd's ranks and join him off to the side. They spoke in hushed whispers and animated gestures.

As they spoke, I watched the men in front of us cautiously. A few birds called in the distance while a small gust of wind whipped up some dirt that breezed by, rippling our clothing. Their eyes were frigid and watching us just as carefully.

The man with the saw spoke suddenly. His words were slow and angry. "Where were you when we *needed* you?"

I didn't break eye contact with him, but allowed a slight cringe at his words. I was surprised when Royce answered for me.

"Sorry, mate. We're here now."

I turned and gave Royce a nod, and he returned it.

The majority of the crowd behind them was watching Eustace II converse with who I assumed were fellow elders, or a council of sorts. I was holding my breath. If they took interest, this could all work. Captain Hael would get what he wanted from these people without harming them.

If this didn't work, Royce, Alomar and I would be blamed for failure. Perhaps Miles, too. And we would be killed for treason against Captain Hael, for certain.

I found myself thinking of Lynn again, her strong, proud features so downtrodden and shattered at the death of Arthur, and Captain Hael's anger and disappointment. He surely would have killed any of the men for doing what she'd done. I wondered about her now. I wondered about what she had been through with these men, how unbreakable her loyalty must have been that she was spared.

Eustace II broke from his council and strode back to us now, and I pushed my thoughts aside. I offered an encouraging smile, and another nod.

"Okay, Penny... what is your surname?"

I shook my head. "No use for one. Not in our line of work."

The Elder frowned for a second, but then continued. "Right. What's the catch, eh? What do you want out of all this?"

I breathed in slowly. Offered a silent prayer to the heavens. "A fee."

Cue visible shifting and mumbling from the crowd.

"And that is?"

Oddly, I hadn't thought about that detail when discussing the plan with the others. I turned back to Miles, who looked very concerned about my next words. He was tapping the side of his scabbard rather nervously.

"Well," I answered, turning back to him, "it's to be determined."

"How often? Weekly? Monthly?"

I sniffed. "To be determined."

"A lot of uncertainty here."

"Not uncertainty," I assured, "just money. That's all it is. Small details. I'm not actually authorized to settle an amount with you. Consider us...an ambassador party, of sorts. I'll report back to our Captain, and we'll go from there."

Eustace scratched his white beard. "How far away is he, this leader of yours? Where are you based? Where are you from?"

"We're located nearby, west of here," I lied. Captain Hael's camp was, of course, to the North at the base of Mount Kovald. This was vitally important. If I had revealed even the direction that the bandit camp was located, I might as well have myself and my friends killed right then and skip Hael's wrath at giving up the outlaws' location.

The man kept stroking his beard.

"Think about it," I said. "A regular fee is nothing compared to what you've been going through. It's like your own private City Watch, yeah?"

The village Elder gave a wily, knowing grin. "Everyone wants something, it seems."

I shrugged and laughed heartily. "Indeed. You want peace. We want coin. With respect, mate, we have to eat too. And pay for weapons. Armor. Maintenance of these things, tools, supplies, not to mention-"

Eustace raised his hand with a smile. "I know. Understood. If you are honest about all of this, and a fee is all you and your lot are asking, then we are indeed blessed."

Royce clapped his hands one time, loudly. "Cheers, then! It's settled!"

Before Eustace could say anything, I grinned and spoke in a soothing tone. "Nothing's final, of course. We will speak with our leader, and see what is to be done. Shall we meet again, tomorrow?"

The nervous and angry buzz of the crowd in Mable's Square had, for the most part, settled to murmurs and soft conversation when they overheard the exchange taking place.

Eustace scratched his jaw thoughtfully and cast a glance over his shoulder at his council. They nodded. He turned back to me, took a final look at all of us, and extended his hand.

"We will see you on the morrow, young man. When the noon sun is highest, yes? We hope you won't disappoint us."

I grasped his hand, trying to snuff out the overwhelming sense of excitement I was feeling. "Of course. I'll report back to our leader."

The old man lowered his voice and leaned a bit closer. "My people couldn't handle a lie like this. The Fates watch you now, Mercenary Penny, because though we are at your mercy, and might not be able to stand up to the likes of you if you are indeed lying, there would most definitely be a place in hell's blazes for such liars. Promises of such salvation cannot be empty."

His words chilled me.

"A place in the heavens sure sounds a bit more desirable," I said through a fake smile.

Eustace II, the Village Elder of Mable, let go of my hand and turned back to his people.

"Fates be with you," he said over his shoulder.

I didn't wait to watch the crowd disperse. In a swift motion, I turned on my heel and rejoined the others as professionally as I could manage.

"Let's get outta here, aye?" I suggested, urgency in my voice. The others nodded their agreement.

The trek back to Captain Hael's camp became an even longer journey than before. We traveled out of sight to the west, in case we were being watched. Eventually our party doubled back toward the Kovald without incident, and nearly an hour later we reached the woods again, confident we had made sold our lie.

"Bloody well done, Pen," Royce said. "Unbelievable. You didn't even seem like yourself. And not that it was a bad thing, no. It was impressive, mate."

I wasn't used to getting compliments, or doing anything right, for that matter. Wasn't accustomed to being courageous, taking control of any situation, playing an important role in something that mattered. I didn't even know how to answer my friend.

"Well, Royce, I suppose I got lucky." I just shrugged.

Alomar tossed back his head and bellowed that loud, hearty laugh of his and clapped my back so hard that I nearly stumbled forward.

"Shut the 'ell up, Penny. You did great. We all did great. It bloody worked."

"Aye, that it did," Miles chimed in. "Now let's see what the Captain has to say 'bout it."

For a moment, I almost preferred a small army of angry villagers armed with sharp instruments of death.

Only for a moment.

CHAPTER 39

Not unlike the first time we arrived at Captain Hael's camp, Royce, Alomar and I were sitting outside the Lodge, twiddling our thumbs, tracing patterns in the dirt and picking at pine needles passively, waiting until we were summoned.

It seemed like so much time had passed already. Three days? Four?

Why couldn't I remember?

Only this time, we weren't newcomers. There we sat under the night sky that covered our land with a thick, wide blanket of stars. The moon shone generously down upon us as it seemed to in those parts, and the silhouettes of trees stretching upward to bathe in the gray light captivated my thoughtful gaze.

It was all so surreal! Just days ago, we were unsure, scared fugitives from the city accidentally helping outlaws, and accidentally doing such a good job that we were accidentally inducted into the clan without any say in the matter. And now, here we were again: unsure, slightly scared fugitives from the city who had potentially done something stupid in ignoring Captain Hael's orders and come up with a grand plan of our own.

Maybe not much had changed after all, now that I thought about it. Unsure, scared fugitives doing crazy and stupid things.

I say we, but really, it was me that was responsible for what had happened at Mable. Alomar started it, but I was the one that took it further... much further. I had come up with an entirely new plan just so we wouldn't have to harm innocent villagers. At the time, it had seemed like a good alternative to what could have otherwise happened, and I had felt exhilarated as I did so... but now that we were waiting outside the Lodge while Miles was inside talking to the Captain, anxiety knotted my stomach.

Now it all felt stupid.

I looked over at Quaid and Gavin, who were waiting along with us. Quaid was staring at me. He offered a forced grin that I didn't return. I looked down at my feet instead, and sank against the wall to a sitting position on the dirt and pine needles.

Gavin was spitting on the blade of his axe and wiping it clean with an old cloth.

Sorley and Ernest had turned in for the night, after Miles had given his consent.

It was then that I remembered Lynn. She had just broken an order that day. Publicly demoted, lectured, reprimanded in front of her peers. We followed up what she had done with rule-breaking of our own. I buried my face in my hands with an exasperated sigh.

"What?" asked Alomar.

"We're dead," I answered flatly. "We are so dead."

Royce shifted his weight. "No we're not, Pen. We'll be fine."

I spat. "He's gonna kill us, mate. What a fool I was."

Gavin just tried to look like he was cleaning his axe more intently.

Quaid sat down on a large boulder and laid his quiver of arrows carefully against it, followed by his bow. The man brushed some dirt off the knees of his trousers, and promptly began brushing the strip of dark hair atop his head furiously, bits of dust falling softly to the ground.

Alomar looked over at the two outlaws. "Oy. What do you two think will happen?"

With a shrug, Gavin looked up in response. "One of two things, mate. The Cap'n will be angry and punish you, or he'll be angry and not punish you."

Quaid shook his head and jabbed a thumb at Gavin. "Don't listen to him. You'll be fine. Don't worry."

Royce seemed to perk up. "Why's that, Quaid?"

The archer stretched loudly. "Because you heard Miles, yeah? Back near the bridge, before we went in. He said there was no way the Captain would punish us, or him, for that matter. Remember?"

I did. It didn't make me feel any better though, and I sighed heavily and gawked upward at the moon.

So, this was an outlaw's life. Death, fear, limited control over the innocent. Danger. So many things I'd always had a thirst to write about, and now that I was living it, it was bloody scary. I wanted nothing more than to flee into the woods, never to return.

"You remember, aye?" repeated Quaid.

Alomar nodded. "I do."

Quaid scooped up his bow plucked lightly at the string before shooting us a wily grin. "Well, if he says it'll be all right, it will be. Miles is one man you can trust. Every word. Am I right, Gav?"

Gavin nodded. "'Tis true. But this is a tricky one, mate. I'm not sure-"

Quaid kicked at Gavin's boot to shut him up, and that was when she entered my mind again.

"What happened to Lynn?" I asked.

Shrugging, Gavin answered rather tepidly. "She's in the Pit. You heard the Cap'n."

"Aye, I heard. But where is this Pit? And what is it, exactly?"

Quaid gave a raspy laugh. "Truth is, mate, we don't-"

Gavin kicked at him to shut him up.

"What?" protested Quaid. "Gav, they're with us now. They have the right to know. Bloody 'ell."

I felt an odd satisfaction in hearing those words.

I also felt an odd sensation watching Quaid while he adjusted the hooded cloak he wore. The man had just witnessed Arthur's death sometime either last night or that very morning, and he was behaving as if it had never happened.

When one lived a life like the one these men led, was this a normalcy? Was death simply an accepted risk? I supposed it was. Many ghastly and disturbing things we had witnessed in the streets of Northroe as orphans had jaded my friends and I, even as children.

Hunger had been a part of life. Dying was an every day affair. We used to even go through the pockets and remains of corpses to see if they'd left anything behind.

It all seemed so long ago. I shuddered for a moment and returned my thoughts to the conversation at hand.

Quaid yawned. "None of us actually know where it is. The Pit, I mean. It's something only officers know the location of."

Royce scratched his dusty blonde hair. "Only the Cap'n and Miles know where? And obviously Lynn?"

"That's right," answered Gavin, lowering his voice. "Keeps us all in check, I suppose. In case anyone gets any bright ideas. That's why there's only two other officers at any given time."

I cocked my head. "The Pit is why?"

Gavin shook his head. "No. Trust is why. Cap'n Hael has a hard time trusting command to others. Hell, trusting anything to anyone else, for that matter. I've been in this company for nearly nine years, mate. I've only ever known of two other officers besides Miles and Lynn."

"Really?" I asked, amazed.

"Aye," Quaid chimed in. "Really."

"What happened to them?" Alomar asked.

Gavin shrugged passively. "One died of some type o' fever just a week before I met this lot and joined up. Unfortunate. I probably would've been able to save the bastard."

My interest was piqued. "What about the other?"

Gavin frowned and looked up to the night sky as Quaid answered.

"The other was one of the blokes who started this band up with the Cap'n. Executed by the Watch, mates. It's a long story, but he sacrificed himself so that Captain Hael and some others could escape during a mission."

Royce, Alomar and I exchanged solemn glances before I turned back to them.

"Where was this 'mission' at? Northroe?"

Quaid shook his head. "No. Near Courtnall, just outside the Heartland. You know it? It's about a two days' ride east from Eisley City."

Royce and I shook our heads, but to our surprise, Alomar nodded.

"Passed through there when we got back from the war. Before we went to hear the King's Address at the capital."

Again, I thought of how much more that man had laid eyes upon compared to Royce and I. A mixture of jealousy and relief met my mind's eye. Alomar had seen much more of the world, but it had come at a price I'd never have to pay.

"Very noble," I managed. "What happened?"

Gavin shot Quaid a look, and this time Quaid took heed before answering me.

"Long story, and if you are to know someday, I'm not the one to tell it. Neither of us are, mate."

"Why?" ventured Royce.

"Well," Quaid started, clearly hesitant. He looked at Gavin.

Gavin rolled his eyes and sighed. "Fine. That man, the officer who gave his life so that the Cap'n and his men could get away, was Lynn's twin brother."

My eyes widened, and my friends and I exchanged glances.

"What was his name?" Alomar asked quietly.

"Donovan," Quaid answered. "Hair and eyes the same shade of dark red. Eerie, really. Ever notice that, Gav, how Lynn's eyes seem to be red-brown? How they light up and all that? 'Twas the same with him."

Gavin shook his head. "Come off it, Quaid. Lynn will kill you."

Quaid seemed to suddenly remember what exactly he was talking about, and now that he'd said too much, decided to treat it as a highly sensitive secret. He cast his eyes downward and fiddled with the wool on his fingerless gloves, tugging at a stray thread.

Royce leaned back against the wall of the Lodge. "Touchy subject then, eh?"

The rest of us looked at Royce, confused.

Gavin coughed. "Say again?"

"Touchy subject, is it? Lynn's brother?"

"I-" Gavin started, before looking at us, then Quaid, then back to Royce with a slight shake of his head. "What do you mean? What's a touchy subject?"

Here we go again.

"Aye," echoed Alomar. "Do tell."

"What's a touchy anything, that's what I wanna know," followed Quaid with a laugh.

Dismayed, Royce motioned for us to shush. "It's, well, a touchy subject. You know, the topic. It's touchy. It doesn't like to be touched."

We all stared.

"So you leave it alone," Royce finished, looking at us like we were stupid. "It's not something anyone wants to touch. Or talk about, rather. So it's like-"

"Oy," I interrupted, "wouldn't it be an un-touchy subject then? Because touchy sounds like it likes being touched, which really contradicts everything you just said."

The other men laughed for a long moment, and Quaid held up his hands as if to pause our laughter. "This whole conversation just got a bit dirty, didn't it?"

Royce snorted dismissively. "Oh, grow up."

Our chuckles turned to howling laughter, and even Royce's features softened when he couldn't help but join in. We chortled on in a carefree stupor caused by an abundance of stress, danger, and fatigue that had all come with a day's work.

The five of us must have become a bit loud. The door to the Lodge just a few paces away whisked open suddenly with so much force that it swung open and bounced roughly off the Lodge wall. Before it could close again with the momentum, Miles appeared in the doorway, followed immediately by Captain Hael himself, who seemed to shine in the moonlight due to the lamellar armor he donned.

We all fell silent immediately.

"Lads, listen up," ordered Miles as he stepped out into the night and stood tall before us. The five of us stood quickly to meet the two men as Captain Hael let the door creak to a close behind him.

The captain folded his arms. "You all learned this about me the first time you set foot in the Lodge and I laid eyes upon you. I don't like formalities. I'll make this quick. I'm bloody tired anyway, and I'm sure you lot are as well."

Quaid and Gavin were the only ones who nodded. My friends and I didn't dare.

I tried to keep my knees from shaking, attempting to remember how the courage had felt when I had summoned it from a dark corner of my heart earlier that day in the center of Mable. Captain Hael's icy blue eyes seemed paler in the starlight as they flickered between the three of us and finally, to my dismay, settled on mine.

"Miles told me what you did today, Penny. I would normally punish any deviation from orders, but you lot made a judgment call this afternoon at Mable that will result in more prosperity than we had planned."

Royce patted my shoulder and gave a triumphant grin. I smiled, though hesitantly.

"We apologize for... for not consulting with you first," I managed. And it was genuine. Suddenly receiving praise from this Captain of men made me want to earn more. I had never felt loyalty to a leader of any sort.

Captain Hael nodded. "Accepted. Since we already killed Tyrius Sewell in Northroe, obviously there won't even be an actual threat to defend those villagers from. Easy coin, easy does it. We may be three men or so down every day since we'll have to keep a constant presence there, but with a steady source of income now, it's worth it. Miles told me everything. Good planning, and good work. Now get some sleep, men. It's late."

"Aye, boss," Quaid answered.

Gavin nodded. "Cap'n."

We were beaming with pride and doing awful jobs at hiding it. Now I caught Miles' gaze and gave a slight nod to him as well, and he returned it. He had told us it would be okay, after all, and Quaid was right. Apparently Miles was a man whose word could be trusted.

Captain Hael was watching Royce, Alomar and I now. There seemed to be a twinkle in his eyes, but I couldn't tell if it was just a trick of the moon's glow.

"Yes, sir," I managed with a grin.

Captain Hael smiled now and gave a nod to Miles, then turned and pulled the door open to the Lodge to retire. But before he stepped in, Captain Hael turned to us.

"I know you're wondering it. Your eyes are asking, though you're not saying it aloud. You're wondering why you weren't punished for carrying out a plan of your own, like Lynn was. You men and Lynn both made your calls. You both acted, no matter how impulsively. The difference is, your actions were in the best interest of this company as a whole. Lynn acted in her own interest, and one of our men was killed. A good man, at that. Remember this well and don't get cocky, lads. Make any brash decisions with undesirable consequences as she did, and you will be killed, by my own hands, Fates willing."

CHAPTER 40

Not long after the Captain dismissed us all from the Lodge, Royce, Alomar and I were seated on the floor of our cabin around the low table, listening to the sounds of the forest night outside and eating a small meal. A magnificent pillar of moonlight reached through our lone window and cast a glowing square on the wall between Royce's cot and my own.

As we ate our hard bread, oatmeal and small bunches of grapes, we spoke in low voices and relived the day's events.

"It doesn't even seem real, honestly," Alomar said, shaking his head. "Just days ago we were drinking at the Raven with Ozlow and Kara and all those crazy drunken bastards."

I nodded, crushing white and red grapes in my teeth and savoring the juice that spilled about.

"Aye," Royce said. "I woke up this morning, mates, and know what happened?"

"You discovered you had drooled on your pillow more than the night before?" I quipped.

"Yes, actually," Royce answered. We all chuckled, and my friend continued. "No, I woke up and... I don't know if it was because of what I was dreaming, or if it was a nightmare, but I didn't recognize where I was."

Alomar reached for his cup of water. "Really? You were surprised at waking up here, or just really didn't know where you were?"

"I didn't know where I was," replied Royce, wide-eyed. "I looked over at you, Pen, and then Al in that hammock, and dawn light was outside the window an' all that, and I sat up and thought, 'Where in the blazes am I?' Was bloody scary, lemme tell you."

Picking a few breadcrumbs from my teeth, I nodded. "You remember the other night, with the story at the campfire?"

"Aye," Royce replied. "Bloody brilliant."

"Thanks, mate. That was the first time I've ever told a story of mine to someone besides Lucille at the Weathered Page, back in the city. Whether it was written down or told in person. I don't count telling you, Roy, about *The Pirate Who Ate Everyone,* which was obviously a bloody mistake."

Royce grinned devilishly.

Alomar stretched out on the floor now and lay back with his hands cradling his head, staring at the ceiling. "Was well done, Penny. It really was. You think you'll ever get time to work on your book around here?"

I froze in mid-chew. I had forgotten all about it since the first night we'd arrived. Hastily I shot to my feet, knocking the table slightly and sending part of the loaf of bread rolling about, and I rushed to my bed and grabbed for my pack.

"You all right, mate?" asked Royce.

I frantically opened my pack and let my eyes dart their way around the contents. A few capped inkwells, two quills for writing, and pages upon pages of parchments and a few rolls of scroll. My eyes widened with relief when I recognized the large stack of pages bound together with the title page that read *The Eagle and the Raven.* My works were indeed still there, and hadn't been tampered with.

I grinned at my friends sheepishly. "Sorry. Just realized, I hadn't checked my pack in a few days. Honestly, I forgot I had it with me."

Alomar cocked his head. "You forgot about your writings, Pen? The stuff you almost got killed over in Northroe?"

"Fates, mate," Royce muttered. "You nearly got hacked to bits by the Watch by going back to that cursed inn to grab those, and now you-"

"I know, I know," I interrupted, feeling embarrassed. "I... don't know how, or why I could just forget. Look. We're here now, and all these things have been happening, and-"

"It's a new life," Alomar finished, still looking up at the ceiling. "I think it's clear that we don't have the time that we used to have, eh? Or at least, our time is spent differently than before."

"That's for sure," I said, gripping my pages with regret. I felt as if I'd betrayed them.

Royce was chewing on more bread and staring off into space. His eyes kept narrowing and then returning to normal, and he began to chew his food slower, and I saw a man deep in thought, reliving something that had passed.

I gave the man a nudge. "What is it?"

He blinked suddenly and looked at me, then at Alomar, and shook his head. "A lot's happened, yeah? So bloody fast, at that."

Alomar and I nodded.

"I mean," Royce continued, lowering his voice, "remember when we saw Arthur and Quaid in the woods? For the first time, I mean? Those blasted bodies floating downriver, and being scared to death and all that? Then suddenly we're here. We're learning about the camp. We're helping chop wood. Arthur and Quaid become our friends. Penny's telling stories around campfires. Then we wake up one morning, and Arthur's bloody dead."

I gritted my teeth. For some reason I thought of Arthur back at the river where we were grabbing the bodies, tossing his head back in bellowing laughter when I told him I'd punched a Watchman. How he'd rushed along the riverbank gracefully, hurtling fallen logs while I had struggled to keep up. The way the man's eyes had been fixed on me the night I told the bandits the story of the Trickster Mirror.

"We knew Arthur for just a couple days," Alomar said, "and in that time we went from... what? Strangers, enemies even, to warming up to becoming good friends, I'd say."

"Aye," sighed Royce. "I liked that one, I did. He and Quaid are good fellows."

I nodded and reached for my cup. Water sloshed about in it as I steadied it in the air. "Oy, mates. Toast, yes?"

Alomar and Royce nodded and lifted their cups as well.

"Here's to Arthur," I volunteered. "And Ozlow. And Kara, and all of those poor souls at the Raven. Almost all of them, at least."

"To the Raven," declared Royce quietly.

Alomar cleared his throat. "Here's to the future," he said. "Because I'm sick of remembering what I left behind in that blasted city. I'm tired of returning to times past, mates. Let's look to the future now. Like Royce said on South Bridge, remember? What are we living for?"

"Aye indeed," Royce answered with a grin. "Cheers, mates. We've got one life, yeah?"

"One life to live."

Our cups clinked and we drank the remaining water welled within and then slammed the simple goblets to the table in triumph, like we were back at the November Raven with mugs of ale.

"Where do we go from here?" I asked. "Do we stay here with these men? Try to leave? I'm having trouble with both options, really."

Alomar folded his arms. "Well, here, we have strength in numbers. Food. Shelter."

"Aye," I answered. "But it's bloody tough living. My hand's still not fully healed and I'm almost dreading the day it's back to normal. Probably be mining some mountain or digging a trench once Miles knows I have two hands again."

Royce nodded. "We have companions and food and the like, but we're not really free, are we? We left Northroe to strike out and find fortune, mates! To travel the land and find adventure!"

I snorted. "We left Northroe because the Watch thought we burned down the Raven, Roy."

"I know, but we were gonna bloody leave anyway, weren't we?" Royce countered. "Remember what I said about Lord Hannady? How a rich man like him isn't truly free, is he, because he's still shackled to his duties and his castle like a prisoner. Can't go anywhere, can he? Not often at least."

"Richest prisoner I ever saw," I said, reaching for more grapes.

Alomar cleared his throat. "Look. If we want to leave here, how are we going to do it? This lot obviously isn't going to just let men leave the Kovald Forest when they could lead any Watchmen or soldiers right back to the bloody camp. Hael's smart. He'd never just let us leave."

I sighed and pondered. "Is it bad if I'm actually liking it here? Feel like I finally bloody belong somewhere."

Royce and Alomar both looked at me with careful expressions.

"I mean, we're doing well, aren't we?" I added. "I'd say we're fitting in. The Captain's starting to trust us. We did well at Mable today, and-"

"Pen," Alomar said, holding a hand up. "Sorry, mate. I know what you're saying. I do, and I'm starting to feel that way too. But listen to me. What you did today for those poor blokes in Mable was brave, and noble. I'm glad we did. I couldn't have cut down innocent people... but we almost had to."

I nodded.

"Think about it," the man continued. "We haven't even been here for a week. So much has already happened, like Royce said. Think about Arthur. And Lynn? One of the officers of the entire company, and she's suddenly not here with us, is she? Off in some blasted Pit."

Royce was nodding, and I let Alomar's words sink in.

"What I'm saying is there's a lot of change in a life like this," Alomar said. "Can't get used to anything because it can all change in an instant. Life's like that, of course, but especially out here. A highwayman, Pen? A renegade? Is that who you want to be? And think about the next time we have to go out on some mission with innocents involved. Mates, we won't be able to save them. Not every time. Especially not without coming off as soft men who don't have the hearts of outlaws. It's too dangerous."

Frowning, I let the man's warning bounce about in my mind. He was right, and I knew it.

"Like I was saying," Royce said, "we have bigger things awaiting us. We've never even seen most of our own bloody country, have we?"

"Most people haven't," I observed. "Most people can't just leave their homes and go sightseeing, Royce. Looking for 'adventure' and the like."

"Exactly," he returned. "We're not most people, are we? We're very like Captain Hael and his company here. No homes and nowhere to go. But we don't have to be looters and killers, either. Nor do we want to be."

I nodded. "Well, 'tis true. I don't want to kill or rob anybody."

"That's what we have to do to live here," Alomar said. "To be with these men, we have to be open to taking part in what they do. And I'm sure we don't want to be cutthroats, do we?"

Royce took a bite of bread. "No."

"And you, Penny?"

Sighing, I looked back down the pages of my works. "Definitely not."

"We can't have one without the other," murmured Alomar. "We can't just lay up here and eat the Captain's food and sleep in their cabin without doing some of their dirty work too. So now I think we all agree, eh? We have to figure out a way to leave this place."

I nodded, and Royce lifted his empty cup.

"I agree, mate. But how will we do it?"

Alomar sighed and strode over to lie up in his hammock. "Not sure yet. Too dangerous to just try to sneak away. These men are good at keeping their camp under constant guard."

I sat on my cot. "Remember the bodies in the river? All their throats had been slashed, and Arthur and Quaid said that the Captain couldn't find out."

Both men looked at me, trying to see where I was going with this.

"Did we ever hear about that again?" I asked. "I mean, they said never to mention it, but it's like it never happened. Did Hael even notice that five captives were missing from his camp? I don't understand."

"Castor," Royce said softly.

"Eh?"

Royce sat on his cot. "They said it was some bloke named Castor who had cut those poor souls' throats. I don't know about you, mates, but I haven't met a man named Castor here."

Alomar was stroking the stubble on his chin. "Lot of men here we haven't talked to yet. Most of them, actually."

"True enough," Royce replied. He turned to me. "What does it all matter, Penny? What about the bodies and that Castor fellow?"

I shrugged. "I was thinking maybe we could find this Castor bloke and... convince him to let us go, help us escape, or else we'd tell Hael what happened."

"No, mate," Alomar said quickly with a dismissive wave. "Can't do that. Too dangerous to put ourselves at odds with any members of Captain Hael's clan. There's no way blokes like these would let any newcomers make such a threat and keep breathing."

Royce piped up. "Besides, then we'd get Quaid into trouble, wouldn't we? The story would come out to the Cap'n eventually. He'd know Quaid tried to hide it, and Arthur, too."

I stared hard at the night outside our window. "We would tarnish Arthur's memory by doing so, wouldn't we?"

Both men nodded. I settled in under my blanket, closed my eyes and listened to the gentle winds rustle through the trees and pass over our cabin.

"Let's get some sleep, eh?" I said wearily. "Probably going to have to go back to Mable with the Captain tomorrow to make good on our deal with those villagers."

The three of us gradually sank into a sea of sleep, hopeful good dreams would be waiting beneath the surface. I don't remember if I dreamed that night, but regardless, in those fleeting moments in which one chases sleep's promise, none of us had any way of knowing what was coming at dawn.

* * *

The faint orange glow of early sunlight seemed to mist about at the glass of our cabin window before streaming in. I don't know what caused me to wake, but through tired eyes I glimpsed the dawn sky and trees and pulled my blanket tighter around me. I thought I could hear voices of men in camp, already up and about and going about their daily duties and activities.

Awfully early for breakfast.

Sitting up in bed, I looked at my friends. Alomar was fast asleep. I still hadn't quite gotten used to the sight of a man sleeping in a net hanging from a ceiling. Royce was snoring loudly, and I cringed when I saw that a glorious puddle of drool had dampened the man's pillow.

There was a loud rapping on our door.

"'Oy lads! Wake up. Coming in!" came Miles's voice.

Startled, Royce's eyes shot open, and Alomar sat up groggily with a yawn. I propped myself up on my elbow and squinted my eyes at the door, trying blink the sleep away from them. The door swung open and Miles stepped in, his boots thudding heavily on the floorboards.

"'Ey there," Royce managed.

"We have a problem, and we have to react quickly," Miles said. "All sentries are on high alert and the guard at our perimeter has been doubled."

Alomar sprang out of his hammock with shocking speed. "What's wrong? Will we need weapons?"

"You will, Alomar," answered Miles. He looked at Royce and I now. "As for you two, you both are returning to Mable with a small squad of men to finish the deal with Elder Eustace. Alomar, since you're a veteran and can fight, you'll be going with the Captain and a small war party, heading north. We recently-"

"Wait!" I blurted out. "We're splitting up?"

Royce looked at Alomar with a worried look, then to Miles. "Did you say 'war party,' Miles?"

Miles held up his hand. "Aye, I did. Listen to me. Tyrius Sewell had a larger following in Northroe than we knew. They're angry at the deaths of he and his men there, and they have decided to retaliate. We are going to-"

"Fates!" I uttered. "What, a damned battle, is that it? With swords and axes and blood and all that? I can't fight!"

Shifting impatiently, Miles shook his head and backed outside, propping the door open with his boot. "You're not fighting. Alomar and myself and the war party are."

"B-but... isn't there a way to avoid... wait, how do they know where to find us?" I sputtered. "How would they even-"

"Enough!" Miles barked. "Your questions will be answered shortly. We're all gathering for a meeting at the fire circle, so make haste. Ruben readied the gear you'll each need, so get up and get to the fire circle."

"Wait, mate," Royce said quickly. "One last question. If you and Cap'n Hael are going to a fight, who's going with Penny and I and the other men to Mable?"

At that moment, Miles stepped back and opened our cabin door even wider, and to our surprise, Lynn strolled into view.

"Mornin' to ya," she greeted.

Lynn leaned sideways in the doorway and folded her arms, resting her weight on the frame as she swept her red-brown eyes over the three of us.

Speechless, I found myself checking her, looking for any signs of pain or horrid torture in wherever this Pit had been. One cut, a bruise, a gash or sign of harm.

I couldn't find any.

The woman brushed some dark red hair from her eyes. I noticed she even wore her 'colors,' or insignia band, once again. Apparently Lynn and Captain Hael had made amends. Either that, or our situation was exceptionally dire.

"Penny, Royce. Miles has told me everythin'. I'll be goin' with ya to Mable," the woman declared. "Gavin will be joinin' us as well. Quaid if we're lucky."

Royce and I nodded.

Miles coughed. "Quaid will be with us, Lynn. Captain's request."

The woman shrugged and turned back to my friends and I. "Well, it'll be the four of us then, eh?"

I just nodded.

Lynn looked to Alomar. "Alomar, you better get sorted out with your weapons and armor. The patrol's leavin' soon. Good luck to ya."

With a nod, Alomar looked over at us. "You two... be careful. All right? Don't do anything stupid."

Laughing, Royce shook his head. "You know we will anyway, mate. We don't need you around in order to be stupid."

"Take care of yourself out there, Al," I said solemnly. It didn't feel like enough, and looking back now I wish I'd said something better to my friend, but things happened so quickly. Without warning, at that. There just wasn't time.

Alomar was pulling on his boots when Lynn looked over and stared at me for a few moments before speaking.

"Somethin' wrong, Penny?"

I hesitated, but answered. "The three of us having to split up. I don't like it."

Lynn gave a slight smile. "First time for everythin'."

Royce was hastily pulling on his boots, and seeming to have a difficult time of it. "Well, Lynn, it's the second time really, since we had to split up in the city before we came here and all that, see? So I believe it would be 'Second time for everything,' as it were."

Lynn blinked. "Your right boot doesn't go on the left foot. Hurry up."

- PART THREE -
In which fear, peril and love all conspire against me

CHAPTER 41

Out of our cabin we went, following Miles and Lynn to the fire circle. I heard low booming of thunder in the distance and looked up to see the dark sky, an equally beautiful and foreboding display of blacks and grays splashed across the heavens' canvas. There was a strange feeling that was foreign to me then, and I realized I'd been experiencing unknown sensations for the first time quite frequently since Royce, Alomar and I had left Northroe and our pasts behind.

I couldn't stop looking at Alomar, and it dawned on me that this edgy, anxious, worrisome feeling was dread. Dread for my friend, knowing that he was on his way to a battle I knew nothing about. My nerves were upended at the thought of being separated from either Alomar or Royce, and I realized then that Alomar's presence had always provided a certain sense of security. The man had been a soldier. He had always been there to protect and provide guidance.

Now, he wouldn't be.

I tried picturing my friend fighting some nameless battle in the forest, alongside brigands against other outlaws. It felt so unnecessary and very wrong. Alomar had put in his time abroad and now faced the prospect of death against his own countrymen, whomever they were. I tried imagining what I would do if he didn't return. What Royce would do. How much would change.

The thought of losing Alomar was painful.

I watched Alomar's face as we trudged through the camp, and felt the first sprinkles of light droplets of rainfall. He looked cold and solemn. His face was not one of ferocity or determination, but rather thoughtfulness and insight. It wasn't as if the man hadn't prepared for battle before, but I worried for him in these circumstances. I knew the Dekkan War had taken its toll on his soul, and I found myself watching for signs of breaking, something that would hint that he would have trouble handling the situation presented to him.

Alomar showed none.

The rain began to fall harder, and his short-cropped hair atop his head glistened with the water. As he always did, my friend smoothed the top of his head over with his hand, his eyes wandering in thought.

The fire circle was just ahead, and it was an impressive sight. Every bandit in Captain Hael's clan was present except for the sentries at the perimeter and out in the woods. Fifteen men stood at Captain Hael's side, huddled together and shifting about in the rain. The only thing uniform about the brigands was the earth-green insignias they all wore. The rest of their apparel varied from one man to the next, mostly leather lightweight armor and the occasional byrnie – a short-sleeved chainmail shirt – worn over a long-sleeved, hooded coat.

We reached the gathering. Miles immediately strode to Captain Hael's side. Lynn touched my shoulder momentarily.

"Just listen for now," she instructed.

I spotted Sorley and Ernest over to the left of Captain Hael, donning their studded leather armor. They flashed me a nod as my gaze met theirs. To the right of the war party, I saw Quaid busy fiddling with the string on his bow, making adjustments on his deathly instrument.

Footsteps plodded up to the left of Royce and I, and Gavin reached our side, giving my friend a nudge and shooting me a grin.

"G'morning," he offered sleepily.

Captain Hael gave a nod in greeting to us and proceeded immediately, skipping formalities as true to his form.

"Men, hear me briefly. That sod Tyrius had a larger band in Northroe than we thought, and they aim to sweep these woods in search of our camp and avenge his death. Thanks to our eyes in the city, they won't set foot within a few hours' walk of here. This is your home, and mine. Are we going to let that filth threaten us?"

A roar rang out from the men around us in response.

Hael smiled now. "Didn't think so. They think we're some band of common thieves, just like them. They don't know our history. How long we've been set here in the Kovald. They know nothing of us, and Fates willing, they'll learn a thing or two about us before dying today. Now, they are to strike out from the city and enter the Kovald around noon, when the sun is highest in the sky. They seek to spill our blood and burn our homes to the ground. What say you to that?"

More shouts rang out, and steel of all sorts flashed in the air as weapons were lifted in reply. I saw some of the men shifting their weight back and forth on their feet and realized they were getting riled up, eager for action.

"Our war band," Captain Hael said gruffly, "will trek north by northwest now to meet these fools. You will cut them down on sight, and you will show absolutely no mercy. No prisoners will be taken. How many of you are veterans of this nation's fine army?"

A shocking number of hands gripping weapons shot into the sky with cheers to match. I heard Alomar give a yell similar to the one I'd heard him utter in the tavern when he had been fighting Tyrius and his companions. I turned to see his face alive with a fierce expression, his teeth clenched, reaching for the stormy clouds above with a mighty closed fist. Admittedly, I was startled at him chiming in with the others, but I also found myself in admiration of the man.

Captain Hael was nodding now with a wily grin as he raised his own hand. "Aye, men. That's right. And our spies in Northroe tell that of the score-and-a-half of men on their way, only one served in the Eislian ranks, and he will be easy to distinguish as their captain. We take him out of the battle, and the rest will be cut as wheat to a scythe."

As the men cheered again, my eyes widened. When I saw the actual number of veterans present in Captain Hael's camp, it surprised me. I had known many of them had served, but I supposed seeing them all in one spot solidified it in my mind. No wonder the City Watch and Lord Hannady's men hadn't gotten the best of Hael and his men yet... they were too formidable. I wondered why the Eislian army hadn't been called in to sweep the Kovald, as surely that would have been the only way to rid the world of Captain Hael's company.

I found myself reminded of my own story of Captain Kade and his outlaws that I had told to the men around the fire.

"We have worked too bloody hard to earn what we've built here!" thundered the Captain. "Those cowardly, double-crossing wretches can't match your blades, your wits, or your courage! We have been through too much as a company to let these blights come and trample it all! Let us see their efforts fail, aye?"

A chorus of enormous, ferocious roars erupted from the fire circle. Even I found myself nodding. My heart was starting to beat faster as I felt myself being carried away by Hael's charisma. The man had a tremendous talent for speech.

Before I could venture another thought, the Captain turned his gaze toward us and pointed an outstretched arm, scimitar in hand.

"Lynn! Step forward."

Royce and I, perhaps not conscious about doing so, stepped away from the woman as she slowly obeyed, her eyes fixed on Hael's. She stood confident and with poise, and I saw the gazes of the other men immediately divert to watch her. Rain streamed down her forehead and face as it began to fall even harder now, and her red hair that flowed out from under her bandana was soaked, looking darker than usual.

"Men," Captain Hael proclaimed, "I have pardoned Lynn for her earlier actions. I deemed them rash, but she was concerned about our comrade Tambor being held prisoner in Northroe, in the midst of a city still teeming with those loyal to Tyrius. Lynn is still my respected lieutenant, whom I trust, and let me declare for all: this will not change. Perhaps after this is over, maybe, we can devise a way to get Tambor out of that forsaken cell. Lynn, welcome back to the company."

Hearty cheers sprang forward from the brigands. Lynn beamed and saluted the Captain, who returned it in kind. "Thank ya, Cap'n."

"Oy! Here's to Lynn!"

"To Tambor, likewise! Cheers to his wellbeing'!" cried out a man.

Sorley stepped forward with a wild grin. "To the Master Chef!" he shouted, raising his weapon.

More men cheered.

"To the Chef!"

"Here's to the Chef's return!"

"Three cheers for Lynn!"

The campground was alive with excitement, and the peculiar thought that just days ago I would have been scared to death at the sight of these men entered my mind. Now, I was in their midst, cheering with them.

The seeds of change sure sprouted baffling results.

I looked over at Gavin. "'Chef,' Gavin?"

Gavin grinned. "Tambor's the best cook any of us ever met. That man could make the dirt at your feet taste wonderful, mate. He's the Master Chef, and rightfully named so."

"Wait," Royce whispered, "you're saying they're holding our cook prisoner?"

Gavin nodded.

Royce narrowed his eyes. "The bastards."

I found myself chuckling, and I looked up to Alomar at my right. His eyes were still flickering between Captain Hael and Lynn.

"Now, shut it and listen up!" bellowed Captain Hael, and the shouts and cheers gradually subsided. "Our newcomers earned us a new trail of coin to be followed. It requires a meeting with the Village Elder at Mable today, at the same time of the battle. One of our officers must be present for the meeting, and that will be you, Lynn."

I thought I saw Lynn clench her jaw momentarily, perhaps in disapproval, but she nodded. "Aye, Cap'n. We'll get it done."

Hael nodded. "As soon as the deal is struck with those villagers, report back here and await our return. Miles, our party will take four of the horses. Lynn, you will take the remaining two."

So we were taking the horses this time. I found it interesting that we hadn't taken horses for any earlier endeavors, and then I found myself thankful because I had no idea how to ride one, and neither did Royce. The three of us had never been wealthy enough to afford one, but Alomar had a wealth of experience on horseback in Dekka, serving with the 2nd Cavalry.

I then realized that there would be four of us and two horses.

"All right then!" thundered Captain Hael. "War band, check your gear! Miles and Sorley, inspect your men's armor and weapons one last time. Lynn, you and your lot meet Ruben outside the armory. He'll have your gear ready. Attention to detail, men! Take stock and move out, understand?"

Lynn nodded. "Aye. Give 'em hell, Cap'n." She hastily found her fellow Lieutenant in the crowd, and called to him. "Oy, Miles!"

Miles looked at Lynn with a grin.

The woman pointed, playing at threatening. "You better get some o' those bastards for me."

The bald man laughed heartily and gave her a wink before turning to motion for his men to round up and get moving. Lynn turned on her heel and strode immediately toward the armory.

Royce and I were left with Alomar.

"So then, this is it, eh?" Royce said solemnly. He clapped his hand to Alomar's shoulder. "You all right, mate?"

Alomar was oddly nodding, and a strange twinkle glinted outward from his eyes that I'd never seen before. "I think we'll be all right, mates. Especially if what he said was true, about them only having one veteran in their company."

I stared at the man for a long moment before sighing, not knowing exactly what to say.

Alomar looked at me squarely. "There's nothing any of us can do about it, Pen. I'm going to a fight, you're going to a business meeting. We've got our jobs to do. Focus on that, and only that. Otherwise, worry and fear inch their way in, and we can't have that, understand?"

I nodded, feeling noticeably numb.

"Let's go!" shouted Miles. "War party, on me! Check your gear!"

A panicked, hurried sensation overcame me as Alomar strode away from us. He ventured one last glance back at Royce and I.

"I'll be fine, mates. I've seen worse fights. Don't worry about me. Just do your job."

Royce stepped forward and nodded briskly. "We will. Take care, Alomar!"

"Aye," I forced. "We'll see you soon, Al."

Alomar just grinned and melted into the crowd of armed men forming up around Captain Hael and Miles.

"Oy!" came Lynn's voice, shouting to us against a roar of thunder overhead. "Come on, you two."

Without hesitation, Royce and I hurried after the woman, who was already well ahead of us with Gavin.

CHAPTER 42

"Why don't we get any armor?" I asked, dismayed. "Where's our chain mail?"

Royce, Lynn, Gavin and I stood inside the armor shed with Ruben the Weaponsmith, listening to the patter of rain on the roof start hitting harder, turning into one steady noise that droned onward amidst more thunder.

"We're not goin' to a battle, you oaf," Lynn said. "We're goin' to talk to an old man at a village. The 'ell we need armor for?"

I sniffed. "The others get to wear armor."

Gavin chuckled with a roll of his eyes, and Lynn shook her head, though with a slight smile.

"Be glad ya get these cloaks at least. The hood over your head will help with the rain, so hopefully ya don't come down with a blasted cold before we get to the village," Lynn said.

Ruben nodded. "Right, so here we have it. Four packs, one for each of ya. You each get a flask of water, some scraps of food and the like. Each of you has some food: carrots, berries, some leaves of lettuce in there as well as a small roll of bread. Enough for two meals... plenty for the journey. Lynn, the Cap'n said to give ya this."

The man reached behind a rack of old, rusted swords and lifted up a purse the size of a man's fist. It jingled noisily with what sounded like coins as he handed it to Lynn.

"Coin? What for?" she asked.

Ruben shrugged. "Just in case they need extra... motivation. Or, if the situation is right, you can present it to 'em as a gesture of good will, aye? You be the judge."

Lynn frowned and placed the small coin purse inside her pack.

"Extra canteen here, in case for some Fates-forsaken reason you lot run low on water," Ruben said, producing a large, circular tin flask of water that was fixed on a strap. The strap buckled like a belt, meant to be slung over one's shoulders or back. Ruben handed it to Royce, who first put on his backpack, and then slung the water canteen across his back. It hung awkwardly, caught up on the pack, and Ruben stepped forward to help adjust the equipment before turning to Gavin.

"Gav, how's your kit? Medicine, bandages and the like?"

Gavin loosed the satchel he always carried from his shoulder and quickly set it to the floor. In an instant he was kneeling and rummaging through its contents.

"Looks good, Ruben. Though I could use a couple extra needles. More sutures, too. We have any extra myrrh?"

I looked at Royce and raised my eyebrows. He just shrugged, so I turned back to Gavin.

"Myrrh?" I asked, as Ruben handed a tiny sack of what must have been myrrh to Gavin.

"For wounds," Gavin answered. "Cuts and gashes."

I folded my arms and shot Lynn a challenging look. "I thought we weren't going to a battle."

The woman snorted. "We're not, but it's Captain Hael's first rule. Always be prepared."

"Then where's our armor?" I demanded.

Lynn glared. "Shut it."

Gavin dropped the myrrh herb into his satchel. "Could use some lavender too, mate. And some wormwood. And mint. Thomas had that nasty stomach pain the other day. Used the last of what I had."

Ruben sighed lazily. "Let me get the needles and sutures first."

"Oy," asked Royce, "what's the lavender for?"

I watched Gavin for his answer, genuinely curious as well.

"Helps with headaches," answered the man. "So do sage, rose, and bay, but I've got plenty of those."

Royce scratched his chin. "What do you need lavender for, then?"

Lynn sighed. "You two are just full of it today, aren't ya?"

Ruben eventually fetched all of Gavin's supplies, and Gavin gathered them inside his satchel before taking the pack issued to him. Clothes were waiting for us: thick overcoats that we could wear over our current clothing, and warm cloaks with hoods to cover our heads in the rain, which we pulled over ourselves snugly. Royce and I were given pairs of gloves. They were warm and thick, made of wool and dyed dark as night. The tips of the fingers were cut off, and the tips were slightly frayed, as if they had been used before. They fit snugly and insulated my hands.

"Sorry we didn't get ya gloves sooner," Ruben said. "Didn't think of it."

Lynn lifted a pack over her shoulder. "That it then, Ruben?"

The Weaponsmith nodded. "The lot of ya is looking good to go, Lynn. Your horses have their saddlebags already situated with some extra supplies. You won't be gone long, so it's not much of a matter anyhow."

Lynn nodded. "Thanks, Ruben."

"Aye. Good luck to ya. Hurry back, yeah? We could use extra sentries while the war band is out."

The woman nodded again. "Will do. Let's get goin', boys."

We made our way back out into the rainfall to where our two horses waited. One was the gray horse we'd seen Lynn ride into camp the day Quaid and Arthur brought us in. The other horse had a walnut-brown coat of fur with white patches on its face. Their breath misted about in the air as they snorted and whinnied their greetings to us.

Lynn strode up to the gray horse and embraced the animal in greeting, lovingly moving her hands about its face. She spoke in a low voice with a brilliant smile, and I saw that her words were soothing the horse almost immediately. The animal grew quiet and met the woman's eyes with its own, nudging its face against hers.

I was staring. Something about what I was seeing struck me, and I felt a strong drawing to Lynn as I watched her. Her smile was disarming. The light in her eyes enchanted my own. I felt a quicker beating of my heart and momentary shortness of breath. She looked beautiful in the rain, exhibiting kindness and pure warmth. These weren't qualities I'd really seen in her yet, except for when she had interacted with her dog, Ember, on the day she'd spoke to me in the cabin.

Where did all that come from? Wasn't it odd to be so taken by a woman who was dressed more like a man than a fair maiden?

Someone gave me a rough prod, and I snapped out of my daze and blinked the rain away from my eyes to see Royce glaring at me and shaking his head in disapproval.

"What?" I muttered stubbornly.

"Don't think now is the time, Pen."

"Was I really that obvious?" I whispered.

Royce snorted. "Painfully."

"Eh?" asked Lynn, turning to us. "I couldn't hear ya."

Both of us shook our heads vigorously.

"Was nothing."

"Aye. Nothing at all."

"Um, look at these clouds, eh?"

"Quite right, Penny."

Lynn frowned and turned back to her steed. She stood on her tiptoes and reached up to the saddlebag, inspecting her gear. Gavin went to his brown horse and presented it with carrots. The animal gratefully ate from his open hand while the man encouraged it kindly before looking back at us over his shoulder.

"Let's get it over with then," Gavin declared. "Who's riding with who?"

Both Royce and I immediately started for Lynn's horse, bumping each other's heads roughly.

"Blast!" I winced, rubbing my temple. "Bloody dangerous, you are!"

Royce was clutching his head as well. "I'm riding with Lynn. The lady needs worthy company, know what I mean?"

Horrified that we had suddenly exposed our thoughts on the woman, I looked at her and was surprised to see a gentle smile cross her lips, almost as if embarrassed. She shook her head and looked away, seeming to force her attention back to her horse.

Gavin was hooting with laughter. "Well, then. Don't all rush for me at once. What's wrong with me anyhow?" he asked with mock confusion. "Oy, Lynn."

The woman turned. "Yes, Gav?"

"Am I not the most handsomest man ever to walk these parts, in all o' the Fates' history?"

Lynn laughed now. "'Tis true, aye. Clearly these two don't know the *handsomest* man in all of Eisley when they see him."

Laughing louder, Gavin stroked his black beard with a shake of his head. I remembered to breathe again, and upon doing so, realized they were both joking.

"That's all good and well, aye," Royce replied, not missing a beat. "What if a bloke like myself happens to prefer women? Gavin, not to say you're not the most handsome bloke I've ever seen. But I'd much prefer to ride with the lady."

Both Lynn and Gavin were laughing now, but all I could do was glare at my friend for vying for the spot that I desired with the woman that charmed me so effortlessly. Wasn't that how it always worked, though? A woman could grab ahold of a man's heart, his very soul, with nothing but a look, a twinkle in the eye, a show of bare skin.

But this was different! I was finding myself more than just in admiration of Lynn.

I was curious about her. I yearned for an open, honest conversation with the woman. I wanted to know more about the kindhearted, pure side of her that I had just caught a glimpse of. I wanted to speak with her, to learn of who she really was underneath her tough exterior.

Lynn was still smiling. Still! I hadn't seen her smile so much. Her eyes flickered between Royce and I, and she suddenly leaned in close toward her horse and spoke softly into its ear. The woman wore a mischievous grin, and her eyes sparkled dangerously. My heart tightened slightly when her gaze fixed on mine.

"Right then," she said matter-of-factly, straightening her posture. "Anijo says the Storyteller rides with me today."

My eyes widened stupendously. "He does? I mean, I do?"

"Anijo?" asked Royce.

Lynn grinned. "Anijo is the horse's name, and he has spoken, ya see?" She stroked the animal's face affectionately, still speaking to him.

Royce snorted. "Alas, Anijo may not be as noble as you'd think. Especially with a name like that, for he has chosen poorly on this day."

Lynn shook her head and beckoned me to her. "No, Royce. Anijo's never wrong."

"But the beast didn't speak a word! The horse can't talk!"

Lynn folded her arms and cast a piercing stare toward the man. "You're right. I'd just prefer the Storyteller ride with me. How's that suit ya?"

I flashed Royce a discreet wink. He brushed back his long, dusty brown hair and tossed back his head to laugh at the stormy skies before giving a dismissive wave of his hand.

I was absolutely dumbfounded. I felt awkward, like a young lad who was too shy to tell a girl he liked her, but my heart soared at the notion of Lynn favoring me over another man... even if it was over something so trivial.

"All right," Lynn declared loudly, "enough o' this. We have to get movin'."

"Lynn?" I asked, trying not to sound meek.

"Eh?"

"Stop calling me 'Storyteller', yeah?"

The woman flashed me a crooked grin. "Okay then, Penny."

Just her voice uttering my name sent small tinges of excitement surging through me. As she climbed onto Anijo and into the saddle with grace, I hoped I didn't make it too obvious that I was hanging on her every word and action. It couldn't be healthy, after all.

"C'mon," she said, still smiling. Lynn leaned forward and outstretched a gloved hand. I took a little running start and met her grasp, hopping upward and landing messily onto the horse. The woman laughed as I tried to situate myself behind her. Both elated and horrified that my hands would touch something they weren't supposed to, I awkwardly adjusted myself on the horse's back and finally was seated comfortably.

"Hands around my waist," Lynn said. "Hurry now."

Swallowing hard and feeling the tremors of my heartbeat, I gingerly did so. As if to echo my earlier thoughts, Lynn turned to me with a straight face.

"If I feel your hands go up or down any more than that, to someplace they're not supposed to, by the Fates I swear I'll cut 'em off, ya hear me?"

"Aye," I answered, totally abashed. "By the Fates. Got it."

Lynn gave a shrill whistle and we were off, thundering through the woods on horseback. I ventured a glance behind me to see Gavin and Royce riding close on our trail, the thud of hooves kicking up dirt and mud in their wake.

I nearly lost my seating as Lynn urged Anijo into a full jump over a fallen log. With a shout, I turned to face forward again and held on for my life. We landed smoothly enough, and I rocked about slightly before realizing I was clutching Lynn's waist perhaps a bit too tightly.

I loosened my grip on the woman. "Uh... sorry."

"Watch your hands, or else I'll keep callin' ya 'Storyteller.' There's your ultimatum, got it?" she called back as we raced on through the storm.

"Got it!" I shouted back, and the rain began coming down even harder.

What in the blazes was going on here with Lynn? It was as if she suddenly didn't mind my presence all that much. Or even liked me, at that. She wasn't shy about choosing me to ride with her, even doing so playfully, I daresay. I was excited, and I replayed her fancying words and flirtatious smiles in my mind as we rode on. I was also hesitant to do so, trying to quell my hopeful heart in its tracks even though it fluttered stubbornly. Lynn's behavior was so sudden, and it didn't seem to make sense. I hadn't seen her act this way toward any man in camp... and she chose to act in this manner with me, of all men? I didn't understand, but I suppose that when it comes to men and women, sometimes we're not meant to. At least, just not right away.

Perhaps I was looking too far into it all.

*   *   *

The journey south to Mable through the dense woods and thickets of the Kovald took a fraction of the time required when we had trekked by foot the day before with Miles and his men. Amazingly, the rainfall was now heavier than ever, and thunder rolled across the heavens. The storm lit the sky with lightning, and an unrelenting fog formed quickly in its midst, so thick that everything in sight seemed to fade away to nothing.

"Whoa, now," uttered Lynn, pulling back gently on the reins. "Slow it down, Anijo."

Her horse obediently slowed pace to a trot.

"Penny," Lynn called out over the rain, turning back toward me the best she could in the saddle, "are we gettin' near? Can ya recognize anythin'?"

Rain was rolling off the hood covering my head. Shielding my eyes from the storm, I peered forward and surveyed the surroundings.

"I can't tell," I said, squinting as if that would help me see. "Fog's too heavy."

Gavin and Royce trotted up next to us.

"Oy, Gav!" called Lynn. "What say ya? We have to be gettin' close, yeah?"

Nodding, Gavin leaned forward in his saddle to stroke his horse's face, trying to comfort the animal in the midst of the storm. "We should be, aye. I'm guessing the river is very near, but we just can't hear it over the blasted rainfall. Want me to scout ahead?"

Lynn bit her lip and surveyed the foggy woods around us before shaking her head. "This mist is too great. Let's stay together for now."

Gavin nodded.

"Oy, look!" Royce said suddenly. We all turned to him to see him pointing to the right. "See that? Those trees? Isn't this where we all huddled up and went over the plan with Miles and the other blokes before going to the bridge?"

I turned and saw a large formation of trees at the edge of a thicket. Foliage was strewn about at their bases and stretched onward to another cluster of pines, clumping around their trunks as well. Most importantly, I recognized the large oak at the center of the first formation, it's trunk twisted and blackened by a lightning strike.

"Aye!" I called. "That's it!"

Gavin nodded. "'Tis true. That means the small bridge is just up ahead, south."

We headed southward at a slow and steady pace, not wanting to risk injury to the horses or ourselves. Lightning flashed again overhead, startling both animals. Lynn was quick to soothe Anijo and spur him onward gently, and Gavin and Royce followed in our wake as we trotted slowly through one last thicket before the edge of the tree line came into view.

My curiosity got the best of me, and I tapped Lynn's shoulder. "Oy! What's the other horse's name, that Gavin rides?"

"That one is Darius," the woman replied. "We caught him wild out near Stratton, years ago. Named him after the man who tamed him. Darius was a good man."

"Was?" I asked.

Lynn gave Anijo a pat as we trotted on, pausing for a long moment before answering. "The Watch got him. Over in the Heartland, just east of Eisley City." She sighed. "They hung him, and there wasn't a bloody thing we could do 'bout it."

I clenched my jaw. "Sorry."

Lynn only shrugged. "What can ya do? The past has passed, as they say, and... hoy there, look at that! The bridge is just up ahead."

The woman held up her hand and motioned for Gavin to ride up alongside us again. A moment later, both horses were abreast of each other and Lynn was speaking.

"Give me a moment. I'm gonna go ahead and have a look, just in case," she said. "Just wanna scout the area."

Gavin nodded. "Right. But don't be too obvious, Lynn. These folks are rather jumpy. Ya heard about them massing up in the Square and all that. Let's not give 'em the wrong impression about why we're here."

Lynn sprang smoothly out of her saddle and touched her feet to the ground, shooting Gavin a hurt look.

"Come now, Gav. Is 'Careful' not my middle name?"

Grinning, Gavin cocked his head. "Didn't know you had a middle name, miss."

"Well, I don't," Lynn replied. "But if I did, 'Careful' would be it. Hey, Penny, toss me that satchel that's bound up with the other supplies? The burlap one. It should be... aye, that one."

I removed the satchel from the saddlebag and dropped it to her cupped hands. The woman quickly unbound the small package and lifted out a long tube with a glass lens.

"A spyglass?" I asked, impressed.

"Where'd you get that?" I heard Royce ask. "Bloody expensive."

"We have our ways," Lynn answered. "Be right back. Don't leave without me."

Gavin chuckled. "Wouldn't dream of it."

The woman trudged away from us toward the bridge and broke into a light jog. I watched her disappear into the fog, so thick that we couldn't see to the other side of the bridge. I found myself admiring even the way she moved. She was nimble and athletic, even running with a grace that eluded my own.

I closed my eyes and shook my head. I felt like a lovestruck youth again, and it was starting to annoy me. We had a job to do here, as Alomar had pointed out earlier. We had to get it done, and done right, at that... and here I was, a grown man getting hung up on the woman's every word and action.

Alomar... how was he? I pictured him with that absolutely fearsome, stone-cold look of his, setting the very forest on fire with his eyes as he gazed upon his enemy. He was a strong, massive man who could hold his own in any fight. He had faced down foreigners in their own land and come out victorious. I knew that Eislian soldiers were near unmatched the world over, and yet I couldn't help but worry for my friend. A worry sprang from the well in the pit of my stomach, and I tried to squelch it before it spread.

"Oy, Pen!" called Royce through the rain. "How in blazes did you pull it off?"

I shifted on Anijo anxiously. "Pull what off?"

"Ha! 'Pull what off?' he says," laughed my friend. "You have the woman of the company fawning over you now, do ya?"

Recoiling, I shook my head. "She... is not *fawning* over me, you oaf." I was very conscious that Gavin was present for this conversation, and glanced at him nervously.

Royce was alight with mischief as always, and nudged the man beside him. "Oy, Gav. May I call you Gav?"

"You may."

"Right, then. Gav. How is it that Lynn chose my friend the Storyteller here, over an obviously handsomer bloke like myself? And not to say, of course, that you're not still the Handsomest Man In All of Eisley. But come on, mate. Is this normal?"

Gavin gazed at Royce, unflinching. "I suggest you focus on what really matters here, and keep your eyes and ears open."

Royce grimaced at the man's words, but obeyed.

Gavin leaned forward, peering through the rain toward the bridge that Lynn had disappeared across. He stroked his bearded chin thoughtfully before dismounting Darius and feed him more food from the palm of his hand.

Suddenly my youthful yearnings for the woman were being overcome with anxiety and fright. If she did have feelings for me, as odd as that felt, what would the other men in the company think? Why wasn't she already taken, now that I thought about it?

I silently scolded myself and shoved the thought from my mind. There was no way a woman like her would fancy a man like myself. I wasn't stupid. I berated myself for letting these wishful thoughts continue and take form in my mind.

Movement on the bridge caught my eye, and all three of us snapped our gazes southward to see the shadow of a woman fade into view through the fog. It was Lynn, and she was jogging toward us.

"Oy, are we all set?" called Gavin.

Lynn didn't answer. Without slowing pace, she rushed straight to the side of Anijo and started rummaging through the saddlebag.

"Penny, get down," Lynn ordered. "Hurry. You too, Royce!"

I clumsily got down from my perch atop Anijo and watched the woman nervously, exchanging glances with Royce.

"What is it?" Gavin asked, his tone changing.

"Dunno," she breathed. I realized she was reaching for one of the spare swords that hung from the gear bag, and she unfastened it from the strap. It was a short sword with a steel blade, much the same as the ones Eislian soldiers favored in battle. She thrust it toward me.

"Take it," she urged. "Hurry."

My eyes widened. "What's wrong?" I asked. "What did you see?"

Lynn's eyes narrowed. "Take the sword. I'm not messin' about."

I obeyed, most reluctantly. "I... I don't know how to fight. I've never swung a sword in my life."

The woman snapped her fingers and motioned to Gavin. Understanding immediately, Gavin loosed his backup axe, a large hatchet smaller than the weapon he usually favored, and handed it to Royce.

"Ma'am Lynn," Royce said slowly, "what's wrong?"

My heart beat with fright. Why was she giving us weapons? What could possibly be happening in the village?

Lynn didn't answer. She was going through her pack, hastily looking for something. I saw the looking glass hanging at her belt. Her eyes found mine, and she saw me still holding the sword and scabbard in my hands.

"Fasten that to your belt," she said. "Blazes, c'mon!"

I immediately set about doing so, trying to ignore the fear building up in me.

Gavin finally stepped forward. "Lynn. What did you see, lass? What's going on?"

Lynn stood and adjusted her backpack so it fit her snugly. Her red-brown eyes shone with an edge I hadn't seen before. The woman bit her lip and she looked at the three of us men for a long moment before finally replying.

"I don't know what the devil's goin' on up there," she said, motioning behind her toward Mable, "but somethin' ain't right. Tie the horses up here. Fasten your gear tight, and we go carefully, aye? The quieter, the better."

CHAPTER 43

Lynn and Gavin left their two horses behind with a bite of food and words of comfort before we set off for the village. Wind and rain whipped through the air and rippled our cloaks as the four of us hurried across the bridge leading to Mable. Thunder dashed the dark clouds above.

Up ahead, the village cottages, houses and various buildings loomed like big ominous ghosts in the fog, slowly taking shape as we neared. We were on the dirt road, which led southward and cut straight down the middle of Mable, with the village's premises lining both sides of it. I could see the Village Square up ahead, where the road widened considerably at the center of the settlement before narrowing once more, further south. It was so foggy that I couldn't yet see the statue above the well in the middle of the Square, or the large manor we had seen the day before.

Stopping suddenly, Lynn motioned for us to dart to the right, and we obeyed. We still hadn't quite entered the village itself, and I realized she didn't want to head straight in like our party had the day before. We still had to cross a decent stretch of open ground, and Lynn and Gavin jogged ahead with Royce and I trailing behind closely.

I slipped momentarily in the mud and regained my footing, stumbling into Royce. My friend steadied me and urged me on, and we followed Lynn and Gavin to the outskirts of Mable, finally reaching and hiding behind an old two-story barn. An old peddler's cart, worn and splintered with age and missing one wheel, sat in a wooden heap directly beside the barn, leaning against the wall. Three large barrels lined the front of it as well as some various tools.

It was there that we hid.

Hunkering down low behind the cart and barrels, and using the barn as shelter on our right, we surveyed the scene. Peering through the rain, I could see nothing but dark, heavy gray mist, broken up here and there by shadowy silhouettes of buildings nearby. I could only see a few, at that. The fog was so thick that a hundred paces or so in each direction was shrouded too heavily for eyesight to penetrate.

Lynn had her spyglass out again and tried sweeping the area, but a brief moment later she cursed and gave up.

"Too much fog," she hissed. "Do ya boys see what's wrong here?"

Royce was on my right, and he looked at me and shook his head slightly. I looked back at Gavin. He had readied his large axe with both hands and rested warily against the barn, watching behind us.

Lynn was on my right, against the corner of the barn. The woman nudged me and leaned closer so that I could hear her over the rain and thunder.

"What do ya see, Penny?"

I shook my head, puzzled. Then I realized what she was getting at, and it was suddenly very obvious.

"There's nobody here," I murmured.

Lynn nodded. "Aye."

"Did you see anyone at all when you first came up here to scout?" asked Royce.

The woman shook her head.

Royce cocked his head in question. "Then why the grave show when you came back to us? Telling us to arm up and all that?"

"'Cause," Lynn answered, "I saw a horse riding off to the west. Its rider was dead. The man was hangin' off the poor beast before he was finally shaken off. Tumbled and rolled across the ground and the beast kept goin'."

All three of us men looked at the woman. I felt a sudden sense of urgency and danger.

My eyes went wider than I'd have liked. "Didn't see anyone else, did you?"

The woman shook her head. "No. But that's not what's worryin' me right now."

Royce glanced at her looking glass laying in the dirt beside her. "Are you worried because you can't see a damned thing?"

Lynn sighed and took one more look through the glass before shaking her head. She reached behind her and gave Gavin a tap, motioning for him to look where she pointed, and she pointed out toward the Square for all of us to see.

"That's where the body fell off," she said, her words laced with tension. "It's not there now. Someone already moved it."

Gavin's eyes narrowed. "Maybe he wasn't dead."

"The back of the man's shirt was soaked with blood. I know a dead man when I see one."

My blood chilled, and thunder erupted somewhere in the distance. I suddenly felt like I was being watched, and I flipped my head this way and that in an effort to seek out any would-be onlookers. I saw nothing but fog, misty buildings, and grassy fields that faded into mist. Royce, now also keenly aware of his surroundings, crouched even lower.

"So, someone's here," Gavin mused, sinking low against the barn wall. He tightened his grip on his axe. "Think it's Tyrius's men?"

Lynn was shielding her eyes from the rain as she peered out toward the Square again. "Could be. No way of knowin'. But we have to find out."

"What?" I asked, trying not to show fear. "Why don't we just turn around? Let's just leave, aye?"

Nobody answered me. For a long moment we sat in the safe haven of ours behind the old cart and barrels against the barn, thinking hard on Lynn's words. I tried to catch Royce's gaze, but he was too busy watching the way we had come.

Lynn finally spoke. "I'm going inside," she said, patting the wall of the barn. "Gonna have a look."

Worried, I frowned. "Just you?"

She nodded. "Penny, I want ya to keep your eyes ahead, on the Square. Royce, keep watchin' the way you're lookin', back north. Gav, you have our backs, yeah? Watch west."

"Aye," Gavin nodded. "And you watch yourself, got it? I hear anything bad in there, I'm comin' in."

Lynn smiled wryly. "I'll be fine. Eyes open, boys. Remember, if that fog clears up, whoever's out here can see that much easier too, got it? So keep low."

We all nodded. Lynn stood slowly and gripped the front of the cart with her gloved hands and stood there, seemingly frozen for a long moment while she took one last look around. Then without a word she sprang up and lifted herself up and over, landing with a soft splash of mud, and swiftly disappeared around the corner of the barn, hugging the wall. I thought I heard the barely audible creaking of a wood door opening around the corner and out of view, and I assumed it was Lynn entering the building.

We listened breathlessly while straining to see through the fog and survey the area. All we heard for a few minutes was the steady, strong rainfall descending upon the land around us. Wind ruffled our cloaks and added bite to the cold air, and I pulled my cloak tighter about me as I kept watch toward the Square. My eyes flickered this way and that. I could have sworn I saw a misty figure dart by in the distance, but I blinked rapidly and there was nothing. Wiping the rain from my eyes, I redoubled my efforts, straining to see clearly.

Royce decided to get prone on the ground and did so very slowly, never taking his eyes off the northbound country toward the bridge we had crossed earlier. After he settled into what must have been the most comfortable position available in the soaked, cold mud, he didn't move a muscle. Perhaps Royce remembered the consequences of doing so, days ago in the woods when he had made the slightest movement and it gave our positions away to Arthur and Quaid.

"Oy, mates," I heard Gavin say as lowly as he could over the rain. "Don't bloody blink, got it? I've got a bad feeling about this, I do. Keep your eyes open. Don't forget your weapons, either."

His words scared me more. A seasoned bandit was watching my back and was apparently as troubled as I was by what we had seen... or hadn't seen... so far. Gavin's words provided little in the way of comfort.

I swallowed hard and kept my gaze ahead, sweeping the foggy buildings and watching the windows and land around them for any signs of movement. It was then that I realized the fog was so thick that someone could be standing with their noses pressed up against the windows in a building across the way, and I probably couldn't see them from where I was.

A couple more minutes passed. The rain continued its downpour. I began to grow uncomfortable and shifted slightly. The hood of my cloak was pressing down on my head with the weight of rainwater. I grew uneasy when we didn't hear from Lynn for yet another minute or so. I sidled right, to where she had been perched, and pressed my head to the wall gently to try to hear the slightest noise from within the barn, but it was to no avail. The rain was too loud.

"Pen," Royce said suddenly. "I don't like this, mate."

I clenched my jaw. "Did you see something?"

"No. I just don't feel right. Something's wrong."

"I know. I don't like it, either."

"Pssst."

All three of us jumped and whirled about, eyes wide and in search of the source of the whisper. My heart just about jumped up into my mouth. Looking up, I saw Lynn peering down at us through a window on the second floor of the barn.

The woman beckoned. "There's nobody here. Hurry inside!"

We hesitantly got to our feet, checked our surroundings before moving, and then hopped over the cart and quickly moved through the front door of the barn.

Gavin shut the door immediately, and before I could get a chance to take stock of the barn interior, Lynn grasped Gavin's shoulder and nodded toward the back of the barn.

"This way. Have to show ya somethin'. Penny, you and Royce watch the door, aye?"

"I thought you said no one was here?" asked Royce.

Lynn glared. "Just watch the door. We'll be right back. C'mon Gav."

I watched Lynn and Gavin navigate through discarded debris, storage barrels, old crates of tools and small heaps of hay as they moved to a small room at the rear of the barn. My eyes wandered to a large mound of straw in a corner.

It was stained red with splotches of blood that trailed away from us toward a steep, rickety old staircase leading upward to a trap door. This opened into the second floor loft.

For a moment, I considered venturing upstairs in a show of bravery. Lynn might appreciate a man who could think for himself and take action, after all... but at that moment, she and Gavin strode back into our presence from the back room. Lynn's lips were pursed, and Gavin was frowning, both deep in thought.

"Come with me," Lynn whispered, her eyes betraying her anxiety. "Quickly."

Gavin hefted his axe. "I'll watch the door."

Royce and I followed Lynn into the next room, which had once been a small stable. We passed by abandoned stalls until we reached the far wall. A pile of hay in the corner next to an old workbench had been recently swept aside, revealing a wooden trapdoor leading below ground.

The edges of the trapdoor were caked with dried blood.

"Skies be cursed," Royce breathed.

"Just take a look," Lynn requested. "I was already down there. It's safe."

She opened the trapdoor and stooped low to cradle it during its descent so that it didn't slam loudly to the floor. An old wooden ladder led down into a dimly lit cellar.

The three of us soon descended the ladder and stood in the basement. A torch was lit in its sconce, casting flickering shadows about. The only object in the cellar was a battered, empty bookcase propped awkwardly against the wall next to the torch.

"Was this torch already lit when you came down here?" I asked.

"Aye. Look over here now," Lynn instructed. "On the other side o' this shelf."

Royce and I obliged. He peered around the bookcase first, stopped cold, and abruptly backed into me.

"What the devil is it?" I asked breathlessly. "What'd you see, Roy?"

"Just look for yourself," Lynn demanded impatiently.

Royce stepped aside with a sorry look on his face, and I obeyed, venturing a look around the discarded bookshelf.

My eyes widened at the sight of three bodies strewn in a heap on the stone floor: a man, a woman, and a boy. The unfortunate souls had wounds on their bodies obviously inflicted by blades of some sort. The child couldn't have been more than ten years old.

"Fates," I uttered.

Lynn was nodding. "Aye. I wanted you to see for yourselves. Killed the boy, they did. Takes a special kind of heartless wretch to do so."

Royce stared hard and looked to us, eyes alive with fire.

"Who did this?" he asked coldly.

Lynn shook her head. "Well, we just got here. Dunno yet. But there's more."

"More?" I asked, looking around. "Bloody hell. Where?"

"Up in the loft," Lynn said grimly. "Follow me."

Soon we were upstairs and walking quickly back into the front room, where Gavin was watching the door intently.

As Lynn turned swiftly to ascend the staircase, I met Gavin's gaze with my own. It was brief and wordless, but a solemn understanding passed between us. Something in Mable was amiss, and we all had the unmistakable feeling that only the surface had been scratched.

The loft above, bare and featureless, was quite large, tall enough so that we didn't have to stoop very low. The rainfall's muffled *pitter-patter* began to ease its relentless washing of the barn roof. Lynn wasted no time in stepping to the circular window overlooking the Village Square outside. She crouched to one knee and motioned for us to do the same.

"Look out there," she ordered, handing Royce the spyglass, "toward the well an' the statue."

Neither Royce nor I obeyed. We were staring at two more corpses of villagers, both men, heaped in the far corner of the loft in a bloody mess.

Lynn clapped hands to both our shoulders, bringing our attention quickly back to her. "Oy! Focus, you two!" She gestured to the spyglass that Royce clenched tightly in his grip, and my friend nodded knowingly. He brought the spyglass up to look out the window.

I peered out too, and thought I could barely discern a silhouette of what must have been the statue out in the center of the village, but the fog and rain made it extremely difficult to confirm. I turned my gaze to Royce and watched his face intently as he looked through the spyglass.

Royce's eyebrows raised in clear alarm, and his mouth opened slowly. He lowered the spyglass, clenched his jaw, and looked again.

I shivered. "What do you see, Royce?"

Royce shook his head slowly. "We need to get out of here. Right bloody now."

"Calm down," Lynn scolded. "Penny, take a look. Quickly."

Steeling myself for whatever might have met my eyes, I obeyed and looked through the lens. I could see much further than before. It took me just a moment to find the well and statue at the center of the Village Square despite the rain and mist. Steadying my grip on the instrument, I peered intently through, and my blood turned cold at the sight that met my eyes.

Four bodies, nooses tight around their necks, hung lifelessly from the stone arch over the well.

CHAPTER 44

"Back downstairs," pushed Lynn. "We don't know if we've been seen or not."

"Don't talk like that, eh?" Royce muttered.

It was true though, and as we trailed behind Lynn back downstairs to the storeroom, that was when the gravity of what we were facing really pressed down upon me. My breathing quickened, and my heart thumped furiously. Whoever was responsible for the savagery we had seen was somewhere out there in the rain and fog, veiled by the storm's darkness... and they could know we were in the village.

They could be right outside, waiting for us.

I wondered if the brigands of Captain Hael's band came across situations like this often. Lynn and Gavin were nervous and highly alert, but if they were scared, they hid it well.

Unveiling the hood from my head, I strolled to a sturdy crate and sat upon it, my sword and scabbard briefly preventing me from doing so comfortably.

My attention was suddenly on my weapon, and the desire to sit drifted away. I stood and reached down to unsheathe the blade. It rasped out of the scabbard, and I was careful to try to draw the sword quietly. The weapon was very light, and I could see a hazy reflection of my face in the steel.

We stood in silence, and Lynn folded her arms and started pacing about, biting her lip in thought.

"I don't know h-how to fight," I stammered finally, gazing at the short sword in my hand. "I've never-"

"Swing it," Gavin replied sarcastically.

I forced a chuckle, but my grin quickly faded. "Seriously. I've never used a blade."

Lynn's eyes shot over at me in surprise.

Gavin frowned. "Never?"

I shook my head.

"How the 'ell did you blokes get away from the Northroe City Watch?" the man asked incredulously.

"Got lucky," Royce answered for me. "Didn't need weapons, as it turned out. Story for another time, aye?"

The way my friend's voice trembled slightly was troubling. Royce was usually optimistic, perhaps even annoyingly so, but his words were plagued by worry.

"Here's the plan," Lynn said lowly. "Listen. We have to go back outside, whether we want to or not – but we have to figure out what the devil's goin' on here."

I gawked in dismay.

"What's the plan then?" asked Gavin.

"Let's search some more. Check some o' the other buildings. Cottages and the like."

"Whoa, now," Royce interjected. "Why? Let's just bloody leave!"

"We can't," Lynn answered. "What if there are other people here? Being' tortured, or worse?"

I snorted. "Now you grow a conscience? After Northroe?"

"There were no children in that tavern!" Lynn hissed angrily. "Somebody is killin' these villagers. Not only do I wanna cut out the eyes o' the bastard that would gut a child, but these people are also supposed to be steady income for our camp, remember? The more blood that's spilt, the more coin disappears."

I closed my eyes and grappled with her line of thought. The woman clearly felt for innocent people, but only if they were children. Apparently she had a problem with unarmed men and women being killed, but only since they represented a way to make money.

I shook my head. "I don't know, Lynn. This is dangerous. We should've brought the horses."

She scoffed in frustration. "If we'd brought the horses, whoever's out here would've heard us comin' before we even reached the barn. We can't just return to the Cap'n and tell him what we've seen, and then inform him that we were too bloody scared to look into it, yeah? The lot of ya better not forget, your friend is out there with the Cap'n and Miles, probably about to fight to the death right now, hear me? There's no quarter for cowards!"

Her words served as a stark reminder of Alomar's circumstances. Royce and I exchanged glances, and I sighed. "Fates be with them."

Lynn nodded. "Aye. Let's not dally about."

The four of us scurried out of the barn, braving whipping rainfall as we jogged to a small cottage just fifty paces or so south of the barn. With Lynn in the lead and Gavin bringing up the rear, we all slid to a stop in the mud and pressed ourselves to the wall of the small building, anxiously looking in all directions.

The sensation that someone was watching us was overwhelming, and I couldn't put it to rest. I was narrowing my eyes, trying to pierce through the fog to spot any suspicious activity, fully expecting to see some phantom drift along in the mist.

There was no old cart or weathered barrels to hide behind outside of this cottage. Though we were pressing ourselves to the wall to keep a low profile, I felt exposed. Lynn carefully peered around the corner of the cottage, and then turned back to us.

"From now on, nobody go anywhere alone, aye? Inside we go, boys. On me, got it?"

After Gavin explained to Royce and me what 'on me' meant, we spent the next half hour dashing through the rain and searching the village.

Cottages. Four small houses. An old woodworking shop. Small shanties. A deserted stable. Quick inspections were conducted amidst the storm, our anxiety as evident as the rolling thunder overhead...and not one soul was found. Only abandoned establishments greeted our brandished weapons.

We reached an old, decaying house within sight of the enormous manor in the Village Square. A lone tree cast a gnarled shadow across the front door, and its branches scraped against the top of the home in a ghostly whisper. One window next to the door seemed to glared at us.

Lynn and Gavin ducked low to keep themselves out of view of anyone at the window and moved quickly to the front door. Royce and I mimicked the tactic. As we readied up at the entrance, I frowned up at the tree, feeling as if it were waiting for us to turn our backs.

Lynn held up her hand, counted down, and we stormed through the doors of the house, Royce and I careful not to hinder the process. Once inside, I immediately shut the door. Lynn and Gavin fanned out and moved swiftly through the home, their weapons swaying in rhythm with their calculated movements. Royce followed.

Inside was normal enough. A washing basin filled with dirty dishes, a small workbench, an old, iron sword hung above a fireplace, a stack of folded linens in a straw basket.

The long, oaken banquet table was what caught my eye.

Most of the wood chairs were pushed in neatly, awaiting any takers, but three others were overturned on the stone floor. The table was set, complete with food and drink. Three plates were still filled with mostly untouched food. Half-eaten rolls, breadcrumbs and bits of vegetables littered the tabletop messily. An inexpensive goblet lay on the floor, and red wine stained the stone.

Among the food and broken dinnerware, I could see specks of blood.

"Pssst!" I hissed, frantic to get the others' attention.

Lynn turned abruptly, the others halting as she did so. Wide-eyed, I gestured feverishly to the table and the blood.

The woman just nodded, and motioned for me to keep watch at the front door. Apparently, blood on the table was old news.

Feeling a little silly, I steadied myself and looked to the entrance. I felt dangerously exposed by the large front window next to the door, so I sidled off to the side and sank down to a crouch against the wall, leaning against it. When I was satisfied I was hidden from any prying eyes outside, I stifled a yawn and listened to the rainfall outside.

Royce joined me shortly after, sitting down next to me with a grunt. "Lynn told me to join you. No one is to be alone at any time."

I nodded. "What do you think is going on?"

"I don't know, Penny. I wish Alomar was here."

"Aye. I hope he's okay."

Royce stretched. "That man has been through too much to fall to some ragtag bandits. He's too strong. They won't touch him."

We both chuckled, though it was forced. Thirst set upon me, and I found my tin water flask in my pack. I chugged greedily, cherishing the cool water washing my dry mouth.

"Don't drink it all at once, mate," advised Royce.

I snorted. "Of course not."

As I twisted the cap back on, I gasped when the tin flask slipped from my fingers, clattering to the stone floor loudly and rolling away beneath the banquet table.

Both of us cringed at the commotion, and I felt as if all of Eisley heard my folly. Neither Lynn nor Gavin came running, and I wondered how they were faring as I sullenly scooted forward on my hands and knees to retrieve the flask from under the table.

I reached for it, and something warm splashed onto my hand. It was blood, and instead of erupting into panic, I slowly tilted my head upward. Under the table were two small, bloody handprints, those of children. Blood streaked away from the prints and toward the end of the table, as if a young soul had been dragged away at this odd angle, clutching madly for life.

I swore and felt myself pale in fright. Turning to Royce, I opened my mouth to inform him of the grisly sight, but shock snatched the words from my mouth and speared my heart.

A man was outside the house, pressing his face against the glass of the front window. He wore a vacant stare, his eyes fixed on mine.

CHAPTER 45

"R-Royce-" I stammered, pointing frantically at the window.

"What?" he breathed, standing immediately.

I stood hastily, forgetting I was under the table. My head bumped into it violently, shaking the table on impact and knocking dishes noisily about. The ruckus rang out through the whole house.

Royce cursed. "What are you doing!?"

Clutching my head in pain, I regained my footing and looked to the window wildly.

There was nobody there.

"I s-saw someone there," I whispered.

"You what?"

"I bloody *saw someone,* there in the window!" I spat.

Royce spun quickly, though the ominous face was gone. Lynn and Gavin came hurtling back to us through the house, weapons ready. They slid to a stop when they came into view, their eyes searching us vehemently.

"What happened?" Gavin asked.

"We heard a crash," Lynn breathed. "You boys okay?"

I took a deep breath, summoning dignity. "Look. I dropped my flask, and there's blood under the table, and the man was staring at me, and-"

Lynn's eyes simmered. "A man was outside? He saw ya?"

"Aye," I nodded. "By the Fates, he was just staring at me!"

Without a word, Lynn readied her blade and ventured a long look out the window.

"He's not there now," I said, shuddering. "Scared the life right outta me."

Gavin stepped forward. "This ain't good, Lynn. They know we're here, now. At least, someone does."

Still looking out the window, Lynn's eyes fell downward, and she cocked her head inquisitively. "Maybe. Maybe not. Gav, come help me. Leave the axe. Royce, hold the door open for us, okay?"

Royce cleared his throat. "Um, what? What is it?"

Without answering, Lynn sheathed her sword, shoved the front door open roughly and stepped out into the storm, Gavin right on her heels. Royce followed and stood in the rain, holding the door open obediently while they ventured outside. I was shocked when Lynn and Gavin came back inside, carrying a man who sagged limply in their grasp.

It was the same man I had seen.

"That's him!" I managed in disbelief.

Royce closed the door behind our companions as we knelt carefully to lay the man facedown on the floor. It was then that I saw a large knife protruding from his back.

"You weren't kidding," Lynn remarked, her eyes narrowed at the man's face. Without hesitation, she closed her gloved fingers around the knife's handle and yanked it from the blood-soaked shirt.

I winced, keeping a comfortable distance and not wanting to go near him.

"Is he dead?" Royce asked.

Gavin nodded. "Aye. We checked. Besides, if a man says nothing as you pull a knife from his body, there's a good chance he's dead. Or, he's knocked out to oblivion. But probably just dead."

I cursed loudly. "What in blazes is happening?"

Lynn turned the man over onto his back. I didn't recognize him, not even from the meeting with the villagers from the previous day. His eyes looked glazed over, his final expression pained and sorrowful.

"A throwing knife," Lynn murmured.

"Did you find anything else in the house?" asked Royce.

Lynn stood and motioned for us to join her safely out of view of the window, in a corner of the room. We did so, leaving the dead man on the floor near the door.

"We didn't find any bodies, but we found blood. Lots o' blood, actually," she replied lowly. "Must've been at least three or four people tortured in that back room, but no bodies."

Gavin sighed. "Someone was on a mission, that's for sure."

"I don't understand," came Royce. "We were just here yesterday. What could've happened?"

"And why on earth haven't we seen one soul during all of this, save for this poor bloke at our feet?" I asked.

Gavin leaned on his large axe like it was a cane. "I think there's a good bit o' danger here, Lynn. Perhaps we should leave."

I nodded my agreement, trying to urge Lynn to comply with my eyes, but she wasn't looking at me. She was peering out the window somewhere into the Square.

"I think you're right," the woman said finally. "Perhaps I made a mistake. Somethin' has definitely gone horrid here. We should return with more men."

As Lynn uttered those words, the rain eased its merciless cascade to a steady, light drizzle, plinking off the roof's shingles above. She rejoined us in the shadows, and we fell into a few minutes' silence, punctuated only by the rainfall's chorus. I continuously glanced toward the rear of the house, half-expecting someone to charge us maniacally from the darkness.

"What if whoever killed this bloke is right outside, waiting?" I asked. "There isn't another way in here, is there?"

Lynn shook her head. Gavin stepped carefully over the dead man and edged slowly to the window. After a few moments, he turned to us.

"The fog's clearing up a bit."

While Gavin eyed the storm outside, the rest of us took the opportunity to chance a drink and quick snack. Water, hard rolls and fruit were unpacked and consumed in contemplative silence.

"Oy, now," Gavin said after a few minutes. "Fog's lifting, indeed. I can see the hanged men now with ease, and the other buildings." The man's forehead furrowed with realization. "Could be a bad thing."

"Why?" Royce asked, his mouth full.

"Because," I answered knowingly, "that means it's easier to see outside now, but that means that whoever, or whatever's out there, will be able to see us just as easily."

Lynn nodded grimly. "Aye. And it's a whoever, not a whatever, Penny. No creatures of children's stories roam these parts, last I checked."

"Last you checked, sure," I quipped with a small laugh.

The others glared at me, and I shrugged apologetically.

"Lynn?" Gavin asked.

Lynn exhaled deeply. "We should leave. If we wait too long, the fog could clear even more."

Royce and I nodded, and Gavin wrung his grip around the shaft of his axe again as he took another peek outside.

"Let's go. Back the way we came," Lynn ordered.

Gavin pressed the front door open quietly, allowing the smell of soaked dirt and pine to flow in around us. The man had barely leaned out for another look around when I saw his eyes narrow before widening. His entire body stiffened at the sight of something outside.

"What is it?" I hissed.

"Gav?" Lynn tried. "What do ya see?"

The man pulled the door shut slowly, stepping away from it and the window again and motioning for us to follow. We complied, anxiously awaiting an explanation.

"I just saw somethin'. A light, up on the second floor of that manor. One of the windows on the top floor was aglow with what looked like torchlight. Because it was moving. Soon the window was dark, but the one to the right was illuminated, and then the one after. Like someone walking through with a torch to guide them."

We all studied each other, as if our troubled faces held all the answers.

"Could be the killer of all these folks," Royce mused aloud.

"Or killers," I echoed. "They could be gutting some poor bloke up there right now!"

Gavin frowned. "Maybe. But we don't know anything 'bout what's going on! We don't know why this is happening. Who, or how many, are responsible. We don't know where all the blasted people are."

I was overcome with a pulse of urgency, accompanied by nervous fear and guilt. What if another poor soul was meeting a grisly end as we spoke?

"Maybe there are folks hiding in the other dwellings?" Lynn offered, herself unconvinced.

My jaw tightened. "Or they're all dead. Everyone."

Gavin frowned. "Like some angel o' death descended from the clouds and decided to go door-to-door and kill everyone here? Dunno 'bout that."

Suddenly impatient, Lynn held up her hands. "Enough o' this. I'm tired of walking around like a scared pauper. The Cap'n sent us here to strike a deal to protect these people, and that's what we're gonna do."

"Lynn," I said slowly, "we don't even know if-"

"Penny," she interrupted, "we know nothing, and that needs to change. Cap'n Hael and the rest o' the men are fightin' it out right now, and the least we can do is get our jobs here, aye? Steady coin depends on us. We're goin' to the manor. Right now."

Royce coughed. "Ma'am Lynn, I don't-"

"She's right," Gavin defended. "The Cap'n wanted us to finish the deal with this village: their coin for our protection. Bunch o' these poor sods are already dead. Not a good start, eh? We have to at least find out what's going on."

Lynn stood by the door, and I saw her draw her sword from its scabbard with a mighty ring of metal against sheath. "Weapons ready." She looked back at me, then Royce. "Really, neither of ya have ever used a sword?"

I shook my head. Royce did too, a bit more reluctantly.

The woman furrowed her brow in vexation. "We've gotta get you two trained. Bloody 'ell. Just hack away if some bastard tries to kill ya."

Gavin was already clutching his mighty axe, and Royce and I unsheathed our weapons with slight hesitation. Lynn shouldered the front door open slowly, leering outside to search for any sinister signs amidst the light rain and mist.

"Here we go. Stay close, and don't stray from the group. You boys ready?"

We nodded, and I followed my companions out into the rain, trying to fortify my nerves as we raced through the mud. We carefully circled the western edge of the Square, pausing cautiously at each dwelling we reached to take stock of our surroundings. I kept glancing at the manor house in the distance, studying the windows that lined the first and second floors of the building and wondering if I'd see the glow of light that Gavin had reported. The manor remained dark and lifeless, haunted only by the ceaseless storm outside.

Moments later, the four of us huddled together behind a simple house at the corner of the Square, a short distance from the looming manor. We swiveled our heads about, taking stock of our surroundings. The veil of fog and rain thickened, and I pulled my cloak tighter around me as if it would make a difference.

At the rear of our group, I was watching our backs for telltale pursuers when Royce tapped me urgently.

"Look! The light!"

I twisted my head and saw a haunting glow in a window on the top floor of the manor. It didn't move, as Gavin had reported – instead, we looked on in astonishment as the mysterious light flickered on and off in quick, steady intervals.

"You all remember how we were considering leaving?" I asked. "I'm thinking that was a good idea."

Lynn glowered at me. "Someone inside might need our help. C'mon!"

* * *

Moments later we came to a stop at the large doors at the front of the manor house, leaving a trail of muddy footprints in our wake. I didn't like the way the dark windows seemed to scowl down at us. The stone walls loomed high and forbade entry, and I was wary of what we might find inside. I recalled watching the Village Elders and their council leave our meeting the previous day, trudging up to the manor's doors and disappearing inside.

Lynn reached for the door handle, chancing another look behind us out at the misty oblivion. "At least if anythin' happens, the walls are thicker here. More defensible."

I made sure my wits were about me as Lynn motioned to get ready. We took up our positions at the large doors and on her countdown, moved into the manor house as quickly as we could. As Royce and I stepped in, Lynn and Gavin winced when they shut the doors with a loud, solid *thud* that sounded off and echoed into the rooms and halls of the dwelling. The storm sounded muffled from within the manor, and the building was somehow even larger on the inside than I had expected.

We were in a confined entryway, leading just ten paces ahead to another tall, closed door. A copper ornamental plaque on the wall read *Mable Manor - Elder Council.*

Smooth wood flooring welcomed our boots, and I looked up in admiration at the high stone ceiling. We slowly filed forward to the tall door. Lynn opened it as quietly as she could, but we all cringed as the door creaked loudly with age.

A great hall of sorts greeted us, eerie and beautiful.

A large banquet table stretched ahead, through the center of the hall, flanked by numerous chairs. Large windows lined both walls, curtains drawn to allow the overcast daylight in. A stone staircase to our right led upward, winding out of view to the second floor. A large fireplace, its decorative stones cracked and weathered, kept watch over the empty hall faithfully.

The table was bare, save for unlit candles spaced evenly across the top. It looked strange to see a large banquet area so plain and featureless.

Another set of large double doors faced us from a distance at the end of the great hall. Numerous closed doors lined both walls, like sentinels standing guard.

"Looks even bigger inside, doesn't it?" I remarked.

Lynn nodded. "Aye," she whispered. "The light was upstairs, so we should-"

Her voice trailed off, for the faint sound of wood creaking taunted us from behind.

The entryway.

All four of us froze and snapped our gazes to the front door just paces away, eyes wide with urgency. Lynn moved forward rapidly, tapping Royce on the shoulder and gesturing for him to watch the stairs.

My friend nodded reluctantly.

The unmistakable groaning of the doors being opened very slowly jarred our senses after being seemingly alone in the village for a lengthy time. Lynn and Gavin exchanged a flurry of hurried hand signals. Both shed their cloaks, letting the garments fall softly to the floor, and I realized they were opting for mobility in preparation for a fight.

They stood on both sides of the door, weapons ready for ambush. I nudged Royce, and we hastily joined Lynn and Gavin on the edges of the doorway. We released our packs and cloaks, imitating our seasoned companions' examples.

I held my breath as the door opened slowly, creaking in hesitation. Whoever was on the other side of it had definitely seen us enter the manor, clearly exercising caution.

Gavin stepped forward, raising his battleaxe, but he never got a chance to deliver a blow. The door was thrown open roughly, slamming into the man's face.

CHAPTER 46

A splintering crack erupted as Gavin was knocked to the floor. Lynn growled and rushed to his aid, narrowly avoiding the other door as it, too, careened inward.

Numbed with shock, I watched a large, armor-clad man barrel into our midst with a rallying yell. Lynn stood over Gavin and swiped at the attacker with her blade, but he countered swiftly.

Gavin scrambled to his feet, grasping his axe desperately from the floor. His eyes filled with fear, seeing something through the doors that I could not.

Another armored man shot into the hall.

And another.

Gavin and Lynn frantically backpedaled in our direction before turning on their heels to make a mad dash for our position, at the foot of the steps leading upward.

To my horror, three more armor-clad men joined their companions.

Royce cursed and raised his sword in a shocking show of bravery. Without thinking, I did the same. We screamed ferociously, dashing to meet Lynn and Gavin midway in their brief retreat. When we reached our companions, they turned to face our attackers.

The six men grudgingly halted their charge at the sight of the four of us standing to meet them, our weapons readied. I felt like my heart would cease beating, and I donned the fiercest glare I could manage, hoping it masked the trembling fright seizing my being.

Both sides squared off, studying each other frenetically. The men in front of us reminded me of Captain Hael's men back in the Kovald. Their skin was tanned, their faces weathered. Scars could be seen here and there. Blood, most likely that of the villagers we could not find, was splotched about their armor and clothing. Speckled across their faces. Staining the blades of their weapons.

These men looked like they had just emerged from a castle siege.

It was then that I understood that Lynn and Gavin's stalwart presence was what was delaying a battle. Had these armored men known how utterly hopeless with a sword Royce and I were, we would most likely be scrambling for our lives.

I'm going to die.

One of the men stepped forward menacingly. Short-cropped, light blonde hair complimented crystalline eyes, blue as a bright sky. He clutched a sword in one hand, and a small javelin in the other.

"Who the hell are you?" he challenged.

Lynn scoffed. "You first."

The man seemed unaffected by Lynn's counter. His eyes were alight with something beneath the surface, and my blood chilled when I realized he was completely fearless.

"Wrong answer."

Before fear could even begin to paralyze me, our enemies surged forward. We raised our weapons to meet them. The icy leader hurled something at the floor between both parties. A loud hissing sound crackled, and thick smoke plumed forward, bursting in every direction.

A javelin parted smoke and whisked through the air at my face, in the center of our midst. I instinctively jerked my head aside, but the speared tip glanced across my cheek. I yelped, and Gavin called out a warning as another javelin streaked through the smokescreen toward us, immediately followed by two of our enemies.

One of the men rushed toward me as I stumbled backward, frightened and taken aback. Lynn darted to my aid. Steel rang loudly as blades connected.

Out of the corner of my eye, I saw three armored figures surge toward Royce and Gavin. Grunts and yells echoed through the hall as both sides collided.

The nameless leader of the enemy band tore through the smoke with frightening speed and lunged for Lynn with a vicious stab. Still fighting off the other man, Lynn saw the impending attack and tried to reel away to avoid the thrust.

She was a moment too late.

Lynn cried out as the man's blade caught her shoulder. Her voice echoed off the walls of the great hall and chilled my blood. I heard Gavin yell in anger from somewhere to my left, amidst the frantic fighting.

I snarled and charged forward. Lynn clutched at her shoulder and sliced upward at her assailant. The blonde-haired man barely deflected it. As he did, the other enemy lifted his blade dangerously.

Before he could deliver his blow, I dove and tackled the man with a grunt. The impact with his armored body jarred me, and we rolled violently across the floor. I heard metal clattering away from me.

My sword!

Dazed and dumbfounded, I rolled onto my back.

My opponent was already to his knees. From there, he grasped his trident with resolve and speared it violently downward. Miraculously, his attack landed high, catching the stone floor above my head. The impact of metal upon stone so close to my head rang in my ears.

I kicked wildly and caught the man on his nose. He recoiled and yanked his weapon back upward to try again. As he did so, the prongs hit the top of my head and raked roughly through my hair. Blood warmed my scalp as I cried out in pain.

When he raised his weapon for another try, a bloodcurdling shout stopped him cold. Lynn's sword flashed furiously and caught the man in the neck with a nasty crack of bone and flesh.

I was overjoyed at the man's demise, and yet sickened by the sight. I didn't have time to be confused, for a shade of a man materialized from the now-dwindling smokescreen.

The crystal-eyed leader of our enemies strode swiftly toward us both. He was not enraged at the sight of his dead companion. His eyes seemed glazed over, completely fixed on Lynn.

Lynn yanked her blade from the dead man and turned to face the blonde-haired ringleader.

"Gav?" she called anxiously, directing her words over the armored man's shoulder and toward the staircase. "Royce?"

No one answered. Two more of our adversaries emerged from where Gavin and Royce had been fighting, coming to join their commander's side as he stopped in front of us.

I got to my feet unsteadily. Blood trickled down my temple and forehead. Lynn stood valiantly beside me, her left arm sagging limply, her right barely able to lift her weapon.

"Roy!" I tried. My yell echoed through the hall, but no reply came.

"Your friends are as good as dead," the man said icily.

I wondered why *we* weren't dead. The last of the smoke dissipated behind our aggressors, and I saw no one beyond it, friend or foe. Only the half-opened doors to the manor greeted my hopeful eyes.

One of the men stepped closely to his boss. "Perrault, shall we join the pursuit?"

Lynn and I exchanged brief glances.

Perrault, the reaper of a man before us, drew in a deep breath. "Aye. Shouldn't last long anyway."

"Shall we take prisoners?"

A glimmer of hope ebbed between my labored breaths. Royce and Gavin had escaped!

"No," Perrault said with a taunting smile. "Kill them on sight."

Without warning, Lynn surged forward with the last of her strength and swept her sword toward Perrault's neck.

Perrault easily caught the woman's feeble swing with his own, knocking her sword away. In one motion, he slipped his arms around her and whirled her about to face me, his blade at her throat.

"No!" I shouted in alarm, eyes wide. "Don't!"

The man watched me curiously. "How did you all know we were here, in this stain of a village that nobody cares about?"

Lynn struggled in vain against Perrault's grip. The look of desperation on her face pained me, but also infused me with a sliver of courage.

I squared myself, set my jaw, and said nothing.

In a swift, fluid motion, Perrault abruptly retracted his arms from Lynn, stepped back, and slashed her back with his sword.

An animalistic roar escaped me, and Lynn cried out before slumping to her knees.

I ambled forward to Lynn's side, ignoring Perrault and his men, and gently grasped her shoulders, trying to catch her gaze.

"Relax, now," Perrault instructed in a deathly whisper. "I didn't kill her... yet. You could say I gave her a slice of life."

Seething with fury, I craned my neck to look up at to the armor-clad man.

Perrault met my stare without difficulty. "Take them downstairs and lock them in the cellar. We can't have their friends telling the world we were here. Prisoners might be useful."

CHAPTER 47

Perrault turned from us and strode passively away, out into the rain and fog. His two men prodded us off through the hall, alongside the banquet table. One man led while his companion brought up the rear, keeping a wary eye on Lynn and me.

The woman sagged weakly against me, her arm around my shoulders. I supported her weight the best I could, growling as the man behind us pushed me forward with a gloved hand.

We were guided through one of the many doors in the great hall, which led to narrow stairs stretching downward into darkness. Our lead captor lifted a lit torch from its sconce and illuminated the way as our little party descended until the narrow corridor widened into a large, open cellar.

Oddities were cluttered everywhere. I saw tall bookshelves, some empty while others had been stuffed with dusty volumes. There was an abundance of old furniture, much of it covered by large sheets that had been overcome by dust. Aged mattresses, frayed and abandoned, leaned in stacks against the far wall. Timeworn blankets and linens had been rolled and stacked clumsily in baskets, which were strewn about here and there.

The torchbearer set the torch in another sconce upon a large stone pillar at the center of the cellar. The fire's soothing glow faded toward the edges of the large room, so that shadows watched us from every direction.

The other man let our packs slide off his shoulder and hit the stone floor. "We see you've brought herbs and such." He looked at me menacingly. "Get her patched up, lad. A prisoner is no good as a corpse."

"Oh, and if ya try to come back up those steps, we'll end ya," the other man growled. "Test us on this."

With that, our captors withdrew to the stairs and left us alone in the dimly lit cellar. Only defeat and the warmth of blood kept us company.

* * *

Lynn's breathing had become alarmingly labored, and her fingers clutched at my shirt as her strength waned. I spotted a long wooden table propped clumsily up on its side, wedged between a discarded armoire and bookcase.

"Hang in there," I encouraged, easing her toward the central pillar next to the torchlight. "Be right back."

"Aye," Lynn managed.

She leaned raggedly against the stone while I hurried to the old table. I eyed her nervously as I maneuvered it out from the clutter and set the table upon its legs. Wood scraped upon stone, echoing its disturbance through the cellar as I moved the table into the torchlight.

"Penny?" Lynn mumbled weakly.

"Fates," I uttered, leaving the table and stepping to her side. She slumped downward, and I had to crouch to absorb the sudden fall.

"There you are," I breathed, lifting her back up. "Careful, now. Sit down, yeah?"

She obeyed, hunching forward and resting her elbows on her knees. Blood trickled down her hand from beneath her sleeve, down from the wound she had received in her shoulder.

I retrieved our packs, then hurried to the stacks of sheets and other linens nearby, rummaging through until I found cloths and sheets not caked with dust. Satisfied, I hurried back to her, and nearly tripped over an old straw basket.

The woman chuckled, but her small laugh was cut short when she cringed and bent over again in pain. Alarmed, I knelt at her feet and pressed her gently back upward. Her entire right sleeve was stained in blood, and I followed it upward until I saw ripped fabric across her shoulder.

"I can get it," she said suddenly, reaching for the cloth in my hand.

"Like hell. You can barely sit up straight."

"Really. I'll g-get it."

I looked up at her squarely. "Let me. Just relax."

The woman sighed, and I reached for the tear in the fabric with my fingers, trying to separate it, when Lynn suddenly arched her back in pain, trying unsuccessfully to mask a small cry with the palm of her hand.

"Blazes. I'm really hurt this time," she uttered, sounding surprised.

I raised my eyebrows. "This time?"

She had begun to perspire. Lynn reached up with her good hand, unfastened her bandana quickly and tossed it aside, letting her dark red hair fall to her shoulders. "What's my back look like?"

I sat next to her on the table and craned backward to have a look. Torn fabric of her shirt ran in a fine line from near the top of her right shoulder, down and across her back to just above her left hip. I cringed when I saw her wound. The skin seemed to part slightly with each breath she took, exposing hot blood that seemed to simmer along the entire length of the gash.

I breathed in deeply. "Not good."

The woman let out a small gasp of a laugh, pain creasing her face. "Was afraid o' that."

"What do I do?" I asked. "I don't know about those herbs and medicines and the like." I narrowed my eyes in realization. "Wait, doesn't Gavin have all the herbs?"

Lynn shook her head. "I have some, too. Gav always gives me extras. Oy, Penny? Don't turn around until I tell ya to."

"What?"

The woman reached down gingerly to the bottom of her shirt and tugged it upward, revealing a slender waist and toned belly. "I said don't bloody look yet."

I guiltily jerked my gaze away from her and opened her pack on the floor, studying its contents. The rustling of fabric and shifting of her boots against the stone floor. "Okay. You can, um, look now."

Turning slowly, I saw that she had drawn one of the clean sheets protectively around her, leaving only her shoulders and collar exposed.

In the glow of the torchlight, I could see the tone of the muscles in her arms and shoulders, which were lean and strong, though not masculine. I recalled observing this briefly the night she had crossed my path in Northroe at the November Raven.

I stepped to her, vowing to focus and prove myself useful. Her back was to me now, and I grimaced at the line of blood staining the sheet wrapped around her.

"Tell me what you want me to do."

She stood, wincing. "Hand me some gauze, yeah? Spread a couple sheets out on the table."

As I covered the table with layers of sheets, Lynn bandaged the wound on her shoulder with gauze, declining my help as she wrapped it tightly. She then lay down on her belly, allowing her back to be exposed, and stretched out on the table before electing to kick her boots off.

I dragged an old crate next to the table and placed the contents of the small medical kit in Lynn's pack atop it.

The gash on her back terrified me.

"Gotta get this bandaged up," Lynn said. "Do ya see a small jar with goldenrod in it?"

"Goldenrod?" I echoed. I knew it was a flower. That was the extent of my expertise.

"Should be yellowish in color," she said shakily. "Curses, I can barely speak."

I found the jar and glanced at the woman, nervous at the way her voice was faltering.

Lynn sighed. "Ever done anythin' like this before?"

I swallowed and shook my head. Her wound was long, it was deep, and the prospect of going anywhere near it made my stomach lurch. For Lynn's sake, I tried to appear confident, all the while fairly certain I was failing at doing so.

"Can ya give me your belt, really quick-like?"

Puzzled, I fumbled about as I undid the buckle and slid it from the loops around my trousers. My hands were shaking with fear in light of the task that loomed over me. I coiled the leather belt and handed it to her.

"Why?" I asked solemnly.

She shrugged. " Helps to have somethin' to bite down on. I don't do pain very well."

"Could've fooled me," I offered.

Lynn smiled briefly and unfurled my belt, taking a deep breath as she lay back down flat to the makeshift gurney. "Goldenrod?"

"This the one?" I asked, producing the jar with a white cap.

The woman shifted slightly. "Aye. The flowers have been ground down to a powder and mixed with some aloe gel. Dab away the blood with a cloth, yeah? Disinfect it with the vinegar, first."

Gulping, I did as she told me. I began to run a cloth carefully along the length of her wound, blotting away blood on her skin that was outside of the cut itself. Lynn tensed visibly.

"Penny, ya have to cleanse the inner part of the wound first, then work outward," she uttered. "Helps prevent infection."

Biting my lip, I reached for a new rag and followed her instruction, applying pressure firmly.

Lynn stiffened and hissed in pain. "Not so hard!"

"Sorry," I sputtered, immediately letting up on the cloth. I pressed it lightly to the wound, let it soak up blood for a few moments and then moved upward. The progress was dreadfully slow, but I was thorough and careful in my efforts. Her wound seemed a bit cleaner by the time I was done.

Lynn gathered herself with a deep breath. "Okay, Penny. I need ya to apply that healing gel to the cut, okay?"

I cringed.

"Make sure it's clean first, aye?"

Nodding, I applied vinegar to a new cloth, then soaked it lightly with the healing gel.

The wound was nasty, etching deep into the woman's back. I collected myself and proceeded cautiously, blotting the gel as lightly as I could onto the cut, starting from the lowest point as I had before.

Lynn tensed her back. Her breathing was heavy, and her teeth were clamped firmly on my belt.

"I'm sorry," I whispered.

She shook her head and let the belt drop from her mouth. "No avoidin' it. Just wanna get this over with."

Lynn bit down on the belt again and I continued on, smoothing the healing gel over her wound as gently as I could. Her low, agonized moans and growls made me cringe, and I started sweating as I made my way up her back, dressing the cut thoroughly.

When part of the wound started bleeding again, I had to look away for a moment, blinking rapidly and desperately trying to quell an intrusive nausea. A few breaths later, I pushed myself back to work.

The gel made her gash look shiny in the torchlight, like a thin film of sorts was covering it. I suddenly felt lightheaded and oddly detached from the situation, like it was all a dream I would soon be free from. The point of contact, where Perrault's blade had first connected, was the widest part of the wound, and most difficult to treat. I blanched but maintained my composure, reminding myself that it was Lynn who was faced with the tougher part of this trial.

I finally finished, set the jar down and watched the woman wordlessly. Her breathing had quickened. Her back was covered in perspiration, rising and falling softly with her swift breathing. Goosebumps had broken out on her skin, and Lynn started shivering.

"I'm sorry," I said yet again.

"Don't be," Lynn managed, and to my surprise she was trying to sit up. "Look away again, please."

I did, and the table creaked as I heard her moving about.

"Okay," she breathed. Her voice was dangerously weak. "Get the gauze."

Turning back to her, I saw that she now sat up with her back to me, and was hunching forward. The blend of perspiration and goosebumps on her skin worried me.

"You cold?" I asked.

Lynn nodded. "But first we have to bandage this up. Quickly, now."

"Aye. Show me what to do."

She instructed me to sit on the table directly behind her, on my knees. Lynn took hold of the strip of gauze, and I brought the roll around her back, wrapping it under her arm. I transferred the roll of gauze to her waiting hand, and she wrapped the bandage around her chest, feeding the roll from her right hand to her left. In this way, I could help, and she maintained her dignity.

Minutes later we were nearly done applying the bandage. It covered most of her upper body, wrapping under the pits of her arms snugly and winding down to her belly above her hips, covering the front, sides and back of her torso nearly entirely.

Minutes later, we were finished. Lynn stretched her arms about warily, testing the elasticity of the gauze wrapped around her torso. Pleased, she turned to me with a smile. "You did well, Penny. Thank you."

I couldn't help but grin. "Well, as you said back at camp, first time for everything, right?"

The woman nodded, and hugged herself tightly. "Fates, I'm cold." Wincing, she curled up on her side in discomfort. I hastily scooped up a few more sheets, fearing she was catching a fever.

"Just get some rest," I said, hoping my voice was soothing. I unfurled a sheet and draped it over her, followed by two more.

"Be careful," Lynn said. "Watch the stairs. If they come down, then-"

"Quiet now," I whispered, giving her shoulder a delicate squeeze. "I've got my sword. Those bastards try anything, they'll be sorry. Just close your eyes, Lynn. I've got it covered."

Who am I trying to fool?

Lynn obliged, and I watched her rest, her chest rising and falling with her breathing. I was shocked at how beautiful she looked even in the state that she was in. She looked like a different person entirely without the leather armor and bandana. Royce and I had observed her beauty before, but now it was strikingly clear to me that Lynn was the most charming woman I'd ever seen.

Her demeanor was a bit rough, but I could picture the fleeting moments when her guard came down, where I had glimpsed what she was like before she had become an outlaw woman. A hearty laugh, a defenseless smile, the look of wonder on her face the night I told the story around the fire, her seemingly flirtatious behavior on the ride to Mable... all of these and many other moments since we had joined Captain Hael's camp were enigmas, lights in a muddled night.

I shook my head and closed my eyes for a long moment.

You've gone and done it now, Penny. Fallen for the most dangerous woman you've ever known. Who also happens to be an officer in a bandit clan. And is being held captive with you in the cellar of a manor in a village where everyone's probably dead.

Brilliant.

Sighing, I stood and drank from my flask of water, intending to get acquainted with our newly awarded prison. I removed my coat and set it over Lynn, making sure to cover her bare shoulders, and then turned to begin the tour.

"Penny?"

I turned on my heel immediately to see Lynn smiling up at me. "Aye?"

"You did really well today." Her smile grew wider. "I mean it."

I shrugged, albeit sheepishly.

"You didn't hesitate up there," the woman continued. "And you really pulled through with patchin' me up. Thank ya."

I felt my face flushing red, and tried not to beam excessively with joy. I grinned at her and dipped in an exaggerated bow. "Pleasure was all mine, miss."

Lynn snorted with laughter and rolled her eyes before closing them to rest. I watched her curl back up under the sheets, leaving me alone in the torchlight with thoughts that nagged incessantly, and questions without answers.

CHAPTER 48

I spent a lengthy amount of time, one that I did not bother trying to measure, investigating the cellar. Though I assumed it would be a wasted effort, I searched the musty basement for an exit, praying for a means of escape. Finding nothing, I slowly scoured over the odd junk and debris cluttered about in search of a weapon.

My search came up empty. As I watched Lynn sleep beneath the sheets, I sank against the stone wall to the floor and hung my head in dejection. Even if I had found a weapon, what could I possibly do? I stood no chance against the mettle of the men upstairs.

The men upstairs.

Perrault's frigid eyes disrupted my thoughts, driving defeat deep into my heart.

Who was he? Why had he and his men come to Mable? Where had all the people gone?

How much time did Lynn and I have? Not much, likely, for we had been given no food or water.

Frustrated, I got to my feet, trying to ignore the fatigue clawing at my body. I wanted badly to sleep, but I vowed to watch over Lynn while she rested. The sound of her voice crying out in pain when she was stabbed kept replaying itself in my ears, no matter how hard I resisted. The image of her being cut down in front of me, eyes wide and surprised, flickered before my mind against my will.

Shouldering the thoughts away stubbornly, I scratched the stubble on my chin. Was Alomar still alive? Did the battle go in our favor, or in that of Tyrius's men? What had become of Royce and Gavin? If they survived, and got back to camp, would Captain Hael come to our aid? Would Lynn and I be dead before that time could ever hope to arrive?

The wretched possibilities of my friends being dead churned my stomach. Distress overcame me, and I paced on through the cellar thinking I would cry, but no tears came. Royce and Alomar were brothers to me.

"No," I pleaded quietly. "Fates, please! No. I couldn't bear it."

I chewed on my lip, burdened by all that had transpired and the notable amount of questions that were, for the moment, denied answers.

Whether hours or long minutes passed, I did not know. I was already getting accustomed to the dank air of the cellar, and the dark shadows dancing at the edge of the room at the torchlight's command seemed like they were closing in.

I cast a sorrowful glance at Lynn. She slept as peacefully as one in her condition could. Before long, I moved to the stairs and chanced a look up. It was too dark to see the door leading to the banquet hall at the end of the steps.

Cursing inwardly at our predicament, I navigated my way through the dark twists and turns formed by old debris and discarded furniture, intending to return to Lynn's side.

I suddenly felt dizzy. My vision blurred.

Puzzled, I had to steady myself with one hand as I nearly pitched forward onto my face. Warm blood trickled down my temple and cheek. I carefully put two fingers to my face and felt upward toward my hairline.

A steady stream of blood met my probing fingers.

Blinking rapidly, I got to my feet shakily and trudged back toward where Lynn was, holding my head and trying not to bump into everything. Blood seeped from the top of my head, through my hair, down my cheek and jaw, and dripped to the floor. Alarmed, I stumbled groggily into a shelf and nearly knocked it clear over.

I had somehow completely forgotten about the head wound dealt to me by the trident during the struggle at the entryway. Between focusing on dressing Lynn's wound and my futile bout with myself in dealing with our circumstances, I had apparently been able to ignore it.

Now, however, the gashes atop my head throbbed intensely, and I was losing an unhealthy amount of blood.

Seconds later, I staggered into our part of the cellar. Lynn was still beneath the sheets, sleeping soundly. The glow of the torchlight seemed to grow duller before my eyes, but it was my sight that was fading.

I swiped a cloth from the stack of linens in the corner and pressed it to my head, dropping to my knees. I hissed with pain, surprised at how much it hurt when I had been able to ignore it for so long.

My eyes found Lynn, only able to focus on her red hair in the light. My sight grew clouded. Strangely, I thought of our fallen comrade Arthur, and if the grisly deaths I witnessed today were anything like the way he met his end. I swayed backward dizzily before fainting to the stone floor.

CHAPTER 49

I awoke to a cool, damp cloth being pressed gently to my temple. Lying on my back, all I could see was part of a palm resting on my forehead, dabbing at my wound. I blinked rapidly, trying to clear the fog from my eyes, and began to prop myself up on my elbows.

"No, no," I heard Lynn's whisper. She put her free hand to my chest and eased me back to laying flat on my back. "Stay still, Penny. This is quite nasty."

Her voice sounded sweeter than usual. Maybe it was because I couldn't see her since her healing hand was in the way. Perhaps I was just growing dumb from admiration.

"Bloody hurts," I muttered groggily. "How long was I out?"

"I'm not sure," the woman answered. "Don't even know how long I was asleep, but I woke up and saw ya on the floor. Scared me half to death. Thought someone had got you at first, but turns out ya fainted. And I can see why."

I sighed. "Indeed." I realized that it was I who now lay upon the table, new sheets and all.

Lynn adjusted her hand so that I could look up and see her face. My breath caught in my throat. She hovered over me, her eyes narrowed in concentration and concern, intent on the cuts on my head. Her silent breaths were warm against my skin.

"That blight got a good hit on ya," she remarked, shaking her head.

"It was a trident."

"I can see that. Luckily it wasn't worse."

I shrugged. "I was too fast for him."

She chuckled at my quip. "Okay, hold the cloth in place for a moment."

I did, trying not to wince in front of her, and Lynn got up and rounded the low table. I watched her, trying to get a glimpse of her back to see if there was any difference in her wound. As she knelt to her pack, I saw that small splotches of blood following the line of her wound had stained the gauze wrap, though they were few and far between.

She gathered a few materials I didn't recognize, grabbed the healing gel, and placed them on the table next to me. My eyes widened when I saw a pair of scissors.

"Oy, Lynn? What are the scissors for?"

Lynn stepped around me out of view, and I heard the scraping of the crate against the stone floor. She placed it close behind me, right up against the table and sat so that I saw her upside down, leaning over me.

"Have to cut your hair a bit."

"Why?" I tried sitting up, but she grabbed my shoulders firmly and pressed me back down.

"Relax," she said. "I'm gonna have to fix ya up. But I can't get to the wounds 'cause your hair is in the way."

Truth be told, I didn't care about my hair much anyway. I wasn't exactly known as a fashionable one back in Northroe.

I grinned wryly. "You all just carry pairs of scissors around?"

"When we can. Like the Cap'n says, be prepared for anythin' that may come. I'd say this blasted village is a good example of why he's right."

"What for, though?" I asked, genuinely curious. "The scissors, I mean."

"Well, for wounds mainly. If we can't get to 'em, like right now, we cut away what's preventing access."

I let what she said sink in. "How often do you or the others get hurt, Lynn? How often do you get into battles and whatnot?"

The woman smiled and put a finger to her lips. "Hush, now. Let's get this done."

"I want to know," I replied stubbornly.

Lynn moved my hand and the bloody cloth out of the way, and I heard her scoot the crate even closer to the table. "More often than you'd think. I need you to come my way a little bit, yeah? Hang your head off o' the table."

I did so slowly. She had found an old pillow, which she placed on her lap, propping it up for my head to rest on. Her hands cradled my head, and I felt involuntary shivers shoot down my spine when I looked up into her eyes. She brushed her fingers softly through my hair, determining where she was going to cut, and I heard the *snip-snip* of the scissors.

It's now or never, Penny.

"Why didn't you just have me cut your shirt then?" I asked. "Rather than take the whole thing off and torture me so. I am a man, after all. You should know better, as a rather pretty woman."

The *snip-snip-snip* of her scissors paused, and her eyes met mine for a long moment. Somehow I mustered the courage to not look away. She looked stunning in the torchlight, and to my surprise a wide smile crossed her face.

"Because," she said, continuing cutting, "I really like that shirt."

We both chuckled, and I tried to keep still as she worked. I wondered if it was my imagination, but it seemed like her cheeks had flushed with embarrassment at my remark. Her eyes were now hard with concentration, and she was sticking her tongue out to one side of her mouth in utmost focus. I could feel her cutting close to my scalp, and it made me nervous.

"How did you come to be in Captain Hael's company?" I asked. "For how long, now?"

Lynn reached for the cloth, and I winced when she dabbed gently at one of the gashes on my head. "You first."

"Eh?"

"You first," she repeated. "I asked ya in the cabin the other mornin' about how you and your friends went from Northroe to suddenly helpin' Art and Quaid fish dead bodies outta the Keska. And tell me how ya decided you wanted to become a Storyteller."

"Writer."

"'Twas what I meant."

I groaned. "That's a lengthy story. Surely yours is better."

"Nope. Don't cause me to accidentally open your wound further. I'll do it."

My eyes widened. "You probably would. Well, 'tis a tale of boredom, dissatisfaction with life, and sorry coincidence. Are you sure you can handle a story like such?"

Lynn grinned, her eyes twinkling with the torch's flame. "Sounds like an epic. Good thing you're a Storyteller. Tell me exactly: what is the difference between a Writer and a Storyteller?"

"Writer-in-Training," I corrected diligently. "I'm not a full-fledged Writer until one of my works is published."

She rolled her eyes. "Come, now. I wanna know everything, from start to finish."

"Fine. But if we're going to be here that long, might as well just cut all of my hair. Make it even and whatnot."

Lynn snorted. "Do I look like a barber?"

"Well, yes, with those scissors. Although you're a fair bit prettier than the barber I knew back in-*ouch!*"

The woman leered over me, bringing her face closer to mine with an evil smile. "I can cause ya unspeakable pain, Storyteller."

"Don't call me that," I complained, reaching for the wound atop my head.

She batted my hand away and pressed the damp cloth to where she had brushed a finger roughly against the gash – accidentally, of course. "C'mon. Let's hear it."

* * *

Amidst the snipping of her scissors, I relayed everything, from my arrangement with Jacques and my feud with Trenten at the Windfarer's Inn, to the sudden letter from Royce's father, which he had set aflame, and even the conversation my friends and I had on South Bridge about the winds of change.

I told Lynn of how I met Royce, his older brother Trev, and Alomar in the streets as homeless children, some of our adventures, and of how Trev and Alomar had been seized by the patriotic call of duty when we were older and Eisley declared war on Dekka.

As I relayed my tale, the Storyteller in me took over very early on, and I spoke with fervor and grand words that coaxed reactions from Lynn. Wide smiles, narrowed eyes, hearty chuckles and angry clenching of her jaw met my tale.

The rhythm of her scissors slowed when I reached the night the November Raven burned to the ground. In stubborn respect for the truth, I told of laying eyes upon her for the first time. Of Alomar's dejected drunkenness at the unfaithful actions of Corrine, and the unbelievable coincidence of Tyrius Sewell being the man she was involved with.

Lynn stopped cutting altogether when I told her, although hesitantly, of the series of chaotic events that took place after she stole out of the Raven and into the night. The poisoned patrons dying around us, the tavern imploding on itself in the rage of fire.

After I informed her of our chance meeting with Arthur and Quaid in the woods, and our utter surprise when we recognized her as she rode into camp, Lynn exhaled deeply, shaking her head.

"When I saw the three of you just waitin' outside the Lodge, lookin' at me, I couldn't bloody believe it."

"Aye," I agreed. "We didn't know what to think. Alomar didn't even believe it was you."

I lay in silence, listening to the cadence of her scissors, reflecting on the fact that the lives of my friends and I were practically unrecognizable compared to what they had been just days ago. Now I was in a basement with a woman who was a stranger to me not so long ago. We had somehow traversed complication and chance, bridging the gap between strangers and companions.

It just didn't seem real.

With my head resting on the pillow at her lap, I found myself trying to avoid looking at Lynn. Not that it was awkward anymore – once you treat someone's wounds and have their blood on your hands, I suppose shyness around that person disappears. I could have simply watched her face while she worked, but I knew better.

"Penny," the woman said quietly, "you know, Royce and Alomar are right. About ya bein' a good Storyteller."

I felt heat begin flushing my cheeks red. "Ah, well... I try. I don't know if I'm that good, yet, but I want to be."

"You are!" Lynn said, putting down the scissors on the tabletop. "Did ya see the men 'round the fire the other night while ya told us 'bout the Trickster Mirror? They couldn't take their eyes off o' ya! Not one of 'em! Neither could I."

My heart swelled with pride. I didn't bother suppressing the smile that crossed my face. It felt amazing to hear someone say that I was good at the one thing I loved to do more than anything in the world. It was a beautiful thing, and to hear it from Lynn made it that much more so.

As she took the cloth and pressed it delicately to the gashes atop my head again, I swallowed hard before speaking.

"Thank you, Lynn. Truly."

"You're welcome."

"Do you want to know something that I wasn't ever going to tell you?"

The woman's red-brown eyes found mine, and her eyebrows raised slightly. "Maybe. What is it?" she asked with the faintest hint of a smile.

"I knew everyone was enjoying the story, and it helped me tell it. It was fun, really. But I was mostly paying attention to you. I wanted you to like it."

Lynn's gaze didn't falter. She watched my eyes without a reply, a soft grin forming on her lips.

"No pressure or anything," I laughed.

The woman chuckled and brushed some hair from her eye. "Indeed."

"I was worried about you, Lynn," I divulged. "When you went to the Pit, men were talking all around camp. I thought maybe you'd be hurt, or... worse. When you came back to camp for this Fates-forsaken mission, I was looking at you. I was trying to see if you had been hurt, I mean. Or injured, or... well, I guess hurt and injured are the same thing, but-"

Lynn's eyes narrowed slightly, but she was still smiling. I recognized the look of a woman trying to understand exactly what a man was telling her... trying to determine if there was a deeper meaning behind my words.

I drew a deep breath. "What I'm trying to say is, I was just glad you were okay."

Her forehead wrinkled slightly as she took in my words, eyebrows arching as if she was growing sad.

"Penny," Lynn whispered at last. "I'm goin' to tell ya somethin', but if we ever make it out o' this cursed village alive, you can't utter a word. You cannot tell one soul, understand?"

I frowned. "Is it bad?"

"Depends on how ya look at it. But ya can't tell anyone in the company. I could get in trouble, understand?"

I steeled myself and nodded, trying to figure out how this related to what I had just revealed to the woman.

Lynn took a deep breath. She slipped her hands around my face and leaned over me to bring her face closer. "Can't tell anyone, okay?" she repeated. "Never, got it?"

"I understand," I answered patiently. Her fingers upon my face made warmth ripple through my heart. I kept my composure.

She paused, and her eyes wandered off to the torchlight as though asking its permission to speak. She finally looked back down at me.

"Penny, there is no Pit."

I raised my eyebrows. "What?"

"There's no Pit," Lynn repeated. "It doesn't exist. We don't have some jail, or dungeon, or anything like it."

I absorbed her disclosure. "Why not? Captain Hael said there was a Pit. Everyone says there's a Pit. Wait... are you saying none of the men know?"

Lynn nodded. "Cap'n Hael uses it as a way to keep the men in line. Only Miles and I know that it's fake. Only the Captain's two lieutenants know at any given time. We have to vow never to tell anyone."

"Why are you telling me?"

"Well, you were so... worried, and I don't want ya to have to worry about me, Penny."

I nodded slowly. "Where did you go, then?"

"The Cap'n told me to take the rest of the day to collect myself. Clear my head, so to speak. I took Anijo and rode up the mountain to a hidden path an hour's ride from camp, see. It's a retreat of sorts, you could say. Mainly for the Cap'n, but he lets us officers use it every once in a while. Again, no one knows about it, so you better not tell anyone, Penny Daulton, or I swear I'll-"

"You remember my last name?" I interrupted with a wily grin. "I thought you told my friends and I to forget about surnames?"

Lynn hesitated for the slightest moment. "Maybe I made it a point to remember yours."

I smiled widely, unsure if I should venture a response. The two of us sat in silence for a long moment. Our dire circumstances seemed to be at a distance, somewhere far away, an illusion in our musty, dark prison.

"Ya know," Lynn finally said, her voice growing coarse. She cleared her throat again, I realized the woman was nervous about what she was about to say.

"What?" I coaxed softly.

She smiled, and her eyes wandered off to a better time. "When I was young, my father would invite my uncle and friends o' theirs from the mill they worked at to our house. I would help my mother in the kitchen while the men would drink and talk. My mum didn't like my father goin' to the tavern anymore with my uncle. They both had problems with rum, see. They drank it like water and... well. It wasn't good, I'll say that."

I just nodded.

"Anyway. When my uncle came over, he let me sit on his knee while he told us stories 'bout the most amazin' things, Penny. Giants, castles that sat atop clouds, treasure hunters... my favorite was about a little girl who had a horse that grew wings, and it could fly."

My eyes were fixed on hers, alight with wonder. Hearing about a fellow Storyteller, especially one that had been family to Lynn, piqued my interest. The stories sounded incredible! Castles that were built upon clouds? I had never heard of such a thing, not even in the storybooks I had read!

"Some of my best memories as a lil' girl are of the stories my uncle would tell to me, my father, my mum, everyone else there. It made everything' sound so wonderful, ya know? Like anythin' could happen in the world, that there were wonders like those he spoke of hidden across the lands and deep in oceans. I knew I'd see 'em all someday. I'd find 'em and have great adventures."

"Great adventures, aye," I echoed in wonder.

Lynn looked down at me, a soft smile tugging at her lips. "Hearin' you tell your story to all o' us the other night made me feel like I used to, Penny. It reminded me o' what it was like to dream, you see? You made me remember who I once was, and the warmth I felt with my family during those days. It was wonderful, truly. First night I slept soundly without nightmares in a long, long time. You're a great Storyteller."

I smiled widely, overtaken with joyful surprise. Even if I had wanted to reply, there was nothing I could say. Perhaps things were better left in silence. I did my best to hold the woman's gaze as she stared down at me.

Lynn slowly leaned downward and tilted her head, her face close to mine, and kissed my cheek lightly. Her lips were soft upon my skin. It sent a tingling wave washing over my entire body. My heart remembered to beat, and it began racing.

Lynn smiled down at me. "That's very good of ya by the way, for worryin' 'bout me like that."

I swallowed hard, trying to remember how to speak. "I-I, um, well... for what it's worth," I sputtered, "the others were worried too. Not just me. But especially me, actually. Way more than them."

She laughed sweetly. "Ya know, shorter hair suits you. Very spruce."

I smiled sheepishly. "Thanks?"

Lynn seemed to realize she had been looking me in the eyes the entire time, and looked away as casually as she could. "Right. Well, I'll finish later. Need to fix you up first, okay? That bastard caught ya really good."

"Okay," I replied nervously.

Lynn carefully leaned to the side to grab the healing gel, and, to my dismay, a needle and sutures.

"Whoa, now," I groaned, sitting up.

"No," she whispered, reaching to bring me back down. "I have to close the wounds."

"I can't, um, I've never had to, I mean, stitches?" I rambled, horrified. "Come on Lynn, I-"

"Shush. You helped me, remember? And there was much more blood."

I frowned. "Well, aye, but-"

"No 'buts' Penny. Lie back down." She shot me a brilliant smile. "I'll be gentle. Just gotta apply the vinegar, as an antiseptic. Then the goldenrod and aloe gel, and-"

"But you didn't need stitches!" I blurted defensively.

Lynn rolled her eyes and took a deep breath. "I'm not letting someone who's never handled a needle and sutures in his life stitch me up. No offense. I'll take my chances and wait."

"None taken."

"Lay down, already. Let's get this done. After I'm finished I'll cut the rest o' your hair." Her tone turned playful. "Doesn't that make things better?"

"Oh, absolutely."

Ignoring the queasiness in my stomach, I lay back down and let my eyes dart about in fear as I felt the woman work on my wounds. The vinegar and healing gel stung, but I soon felt a tingling relief. A few short moments later, I saw Lynn nimbly pluck a needle from the medical kit and get the sutures ready.

Lynn leaned in to begin her work. "You'll be okay, I promise. Ready?"

I sighed. "Let's do this."

CHAPTER 50

I don't know how long I slept after Lynn finished treating the two gashes atop my head, but I awoke feeling much better than when I had come to after fainting. Timidly testing the top of my scalp, I was shocked to not feel the messy tousle of hair that usually covered my head. I ran a finger very lightly across the threaded sutures that closed my wounds, and I was amazed that they didn't hurt immensely to the touch.

Sitting up, I took stock of the dim basement and saw Lynn sitting nearby on another crate. She had pulled her shirt back on, and oddly the bloodstained garment didn't bother me the way it once had. The woman was biting her lip thoughtfully, leaning forward with her elbows resting on her knees and cupping her chin with both hands.

"Everything okay?" I asked.

Dashed from her thoughts by my voice, her eyes flickered to me and she smiled. "Finally up, are ya? You must've slept half a day."

"Really?" I asked.

Lynn shrugged. "Don't actually know. It feels like hours and hours are passin' by, but we have no way of knowin'. We might've been down here two days already... or a few hours. How do ya feel?"

I swung my feet off the table and touched them to the cold floor, next to where my boots waited for me. "Better. Thanks for your help, Lynn."

She nodded. Her jaw tightened, and her features sank into thought.

I sat up groggily, wincing at the soreness that riddled my entire body. The small cut where the javelin had glanced my cheek itched, and I pressed a finger to it carefully.

"Anything change?" I asked.

Lynn shook her head. "Not a peep from upstairs. Can't for the life o' me figure out what in blazes is goin' on."

"Aye." I swung my legs over the edge of the makeshift bed carefully, leaning forward on my elbows. "Who are those men up there?"

The woman shrugged. "Not a clue. Never heard o' this Perrault bastard, either. No idea what they're here for."

"Why kill the villagers?" I mused aloud. "And where on earth could they all be?"

Lynn shook her head slowly. "I don't know, Penny."

I scratched briskly at the stubble on my chin. "Wait... do you think Perrault works for Tyrius? What if it's payback?"

"For what, Tyrius's death? The villagers didn't kill him. I did. Besides," Lynn continued, "Tyrius was a weak-hearted bully when it came right down to it. All talk and no grit. Men to do his dirty bidding for him, see. A man like this Perrault bloke would never take orders from the likes of Tyrius."

I sighed. "None of this adds up."

"Indeed."

I watched Lynn, prying for signs of pain or discomfort. "How are you feeling?"

Lynn managed a smile. "As good as I can feel, given my condition. Much better than before, thanks to you."

"That blight," I cursed. "Can't believe he cut you when you were unarmed. Your back was to him!"

Lynn sighed. "I keep thinking o' all the things I could have done differently back there. We might not be locked away in this blasted cellar."

I wanted to refute her words, but I knew the effort would be pointless. The two of us sat in the flickering torchlight for some time. Though words weren't spoken, the air was heavy with our thoughts, and the reapers upstairs tugged at the corners of my mind.

"We need to get out of here," I whispered.

"There's no way."

"There's got to be."

"I checked, Penny. We've got nothin' down here." Lynn frowned and brushed red hair from her eye. "Tested the door upstairs. It's locked. We don't have weapons, anyhow."

I raised my eyebrows. "In your condition, would weapons make a difference?"

"My point exactly!" she flashed angrily. "There's nothin' we can do."

I opened my mouth, wanting to apologize, but I couldn't find the appropriate words. A few more silent moments passed, and the faces of our friends forced their way to the surface of my thoughts.

"I wonder how Royce and Gavin are doing?" I murmured.

Lynn twiddled her thumbs. "Tryin' not to think about it, to be honest."

"Why not?"

She shrugged. "Penny, there's a chance that they... didn't make it. A good chance, at that."

"No," I huffed.

"No?"

"If there's a chance, I have to believe they're still alive."

"Ya need to prepare yourself for the worst."

"Listen!" I snapped, standing. "Look at us. We're still alive, aren't we? Perrault hasn't hacked us to pieces yet. That has to count for something, Lynn. Besides, if Roy and Gavin are out there somewhere, even escaped, don't you think they'd come back for us? Wouldn't we come back for them? I can be prepared for bad news, sure, but I'm choosing to believe they made it until I find out otherwise. And you should, too."

Lynn grew quiet and didn't divert her hard stare from my eyes. Her wounded arm hung at her side, and I saw her shake it as if it was bothering her. A lengthy moment passed with nothing but the crackling flames of the torch to be heard.

She finally smiled. "You're a good man, Penny Daulton."

I was slightly stunned by her compliment, but I tried not to show it. "If we make it out of this alive, this is all going to make for a great story someday."

The woman's face brightened slightly, and she laughed while rolling her eyes. "You would think about writin' this all down right now, wouldn't ya?"

I grinned, but it faded when I blurted out my next question. "Who is this 'Tambor' that's locked up in Northroe?"

Lynn's features recoiled. "That was outta nowhere."

"I know," I said sheepishly. "But you seemed hell-bent on rescuing him. Even when the Captain said not to and all. I... was just wondering if you'd be that determined to try to save any of the other men in the company."

She studied my face for a long moment, eyes narrowed. "You sure that's all you're wonderin'?"

"Aye."

"It seems like there's more to it than that," Lynn said, folding her arms and wincing with the movement. "Sounds like you're afraid o' who this man is, or what he might mean to me."

My heart fell. "So he does mean something to you, then?" I blurted out, cringing after I did so and feeling dumb for the outburst.

Lynn glared at me and stood suddenly. "It doesn't matter whether Tambor means somethin' to me personally or not. I'd do it for any o' the men. I wouldn't bloody leave anyone, you neither, to rot in a cell, ya hear me? What's your problem all o' the sudden?"

I bit my lip and raised my hands defensively. "I'm sorry Lynn, okay? I'm sorry. I didn't mean to-"

"Now that," Lynn interrupted, pointing an accusing finger, "is a load o' crap. You meant it exactly how ya said it."

"It was just a question!" I protested. I paced for a few heated moments. "Yes, okay, I admit it! I wanted to know! I was afraid maybe this Tambor fellow was close to you. Seemed like you put a lot at stake for him, yeah? I was curious because I haven't been able to take my blasted eyes off of you from the moment I first saw you!"

Lynn's aggressive stance melted visibly at my words, and her forehead crinkled in slow understanding.

"I'm probably an idiot," I muttered, hands out to my sides in surrender. "Probably a fool for letting myself feel that way about a woman before I even knew her name, but I couldn't help it. You know, I was at odds with myself for still being drawn to you even after learning of what you did to all those poor souls at the November Raven!"

The woman's eyes fell to the floor. I felt a sudden pang of regret at the sight. I was breathing heavily and paced wordlessly for a long moment.

"I can't help it," I said. I took a deep breath and tensed my gut in preparation for my next words. "I can't help the way I feel about you, see? I've never met a woman like you, Lynn. You're so damned beautiful. Your eyes are like embers of a fire. Your voice could soothe a storm right out of the blasted sky. You can take care of yourself if you need to, clearly. You're strong, yet you have healing hands. Just the touch of your fingers made me breathless, understand? Do you know what you did to me with just the kiss on my cheek?"

Lynn's mouth was opened slightly, and she seemed paralyzed. Her eyes were fixed on mine, unwavering and astonished at my words. The features of her face turned soft with realization as she took in my words. I had never given much thought to the shape of a woman's face, but if one were to ever be perfect, it had to be the one I was looking at.

I snorted and folded my arms. "It's bloody unfair, really."

Silently, Lynn watched me for such a long moment that it was I who had to divert my gaze away from hers. When I did, she sat back down on the crate and, to my surprise, buried her face in her hands as if she would cry.

Swallowing hard, I shifted uncomfortably. "I... are you okay? I'm sorry."

"*I'm* sorry," she whispered.

"You're sorry?" I echoed dumbly.

She buried her face in her hands again and nodded.

"For what?" I asked, softening my tone. Now that I had revealed the way I felt about her, I suddenly didn't care about getting too close. I dropped to my knees in front of her and put a hand on her knee. "What for?"

The woman dropped her hands from her face, and I saw sadness in her eyes. One lone tear rolled down her cheek, which she wiped hastily. Her eyes were pink with sorrow, and it made my breath catch within me. I wanted to hug her. I wanted to assure her that she was far too beautiful to be sorry about anything, and yet I also wanted to apologize for telling her the truth.

My heart jumped when she leaned close, our noses nearly touching.

"I'm sorry about your friends." A pained look darkened her eyes. "For what I did at the tavern. I regret it, okay? I do."

Not daring to move, I could only blink. I dared not speak.

"You're a good man, Penny," Lynn continued softly. "No man's ever talked to me quite like you have before. You're very... kind with your words," she said, a faint smile crossing her lips.

My heart pumped furiously. Butterflies filled my stomach. "I meant every one of them. I wasn't lying."

Lynn smiled widely and cupped her hands around my face. The touch of her fingers sent shivers trickling down my spine, and I tried not to blink, for I didn't want to miss a single moment of her face being this close to mine.

She drew me closer and kissed me lightly upon my forehead, letting her lips linger there a long moment, running her fingers carefully through my hair. I held my breath and searched her eyes to decipher her thoughts. Her mouth widened into a brilliant smile, and she studied my face thoroughly, tracing my jaw and my chin lightly with a finger. It was almost more than I could bear. My breaths became shorter, and a wave of heat washed over my heart.

Lynn pressed her forehead to mine and closed her eyes. I lost the ability to breathe when she tilted her head slowly, parted her lips lightly and started leaning in close. So entranced was I by the realization that she was about to put her mouth to mine that I find it impossible to put the feeling into words.

I yearned to kiss her.

The moment was dashed to pieces by sharp yells and shouts from above us, amidst a commotion so loud that the familiar sounds of battle echoed all the way down the basement stairs to our ears.

"The hell?" Lynn breathed, releasing my face from her hands and shooting to her feet.

"I don't know," I answered, whirling about to face the stairs, scared and alert. "Blazes, you think they're coming down?"

I saw Lynn reflexively reach for her sword usually in its scabbard at her hip, but urgency crossed her face as she remembered she was unarmed.

"What do we do?" I asked urgently.

Lynn paused briefly. Her eyes swept about, and then met mine. "Wait. Did you hear that? Grab the torch! Follow me!"

Without hesitating, I did, and to my surprise Lynn was dashing for the stairs leading up to the great hall. She bounded up two steps at a time, guided by my torchlight, grunting in pain with each leap. Soon we were nearly to the top of the stairs. The door was just paces away.

"Listen!" she said excitedly.

Sounds of blades crossing, men yelling and wood splintering rang through the door.

"Fates!" I hissed. "Who is that? Who's fighting?"

That was when I heard Alomar's roar, a loud crash, and the sound of a man writhing in pain.

I gasped. "That's Alomar, Lynn!"

"It is!" Lynn exclaimed gleefully.

The sound of men rushing about in a flurry of activity cascaded in, and I nearly jumped for joy when I heard Captain Hael shouting orders to men unseen.

Lynn clapped my shoulder gleefully. "It's the Cap'n! They're here to save us!"

Before we could ascend for the door, it was flung open wildly.

Perrault stood at the top of the stairs, denying us freedom's gate. Fresh blood trickled down his face. He stared down at us with wild, piercing eyes. Shouts of men rushed in from the great hall behind him, and he charged down the stairs toward us with a snarl.

* * *

Lynn and I flinched in surprise before turning to flee back down the steps and into the cellar. The hollers of our friends in the hall were drowned out by the frenzy of Perrault's pursuit so close behind us – the folly of his gear and armor shuddering with each running step made my hairs stand on end. Fear screamed throughout my body.

Just as we reached the cellar floor, I heard Lynn cry out in pain as Perrault shoved her viciously off the stairs and into me, sending us both tumbling about on the stone. My body hit the floor with such force that my head whipped into the ground on impact.

My vision clouded. A hot, flailing panic rose from my chest as I desperately tried to get to my feet to aid Lynn, but found I could not even sit up. Blood from a new cut warmed my face, and the gashes atop my head throbbed. The torch rolled away in a cloud of sparks, continuing to burn indifferently on the floor nearby.

Sounds of a struggle echoed all around me, glancing off the dark cellar walls. I could hear both Lynn and Perrault grunting in pain and desperation, boots scuffing against stone as they grappled nearby.

I blinked rapidly, trying to will my eyes to see clearly. Everything seemed far away.

The rushed steps of numerous men pounded down the stairs. I could faintly hear Captain Hael, Alomar, Miles and other men roaring curses and threats, accompanied by feverish calls of Lynn's name, of mine.

The fighting cries of Lynn and Perrault were growing more guttural and distressed each second.

Get up, Penny!

I dizzily willed myself to a sitting position, just in time to see Perrault swing his sword down upon Lynn.

"No!" shouted Captain Hael as he, Alomar and the others spilled into the cellar from the corner of my eye.

Lynn halted Perrault's hand mid-swing, clutching his wrist weakly.

"Penny!" came Alomar's voice.

I dared not take my eyes away from Lynn and Perrault. I tried to get up, to hurl myself toward Lynn's attacker, but I fell forward shakily.

"Put your bloody weapon down!" Sorley screamed.

Perrault, clearly fatigued, wrapped an arm around Lynn, forcing her back to him. He held her hostage, his blade to her neck, a sight I had hoped to never see again.

The fog began to lift from my eyes. Still sitting, I haphazardly grasped the still-lit torch from the floor, holding it up to cast light upon the scene around me.

Captain Hael, Alomar, Miles, Sorley, Ernest, and others stood in a crescent formation, angled inward toward Perrault. Weapons were drawn, and I saw distress dominating the eyes of each man in a manner I had never seen.

"Listen, you sod!" Miles barked. "You harm her further, you're a dead man!"

Perrault steadied his voice, trying to mask his fear. "If I let her go, I'm a dead man."

"You've lost!" thundered Captain Hael. His scimitar gleamed in the torchlight. "Give it up!"

"Let me go, and I won't slit her throat."

All of Captain Hael's men erupted at once, and Perrault's voice exploded back in a long exchange of threats and insults. I saw Alomar continuously glance at me, not breaking formation.

It was then that movement on the steps caught my eye.

I turned and saw Quaid stalking silently down the stairs, bow drawn and arrow nocked. We locked eyes, and I immediately ripped my gaze from him, understanding his desire to stay hidden.

"Silence!" Captain Hael roared. Everyone present, including Perrault, obeyed.

I watched Lynn carefully. She was breathing heavily, as was the man who held her, both tired from their brief battle. Her forearms were flexed tautly, both hands gripping Perrault's arm in a stubborn but ineffective defense. Lynn's eyes flickered off to the right.

Toward Quaid.

New confidence lit up her eyes. She pursed her lips and let her grip slip from her captor's arm, her hands falling idly to her sides.

Perrault shifted his weight. Narrowed his eyes. "Do you not know who I am?"

An eerie quiet settled upon us, the cellar filled with only the taxed breaths of men.

"A dead man, and nothing more," Ernest growled.

Anger seized our enemy's face. His icy glare challenged us all.

Miles took a step forward. "Enough. You've lost."

Perrault squared himself. "I tell you the truth: harm me, and you provoke death itself. You don't know what you're doing. Fools, playing at a lion's game."

Without warning, Lynn bared her teeth and gnashed down on the arm wrapped around her. Perrault screamed in agony, and the woman exerted more force, tearing violently with sporadic whips of her head.

Her captor's sword hand ebbed, dropping to his side.

Lynn released her grip and swiftly collapsed to a crouch.

Quaid's bowstring snapped. A barbed arrow slammed into Perrault's chest.

Shock grasped Perrault's face ruthlessly as strength left his body. His sword clattered to the ground. The man stumbled back a few paces, mindlessly grasping at the arrow jutting out of his armor, eyes wide.

Before anyone could move, Lynn was already on her feet, swiping Perrault's sword from the floor with the deathly scrape of steel across stone.

Without a sound, she exploded forward and plunged the man's blade into his belly, driving him back into the wall with astonishing force.

Dumbstruck, Perrault's eyes lost focus, unable to meet Lynn's savage stare. She stared him down for a long, wordless moment. His arms began to slump downward. His legs shook.

With a grunt, Lynn pulled the sword from the man and let him slump in defeat to the cellar floor. Perrault's eyes glazed over as his last breath left his lungs.

"Bastard," she spat.

CHAPTER 51

Our time in Mable changed my life. I must admit that to the day I write this, I have had the strange sensation of being confused about what transpired there, battling inwardly on whether I want to remember that period as a mostly positive or mostly negative experience.

Recollections of the greatest fear I had ever known haunt my dreams some nights... memories of moving through the village blindly with Royce, Lynn and Gavin. The stormy ghost-like dwellings of the village combined with the mystery of what had befallen it as we found the blood of those poor souls sometimes overtake my dreams, turning them into nightmares when they see fit.

For all the horrors I had experienced, as close as I had come to losing my life at the hands of Perrault and his men, I also remember the time I shared with Lynn. I remember the way her gentle touch felt, her concerned eyes while she listened to my story, and the way her lips felt on my skin. Surely, such blissful memories would never have transpired at all if we had not been faced with the dangers of that day.

Perhaps to experience truly wonderful things in life, one has to step out and take risks. Brave the darkness and stare fear in the eyes. Maybe more danger equaled greater rewards to be reaped at the end of the day.

That night back at Captain Hael's camp, everyone except those on guard duty on the perimeter and in the woods gathered around the campfire and toasted mugs to our safe return and a battle won against Tyrius's men. Royce, Alomar and I sat with Gavin and Quaid on one side, and Sorley and Ernest on the other. The large and loud circle of men spread out before me, illuminated by the fire's light. Captain Hael, Lynn and Miles were the only ones not present at the moment. Earlier, Gavin had taken a needle and sutures to Lynn's back wound in the Lodge, and I rested a bit easier knowing she would be okay after all.

Our merriment rang out in the woods with unmatched avidity, and we exchanged tales.

I learned that Royce and Gavin had barely escaped, slipping away into the fog. Perrault's men had pursued them but returned to regroup at Mable Manor when they came away empty-handed. Royce and Gavin were able to reunite with our horses near the bridge and ride for Hael's camp at breakneck speed.

Captain Hael's war party returned at the same time Royce and Gavin reached camp. Hael was hastily informed of the situation in Mable, and the war party hightailed it for Mable without delay, hoping to rescue Lynn and me.

"Can't believe you and Gavin made it out!" I said, clapping Royce on the shoulder.

"Aye," he grinned. "Sorry for leaving you two, Penny. We didn't want to."

"Indeed," Gavin interjected. "Royce here was cursing like a sailor the entire way to camp. Pained us to leave ya, it did. But we didn't have a choice. Those blights were armed to the teeth. Knew that if you survived, only way to save you was with help."

I nodded and gave Royce a jesting kiss on the head. "I love ya. You two saved our arses. Did you ever find the villagers?"

Ernest nodded. "We did. There were a few dead, lyin' about in homes here and there. The rest of them were all hauled up inside a large farmhouse on the southeast edge of Mable."

Sorley took a swig of ale. "Perrault had his boys lock them in. Easily a hundred people. The villagers said Perrault's men were gonna burn it down with them all still inside, but Perrault saw the signal."

I cocked my head. "Signal?"

Alomar nodded. "Aye, Penny. 'Twas the light you all saw, upstairs in the manor. They flashed a lantern in signal when they saw you and the others prowling about the village. Turns out it also lured you in."

"And in doing so, temporarily prevented them from setting fire to the barn," I finished, eyes wide.

Alomar shuddered. "Villagers got lucky."

Royce sighed. "We still don't know what in the hell Perrault and his men were there for. The villagers didn't know, either."

I took everything in solemnly, tilting a mug of ale to my lips. "What of the deal? With Mable, I mean?"

"Well," Gavin said, frowning, "the Village Elders were the ones we saw strung up above the well. The village folk have some recovering to do, but they're all the more eager for our protection now. We ended up saving them, after all."

I stretched my arms to my left and right, wrapping both Royce and Alomar in embrace. "Thanks, mates. Truly."

Alomar gave my shoulder a squeeze.

Royce smiled wickedly. "Now you owe us, Pen."

Laughter broke out around the fire just as the smell of something cooked reached my nose. I looked about and saw Ruben making his way into the fire circle with a huge platter of roasted chicken lined with slices of cheese. A cheer rose up from the men when they saw the dish, and I was practically salivating at the sight. Another man followed close behind with a dish nearly identical to the first.

"Is that chicken?" crowed Alomar. "I'll eat all of it myself. The rest of you gotta fight me for it."

Sorley leapt to his feet. "I'll take ya up on that challenge, Alomar. But you can only use one hand, see."

Men chuckled around us, and I heard a voice ask, "Why one hand?"

Sorley thumped his chest. "Ho, now! You shoulda seen this man fight," he said, jabbing a closed fist at Alomar. "By the Fates! Unfair, it was. I'm a mean bloke and I'd think twice before crossing this one."

More chortling sounded off, and Alomar shook his head. "No, no. Worry not, Sorley. As long as I get my chicken, I'll be happy."

Another round of laughing laced with cheers erupted, and Ruben set down the dish.

"All right, lads! Dig in before I make ya."

Ernest stood. "Hold on now! Worry not, Alomar: you'll get your chicken," he declared. He gestured to Royce, Gavin and I. "But these blokes decided to spend the night with those crazies in Mable. They get first pick."

Royce stood eagerly. "No, mate. Only Penny and Lynn were mad enough to want to stay the night there. Gav and I left, having common sense, see. But we'll take your offer."

Minutes later everyone was served and eating heartily. I kept glancing beyond the fire and uphill toward the Lodge, waiting for the Captain and his two officers. Oddly, I felt nervous about Lynn returning. I obviously hadn't said a word about what transpired between us, and I'm sure she had acted in the same manner. Still, I was anxious.

I sighed inwardly as I chewed when it dawned on me that I was afraid that Lynn would choose to sit somewhere besides next to me.

Get ahold of yourself, Penny.

There was no room for petty, juvenile jealousies in this company of men.

Alomar bumped me. "So, Pen. Your first battle. How'd you like it?"

I snorted. "Fantastic, it was."

The man chuckled. "Well, look at the bright side. You survived an actual fight. Now you can use that when you write, aye? It'll make you that much better."

I raised my eyebrows. "True. How are you faring, mate? Lynn and I were thinking about the lot of you in the woods, fighting Tyrius's men." I lowered my voice slightly. "Was it... like Dekka?"

Alomar chewed thoughtfully for a few moments before answering. "Yes, and no. The feeling was the same. The feeling of being in a battle, life and death suddenly being all that matters. But something about it was almost more chaotic, yeah? It wasn't two armies, two trained groups of people in formal combat. It was a blasted free-for-all in the woods between two gangs of angry blokes."

I didn't know what to say for a long moment, but I finally patted my friend on the back. "I'm glad you're all right, Al."

The man nodded, taking a drink of ale. "We didn't suffer one casualty. Hael was right. They were totally oblivious as to who they were fighting."

At Alomar's statement, I recalled Perrault's strange words in the cellar. He had seemed surprised that we didn't know who he was, that we hadn't recognized him by his name alone.

Harm me, and you provoke death itself.

The words kept replaying themselves in my mind. Tyrius's men had been ignorant and foolish in waging battle on Captain Hael in the forest... were we guilty of making the same mistake with Perrault?

Before I voiced my thoughts, I saw three figures coming down toward us from the Lodge. Sorley must have noticed them too, because he lifted his cup to the sky.

"Oy! Cap'n! You and your fancy-arse officers better get down here and drink some o' this ale!"

Men all around laughed warmly and turned to see Hael, Lynn and Miles stepping up to the fire circle. I held my breath when Lynn's eyes met mine for but a moment. She had changed out of her bloody garments and now wore a plain, long-sleeved shirt that she had rolled up past her elbows. Her bandana was secured around her left shoulder and her red hair was tied back.

As she and Miles moved about the crowd, shaking hands amidst the cheers and guffaws of their fellow brigands, I watched no one but her. The fire lit her eyes, and that shining grin of hers was undying. I wondered if no one else felt the way I did about her. It seemed impossible.

Royce, Alomar and I continued eating and drinking and exchanging words with the others, but I watched Lynn from the corner of my eye when Miles took a seat next to Ruben. The woman, however, kept walking, casually treading the outskirts of the fire circle. I stiffened when she neared us.

"Any room for me here?" Lynn asked.

I grinned up at her. "Of course."

Alomar scooted over, and I did likewise, bumping into Royce as Lynn swung one leg over the rock, followed by the other, before sitting next to me.

"Curses," Royce muttered. He leaned forward so that Lynn could see him. "Twice, you pick the Storyteller, Lynn? You could have sat next to *me*. It would've changed your life."

Lynn, Alomar and I laughed loudly. Ruben was hurriedly approaching the woman with a plate of chicken and warm rolls of bread, and she took it from the man.

"Give me poultry or give me death!" Lynn exclaimed, rubbing her hands together. "Haven't had chicken in ages, and could smell it from the Lodge. All I'm gonna do is eat. Don't talk to me."

"You want ale or water?" asked Ruben.

"Don't talk to me."

We all broke into more laughter, including Ruben. "Ale it is," he responded, and fetched the woman a mug.

Gradually the hours grew late, and the fire began to die down. Men would get up and bid us good night, and congratulate us for staying alive and not getting any limbs hacked off before they turned to retire to their sleeping quarters. An hour or so past midnight, the moon was smothered by clouds and all that remained of the fire were a few stubborn embers refusing to die out.

Only Royce, Alomar, Lynn, Gavin and myself remained.

Alomar hiccupped and stood to refill his mug. Royce had left the boulder he had sat upon and now stretched out on the dirt, leaning back on one elbow to watch the dying fire. Gavin drank in silence, and the five of us took in the sounds of the Kovald Forest around us, reflecting on all that we'd been through in the last few days.

"Oy, Royce?" Lynn asked suddenly.

"Aye?"

"When we were down in that cellar, Penny told me about the lot of ya. How ya came to join up with us and whatnot."

Royce shifted to look at Alomar – who was watching me carefully as he put more chicken on his plate – and then shot me a look. "Did he, now?"

I shrugged. "Thought we were gonna die, mates."

Alomar sat back down beside me. "It's fine. The truth is the truth."

I breathed easy and gave an appreciative nod to Alomar, who returned it.

"So what'd you think?" Royce asked Lynn. "Did the Storyteller do us justice?"

Lynn chuckled. "I'd say so. Was quite a tale. But I bring this up for a reason: he told me 'bout how the three of ya were orphans. Told me 'bout your father, Royce, and how he up and left you and your brother in Northroe."

Royce sat up, and said nothing. I grew nervous for a moment. He watched what remained of the fire closely.

"Penny told me about the letter your father sent ya," Lynn said quietly. "The one you burned by candle."

"There anything Pen didn't tell you?" Royce asked smartly, folding his arms.

Lynn ignored the man's jab. "Did ya give any thought to helpin' out your father? At all, I mean, before you burned his letter?"

"After he abandoned Trev and I, and left us to die? No."

The woman said nothing. I cast her a questioning glance, and she looked away from me and up at the stars. After a long silence, Royce whispered something.

"What was that?" Lynn asked.

The man sighed. "I said aye, I did. I considered it, I mean. Answering my father's letter and all. I suppose I am a bit curious about him. What he's like now, where he's been. What his life's about. He probably has another family by now," Royce quipped. No one laughed, and he cleared his throat. "Thought about it, yeah. I want some answers, after all."

Lynn nodded. "Maybe... you should consider doing it someday."

Royce shrugged. "Maybe. Why do you think so?"

"Well, my papa abandoned me and my mum when I was a little girl," Lynn answered.

Taking a sip of ale, I turned to look at her in surprise.

"I always wondered why he did. My mum was beautiful, ya know. The prettiest woman I'd ever seen. Kind as could be. I wondered how the 'ell a man could just up and leave like he did. And, well, I don't mean to impose, Royce, but if I got a chance to meet the man, I'd get right on it. I have questions I'd love to ask him someday. But I never will. It's been over twenty-five years since I saw my father."

"Don't you hate him for it?" asked Royce.

"Aye, I do."

We let Lynn's words hang in the air around us for a lengthy silence. No one spoke, and I put my mug to my lips. After a minute had crept by, Royce spoke.

"Lynn, I mean no disrespect by this. Do you ever wish you could have one more talk with your brother? Just one?"

A heavy wind of uneasy shock rippled across all of us. Gavin leaned forward and shot Royce a ferocious look of disapproval, shaking his head. An awkward silence settled about the air. Alomar and I exchanged glances, and I stiffened when Lynn at last leaned forward to look over at the man.

"I won't ask how ya know about that, but I do. Aye, there's not a day that passes that I don't wish my brother were still here with me. I'd give just about anythin' to hear his voice again."

Royce nodded. "Sometimes I think about my brother, Trev. I wonder what I'd say to him if I were able to speak with him again. If I'd be able to say anything, at that."

We all dwelled on these words while Lynn answered with a wordless, knowing smile. I watched Royce's face carefully as he adjusted the band that tied back his hair. He very rarely brought up his brother in any conversation, and never in front of strangers.

Then again, we weren't strangers now, were we? We had lived with, eaten with, even fought and bled with the brigands of Captain Hael's camp.

Lynn stood and stepped a couple paces away from where we sat before turning to face the four of us men.

"Gav, Penny, Royce," she said with a smile. "Just wanted to thank ya for doin' a great job out there at Mable. Thanks for havin' my back and helpin' get us through it. You all contributed and did wonderfully. I told the Cap'n everything, and he was glad to hear it. Alomar, the Cap'n and Miles told me how well you fought today. Or... yesterday, rather. I wanted to thank ya, as well."

We all smiled and lifted our cups in acknowledgement.

"Sure could've used you in Mable, Alomar," remarked Gavin. "You missed all the excitement."

Alomar shook his head. "Sounds like it was a hell of a party. Too much ale for me."

The five of us all laughed. Before long, Gavin had retired, and Royce and Alomar got to their feet. By habit, I did so as well, leaving Lynn the only one left sitting at the fire circle.

"Time to turn in," Royce said, rubbing his eyes. "Can't keep awake."

Alomar yawned. "Aye, me too. Lynn, good night."

"G'night."

Royce stretched and took a few steps with Alomar toward our cabin before turning to look back at me. "You coming, Penny?"

I hesitated. "Give me a few, yeah? Be there soon."

My friend's eyes lit up with a knowing grin. "Right, then. I see how it is, Lynn. Maybe I should become a Storyteller. I'm missing out."

I rolled my eyes. "Knock it off, Roy."

"Ho, now!" Royce whistled lowly. "Storytellers fight in real battles now, too! Look at you, mate!" He changed his voice into a tone mocking nobility. "From henceforth, on this hour of this... day, and all that, you, Sir Daulton, shall be known as Penny the Brave!"

We all laughed as my two friends walked away. Royce turned one last time. "Oh, and Lynn?"

"Yeah?"

"About my father... I'll think about it."

Lynn smiled, giving a nod. "G'night, Royce."

The woman and I sat alone beneath the stars a few paces apart on different sitting stones, and I found myself not knowing what to say at first. I wanted to bring up what happened back in Mable, but I didn't dare. Instead, I tried to get her to make good on what she had promised.

"Tell me about how you came here," I said quietly. "How you met this lot and ended up here in the woods."

Lynn tipped back her head to the stars and smiled. "You don't give up, do ya?"

"No."

The woman got up and came closer to sit at my side. "Well, you told me your story, so I suppose it's only fair I tell ya mine. At least some of it."

CHAPTER 52

I shifted, looking at the dying fire and waiting for Lynn to begin. The woman took a few sips of her ale and cleared her throat.

"I had an older brother, as you and your friends apparently already know. His name was Donovan. After my mother died o' summer fever, Donovan was the one who looked out for me. Wherever m' brother went, I went. He would get odd jobs, apprenticing for carpenters, blacksmiths, leatherworkers, you name it. When I was old enough to work I helped out as a farmhand, and I was a tailor's assistant for a time.

"Donovan was the one person I could count on to do anythin' for me. He was always there for me, ya see? One time a farmer tried cuttin' my week's wages by nearly five silver 'cause I was the only girl workin' his field. I told Donnie and he marched right down the path out o' the city and showed up at the man's door with this big double-headed axe o' his. He forced that blight to give me the coin he owed me. My brother coulda killed him or robbed him, but he took only what I was owed, and that was it."

"Sounds like he was a good man, your brother," I remarked.

Lynn sighed. "Ah, he was. I miss him so."

"Why have you never brought him up before?"

"It's hard for me to talk about him, honestly."

I nodded. "I understand. You say 'the city.' What city do you mean?"

"We lived in Eisley City, actually."

My eyes widened. "The capital? What was it like?"

"You've never been?"

"No, we were street urchins in Northroe, remember?" I replied. "Never really got out."

Lynn nodded. "Right. Sorry. Well, it's massive! Very easy to get lost. People everywhere, Penny, you wouldn't believe it. Buildings that stretch up to the sky, big manors and estates right in the middle o' the city, gardens and hedgerows strewn throughout... but it was like any city really, in that it could be beautiful, until ya went to the alleys and backstreets. And the King's castle...

by the Fates, it was huge. They built it on a large hill overlooking all o' the city. Sometimes at night my brother and I would sit and watch it beneath the stars, talking 'bout what it must've been like to set foot inside."

I nodded, my imagination spinning a tapestry of vibrant, lush cityscapes that I had never even laid eyes on and only heard of. I wondered what it would be like to behold it in person, with my own eyes.

"Anyway, that farmer ended up reportin' my brother to the Watch, but he exaggerated what happened. He told them that Donovan robbed him and killed his horse so that he couldn't follow... but the farmer actually hid his own coin, smashed up his own belongings a bit and killed his own horse so that when the Watch investigated, the evidence pointed to my brother."

I shook my head, amazed. "That is ludicrous."

Lynn nodded. "It was. Thanks to one of the farmhands bein' a good friend of ours, Donnie found out before the Watch came. He was furious. He woke me in the middle o' the night and we left. We went out into the night with all that we could carry, stole a horse from a stable and rode out of Eisley City, headin' east through the Heartland. We reached the town of Courtnall a day later. It was there we met the Cap'n for the first time."

I perked up at the mention of Captain Hael and shifted my position on the rock next to her.

"The Cap'n and a friend of his were in some tavern that we stopped at, and o' course they didn't know us, and we didn't know them. They were sitting in a corner, bein' all quiet-like, and Donnie and I went to the bar for a couple o' drinks. That's when the City Watch suddenly came in, practically bashin' down the doors. They were askin' everyone if they'd seen two red-haired persons, one male and one female. Amidst the crowd, Donovan took my hand and led me to the back corner where the Cap'n sat. You know that big hat the Cap'n wears, the dark blue one?"

I nodded.

"He was wearin' it then, too. Donnie knew we'd stick out like land in the ocean with our red hair and dark complexion, and he asked Cap'n Hael nicely if I could wear the hat."

I couldn't help but grin, scratching at the stubble on my chin. Lynn saw me and chuckled lightly, her eyes growing sorrowful for a moment.

"Good brother o' mine of course thought about my wellbeing before his own. The Cap'n, being who he is and everythin', instantly caught on to who we were and immediately obliged, standing and settin' his hat atop my head. He even urged us both to sit down with him and his friend in an effort to conceal us from the Watchmen searchin' the tavern. But see, Donovan was a good head and a half taller than I. Though I was sitting down and the hat concealed my hair color, Donnie was still standing tall with that red hair o' his, and the Watchmen spotted us. To be brief, they came at us hard, but the Cap'n and his friend hit back harder. We ended up escapin' town."

Totally immersed in the story she was telling me, I cocked my head slightly in question. "Did Captain Hael already have a company? A band of men?"

Lynn shook her head and smiled. It was the fleeting, occasional smile brought on only by memories far off and long past. "No, but we started the company that very night."

So Lynn was one of the original founders of Hael's clan. I somehow admired her even more than I already had. It was so unorthodox, a woman being mixed up with outlaws to begin with. But being one of the founding members, being in charge, even, just added to the awe of the entire thing.

"The Cap'n had some friends o' course who were interested, and in no time we had a good enough crew. The hard part was earnin' money for our band, ya see. There was a lot o' robbery, pick-pocketing and the like." The woman grinned and held up her hand, twiddling her fingers. "I was the best pickpocket in the land. Caused a lot o' grief in crowded streets. I was the biggest pain in the arse."

I laughed loudly, and lowered my volume when I heard my laugh echo off the trees and bounce back at me. Lynn chuckled with a bright smile.

"Why did Captain Hael assist the two of you?" I asked. "I mean, he didn't even know you."

"The Cap'n hates the Watch. Thinks they're corrupt, pompous, power-hungry little men with armor and weapons. Apparently a Watchman made supreme trouble for his father when he was a lad. Cap'n Hael grew up hating them and the laws they claim to uphold."

"They're not all bad, though," I said.

Lynn crinkled her nose, as if an unpleasant smell had presented itself. "No, I suppose not. We don't even have to deal with 'em hardly anymore, except on occasion. Like when we're saving the arses of a Bookkeeping Storyteller and his friends."

"Hey!" I said in mock protest. "Easy, now."

Lynn laughed and raised her eyes to the cloudy moon and stars in the night sky. I decided not to ask about how Donovan died, and instead watched the sky with her for a long moment when something entered my mind. It was risky. I probably should have discussed it with Royce and Alomar first, but I had a feeling that the moment was right, and I wasn't sure how often I would get the opportunity to speak with Lynn alone.

"I have to tell you something," I said testily, scraping a line into the dirt at our feet with my boot. "Something that, to be honest, I'm hesitant to bring up to you. Or anyone else."

The woman was visibly alarmed, though she tried to hide it. She shifted to a cross-legged sitting position facing me on the large boulder, watching me closely. "Aye? What is it?"

I took a deep breath. "My friends and I... we never intended to stay here. We only helped and followed Arthur and Quaid because, well, they were armed, and we didn't want to die. I don't mean any disrespect. You and the Captain and everyone have done so much for us, and we're really grateful, but... I wanted to be a Writer. Travel the world and record my journeys, write stories that become famous all over Eisley... maybe even the world. Royce wanted to leave Northroe because he believed the only true freedom in life is experiencing the world and what it has to offer. Trek through the lands and see what the Fates set upon us. We were going to go to Saelow Province. They're settling it soon, actually. Royce and Alomar talked of going there to start new lives."

I paused, letting the information sink in for Lynn. Her eyes were fixed on mine, and I saw her face harden with thought as she looked down at her feet.

"I don't see how we can do any of that if we stay here," I murmured. "But now it's difficult, see. I... we like the lot of you. We've grown to know you and the others. And to be honest Lynn, I've been worried about how I would ever tell you this, because I've never... met a woman like you. I've never felt for a woman what I feel for you now. I don't know if I can leave with my friends if they decide to go."

The woman looked up at me, and I saw her features fade into regret. She opened her mouth to speak, but nothing came out.

"I'm sorry," I whispered, my stomach tightening. "The whole thing just turned quite complicated, didn't it?"

Lynn took a deep breath, and her knee was bouncing nervously. I was worried when I couldn't get her to look at me.

"I have to tell ya somethin' too, Penny. Two things, okay?"

I nodded. "Please do."

"First, I knew already. That you couldn't stay, I mean. When I was fixin' ya up back in Mable, and you were tellin' me the story o' you and your friends and your dreams, I knew right then that ya had to leave this place. It was in your voice. I heard the words of a man that knew what he wanted in life, and it brought a smile to my face. It did."

I glowed with a sense of relief. "You knew?"

"Aye. I think I know a way that we can get that done. I haven't told any o' the others this, so you can't either, okay?"

I nodded, scooting in closer. "But I don't want to leave you, see? That's the problem. I-"

"Penny," she interrupted, "let me finish." Lynn sighed and looked as if she was mustering strength to continue, and it worried me. "Like I said, I haven't told anyone this, but the Cap'n was talking with Miles and I before we came down to the fire with the lot o' ya. He wants to try to break Tambor outta jail, which means we have to return to Northroe."

I narrowed my eyes and studied her face hard, trying to find where she was going with this. The woman still wouldn't look at me.

"What's wrong?" I asked.

Lynn looked away, biting her lip fretfully. She looked off to the trees in the distance for a long moment, and I grew wary of her next words.

"We can possibly try to get you and your friends freedom, if you participate in the mission," she said quietly. "In exchange for your efforts at Mable and freeing Tambor from jail in the city, I'm... I'm sure the Cap'n would be open to negotiations."

Steeling myself, I sat up straight. "Is that the second thing you had to tell me?"

The woman suddenly hung her head and ran both her hands through her hair, clearly distraught. She was saying something under her breath, and it looked as if she were about to cry.

"What is it?" I asked, bracing myself. "What do you have to tell me?"

Lynn looked up at me with her beautiful eyes. Her lip quivered, and she sniffled softly. The sight of her trying not to cry broke me. It looked strange on her.

"Tambor... is important to me, Penny. H-he... he and I are..." She sighed heavily and trailed off momentarily. "I'm with him. He's with me."

Lightning struck in my mind. A hammer flattened my heart, and I speak the truth when I say that I felt the wind get knocked out of me. Her words crushed my spirit. My mouth fell open and all I could do was stare off at the dirt.

It couldn't be. Not after what we had been through. Not after the connection we had shared. I had felt it! It was real!

"I'm sorry, Penny. I didn't know how to tell ya back in Mable, and-"

I shook my head. "So you just *didn't* tell me?" I replied weakly. "I've been opening up to you this whole time, Lynn, and you hit me with that?"

Lynn swallowed hard. She reached a hand for mine, but I recoiled away from her.

"I asked you," I said, dumbfounded. "I asked if Tambor... if he was... and you just got angry at me!" I nearly exclaimed. "And then you act like you're drawn to me, getting close and all that, and for what?"

The woman stood, her face seized with regret. "I wasn't actin' at all! I didn't want to tell you about Tambor back in Mable!" She stopped, looking like she felt guilty about admitting the words she had spoke. "I made a mistake, Pen. I-"

"Don't call me *Pen*," I retorted angrily.

"I'm sorry. I don't know what happened back there, in that basement, okay? You just came on so strong, and you were really sweet, and caring, and ya saved my life, and I wasn't lyin' when I said no man's ever spoken to me the way ya did," Lynn rambled, her voice trembling. "And I thought we were gonna die! I didn't think we'd make it out! I shouldn't have. I know it's my fault."

I stood and stared at her, my heart feeling destroyed but alive with hurt simultaneously. Opening my mouth to speak, I merely uttered a strange whimpering noise and shook my head, looking away from the woman.

"Penny," Lynn pleaded, stepping toward me. "Penny, I felt somethin' for ya. I still do. It's not a lie, okay? Back there in the Manor basement, I wanted to be... close with you. But I just can't do that to Tambor, ya see? I'm sorry, but that's not the kind of person I am. And I know you're angry with me now, but you're the same, Penny. You're like me. You couldn't do that to the woman who loved you, and I know it."

Where had this sudden set of morals come from?

I cursed. "Ah, Fates. I should've known. Why else would no man in camp go near you? I'm such an idiot."

Lynn tried to reach for me again, but I bristled at her approach.

"I'm so sorry, Penny. I don't know what else to say. I'm not lying. I feel somethin' for ya, I do. I feel a lot for ya actually. But I just can't do it."

"Stop," I said through clenched teeth. "You think you're making it easier, talking like that?"

She grimaced, still holding back tears.

A wave of anger, of embarrassment, of sadness and misery swept over me, flooring my heart. My chest hurt and my face burned, I was swimming in an ocean of self-loathing and frustration, and I put all the blame on Lynn.

So I did what any man not thinking clearly would.

I spun to her, wrapped my arms around the woman's waist, pulled her close and kissed her fiercely. Her soft crying faded as I pressed my mouth to hers, and I felt her lips part for mine. They were soft and warm, seeming to fit my own perfectly. Lynn's arms hung limply at her sides at first, but I felt one of them take hold of my shoulder, pulling me to her while I drew her waist to mine, as if we could be closer.

We kissed for a thunderous moment in the middle of the campground, uncaring of who was watching, when she suddenly drew away from me with a confused, frightened look in her eyes.

Lynn shook her head. "I can't, Pen."

I extended my arms. "Lynn, please. Don't go."

The woman wiped her mouth and backed away, regret filling her features. Her breathing was rapid like my own. My heart was beating heatedly. We stared at each other for a long moment in the night, the sounds of our quick breathing the only noises I really bothered hearing.

Lynn closed her eyes and shook her head. "I'm sorry," she whispered. "I shouldn't have. You shouldn't have, either."

Before I could answer, the woman spun quickly and strode away from me, walking briskly up the hill toward her sleeping quarters. I watched forlornly as she became a shadow of the night before fading into the darkness.

Dejected, I let my eyes fall to the ground in defeat and breathed out slowly, my gaze wandering and unable to focus on anything. I felt betrayed, yet guilty. I furrowed my brow in grief when I realized that I had just felt and been shown a glimpse of what I would never have. What I was foolish to hope could be mine.

I dismally slumped back down to my seat and put both hands to my head in exasperation, basking in misery and trying to come to terms with what had just happened.

Alone in the night, joined only by the dying fire, I struggled to come to terms with everything I had just heard.

The only way for my friends and I to leave the Kovald on good terms with Captain Hael would be to help the woman I had immense feelings for break her lover out of prison.

That meant returning to Northroe, the city we had worked so hard to escape from.

Additionally, all of this was mere speculation, an estimation of what kind of actions might be worth something in a bargain for departure from Captain Hael's camp forever. He could simply decide to reject our offer and have our heads. After all, he certainly didn't *need* our help in a jailbreak.

How would I tell Royce and Alomar all of this?

I groaned loudly and looked to the night's stars above. "Fates, why do you hate me so?"

CHAPTER 53

Nearly a week had passed since the night I spoke with Lynn alone in the center of the campground. I had not seen her since, and neither had most of the other men. Captain Hael had ordered that she stay in bed and get rest to recover from the wounds she had sustained in Mable, and as a result Gavin had kept a close watch over her. I had seen the man make regular visits to her quarters, always with a bag or satchel or jar of some type of herb or remedy.

Since Lynn had been recovering out of sight for a week, I had heard nothing from her about the deal to be possibly worked out with Captain Hael, of earning our freedom by assisting with Tambor's jailbreak. I had told Royce and Alomar about it, but I had left out any details of the story that revealed my feelings for Lynn, and her feelings for me, brief as they were.

The seventh night at camp after returning in one piece from Mable, I found myself shoving these thoughts roughly aside as I sat with Royce and Alomar in our cabin. The sun was setting outside, and we were sitting cross-legged on the floor around our low table, feasting on almonds, bowls of rice, and dinner rolls with mugs of water,

I scooped a handful of almonds from the bowl and looked back to my journal, a leather-bound book that I had come across for a good price in the Market Quarter back in Northroe a year before. I had written about ten pages' worth about our experiences so far, starting with the day Thomas and Sophie Flannery came to me at the Windfarer's Inn to declare they couldn't pay their rent.

Our travels and experiences had already begun to change the way I looked at the world, even how I looked at myself. The revelation prompted me to start recording our travels.

Royce chomped down on a semi-hard bread roll. "What do you got there, Penny?" he asked, looking at my open journal. "That another book you're working on?"

I shook my head. "No. It's a journal. I'm writing down everything that's happened."

Alomar nodded in approval. "Good. One day you'll be glad you did so."

"Aye," I answered. "And so will you two. We'll get rich and famous, and not have to run around with bandit clans anymore."

"Fates willing," mumbled Alomar. "Tell you two one thing: I want to live by the sea. Big, sandy beach. Palm trees. Crystal blue water. Fishing."

Royce lifted his cup. "Good plan."

I chewed my food for a moment. "I've never seen a palm tree. Only a painting of one. Remember that artist with the long hair who would loiter around the Raven at night?"

"Ha!" Alomar replied enthusiastically. "The painter! I forgot about him!"

"So did I," said Royce. "He was a strange one, eh?"

I chuckled. "Aye, but he was an incredible artist. One night he was in front of the tavern, painting a palm tree against a blue sky and bright sun. I had to ask him what kind of tree it was, and that's when I learned what a palm tree looked like."

Alomar nodded. "Aye, they're beautiful. Dekka had droves of them everywhere you looked. Don't think we have any in Eisley. That I know of, at least. Maybe out west."

I washed down some bread with a swig of water. "He told me he was painting in front of the Raven for inspiration, but it was nighttime in Northroe. No sun, blue sky, or palm trees in sight."

Royce's eyes grew wide with urgency, and he slapped a palm to the table. "I'm tellin' you. We could find that at Saelow. Maybe not palm trees, but a new life, a new sun, a new everything, mates. We need to get out of this blasted camp."

"It'd be the same sun, technically," I needled.

Royce rolled his eyes. "You know what I mean."

"Speaking of getting out of here," Alomar said, lowering his voice, "when the devil is this supposed 'plan' of Lynn's gonna happen, Penny?"

I shrugged. "I don't know. Still haven't seen her since she's been in recovery."

"That's it?" glared Royce. "She just said, 'Oy, Penny m' love, I have an idea that could set the lot of ya free, but know what? I'm not tellin' ya anything about it.' Brilliant."

Sighing, I shook my head. "Don't start with that, 'my love' business."

I hated when they brought Lynn up at all. Since I hadn't told them about what had transpired between us, they obviously didn't know any better when they made prods and jabs about the woman. I couldn't bring myself to tell them. I was also keenly aware that I had tried to win over Lynn over despite her being taken by another man, and Alomar most likely wouldn't have been very approving of my actions because of what he had gone through with Corrine.

Come to think of it, he might very well have killed me.

"Back to Northroe," Alomar murmured.

Royce chewed on some rice, his eyes distant. "Don't know a thing about jailbreaks, do we?"

"I don't know if it's a good idea," I said solemnly. "We're wanted men, for sure."

"Corrine is there," Alomar said. "I miss her, mates. I feel stupid for it, but I do."

I smiled faintly. "You loved her for years, Al. Nothing stupid about feeling that way."

He nodded. "I just want to talk to her. Get to the bottom of it all. Never got to tell her the truth about the Raven." He paused. "Never even said goodbye."

"Who knows?" mused Royce. "Maybe you will, mate. One thing at a time, eh?"

"One thing at a time," agreed Alomar. He lifted his cup. "Toast to our good fortune in the days to come?"

"To good fortune!"

The three of us drank, and I glanced down at the pages of my journal.

"And here's to stories yet told."

PORT MIHKOZA - SAELOW PROVINCE - SUMMER, 1217
Docks Security Office - Captain's Quarters

Commander Paxon of the King's Elite let the leather-bound journal drop to the table next to his mug of ale, half-full. He leaned back in his seat with a sigh and kicked his boots up.

"A 'journal' he calls it," the man muttered. "Damned book weighs ten pounds, it does. Three bloody days to read it."

Lieutenant Griff leaned against the wall next to a large window providing a grand view above the docks. She could see a slight reflection of herself in the glass: shoulder-length blonde hair, brown eyes, and the handle of the sword strapped to her back jutting up above her shoulder. She turned to Paxon.

"That definitely explains a few things, Commander. What happened at Mable, for one."

Paxon nodded. "Never believed those villagers' stories, when we asked about the dead persons. Bunch of bears attacked them randomly? Not a chance."

Griff clicked her tongue. "Also explains why no further harm came to that Watchman at the November Raven."

"Don't get carried away."

"I'm not, sir. Think about it for a moment." Lieutenant Griff pulled out a chair across the table from Paxon. "They poison all those people first, and then set fire to the tavern, even though everyone was already dead inside? And then they risk their lives to drag a city Watchman from the flames?"

Commander Paxon shifted in his seat.

"Doesn't add up, sir."

"What are you saying, Helena?"

Helena Griff squared herself. "It's possible Penny Daulton is telling the truth."

Paxon sighed, exasperated. "Lieutenant, if he's telling the truth, where the bloody hell is this 'Captain Hael' he wrote about, and his band of outlaws? Tell me, how many times did we take a company of troops to sweep the woods surrounding Mount Kovald?"

She frowned. "Thrice."

"What did we find?"

"Nothing."

"Who did we find?"

"Nobody. But with respect, Commander, we've only read the first of Penny's journals."

The man raised his eyebrows. "You're not seriously suggesting we sit around and read this man's books all month long, are you? We have better things to do. Our place is in Eisley City, in King Lidstrom's castle. We did not hunt these fugitives for nearly a year so we could read the rubbish that one of them wrote."

Helena brushed stray strands of blonde hair from her eyes. She stood wordlessly and returned to her perch by the window, watching the busy docks for a long moment.

"Great," Paxon mumbled. "I know that look. What are you thinking?"

"What if they're telling the truth?" Griff answered softly. "What if they were set up?"

"Helena, you don't really think that-"

"Sir," the woman interrupted, "forgive me, but I do."

Commander Paxon stared hard at Lieutenant Griff. The woman matched his gaze with her own, refusing to divert her eyes. A long, silent moment passed between the two. Only the sounds of dockworkers bustling about in the port could be heard, muffled through the office walls.

The knight finally exhaled, as though a weight was lifted from his shoulders. "You're still young, Helena. Yet, you're already my second in command. You didn't get there by fool's folly. I can't think of a single time you trusted your instincts and were wrong."

Griff offered a slight smile.

"That said, we've spent far too long on this assignment. We're not bounty hunters."

"Wasn't supposed to take this long," Griff remarked.

"True enough, but it has. We're needed back in Eisley City. The capital is the Elite's home. We belong at the King's side."

The woman opened her mouth to argue but decided against it. The man was right, after all.

Paxon scratched at his coarse, unshaven jaw. He looked again to the stack of leather-bound volumes on the table. Thumbed open the cover of the next journal. Opened it and let the pages sift noisily through his fingers.

"Sir, please hear me on this," Helena ventured. "We need proof to convict Penny and his associates. We don't have proof. We only have boatloads of hearsay."

"The claims of Lord Hannady of Northroe and Lady Monica of Foye are not mere hearsay, Lieutenant."

Griff shrugged. "Never distinguished between a noble's word and that of a commoner, sir. Everyone should speak the truth, but not everyone does."

The Commander glared at her, but his gaze softened and his lips drew into a smile, making the crow's feet at the corner of his eyes more prominent. "You know, sometimes you're a pain in the arse to argue with."

The woman grinned. "Sorry, Commander."

"No, you're not." Paxon's smile slowly faded. "Lieutenant, I hear you're interested in becoming Captain."

Helena Griff's brown eyes widened, and she made no effort to contain her eagerness. "Well... aye, sir. It would be an honor. Truly."

"You insist on staying here in Saelow, Griff?"

She hesitated. "Aye. Give me some time to pour through Daulton's journals, sir. I'm confident I can get to the bottom of things."

Paxon drummed his gloved fingers on the tabletop and watched her for a long moment, eyes squinting in assessment. "Fine. You can stay. Take a couple weeks' vacation here while you're at it. You've earned that much."

"Thank you, sir."

"But," the man interjected with a wily grin, "there are terms. Stay here and read this man's books, if you must. If you find that your suspicions are right, then innocent men are freed, and you will get your promotion."

Griff tried not to appear excited at the notion. She gave a brisk nod.

"However, if you find Daulton and his companions are indeed guilty, and it turns out I was correct, along with every other blasted government official this side of the Heartland, then you will be passed over for the position of Captain of the King's Elite."

A lengthy time passed as Paxon allowed his terms to sink in. Helena mulled over the man's words, unafraid of being deliberately careful about her decision in front of her commanding officer.

Finally, she met his stare. "I accept your terms, sir."

Paxon whistled lowly. "I must say, I had hoped you would choose differently."

"You said it yourself, Commander. When have my instincts ever been wrong?"

"Careful now, Lieutenant. First time for everything," Paxon scooped his fearsome black helm off the tabletop and pressed it down around his head. "I'm off. I'll leave Jon and Marten with you. Send a courier with your findings to me as soon as you reach a verdict. Don't dawdle."

"Aye, sir."

Commander Paxon gripped her hand firmly. "Two weeks, Helena."

"Understood."

Without a further word, the man strode quickly out into the sunshine, barking orders at the rest of the men positioned around the security office.

Helena took a deep breath and exhaled slowly. She picked up the next of Penny's journals and opened it to read, but quickly clapped the book shut and got to her feet.

The armor-clad woman strode swiftly out of the security office, cherishing the sun's rays on her skin and the sea breeze in the air. Two security officers saluted her, to which she returned a brisk nod in passing before gliding across the dock to the holding cells nearby.

Before she continued this man's story, Lieutenant Griff would meet Penny Daulton for herself.

TO BE CONTINUED...

ACKNOWLEDGEMENTS

I am deeply grateful to all of you who helped me publish this book on Indiegogo.com. Your generosity and belief in this story and me has humbled me. Many more stories have yet to be told, and I look forward to sharing the road with you.

To Jenene Scott, and the rest of the folks at A Book's Mind, for your guidance and for being so open, genuine, and ready to help me, and others, see our dreams become reality.

To my editor, Miguelicuddy, for your hilarious honesty, extraordinary attention to detail, and appetite for adventure that rivals my own.

To Josh Brizuela, for your patience, understanding, and breathtaking illustrations for the cover art and the "One Life to Live" poster.

To Arie Mulich, for your beautiful work on the Map of Eisley. I've been imagining this land for nearly a decade, and you've brought it to life for eyes to see.

To Denny Schneidemesser (Composer), Taryn J. Harbridge (Violin), and Kristin Naigus (Irish Low Whistle), for your wonderful work and performances on *An Eislian's Tale*. I am forever grateful to you for lending your gifts to my book's world.

To Samuel Hurley, man of many talents, for giving Penny Daulton a voice.

To Eljay Peña, for your font detailing on the cover art, and your infinite supply of disarming positivity.

To Jeremy Soule, Hans Zimmer, Nightwish, and Of Monsters and Men for breathing life into the people and places of this novel with your music.

To my beta readers, for all of your input, honesty, and your willingness to spend your time in this world I've created: Brian Austin, Mike Jasinski, Dr. Sheila Murphy, Jason Scott, Luke Holland, Douglas Holland, and David Holland.

To Gary Mulich and Lindsey Schulz, for your kindness, support, and all of your help.

To my friends from Roam Free – you know who you are. Thanks for believing in me all of these years.

To my family, for your limitless love, support, and all the countless times you encouraged me while I talked about 'writing a book someday.'

To my lovely wife, Anyssa. You have been patient, understanding, and endlessly supportive since even before this all began. I'm enormously grateful for the numerous conversations we've had about this story, and your willingness to take a walk in my imagination with me. Your love for me is matched only by my love for you.

    To God and Christ. All is yours, and so am I.

ABOUT THE AUTHOR

Paul lives in Phoenix, Arizona, with his wife. Both are natives of the desert, but dream of traveling around the world.

Fiction and fantasy captivated him as a boy. Classics like *Peter Pan, Tom Sawyer, Treasure Island, Robin Hood,* and *The Time Machine* left an everlasting impression and showed him the wonderful power of the imagination.

Among his favorite authors are Terry Brooks, J.R.R. Tolkien, Michael Crichton, Brian Jacques, and Louis L'Amour. He still treasures children's stories for their limitless nature and dreamlike storytelling.

The setting for this book started taking shape in Paul's imagination back in 2007. A saga unlike any other awaits readers, along with many other tales to be told... years in the making!

Listen to the epic original song *An Eislian's Tale,* composed by Denny Schneidemesser, on YouTube!

FIND ME ONLINE:
http://www.paulhollandauthor.com/
https://twitter.com/pdhollandAuthor
https://www.facebook.com/paulhollandauthor/